CONTENTS

FAVOUR THE BOLD

(THE EMPIRE'S CORPS - BOOK XVI)

CHRISTOPHER G. NUTTALL

The characters and events portrayed in this book are fictitious. Any similarity to real persons, living or dead, is coincidental and not intended by the author.

Printed in the United States of America.

ISBN: 9781695664890

Cover By Tan Ho Sim
https://www.artstation.com/alientan

Book One: The Empire's Corps
Book Two: No Worse Enemy
Book Three: When The Bough Breaks
Book Four: Semper Fi
Book Five: The Outcast
Book Six: To The Shores
Book Seven: Reality Check
Book Eight: Retreat Hell
Book Nine: The Thin Blue Line
Book Ten: Never Surrender
Book Eleven: First To Fight
Book Twelve: They Shall Not Pass
Book Thirteen: Culture Shock
Book Fourteen: Wolf's Bane
Book Fifteen: Cry Wolf
Book Sixteen: Favour The Bold

http://www.chrishanger.net
http://chrishanger.wordpress.com/
http://www.facebook.com/ChristopherGNuttall
All Comments Welcome!

HISTORIAN'S NOTE

I'VE DONE MY BEST TO MAKE THIS BOOK, the first of a series exploring what happens in the Core Worlds after Earthfall, as self-contained as possible. It should be comprehensible without ever having read any of the prior books. However, I would advise you to read *When The Bough Breaks* to set the scene, as it covers Earthfall itself.

CGN

PROLOGUE

FROM: *The Dying Days: The Death of the Old Order and the Birth of the New*. Professor Leo Caesius. Avalon. 206PE.

IT IS DIFFICULT TO SAY, with any real certainty, when the collapse of the Galactic Empire became inevitable. The stresses and strains that would eventually tear the empire apart, sparking off a series of vicious civil wars that would kill uncounted trillions of people, were clearly visible—to those who cared to see—hundreds of years before Earthfall. Indeed, by the time I was born—a mere fifty years before Earthfall—it was unlikely that anything could avert collapse. The best anyone could do was stave off disaster for a handful of years. Eventually—inevitably—Earth collapsed into madness, then death. It took the Core Worlds with it.

The chain of events that led to Earthfall—and the plans made by some, particularly the Terran Marine Corps, to salvage *something* from the disaster—have been amply documented elsewhere. Our historical records are open to debate—and generations of historians have debated extensively—but the basic facts are not in dispute. Reconstructing the events following Earthfall, however, will always pose a challenge. It is very difficult to track the course of events, as the news radiated out from Earth. There were naval officers, for example, who declared themselves warlords… only to be swept away, days later, by the press of events; there were space stations, asteroid settlements and entire colonies that were wiped out, in passing, by one side or another. Governments declared quite draconian measures to control unrest—or secure their power, or remove minorities they found troublesome—and discovered, too late, that they were quite unable to enforce them. There are great gaps in the historical record that will probably never be filled.

It is simply impossible, too, to grasp the true scale of the disaster. Earth's *official* population, before Earthfall, was eighty billion. *Eighty billion!* The human mind cannot imagine so many people. It certainly cannot truly comprehend their deaths in a few short days of nightmarish horror. Nor can it grasp the deaths—millions, billions, trillions—that followed in the days, weeks and months after Earthfall. They died because society collapsed around them, they died because of military action, they died because they were the *wrong* sort of people and the military was no longer around to oppress everyone into behaving themselves…in the end, it doesn't matter why they died. All that matters is that they died.

There were some, even before my birth, who understood that the end could not be delayed indefinitely. First amongst them was the Terran Marine Corps, led—in its final years—by Major-General Jeremy Damiani. Enjoying an independence from the Grand Senate that even the Imperial Navy could not dream of, possessing an infrastructure that was largely free of political interference, corruption and cronyism, the marines were free to make their preparations for the coming disaster. Long before they recruited me—and shipped me to Avalon—they had a plan. It was not a good plan, as Damiani happily admitted, but it was the best they could put together on short notice. It says something about the scale of the problem that 'short notice' was nearly a century.

The first part of the plan called for securing colony worlds, like Avalon.

The second part of the plan involved the Core…

CHAPTER ONE

It is difficult to say when the Fall of the Galactic Empire became obvious to the vast majority of its citizens. The Core Worlders, living as they did in a political, media and social bubble, had no idea of the gathering storm until the empire collapsed and all hell broke loose. The Fringers, on the other hand, had very little contact with the Core and didn't realise—at first—that Earth was gone.

—**PROFESSOR LEO CAESIUS**

Earthfall and its Aftermath

THE CITY WAS UNNATURALLY DARK.

Specialist Rachel Green felt her heart start to pound as the aircar flew towards the distant spaceport, her enhanced eyesight picking out the armed helicopters and skimmers orbiting the installation and watching for signs of trouble. Hundreds of aircars, trucks and buses were heading to the spaceport too, the rats leaving the sinking ship. The news—Earthfall—had arrived only two weeks ago and the planet was already chaotic. The policemen, guardsmen and soldiers on the streets below weren't enough to keep long-held discontents from bursting into violence.

It will be worse when they realise that food is going to run out, sooner rather than later, she thought. Gamma Prime had never been a particularly habitable world, more dependent than most on advanced technology and food imports. There was no way they could feed everyone, now that interstellar trade had gone to the dogs. *And when they realise their leaders have abandoned them, they'll go mad with rage.*

She looked down at the darkened CityBlocks—the power had been cut, only a few short hours ago—and shivered in sympathy. The towering skyscrapers weren't anything as horrific as the endless warrens of Old Earth—*dead* Earth, now—but they were still nightmarish, as far as she was concerned. Generations of people could be born, get married, have children, grow old and die...without ever stepping into the wider world. She wondered, as the aircar adjusted course and flew towards the security zone, if Lieutenant Opal Moonchild would be grateful that Rachel had taken her place. She'd be transported off-world, whatever happened. She'd survive the brewing chaos that would throw the planet into the deepest, darkest pits of hell.

She'll be grateful once she realises she's no longer in any danger, Rachel told herself, firmly. Lieutenant Moonchild had been on long-leave, before Earthfall and the emergency recall of everyone who had ever worn a uniform. *It's I who should be concerned.*

The aircar started to descend, heading towards the landing pad. Rachel took a long breath, calming herself. She always got the shakes before a mission began, particularly one that left her isolated from the rest of the team. She'd known she'd be on her own going in, of course, right from the moment she'd been briefed...but no training and planning could ever encompass the feeling of being completely alone. If everything went to hell, she'd have to punch her way out and hope for the best. And she knew, all too well, that if her cover was blown once she was inside the security perimeter, she didn't have a hope of getting out alive.

As long as it isn't quite impossible, she thought, *I can do it.*

The aircar landed with a bump. The hatch opened. Rachel stood and clambered out, looking around with interest. The entrance was guarded by five heavily-armed men, looking so much like hulking gorillas that she *knew* they were enhanced. Their enhancements probably weren't comparable to hers, but that didn't mean they weren't dangerous. She was mildly surprised their employers hadn't tried to hide the enhancements. They probably had all their licences in order—and no one really cared any longer, in any case—but humans still reacted badly to openly-enhanced soldiers. It saved a great deal of angst if the enhancements were carefully hidden.

One of the guards peered down at her with cold, discerning eyes. "Papers, please."

Rachel removed the biochip from her blouse and held it out to him, trying to show *just* the right amount of unease under his porcine gaze. He took the chip and scanned it, his companions keeping a close eye on her. Rachel braced herself, silently calculating how best to escape if the mission failed at the first hurdle. She'd worn a tight blouse, deliberately, but they weren't eying her like a piece of meat. *That* was worrying. It suggested they were depressingly professional. They'd be harder to fool.

The biochip is perfect, she told herself firmly. *And all the details were inserted into the central databases.*

The guard returned the chip and opened the door. "Pass, friend."

Rachel felt a chill running down her spine as she walked through the door and into a large foyer. Hundreds of men and women—some clearly military, some more likely civvies—were sitting on chairs, or the hard metal floor; others, more impatient, were pacing the room while they waited to be called. Rachel found a seat and forced herself to wait, watching as names were called and people left to pass through security screening. It was nearly an hour before they called for Opal Moonchild. Rachel couldn't help feeling uneasy—again—as she walked through the door and into the security section. If she was going to be caught, she was going to be caught here.

Another guard, a stern-faced woman, caught her eye. "Strip," she ordered, shoving a large plastic box at Rachel. "Put everything, and I mean everything, in this box, then seal it up and walk into the next room."

"I understand," Rachel said. Opal would be nervous, so Rachel acted nervous. "What will they...?"

"Get on with it," the woman ordered. "My shuttle's leaving at 2250 and I don't intend to miss it."

Rachel nodded and undressed hastily, then walked into the next room. Her implants bleeped an alert as soon as the door closed, warning that her body was being scanned right down to the submolecular level. Rachel was torn between being morbidly impressed by their thoroughness and rolling her eyes in disdain. She didn't have to be *naked* for a deep scan. It was probably just a reminder that her life was in their hands, that it had been in their hands from the moment she received the recall notice. She schooled her expression into impassivity as the next door opened, allowing her to walk into the third chamber. Three beefy security guards were waiting.

"The scan says you have a neural implant," the guard said. He kept his eyes firmly on her face. "What's it for?"

"Porn," Rachel said, trying to sound ashamed. It wasn't *easy*. She'd feared they'd detect the *rest* of her implants. "I use it for VR sims..."

"A pretty girl like you needs VR sims?" The guard held up a scanner. "I have to test it."

"Go ahead." Rachel bent her head as he pressed the scanner against the back of her neck, trying not to tense too visibly. If the scanner picked up more than it should, she'd have bare seconds to take them all out before the alert sounded and the entire complex went into lockdown. "I...will it hurt?"

"Stay still," the guard ordered. "It's just a simple ping..."

Rachel smiled as her implants went to work, feeding false information into the scanner while—at the same time—accessing the security systems and subverting them. The scanner wouldn't see anything more than a simple VR cortical stimulator: shameful, as if she'd been caught with a datachip loaded with porn, but hardly illegal. Or dangerous. She could put up with hundreds of ribald jokes if it meant they missed the *rest* of her implants. She wondered, idly, what they'd make of it if they did. They'd certainly have reason to suspect that *something* was wrong.

"What a waste," the guard said. "You wouldn't need such a toy if you were with me."

"If you say so," Rachel said. She crossed her arms over her breasts. "Can I go now?"

"Yeah, sure." The guard pointed at yet another door. "See you on the flip side."

Rachel shrugged, then walked through the door and into a small changing room. A large matron was waiting for her, holding a simple uniform tunic in one hand. Her face was friendly, but her eyes were flint-hard...an anger, Rachel thought, directed at the security goons rather than Rachel herself. She felt an odd flicker of respect for the older woman. She clearly took care of the girls in her charge.

"You alright?" The matron's voice was calm, but there was an edge to it that reminded Rachel of some of her sergeants. "They can be a little... *intrusive*."

"Just a little." Rachel took the tunic and donned it with practiced ease. "Do they have to make us strip naked?"

"They're assholes," the matron agreed. "Buy a girl a drink first, why don't you?"

Rachel had to laugh. "What now?"

"Now you wait for your shuttle," the matron said. She held out one meaty hand. "I'm Grace, by the way. I don't recall seeing you before."

"I've been on leave," Rachel said. Opal had been on leave for over a year, long enough—Rachel hoped—for everyone to forget her. She'd had few acquaintances and even fewer friends *before* she'd gone on leave. As far as the data-miners had been able to determine, there shouldn't be anyone who'd known her assigned to the spaceport. "I only got the recall yesterday."

Grace shrugged. "Wait in the lounge," she ordered. "Have a drink, if you like. We'll be boarding in an hour."

Rachel nodded, keeping her face under tight control as she made her way into the lounge. It was crammed with people, all military or ex-military. They barely spoke...or drank, for that matter. The tension was so thick it was almost tangible. She wondered, absently, where the civvies were going, then decided it didn't matter. She'd made it through the security perimeter. The rest of the mission should be easy.

Don't get overconfident, she told herself, as she found a seat and settled down to wait. *You're not there yet.*

Rachel was used, very used, to waiting, but it still felt as if time was moving slower than usual before they were finally called to the shuttle. The relief in the air was almost palpable. The civilians might be too ignorant to know the planet was doomed, but the military personnel had no such luxury. Blasting into space might be their only hope of survival... no, scratch that, it was their *only* hope. Grace checked her girls were all buckled in before taking her own seat and waiting for take-off. Rachel felt a pang of guilt, mingled with the grim awareness she was probably doing Grace a favour. It was never easy when she *liked* one of the people she was going to betray.

"I hate flying," the girl next to her muttered. "I really hate flying..."

"It could be worse," Rachel said. She'd made a HALO jump through a thunderstorm once, back when she'd been young—well, younger—and stupid. The shuttle might be a military design, built more for practicality than comfort, but it was hardly an *assault* shuttle making a landing on a defended world. "Just close your eyes. It'll all be over soon."

She allowed herself a tight smile as the shaking slowly tapered into nothingness. The shuttle flight was astonishingly smooth, compared to some of *her* flights...but then, someone who'd spent most of her career behind a desk probably wouldn't realise it. Rachel reminded herself, sharply, that *Opal* had spent most of her career behind a desk. She'd probably be scared to death if *she* was on the shuttle. Rachel sighed. She'd left it too late to pretend.

A voice came over the intercom. "Ladies and gentlemen, this is your captain speaking. We will be docking at the shipyard in two hours, thirty-seven minutes. Please sit back and enjoy the flight. Anyone who wants to join the Light Year Club can apply at the front hatch..."

Rachel concealed her amusement as a senior officer towards the front of the shuttle began to shout in outrage. Idiot. He might outrank the pilot, normally, but as long as they were in transit the pilot outranked *him*. He'd be better off waiting until they docked before he gave the pilot the ass-chewing to outdo all ass-chewings. Besides, who cared about stupid jokes when the galaxy was falling apart?

Him, obviously, Rachel thought.

She closed her eyes, trying to sleep. There was no point in doing *anything* until they docked, where...she told herself, firmly, to stop worrying about it. She'd have to improvise...and have faith the rest of the team were in position. They were marines. If anyone could do it, they could. But...she shook her head. There were too many moving parts in the plan for her peace of mind, too many things that could go wrong, but...they'd planned for as many contingencies as possible. And, if all else failed, they could improvise. She grinned as she went to sleep. She was quite looking forward to it.

The shuttle shuddered, snapping Rachel awake. She opened her eyes to see the senior officers already gathering at the hatch, even though it was against safety regulations. But then, the rules didn't apply to senior officers. She snorted, then waited for Grace's command before unbuckling and joining the rest of the girls. One was asking, rather plaintively, about the man she'd left behind. Grace didn't seem to have the heart to tell her that she'd probably never see her boyfriend again.

Unless he's bagged himself a shuttle ticket too, Rachel thought, as they started to make their way through the hatch and into the shipyard. *He might just have a way to get off-world before the shit hits the fan.*

She looked around with interest as they were pushed down to the barracks. Dozens of armed guards were visible, although they carried shock-rods and neural whips rather than automatic weapons. They shoved anyone who didn't move fast enough to suit them, silencing any complaints with brandished weapons. It looked as if things were worsening, Rachel noted, as she did her best to avoid attracting attention. The planet's collapse might have accelerated. Who knew *what* had happened while they were in transit?

"We'll be waiting here until we get reassigned," Grace said, once they were in the barracks and the hatch was firmly closed. "Get some sleep. You'll need it."

A young girl held up a hand. "But what about...?"

"Stay in here and get some sleep," Grace snapped. "Do *not* go out of the barracks."

Rachel took a bunk near the door and closed her eyes, pretending to sleep as her implants reached out and queried the local node. It was locked, but her hacking implants rapidly cut through the node's defences and gained access. She scanned the security files, noting just how many soldiers, spacers and commandos had been assigned to the shipyard. Someone—the planetary governor, perhaps—was determined to keep the shipyard under tight control. It was a shame, Rachel thought, that she was going to steal it from under his nose.

She waited until everyone was asleep, then rose and looked around. Grace slept right *by* the door, snoring so loudly that Rachel was surprised that everyone else *could* sleep. The hatch was locked, probably impossible to open without making a noise. Rachel briefly considered doing it anyway, then shrugged and walked towards the washroom. She'd downloaded a copy of the shipyard's internal plans from the central database when she'd been briefed on the mission. There should be a link to the maintenance tubes just inside the washroom. She smiled as she closed the door behind her, then opened the hatch. It hadn't been locked.

Careless, she thought, *but who would have expected a new recruit to go exploring?*

Her lips twitched at the thought—marines were taught to familiarise themselves with their surroundings *before* the shit hit the fan—as she pulled herself into the tube and started climbing up towards the command centre. It was a tight squeeze, even for her, but she forced herself to cope. She'd been in worse places. It was more of a challenge to open the internal hatches without setting off the alarms. Thankfully, someone had taken down half of the security network. She smiled, rather coldly. No doubt they'd gotten tired of a constant stream of false alarms from people blundering around like idiots.

You only need one real alarm to ruin your day, she thought, as she reached the top of the shaft. The tubes didn't open *in* the command centre, unfortunately. *And this time, the alarm will be real.*

She pressed herself against the hatch, listening intently. There would be at least one guard, perhaps two, outside the command centre itself. That was procedure. She found it hard to believe they'd change *that* much, even if they *were* pressed for manpower. *Someone* would have to tell anyone who got lost that they couldn't go into the command centre...

Bracing herself, she opened the hatch and jumped through. A guard stood by the command centre hatch, his eyes widening with surprise as he saw her. She didn't give him time to recover. She drove her hand into his throat with enhanced strength, knocking him to his knees. He was enhanced too, part of her mind noted. The blow would have killed him if his throat hadn't been reinforced. Rachel didn't give him time to recover. She hit him again, harder this time. His body hit the floor with a sickening crunch.

I'm committed now, Rachel told herself. It had always been true, but... she could have played at being Opal Moonchild until she had a chance to escape, if she hadn't shown her hand so blatantly. *It's time to move.*

She searched the guard quickly, removing both his access cards and weapons, then stood and readied herself. Again. If something went wrong, the entire mission would fail spectacularly...

Smiling, she pushed her hand against the hatch and hacked the access codes.

CHAPTER TWO

Indeed, some worlds were so isolated—so cut off from the Galactic mainstream—that the inhabitants never actually realised the Empire was gone.
—**Professor Leo Caesius**
Earthfall and its Aftermath

SPACE WAS DARK, AS DARK AND COLD AS THE GRAVE.

Captain Haydn Steel *felt* it as the stealth shuttle waited, hovering just outside long-range sensor range of the shipyard. The *enemy* shipyard. It felt odd to be planning an invasion and occupation of what had been, only a few short weeks ago, a friendly shipyard, but the old certainties were gone forever. Earth was gone. The Empire was gone. And he and his men were alone.

No, he corrected himself. *We're not alone.*

He rested in his webbing, watching through the shuttle's passive sensors as they waited for the signal. The plan had seemed insane, when he'd been briefed. There simply hadn't been the *time* to gather more than a handful of marines and throw them at the problem, not when there was no way to know when Earth would actually fall. Haydn had been brought into the Safehouse Cell years ago, after he'd been promoted to captain, but it had been made clear to him that his entire career might go by without ever having to put the Safehouse Contingency into effect. He'd learned to hope that he *would* never have to watch helplessly as galactic civilisation collapsed into chaos. He'd seen the projections. The Empire, for all its flaws, was vastly superior to the nightmare that would sweep over the galaxy when it was gone.

The shipyard hung in front of his eyes, a three-dimensional image that spoke of power and potential, both long-since lost as galactic civilisation started to contract. Gamma Prime had been important, once upon a time. The Imperial Navy had placed a shipyard there that, over the next few centuries, had grown into a commercial enterprise that had rivalled Old Earth herself. Perhaps that was why it had failed, Haydn thought. Earth hadn't been able to tolerate a rival, not indefinitely. The recession had turned Gamma Prime into a dumping ground for old ships, for warships and commercial vessels that had been placed in reserve, rather than being sold to the highest bidder. No one had expected Gamma Prime to become important, once again. But it had...

And if the reports are accurate, he thought grimly, *someone is clearly trying to activate the old ships.*

His eyes narrowed as he contemplated the reports from the Pathfinders. *Someone*—more quick-witted than the usual corporate blowhard—had issued orders for all spacers and industrial workers to report to the shipyards, where...the reports weren't clear on where they'd be going, in the long run, but it was clear that their *first* destination was the shipyard. Haydn wasn't going to knock it—the chaos caused by the sudden demand for personnel had allowed the Pathfinders to get their agent onto the shipyard—but he couldn't help feeling concerned. *Someone* was thinking ahead. *Someone*...might just have a plan that conflicted with Safehouse. And who knew what would happen when the two plans collided?

We might come to terms with them, he thought. *Or we might have to push them out of the way.*

Sweat prickled down his back as he waited, intently aware of the seconds ticking away. There had been no time to plan the mission down to the last millisecond and no way to do it, even if they *had* had time. He would have expected failure, right from the start, if they wound up depending on perfect timing. Instead, they had to keep themselves at the ready for a call that could come at any moment. Or never come at all. If the Pathfinder was caught in transit—the worst possible scenario—the entire plan would fail completely before it even got off the ground. Haydn and his men wouldn't even *know* the plan had failed until it was far too late. They'd have to keep waiting until higher authority finally called the mission off.

And we'd never know what went wrong, he thought, sourly. *The only consolation is that they won't know what happened either.*

He took a long breath, reminding himself—again—that he was a marine with over twenty years of service. He was used to waiting. He was used to being on standby, waiting for a call that came late or never came at all. But…this was no normal mission. They were going to be engaging potential allies, people who might have worked with the marines…people who probably *had* worked with the marines, in happier days. Haydn had strict orders to avoid casualties, as much as possible, but both he and his superiors knew there was no way to guarantee that no innocents would be killed. Only a Grand Senator could be so foolish. If they killed the wrong man…

The thought made him snort in irritation. *No one* was that important, not even Major-General Damiani himself. The engineers and technicians and mechanics and what-have-you on the platforms surrounding the shipyard were important, true, but losing a handful wouldn't be a disaster. Not strategically, at least. But their deaths would be a personnel disaster…he shook his head. He'd do everything in his power to keep casualties as low as possible. There'd already been enough death. If the reports from Old Earth were true, eighty *billion* people were already dead.

And that's just the beginning, he thought. *It won't be long before the Core Worlds start to collapse too.*

He shuddered. Eighty *billion*! He couldn't even *begin* to grasp it. He'd seen death—death had been his constant companion, from the moment he'd dedicated his life to the corps—but death on a small scale, on a *personal* scale. He'd walked through the remains of townships, destroyed by barbarians; he'd drifted through burned-out freighters, crews tortured and murdered by pirates...he'd seen death. But eighty billion dead? He couldn't even *begin* to visualise so many people. It was just...a number. Even the billion or so people on the planet below were just another statistic. The briefing notes had made it clear that most were doomed, whatever happened. Gamma Prime couldn't survive without imports from off-world. Whoever owned the shithole hadn't bothered to invest in some proper algae-farms, damn them. The population would complain about the taste, of course, but at least they'd be *alive* to complain. And there was nothing the marines could do about it, not now. They'd just have to bear witness as the planetary government's mistakes came back to bite them.

And watch as their people pay the price for their misgovernment, he told himself, morbidly. *What* were *they thinking?*

Command Sergeant Mark Mayberry swam up beside him, his face hidden behind a helmet. "We just got word from the observers, sir," he said. "The planet is starting to riot."

Haydn winced. "And the cops aren't doing anything about it?"

"No, sir," Mayberry said. "The cops are doing the rioting."

"Brilliant," Haydn said, sarcastically. He wished he was surprised. He'd grown up on a colony world and he'd been astonished, during his first visit to Old Earth, to discover the cops there were just another gang of thugs, preying on the helpless civilians. No wonder so many people hated and feared authority, even the marines. Authority was just another enemy. "Are our people heading to the extraction point?"

"They're holding position, apparently," Mayberry said. "They seem to think they can bug out before it's too late."

"Let's hope they're right." Haydn had no illusions. Gamma Prime was descending into a nightmare. The mob would loot, rape and kill...unaware that they were destroying their only hope of survival. By the time they realised there was no more food and drink—that there would never be any more food and drink—it would be too late. The entire planet would collapse into an orgy of violence. "Tell them…"

He shook his head. He couldn't micromanage from a distance. He didn't know *what* was happening on the surface, except in the broadest of strokes. And he had no right to give orders to the Pathfinders anyway. They knew what they were doing. They'd get out before it was too late. His lips quirked. The Pathfinders probably had enough firepower to cut their way through any opposition on their way to the extraction point. If law and order had broken down, no one would be organising opposition.

"Keep me informed," he ordered. "And be ready to jump."

"Yes, sir," Mayberry said.

He turned and made his way down the aisle, checking on the men in their webbing. Haydn knew some of the younger marines would resent his attentions, although they all had enough experience to know that it was better to check and check again rather than let a single mistake stand long enough to do damage. Better the mistake was discovered before it cost a life, he reminded himself. They were going into danger…

And until we get the signal, all we can do is wait, he told himself. *And that's when mistakes happen.*

• • •

"Well?"

Ensign Susan Perkins looked up from her console. "No word, Captain."

Captain Kerri Stumbaugh told herself, firmly, that the lack of word—either from the shipyard or the planet itself—wasn't Susan's fault. The people on the surface were the ones who were supposed to send word if things changed, not an ensign who was so young Kerri half-expected her to have milk on her lips. Susan had been incredibly lucky to graduate from the naval academy—and then be streamlined into the Marine Expeditionary Force—before all hell broke loose on Earth. Normally, she would spend a year with the marines before being sent back to the Imperial Navy… Kerri snorted, dismissing the thought. There was no *normal* any longer. The Imperial Navy no longer existed, to all intents and purposes. They were alone.

She settled back in her command chair, trying to project an air of calm as she studied a holographic display that hadn't changed in the five minutes since she'd *last* looked at it. The planet itself was surrounded by orbital installations, hundreds of shuttles and spaceplanes buzzing around like angry bees. It looked as if the entire planet was being evacuated, although anyone who knew anything about interstellar logistics would know that evacuating even *one* percent of the population would be pretty much impossible. The last set of reports had made it clear that the upper crust and their support personnel—everything from spacers to butlers and maids—were being evacuated. The remainder of the population was being left to starve.

Kerri gritted her teeth, trying not to show her anger and contempt. She'd grown up on Tarsus, a world dominated by oligarchies and ruled by politicians who had about as much in common with the people they claimed to serve as *she* did with imaginary aliens from an absurd science-fantasy flick. She'd been forced to watch, helplessly, as all her applications to various naval academies and space training institutions had been declined, while arrogant rich kids had been allowed to enter without taking exams or jumping through hundreds of petty and pointless hoops. It had been the *marines* who'd given her a chance, despite her lack of qualifications. *Their* leaders didn't abandon troops—or support staff—when they became inconvenient. But then, the marines were a meritocracy. She wasn't remotely surprised that Gamma Prime's leaders were running for their lives. Their days had been numbered the moment their former subjects realised the Empire was gone.

Rats leaving the sinking ship, she thought, nastily.

"Captain," Lieutenant Tomas said. "I'm picking up a handful of ships entering the system on a least-time course to the shipyard. They'll be here in seventeen hours."

Kerri leaned forward as a new set of icons flashed into existence. "Do you have an ID?"

"No, Captain, not at this distance." Tomas worked his console for a long moment. "I think four of them are bulk freighters, but I can't be sure. They're moving at quite a clip for bulk freighters."

"I see," Kerri said.

She stroked her chin, considering. Bulk freighters were slow, ponderous ships. They made easy targets for pirates, although they rarely carried anything worth the risk. Unless…Q-Ships? She knew better than to think that converted merchant ships would make good warships, but Q-Ships were different. A Q-Ship didn't have to be fast. It just had to look unable to defend itself until the pirates got within point-blank range. And yet…why would anyone send a Q-Ship to Gamma Prime? What were the remaining ships?

Escorts, probably, she thought. Interstellar trade had been shutting down for the last two weeks, ever since Earthfall. Everyone wanted to wait and see what happened, now that Earth was gone. *And no one would send out a bunch of freighters without being sure they would come back.*

She ran through the calculations in her head. There were already too many variables for her liking, even though she was used to it. *Havoc* was safe, well-clear of any prying sensor platforms that might notice a stealthed cruiser. And yet…Kerri was uncomfortably aware that all hell would break lose if the locals realised they were being watched. Kerri herself would have no trouble breaking contact, if the locals spotted her ship in the first place, but the marines would be in deep shit. The shuttles wouldn't be able to get out of range before they were blown to hell if they were spotted.

And now we have a fleet of newcomers, she mused. *What do they want?*

She looked at the timer. The last pulse from the planet had confirmed the Pathfinder had entered the spaceport…five hours ago, give or take a few minutes. There was no hint the Pathfinder had been caught, although that was meaningless. Kerri had handled enough insertion missions—she'd been in the supporting arms ever since she'd failed Boot Camp—to know that something might have gone badly wrong, without anyone on the outside having the slightest idea. The locals might have caught the Pathfinder... she shook her head. The Pathfinder wouldn't talk, if interrogated, but the mere fact of their existence would be a tip-off. The locals would suspect something. *No one* would go to all the trouble to insert someone into the evacuation queues—and get them onto the shuttles—unless they had *something* in mind. And it wouldn't take much imagination to guess *what.* The shipyard—and the hundreds of decommissioned starships—was the only thing of any real importance in the system.

And it's only a matter of time before the shit hits the fan, she thought. *And who knows what will happen then?*

She glanced at Susan's back. "Record a burst transmission for Commodore Steel," she ordered, giving the Marine Captain the standard courtesy promotion. "Steel. Long-range sensors are detecting at least seven unidentified starships, three of them possibly warships, entering the system. ETA at shipyard is just under seventeen hours, at current course and speed. We will continue to monitor and advise."

"Message recorded, Captain," Susan said. "Compressed and ready to transmit."

"Send it down the laser link," Kerri ordered. No one would be able to detect the laser signal unless they actually managed to cross the beam itself. The odds against *that* were staggeringly high. "And inform me if he replies."

"Aye, Captain."

Kerri forced herself to relax. The unknown ships were a *long* way away. It was unlikely they could do *anything* to interfere, unless the Pathfinder waited *hours* before going into action. Or if they had a drive system out of a science-fantasy nightmare. She'd heard all sorts of stories about advanced technology secretly developed by semi-independent worlds or big corporations...she snorted under her breath. It was absurd. A corporation that developed something new, something game-changing, would have sold it to the highest bidder. A semi-independent world would have used it to make themselves *truly* independent. And besides, it had been a long time since there had been anything beyond incremental improvements in science and technology. She found it hard to imagine there was anything left to invent.

She felt the tension on the bridge start to rise, even though her crew knew that nothing had really changed. She didn't blame them. They'd all been a little unsure of themselves, when they'd heard about Earthfall. Some of the crew had friends and family on Earth, their fates unknown; others, lucky enough to be born on the Rim, feared that they might have lost contact with just about everyone outside the corps. Kerri herself wouldn't have shed many tears if her homeworld collapsed into chaos—she'd lost contact with her family long ago—but she understood. The corps was her home now. She would have regretted losing it.

The console pinged. More shuttles were leaving the planet's atmosphere, heading for the shipyard. Others...Kerri's eyes narrowed as she realised that none of the shuttles were returning to the surface, not any longer. Someone had called off the evacuation...it didn't bode well. A message appeared in her console, sent from the planet's surface...she knew what it said, even before she opened it. The planet had started its final inevitable slide into madness.

Poor bastards, she thought. She knew how dependent the locals were on technology—and imports. *They don't have a prayer.*

She glanced at the timer and winced. Time was running out: for her, for the marines, for the planetary population...a shiver ran down her spine.

Time was running out for everyone.

CHAPTER THREE

Given the time it took to travel from Earth to the Rim—to the handful of colonies that were founded in the last century before Earthfall—this is not too surprising. Very few colonists were ever able, let alone willing, to travel to Earth—they certainly saw no need to keep in touch. News from home was very late, when it arrived at all.

—PROFESSOR LEO CAESIUS
Earthfall and its Aftermath

THE HATCH OPENED WITH A HISS.

Rachel stepped inside, raising the stunner as she looked around. The control centre was massive, a giant circular chamber crammed with consoles and illuminated by holographic displays, but only a handful of people were on duty. She glanced from side to side, making sure that no one was concealed behind a piece of machinery, then opened fire. The stunner hummed as it spat nerve-jangling pulses towards its targets, sending them crashing to the deck. Rachel reminded herself, sharply, to check that her targets were *truly* unconscious before she relaxed. Stunners weren't reliable, not in combat situations. A person with the presence of mind to fake being stunned might be able to do terrible damage, if she gave him the chance.

She heard a howl and looked up. A giant of a man leapt at her, holding up his arms to cover his face. She was sure she'd hit him…she guessed the pulse had struck his tunic, giving him a shock without actually knocking him out. She darted to one side, silently grateful the man hadn't had the common sense to hit the alarm rather than try to fight. If he'd summoned help, the mission would have become a great deal harder. Instead, she rammed a fist into his gut as he landed beside her and followed up with a blow to the head. He was out of it before his body hit the deck. She checked his pulse, stunned him again just to be sure, then hastily checked the remaining bodies. Everyone seemed to be stunned.

Which doesn't mean they won't wake up in a hurry either, she thought, grimly. The *other* disadvantage of using stunners was that it was difficult to predict when their victims would wake up—or, for that matter, what state they'd be in when they *did. I have to hurry.*

She sealed the hatch, made certain there were no other ways into the control centre and checked the office. The shipyard's commanding officer didn't look up from his datapad as she stunned him, his head hitting the desk with a satisfying *THUNK*. Rachel rolled her eyes as she placed him on the deck, wondering just how he'd managed to miss the sound outside his office. The chamber was soundproofed, according to the plans, but not *that* soundproofed. Maybe he'd been reading something absorbing… she picked up the datapad and glanced at it, only to discover that it was a report on shipyard queens. She puzzled over it for a moment, then realised it referred to decommissioned ships that had been cannibalised for spare parts. The CO was lucky the Inspector General's office hadn't carried out an inspection, she noted. He'd be in big trouble if the ships couldn't be readied for deployment within six months.

Or he would have been, if the Inspector General hadn't had other problems, she thought, as she found a roll of duct tape in the maintenance locker. *Right now, the Inspector General is probably dead.*

She bound his hands and feet with tape, slapped a makeshift gag over his mouth, then left him in his office and returned to the control centre.

One of the staffers was stirring slightly, moaning as if he'd gone on a bender the previous night and was now suffering from a terrible hangover. Rachel felt a flicker of sympathy as she stunned him again, then taped him up and dumped him in the centre of the chamber. The other operators were still stunned. She taped them anyway, just to be safe. She was stronger and better trained than any of them, but her enhancements didn't make her invincible. She wasn't stupid enough to think she couldn't be taken down, if she got unlucky. Or if she made stupid mistakes.

She sat down at the prime console and pressed her hand against the sensor. It should have rejected her automatically, but the implant in her palm went to work, hacking its way through a set of civilian-grade safeguards. No one had bothered to update the system in the last twenty years, she noted. She supposed it made a certain kind of sense. The shipyard datanet was a closed system. You couldn't access it unless you were already *on* the shipyard and you couldn't *get* on the shipyard unless you passed through a set of stringent security checks. She rather suspected it would have been harder to get through security if the shit hadn't already hit the fan. The locals had been so desperate to get everyone *important* off-world before it was too late that they'd let her slip through the net.

The system opened up. She keyed through a series of menus, quickly assessing the best way to proceed. It was relatively simple to insert a message into the communicator, then order the entire network to slip into secure mode. She sealed the hatches, shutting down communications between the different compartments. If she was lucky, the locals wouldn't realise she'd carried out a soft coup before it was too late.

And if they do realise, they'll have some trouble dealing with it, she thought. The control centre was a self-contained system, isolated within a mass of hullmetal. Her opponents *might* be able to cut the control links, if they were willing to butcher their own systems, but they wouldn't be able to get to her. Not in a hurry, at least. They'd need a heavy-duty laser cutter to make an impression on the hatch. *And by the time they do, my backup will be here.*

She heard a moan behind her. She glanced back—a young woman was stirring, struggling vainly against her bonds—and then returned her attention to the display. It wasn't hard to shut down the sensor platforms, or to ready the hatches, or to order the shuttles in transit to go doggo and wait for instructions. She had no idea how long it would take the rest of the system to realise that something was wrong, but it wouldn't matter. They shouldn't be able to do anything about it...

I hope, she told herself. She sent the signal, then settled down to wait. *We're about to find out.*

• • •

"That's the signal," Sergeant Mayberry said. "We're cleared to make our approach, plan alpha."

Haydn allowed himself a tight smile. "Take us in," he ordered. "And be ready to jump if necessary."

A thrill of excitement shot through him as the shuttle hummed to life, banishing his previous concerns. Plan alpha was the best-case scenario, allowing them to actually dock at the shuttle ports rather than landing on the hull and forcing their way into the shipyard. He wasn't going to complain, not if everything worked perfectly. He'd been in enough tight spots over the years to know that a nice easy mission was nothing to sniff at. But then, the enemy had no idea they were about to be attacked. It was easy to get an advantage if you attacked without warning.

He snapped orders, watching through the shuttle's sensors as the small craft headed towards the shipyard. The orbital weapons platforms—outdated, but still perfectly capable of blowing the shuttle into dust with a single shot—were shutting down, their active sensors going offline as he watched. It meant nothing—passive sensors radiated no betraying emissions to mark their presence—but he couldn't help finding it reassuring. The closer they got to the shipyard, to vital installations the enemy couldn't afford to lose, the harder it would be for the enemy to deal with them.

Indiscriminate firing within a shipyard was a very bad idea. The enemy would wind up destroying the very facilities they were trying to save.

His intercom buzzed. "Contact in ten...nine..."

Haydn nodded to himself as Lieutenant Joseph Wooten led his men towards the hatch, readying themselves for a hard entrance. He couldn't help feeling a twinge of guilt at *not* leading his company into battle, even though he had nothing to prove to himself or anyone else. It felt *wrong* to let someone else take the risk of blundering into an enemy force and being blown away before realising his mistake. But it couldn't be helped. He understood the logic—better to lose a lieutenant than a captain—yet it still didn't sit well with him. It felt as if he was driving a knife into Wooten's back.

He volunteered for the job, Haydn reminded himself. *And you did plenty of door-knocking when* you *were a stupid greenie lieutenant yourself.*

A low *thud* ran through the shuttle. "Contact!"

The hatch hissed open. Wooten jumped through the hatch, weapon at the ready. Alerts flashed up in Haydn's helmet, warning him that weapons were being fired. He stood, following the rest of the marines as they hurried into the shipyard. A handful of bodies lay on the ground, breathing harshly. They'd been stunned before they had a chance to react.

"No obvious weapons, sir," Wooten reported. "I think they were trying to open the hatch."

Haydn looked up and down the corridor. In one direction, a blast door was firmly in place; in the other, the door looked to have been blown open... he wondered, absently, what had been used to knock it down. The average shipyard worker didn't carry shaped charges, as a general rule. He was morbidly impressed. Someone had clearly reacted quickly, although he doubted they knew what they were doing. There was no point in trying to open one of the outer hatches when there was no shuttle on the other side...

Maybe they didn't know that, he thought. A handful of bodies were carrying rebreathers. *Or maybe they were trying to get onto the hull and make their way to the emergency pods before it was too late.*

He dismissed the thought as his intercom buzzed. A female voice, very familiar. "Code Theta-Alpha?"

"Clear," he said. "Code Emily-Cat-Gwen-Elaine."

"Welcome aboard," Rachel said. "I'll clear you through the blast doors and sealed hatches, Captain, but you'll have to stun everyone you encounter."

"Understood," Haydn said. It was no surprise. "We're on our way."

He snapped orders, deploying his men to their pre-planned targets. The shipyard was immense, but only a handful of sections were vital. The marines would secure the control centre, the power cores and the life support, then give the remainder of the giant complex a flat choice between surrendering and suffocating when they ran out of air. If, of course, the defenders had a chance to coordinate resistance. A team of marines would be able to cause a great deal of trouble before they were hunted down and killed. A team of civilians…

They know the territory, he reminded himself, as they pushed through the first hatch. *They know all the little details that don't show up on the plans.*

He pushed his doubts aside as they passed through a second hatch. A dozen people were behind it, milling around awkwardly. Haydn stunned them at once, without giving them a chance to surrender. He tried not to feel guilty about it. Right now, they were just in the way. They'd have an opportunity to join Safehouse later, if they wished, or be dumped somewhere they might have a reasonable chance to build a new life for themselves. Until then…he pushed his doubts aside as they reached the intership car hatch. It was closed, the cars themselves shut down. He hoped no one had been unlucky enough to be inside them when the power shut down.

"I can call a car for you, if you like," Rachel said. "Or…"

"We'll climb up the shaft," Haydn said, as the marines opened the hatch. "Better not to risk it."

He frowned as he peered into the darkness. "Do they know there's trouble yet?"

"They know *something* is wrong," Rachel said. "There's a lot of panic in the dorms. But so far there appears to be no organised resistance."

"That's something, at least," Haydn said. "Keep me informed."

He scrambled up the hatch, silently cursing the light combat armour under his breath. It was good for a great many things, but climbing ladders wasn't one of them. He supposed he should be grateful they hadn't been ordered to use heavy combat armour. The corridors and passageways were too small. They'd get stuck. He smiled at the thought—he'd hate to be the person who had to write the after-combat report if *that* happened, then sobered. There would be worse consequences than a reaming-out from his superiors...

The hatch opened as he reached the top of the shaft. A handful of guards were clustered around the control centre hatch, trying to hack the lock. They turned, grabbing weapons as they saw him climbing through the hatch. Haydn didn't hesitate. He launched a stun grenade down the corridor, then ducked back down as blue-white light flared. The rest of the team followed him as he scrambled back up and down the corridor. The guards lay on the deck, moaning. They'd done well, he supposed, but it hadn't been good enough. They hadn't had a hope of breaking into the control centre before time ran out.

He keyed his throat mike. "Did they cut the command links?"

"It doesn't look like they thought to try," Rachel said, through the intercom. "I suppose they thought they'd get the bill."

Haydn smirked as the hatch opened, allowing them to take possession of the command centre. Corporate security guards were all the same, fearful of breaking the rules and destroying corporate property...even if they had no choice. No doubt the handful of guards who'd realised something was wrong had hesitated, too scared of the potential consequences to act decisively. Haydn had never had *that* problem. His superiors were smart enough to know there were no perfect options. They would have backed him to the hilt if he'd destroyed something to keep it from being turned against the marines.

He looked around with interest as he entered the chamber. Rachel sat at a console, looking strikingly harmless. She looked more like a computer geek than a marine pathfinder. No wonder the security officers hadn't taken her seriously. They hadn't realised just how dangerous she could be. Or that she'd taken the defences down, practically single-handedly.

"Mission accomplished," Rachel said. She didn't *sound* dangerous either, although there was an assurance in her voice that came with being very good—and *knowing* she was very good—at what she did. "Captain?"

Haydn nodded, then keyed his throatmike. "Teams sound off, by the numbers."

"Target Two secured," Wooten said.

"Target Three secured," Lieutenant Malone said.

"Target Four secured," Lieutenant Lavin said. "Captain, some of the shuttle pilots managed to disengage from the shipyard datanet and escape."

"Good thinking on their part," Haydn conceded, without heat. "Do they pose any threat to us?"

"Unclear, Captain," Lavin said. "There's no hint they carry weapons. But they could certainly raise the alarm."

"Understood." Haydn took a moment to assess the situation. The shipyard was under control, for the moment. It wasn't too likely that the planetary defenders could mount a counterattack, at least before *Havoc* and her consorts arrived. A handful of fleeing shuttles probably wouldn't make any real difference. "Secure the remaining shuttles, then hold the pilots until we have a chance to speak to them."

"Aye, sir."

Haydn glanced at Rachel. "Do you want to give them the good news?"

"No, thank you." Rachel smiled. "I should probably slip out of sight, before they notice me."

"Understood," Haydn said. Pathfinders didn't like publicity. Better the general public thought of them as supermen, with muscles on their muscles, than harmless-seeming individuals who wouldn't attract any attention from security goons. "Do you want to slip back to the shuttle?"

"I probably should," Rachel said. "Grace will have noticed I'm missing, by now. She'll put two and two together."

Haydn nodded. He didn't know who Rachel was talking about, but it didn't matter. Instead, he sat down at the console and opened the intercom. Everyone would hear him, on or off the shipyard. And they would believe… eventually. He just hoped no one would try anything stupid.

"This is the Terran Marine Corps," he said, keeping his voice as level as he could. "This installation is now under our control. Please remain calm and await processing. If you wish to remain with us, and work with us, you will have that opportunity. If, on the other hand, you wish to go elsewhere, we will do everything in our power to arrange it. However, until that moment, I must warn you that this system is now under martial law. Any attempt to impede our operations will result in immediate and thoroughly unpleasant consequences."

He paused, then continued. "My men will open the hatches as soon as possible. When they do, please follow all orders without hesitation. Thank you."

"Some of them will refuse to cooperate," Rachel said, quietly. "The people they were moving to the shipyard aren't used to the iron hand of authority."

"They'll have to get used to it," Haydn said. He'd always found Core Worlders to be silly creatures, but the ones who worked in space—where the slightest mistake could be lethal—tended to be a little smarter. "And if they're not, they can go into the stockade until we're ready to drop them somewhere out of the way."

"If there is anywhere out of the way, these days." Rachel stretched, the moment drawing attention to her tight shirt. "I'll head back to the shuttle now."

"Get some rest," Haydn ordered. "The rest of your team is already on their way."

"Good," Rachel said. "Once they're here, insert a couple into the crowd. Just in case."

"Understood," Haydn said.

CHAPTER FOUR

Indeed, they saw this as a definite bonus! Earth—as has been made clear in other volumes—was not seen as the home of civilisation, or a respected mother, but an official nuisance, source of taxmen, corporate exploiters, social justice wokescolds and people who were—not to put too fine a point on it—thoroughly uncivilised.

—PROFESSOR LEO CAESIUS

Earthfall and its Aftermath

"GO ACTIVE," KERRI SNAPPED, as soon as she saw the first report. "Tactical, bring weapons and sensors online."

"Aye, Captain," Lieutenant Tomas said. New alerts flashed up on the display. "The planetary defences are going online."

"Ignore them," Kerri said. The orbital weapons platforms were formidable, but irrelevant as long as her ship stayed out of engagement range. "Can you locate the defence force?"

"I'm picking up all four destroyers," Lieutenant Tomas reported. "Their drives are powered up, but they're not leaving orbit."

Smart move, Kerri thought. The destroyers were tough ships, but utterly outmatched by *Havoc* and her consorts. They'd do better to stay near the planetary defences than getting themselves blown away for nothing. *I wonder if their superiors will let them get away with a display of prudence.*

"Captain, I'm picking up a hail from the planetary defence network," Susan reported. "They're demanding that we vacate the system at once."

Kerri resisted the urge to say something cutting. The planetary defenders didn't have the firepower to make her withdraw. One didn't have to be a naval officer with fifty years of active service to know that four destroyers would be utterly outmatched if they tried to fight nine heavy cruisers. She'd have problems capturing the high orbitals, if she took her ships against the planetary defences, but as long as she stayed out of range she was effectively untouchable. And she had no interest in trying to capture the planet. Gamma Prime was on the brink of collapse.

"Transmit the pre-recorded message, then close all communications," she ordered. She had no intention of wasting time bandying words with the planetary government. They could stay out of the way, if they didn't want to cooperate. "Helm, keep us on course towards the shipyard."

"Aye, Captain."

Kerri settled back in her chair, watching as the display continued to update. The shipyard really *had* been heavily defended, for a free-floating installation near a Core World. It was lucky they hadn't had to punch their way through the defences or...they might have destroyed the shipyard while trying to save it. Her eyes moved to the hundreds of decommissioned starships, drifting in neat rows just inside the defence perimeter. The ships—and the trained personnel—were the true prize. She just wasn't sure how many of the ships would still be usable.

We'll find out soon, she thought, grimly. *And then we can decide how many of them we want to take with us.*

"Captain," Susan said. "The marines are requesting that we bring the transports into the defence perimeter."

Kerri nodded. "Order them to move in," she said. "And then remain within the perimeter until we're ready to leave."

She forced herself to remain calm as the transports picked up speed, heading directly towards the shipyard. The plan had seemed too improvised, too thrown together on the fly, for her peace of mind, but it seemed to have worked. Letting the planetary government do the hard job of collecting and transporting everyone with military and industrial experience had been a stroke of accidental genius. She might have felt a little guilt at swooping in and kidnapping the experienced people, once they'd been collected, if she hadn't had a great deal of experience with deeply-corrupt planetary governments. She was doing the hapless conscripts a favour. Most of them would probably agree with her. The only ones who'd think otherwise were the people who had relatives on the planet's surface.

"I'm picking up another communication from the planetary defences," Susan said. "They want to talk."

"I'm sure they do." Kerri bit down on the urge to remind the younger woman that she'd ordered all communications to be closed. "We'll talk to them after we secure the shipyard."

"Aye, Captain," Susan said.

Kerri glanced at her back, then turned her attention to the helmsman. "Commander Joaquin. Report."

"We are entering the shipyard defence perimeter now," Commander Joaquin rumbled.

"Hold position, just inside the defences," Kerri ordered. She looked at Susan. "Any updates from the Pathfinders?"

"The last update said they were nearly at the extraction point." Susan frowned. "That was fifteen minutes ago."

"There's no need to panic *just* yet," Kerri said, dryly. The planetary defences had gone to full alert. The Pathfinders might have decided to wait on the ground, rather than draw attention from the orbital weapons platforms. Pathfinders were tough, but a single plasma burst or railgun strike would be more than enough to vaporise their shuttle and scatter their atoms across the planetary surface. "Let me know when they send an update."

Susan glanced up. "Shouldn't we be planning to rescue them...?"

Kerri made a mental note to remind the girl, again, that questioning her superior officers in the middle of an operation was *not* a good idea. "There's no need to panic *just* yet," she repeated. She pretended not to notice the girl flushing bright red. "If they don't get back in touch with us...we'll do something about it then."

She kept her face impassive, even as she thought hard. It wouldn't be *easy* to recover the Pathfinders, not if they were pinned down. Even *trying* might prove disastrous, if the planetary government hadn't twigged to their presence. And...the planet was becoming chaotic. It was quite possible they'd been lost somewhere within the vast planetary charnel house...

Worry about that when it happens, she told herself, firmly. *Until then, concentrate on your duties.*

"Captain, the transports are docking now," Lieutenant Tomas reported.

"Very good," Kerri said. "Hold position and *wait*."

"Aye, Captain."

• • •

"The transport is in position, sir," Sergeant Mayberry reported. "The secondary transport is at the lower docks."

"Understood," Haydn said. He glanced at the hatch. "Open it."

The hatch hissed open, revealing a barracks. It was larger than anything *he'd* enjoyed, as a lowly marine rifleman, although anyone who wasn't used to such accommodation would find it more than a little claustrophobic. The occupants were all women, ranging from girls just out of their teens to middle-aged ladies who looked torn between fear and defiance. They'd heard his message, he was sure, but he had no idea if they believed it. Pirates were fond of pretending to be naval officers until they got into weapons range.

He raised his voice. "Form an orderly line, one by one," he ordered. "If you're carrying any weapons, leave them behind. Anyone found with a weapon will spend the voyage in irons. Make sure you have your ID chips..."

A line formed behind a grim-faced woman who looked to be pushing forty. Haydn studied her for a moment, then ran her ID through the processor and directed her through the airlock and into the transport. She—and her fellows—would be held in stasis until they reached Sanctuary, where they'd have a choice between joining the marines or being sent elsewhere. Haydn was fairly sure most of them would stay, once they realised they would be protected for the first time in their lives. The corps wouldn't take advantage of them.

We'll be offering a chance to help rebuild, Haydn thought, as the line started to move. *How many people could turn that down?*

He felt a moment of grim concern as the barracks slowly emptied. The women had been crammed into the compartment, crammed so tightly they'd practically slept two to a bunk. The mischievous side of his mind noted they'd probably gotten very friendly, but the more practical side found it odd. He passed the duty to Lieutenant Travis and checked the stream of updates from the other checkpoints. There were so many people on the shipyard that the installation's life support must have been pressed to the limit. He knew there was a great deal of redundancy built into the system—the old-timers had been practical engineers, not dreamers—but any *competent* safety inspector would have howled in outrage. For once, he would have had a point. The slightest mishap would have condemned hundreds of people to a horrible death.

"I think they're breeding stock," Rifleman Leyland noted. "They're all young women..."

"That will do," Haydn said. "Concentrate on your duties."

He scowled at the datapad, watching as the numbers slowly added up. There *was* a slight preference in favour of women, young women. Experienced, true, but...odd. He didn't want to consider the possibility that Leyland might be right. A colony couldn't survive without mothers... if he was right, where had they intended to *go*? It wasn't as if they were shipping people to the Outer Worlds, or even to the Rim. It made no sense.

And they didn't recruit young mothers, he thought. *They recruited people with experience.*

He put the thought aside. The mystery would solve itself, sooner or later. Until then…he had work to do.

• • •

Rachel had had a quick power nap, as soon as she'd boarded the marine shuttle, but—afterwards—she hadn't been able to keep from returning to the shipyard. It wasn't *that* big a risk, she told herself. Grace—and everyone else who might have seen her, who might have realised that she'd vanished shortly before the shit hit the fan—had been moved to the transports, where they would be held in stasis until the ship reached its destination. She *looked* like a harmless intelligence officer, not a lethal specialist. And besides, it kept her from worrying about the rest of her team. They hadn't returned to the MEU. She had no idea what was keeping them.

She found her way to a data room and sat down at the console, inputting a handful of codes to unlock the system. The WebHeads had already copied everything—the intelligence officers on Safehouse would dissect it, piece by piece—but she was morbidly certain they'd miss everything *important*. Marines were riflemen first and foremost, yet…even *marine* intelligence officers had a tendency to miss the trees for the forest. Or sometimes the forest for the trees. She smirked, then started to access the files. The corporate shipping manifests were a mess. Someone was probably going to be fired for it.

If their superiors ever find out, she thought, as she opened the first file. *And they probably never will.*

She worked her way through the file—a series of passenger manifests, listing people who'd been transported from the planet to the shipyard—hoping that *something* would leap out at her. There was nothing, apart from an ever-growing list of evacuees…it was astonishing, she noted, just how *many* experienced personnel had been living on Gamma Prime. She would have expected anyone with any *real* experience to realise just how fragile the planet's ecosystem was and run away, right to the edge of explored space if necessary. Had someone been inviting them to move to Gamma Prime? She couldn't find any record of it. The Imperial Navy's interest in the system had waxed and waned as resources rose and fell. The corporations hadn't been much better. There was little to attract anyone, save perhaps for vast land grants. But those weren't enough to attract *everyone.*

Odd, she mused. She flipped through another set of files. A marine—Captain Steel, she noted—had raised questions about just how *many* people had been transported to the shipyard. She felt her eyes narrow as she checked the figures. How the hell had she missed *that*? There were too many people on the shipyard for anyone's peace of mind. *Why didn't they send the evacuees to the orbital habitats?*

Her mind raced. The habitats were big enough to take all the refugees, without pushing their life support into the red. Sure, there'd be a little crowding...maybe *that* was why they'd been sent to the shipyard. The habitats were owned by the great and the good, people who would complain if they had to share their homes with their social inferiors... people who wouldn't know the difference between whiskey and gin if their lives depended on it. But...who *cared* about what the rich thought, after Earthfall? Trillions upon trillions of credits had been wiped out, when the interstellar economy collapsed. The planetary government could have forced the rich to take evacuees...at gunpoint, if necessary. There was no solid reason *not* to put them on the asteroid habitats. Transporting them to the shipyard was an unnecessary risk.

And that means there must be some reasoning behind it, Rachel mused. She'd served long enough to know that something might make sense to one person and, at the same time, be utterly absurd to someone else. *What were they thinking?*

The more she looked at it, the less sense it made. They'd moved too *many* people to the shipyard, too many to handle easily...if they'd wanted to bring the shipyard back to full production, and bring the decommissioned ships back into service, they'd actually brought too *many* people. They'd be tripping over themselves when they tried to organise their people to actually *work*. She frowned, puzzling it out. It made no sense...

And then it hit her.

"This isn't their final destination," she said, out loud. She kicked herself, mentally. She should have seen it right from the start. The planetary government had been gathering the evacuees so someone *else* could collect them and...and transport them elsewhere. She felt a giggle escape her lips, despite her best efforts. "And we came and stole them before they could be collected."

She keyed her intercom. "Commander, this is Green. What happened to the CO?"

"He's in the brig," Commander Walters said. He'd taken over the shipyard, once the remainder of the MEU had arrived. "Do you want him?"

"I want to have a few words with him," Rachel said. "Can you clear me for access?"

There was a long pause. Rachel knew what Walters was thinking. Technically, the CO had to be held until higher authority could decide what to do with him. He wasn't supposed to be interrogated. But...Rachel was a Pathfinder, with wide authority to do whatever she thought was necessary to get the job done. She wondered, absently, if Walters would forward the question to Captains Steel or Stumbaugh or...make a decision for himself. Walters wasn't a marine. He was just...an auxiliary. He might not have the nerve to say yes or no.

"I've cleared you," Walters said, finally. "Make sure you record everything."

Teach your grandmother to suck cock, Rachel thought crudely, as she rose and headed for the hatch. *You could have been a little more decisive...*

She pushed the thought aside as she reached the brig. A handful of senior officers and corporate managers had been captured and, in accordance with standard convention, held separately from their men. She checked the pickups—the CO was sitting on a bench in his cell, his head in his hands—then opened the hatch. He looked up, his eyes narrowing when he saw her. She saw cold calculation, just for a second. She hoped he'd have the sense to realise he didn't have a hope of escape, even if he somehow managed to subdue or capture her. The entire shipyard was in unfriendly hands.

His eyes glared at her. "What do you want?"

"I have a question," Rachel said. "Who was intended to collect the evacuees?"

She had the satisfaction of seeing his eyes open with surprise, just for a second. "What...?"

"You gathered them all here," Rachel said. "You put your life support at risk...the only reason that makes sense is that someone was coming to pick them up. Who?"

The CO looked at the deck. "I won't talk."

"Someone will," Rachel said. There were ways to prevent someone breaking, under interrogation. Implants, conditioning...it wasn't that difficult. The CO probably had at least *some* conditioning. It was fairly standard among higher-level types. "What do you think is going to happen to you, when we send you back? They're not going to be very pleased with someone who lost an entire shipyard to a single attacker."

"Hah," the CO said.

Rachel allowed her gaze to harden, willing him to believe. "If you tell me freely, we'll give you a free ticket to wherever you want to go. And some trade goods, if you like. If not...you'll go into an interrogation lab. Maybe we can break you. Maybe your brain will start melting and leaking out of your ears instead."

"Fuck." The CO looked from side to side, as if he expected someone to come riding to the rescue. "They'll kill me."

"We might kill you, once we get you in the lab," Rachel pointed out. She had no idea if she was bluffing. Her superiors might sanction an extreme interrogation, or they might not. It wasn't as if the CO was a terrorist who deserved to die slowly and painfully. He'd been doing his job when he'd been captured. "But if you cooperate, we'll make it worth your while."

The CO eyed her for a long moment. "You have authority to make a deal?"

"Yes." Rachel met his eyes, evenly. "Talk now and we can deal. Talk later…and, well, whatever is left of you will be dumped on a penal world."

"Fine," the CO said. "You'd better give me a new ID, after this."

"We can do that," Rachel said. "Talk."

CHAPTER FIVE

It is therefore unsurprising that vast numbers of distant colonies effectively slipped out of the Empire's control long before Earthfall, even though—in theory—they remained part of the Empire. It was difficult, almost impossible, for the Empire in its waning years to impose itself on the colonies.

—PROFESSOR LEO CAESIUS

Earthfall and its Aftermath

"CAPTAIN," TOMAS SAID. "The unknown ships are reversing course."

"Interesting," Kerri mused. "Did someone signal them?"

"Unknown." Tomas glanced up at her. "We didn't detect any radio transmissions, but they could have used a narrow-beam or a pinpoint laser..."

Kerri nodded, curtly. It would be difficult to use a laser to communicate at such a distance—the bulk freighters were tiny, on an interplanetary scale—but it wasn't impossible. She hadn't had time to deploy a network of sensor platforms to watch for narrow-beam communications...not, she supposed, that she could have done anything about it if she *had* detected a transmission. The unknown ships were well out of range. She could detach a cruiser or two to chase them, but they'd be over the Phase Limit *long* before her ship could run them down.

"Keep an eye on them," she ordered. The unknowns would go, as silently as they'd come. "Do we have an update from the shipyard?"

"Yes, Captain," Susan said. "The advance parties state that a third of the decommissioned ships are either serviceable or can be returned to service relatively quickly. They're already moving the personnel to the transports and they're ready to depart on your command."

"Assign *Pollux* and *Nemesis* to escort the transports home," Kerri ordered. She had no idea how long it would be before things changed, perhaps for the worse. Gamma Prime wasn't *that* isolated. Sooner or later, one of the warlords would remember the shipyard and send ships to take it. "When can they get the ships underway?"

"They're detaching tugs and worker bees now," Susan said. "They think they can get the ships moving in a few short hours."

Kerri nodded. The ships wouldn't be combat-worthy, of course, but at least they'd be away from Gamma Prime. She'd take them to a concealed shipyard, where they would be refitted and prepared for deployment. A handful would probably have to be cannibalised to keep the rest underway, but...she shrugged. It didn't matter. The ships would be refitted well before crews were assigned to them. There would be no one to complain about *their* ship being sacrificed to keep the others alive.

Which was always a problem, back in the day, Kerri thought, wryly. *The Imperial Navy had too many captains with political connections to get anything done.*

She allowed herself a moment of amusement, then sobered. It wasn't good news. The Imperial Navy had *also* had a lot of very capable, very competent officers who'd never been promoted to command rank because they lacked political connections. Their ambitions had been stifled, their resentments growing even as the empire they served weakened. How long would it be, she asked herself, before some of those officers realised they could just *take* the ships they wanted? How long would it be before even *more* warlords appeared on the galactic scene?

Probably not too long, she told herself, grimly. *And some of them will have enough firepower and supplies to become a major threat.*

"Captain," Susan said. "I'm picking up a signal from the planetary government. They want to negotiate."

"Really?" Kerri considered it for a moment. "What do they have to negotiate *with*?"

"I don't know, Captain," Susan said.

That was a rhetorical question, Kerri thought, wryly. The poor ensign wasn't experienced enough to realise it. She was luckier than she knew. There were officers who wouldn't have hesitated to tear her a new asshole—hopefully metaphorically—for daring to answer the question. *They don't have anything to offer us, not now.*

She leaned forward. "Have we heard anything from the Pathfinders?"

"No, Captain," Susan said.

Kerri frowned. If the Pathfinders had been caught, or simply pinned down...it would cause some problems. She might have to negotiate for their freedom. But...she shook her head. The planetary government wouldn't play games, if they knew they had leverage. They'd make it very clear that they knew they *did* have something to bargain with. Kerri wasn't sure what she'd do, if she did have to negotiate. Her orders didn't give her much leeway.

"We wait," she said, calmly.

She felt an odd unease as she surveyed the holographic display, even though she *knew* there was no reason to worry. No logical reason, at least. There was no force in the system that could match her, as long as she didn't go too close to the planetary defences. She'd be in some trouble if she wanted to *take* the planet, she admitted coolly, but thankfully she didn't have to do anything of the sort. And it would be a long time before forces arrived from elsewhere to dislodge her. It would have taken weeks to get a relief force organised, back in the old days. Now, it was anyone's guess if anyone would care enough to bother.

The old days, she mocked herself. *They were only a few short weeks ago.*

Perhaps *that* was the root of her unease, she considered. She could *feel* the seconds ticking by. The universe she'd grown up in was gone. All the old certainties were gone. The old rules no longer applied. She'd seen some of the reports, back before the squadron had been dispatched to Gamma Prime. Earth had merely been the first world to fall. Death and devastation were sweeping across the galaxy. She could no longer rely on anything and she knew it.

I can rely on the corps, she thought. *And they can rely on me.*

"Captain," Susan said. "I just picked up a burst transmission. The Pathfinders are on their way."

Kerri let out a breath she hadn't realised she'd been holding. "Have them brought onboard, when they arrive," she ordered. "And then we can start preparing to vacate the system."

"Aye, Captain."

• • •

Haydn felt as if he'd gone beyond mere exhaustion as he walked through the empty shipyard, checking—again—that they hadn't missed anyone as the engineers and techs steadily stripped the installation of anything useful. The Imperial Navy had designed the shipyard to make it easy to dismantle and move elsewhere, given enough freighters and technicians, but the corporate bosses hadn't been as farsighted. *Their* additions to the original design were proving a nightmare, causing delay after delay as each non-standard installation was either dismantled or pushed to one side for later attention. Clearly, *they* had never heard of the KISS principle. Haydn wasn't surprised. Corporate bureaucrats weren't known for caring about anything beyond their monthly profit margins.

He stopped outside a transparent blister and peered out, into the icy depths of space. The stars burnt in the darkness, utterly unconcerned about the affairs of man. It still surprised him, at times, that they didn't twinkle in space, although he knew the stars only seemed to twinkle because of atmospheric distortion. A handful of lights could be seen as the technicians worked on the ships, powering a handful towards the edge of the defence perimeter. They'd be moved or towed to the Phase Limit, once the remainder of the shipyard had been stripped. By then, Haydn was fairly sure he'd be well on his way to his next deployment. There were more fires to put out than there were marines to piss on them.

"Captain Steel?"

Haydn turned and blinked in surprise as he saw a young woman making her way towards him, wearing a standard shipyard tunic. She looked... harmless, almost *too* harmless. She was practically the very model of a nerdy girl, so shy and retiring that she was practically unnoticeable. No one would pay any attention to her. And yet...his eyes narrowed as he picked up a faint sense of *danger.* His instincts knew she was trouble, even though he couldn't put it into words. And then he realised who he was looking at.

"Specialist Green," he said. He shook his head in quiet admiration. He'd *met* Rachel Green and yet .. he almost hadn't recognised her. It was astonishing what a handful of tiny cosmetic changes—and a marked shift in attitude—could do. "What can I do for you?"

"You're out here, alone?" Rachel stood next to him, staring out into space. "Where are the rest of your team?"

"Half of them are catching some rest," Haydn said. "The remainder are on standby, waiting for something to happen. I should be resting too."

Rachel shrugged. "I was interrogating Commander Anshan."

Haydn lifted an eyebrow. "Anshan?"

"The CO—the *former* CO." Rachel smiled, as if she was reliving the moment when she'd taken Anshan's shipyard from under his nose. "He had a few interesting things to tell me, once I promised him safe passage somewhere else."

"Really?" Haydn was mildly surprised the shipyard had been in the hands of a *mere* commander. Gamma Prime was hardly a tiny little colony on the ass-end of nowhere. It wouldn't be hard for *someone* to make money while they counted down the days until they could go home. "What did he say?"

"We thought they were moving essential personnel into space before all hell broke loose, down below." Rachel jabbed her finger at the deck, as if the planet was directly below the shipyard. "I thought they were bringing too *many* people to the shipyard. They were pushing the safety limits to the margins, about as far as they would stretch if something didn't go wrong."

Haydn nodded, slowly. Put that way, it sounded odd. No one in their right mind would risk pushing their life support too far, even if they kept the system in perfect condition. And, on a shipyard that had practically been written off years ago, he wouldn't have trusted the life support any further than he could throw the entire installation. God alone knew how many components had been left in place, well past their replacement date, or simply cannibalised to keep another part of the giant structure alive. Transporting tens of thousands of people onto the shipyard would have been a dangerous gamble. Haydn wouldn't have taken it unless he was desperate.

"Why?" He glanced at her, sharply, as the pieces fell into place. "They were being moved onwards, weren't they?"

"So it seems," Rachel said. "Commander Anshan believed the evacuees were going to be transported to Hameau."

"Hameau," Haydn repeated. It meant nothing to him, but it wouldn't be the first time trouble came out of a system he'd never heard of. A lifetime spent travelling from trouble spot to trouble spot had convinced him that *anywhere* could turn troublesome, given time. "And they were going to be transported...when?"

"Soon," Rachel said. "We beat them to the punch."

"Good," Haydn grunted. It was disturbing, the more disturbing the more he thought about it. They'd been in a race, without knowing it. The only upside was that whoever had been on the other side had clearly been unaware of it too. He supposed it shouldn't have surprised him. Gamma Prime was an obvious target for someone who realised the Empire was nearly extinct. "Why?"

"Presumably, they did it for the same reason *we* did." Rachel shrugged, expressively. "They wanted to put the evacuees, all the trained and experienced personnel, to work."

"Yeah." Haydn rubbed his scalp. It felt itchy after hours in combat armour. "We'll have to inform our superiors."

"Yeah," Rachel echoed. "And then...what?"

Haydn smiled. "Someone a bit higher up the food chain will have to make *that* call."

"Belinda Lawson's report stated that other people were making contingency plans of their own," Rachel said, as if Haydn hadn't spoken. "We could find ourselves clashing with *others* who weren't caught by surprise."

"Belinda?" Haydn shrugged. It didn't matter. "It was predictable."

But was it? He'd moved from trouble spot to trouble spot—yes, he had—and he'd *seen* the Empire's steady decline. And he'd grown up on a world that made Earth seem like a nightmare of steel and shadows, where the crime rate was so high that people just shrugged off things like being mugged or raped or watching their relatives being murdered right in front of them...he shook his head. People could get used to anything. They might not have realised the Empire's days were numbered.

And anyone with the power to do anything about the coming fall might keep it to themselves, Haydn thought. Only a handful of marines had been briefed on Safehouse before Earthfall, before it had become impossible to keep the news from the rest of the corps. *Who started collecting experienced personnel as soon as the news reached them?*

He put the thought aside. "Our superiors will have to worry about it," he said, calmly. "We have other problems right now."

"True." Rachel grinned. "I have to rejoin the team."

"I'm glad to hear they got out safely," Haydn said. "Have you made a report to the CO?"

"I passed it up the chain," Rachel said. "But you're right. Someone with more brass on his shoulders will have to decide what to do with it."

She turned and hurried off. Haydn watched her go, feeling torn between two contradictory impressions. Rachel was harmless, utterly harmless... and, at the same time, a deadly warrior with enhanced strength and speed. It was difficult to rid himself of the former impression even though he *knew* she was tougher than him. She would have been hard to handle even *before* she'd been enhanced. He would have bet half his pay packet she had a few weapons hidden under her pale skin.

If I still get paid, he thought, wryly. The marine banking system was still intact, as far as he knew, but he wasn't sure if his bank balance meant *anything*. Earth was gone. The interstellar economy had practically evaporated. It was quite likely that everyone's banking datachips were worthless, now that the banks were gone. Their owners couldn't even use them to wipe their asses. *Do I even have any money left at all?*

He shook his head. Under the circumstances, it didn't matter.

• • •

"Captain," Tomas said. "The captured ships are ready to depart."

Kerri nodded. It had taken longer than they'd promised—four days, instead of two—but thankfully no hostile force had turned up to force her to cut and run. She'd had visions of being faced with a choice between destroying the ships herself and letting them fall into potentially-hostile hands...she hadn't wanted to do the former, yet she'd known she *couldn't* do the latter. She promised herself she'd make a prayer of thanks, later. She knew she had a great deal to be thankful for.

"Order the flotilla to start moving, as planned," she said. "And then send our farewell message to the planetary government."

"Aye, Captain," Susan said.

"Helm, keep us on station," Kerri added. "Tactical, watch for trouble."

She turned her attention to the planetary display, wondering if the government would do anything—anything at all—to impede their departure. Hundreds of messages had been received and logged, ranging from threats to promises and pleas. Kerri had ignored them, right until the moment she was ready to leave. If the planetary government cooperated...she shook her head. It was hard to be sure, now the forward teams had been extracted, but it was fairly clear that Gamma Prime was doomed. The orbital installations would wither and die shortly after the planet itself.

They'll be eating themselves in the streets, she thought, numbly. Her stealthed probes had noted fires burning out of control, entire CityBlocks collapsing into rubble...Earth had always claimed the CityBlocks were so stable that nothing, not even a nuke, could bring them crashing down. She wasn't surprised they'd been wrong. *And their deaths will pass unnoticed as the chaos spreads wider and wider.*

She allowed herself to relax as the flotilla picked up speed, heading up above the system plane as it headed to the Phase Limit. They were safe, now. The mission had been carried out perfectly, from start to finish. There hadn't been any casualties on either side...she shuddered. *That* wasn't entirely true. The entire planetary population was about to become a casualty. She knew it wasn't her fault, that the population had been doomed from the moment the government had started cutting corners, but it still grated on her. It would be worse, she supposed, if she could truly grasp how many people were about to die. They were just...numbers.

And they're a drop in the bucket compared to Earth's teeming billions, she thought, glumly. *And those teeming billions are all dead.*

Tomas cleared his throat. "Captain, the charges are ready for detonation."

"Confirm that everyone got off the shipyard," Kerri ordered. It went against the grain to destroy whatever they couldn't take with them, but she was damned if she was leaving anything behind for their unknown rival. "Once you're sure, send the detonation command."

"Aye, Captain." Tomas worked his console. "All present and accounted for."

"Then send the command," Kerri said. "Now."

She returned her attention to the display, watching as the shipyard icons winked out of existence. It was so...sterile. There was no hint of the nuclear megatonnage tearing the shipyard apart, atomising the facilities and melting the handful of remaining starships. They would be well beyond repair, if anyone cared to try. It would be cheaper and easier to build an entirely new fleet from scratch.

But it may be a long time before anyone can, she mused, as her fleet picked up speed. *The interstellar economy is gone.*

CHAPTER SIX

This was both good and bad for the colonies themselves. On one hand, they were designed to be self-sufficient, at least in the essentials of life. Most colonies could and did feed themselves; indeed, many worlds produced a significant food surplus that, in happier times, might have supplied off-world asteroid mining colonies, cloudscoops and other installations.

—**Professor Leo Caesius**

Earthfall and its Aftermath

IT HAD OFTEN SURPRISED Major-General Jeremy Damiani, Commandant of the Terran Marine Corps, that Safehouse-I had never been colonised, let alone developed, even though it was relatively close to the Core Worlds. A lone moon orbiting a lone gas giant, the only object of interest within the otherwise useless system, it should have drawn some attention. But then, there was little to draw settlers and tourists to the system. Anyone who wanted to set up a hidden colony would prefer to be a great deal further from the Core.

He stood by the transparent hullmetal window and stared over the plain. The views were spectacular, if nothing else. The gas giant hung in the sky, a giant blue orb that utterly dominated the tiny moon; the lands below the window looked strewn with white snow and ice. It looked charming, if one didn't know the surface was largely composed of liquid nitrogen. The installations the corps had established, over the years, were buried well beneath the ground. They wouldn't be easy to detect, even if the system was searched thoroughly by an entire fleet. Safehouse was practically undetectable.

Or so we tell ourselves, he thought, grimly. The Slaughterhouse was gone. It hadn't *just* been bombarded from space, although that would have been more than enough to render the world useless. The atmosphere had been thoroughly poisoned, rendered so antagonistic to human life that anyone who set foot on the ruined world without heavy-duty armour would be dead in a few short hours. *If Safehouse is discovered too soon, whoever wrecked the Slaughterhouse will come for it too.*

He gritted his teeth as he watched snow being blown through the air by a gust of wind. He'd taken control of the contingency plans from his predecessor, when he'd been promoted to Major-General, but...he'd always hoped he wouldn't be the one who actually put them into action. The Empire had been failing for years, yet...he'd dared to hope he'd see out his entire career before it finally collapsed. But he hadn't been so lucky. He'd been the man on the spot when the shit hit the fan.

And, no matter what we do, trillions of people are going to die. There's nothing we can do to stop it.

The thought gnawed at him, mocking him. He'd spent his career fighting to protect a population that, all too often, regarded his men as wolves in human form. And yet...he'd failed, in the end. The people who had been safe and warm because men like *him* had been ready, willing and able to commit violence on their behalf were no longer safe.

The news was a constant liturgy of horror. Earthfall had merely been the start. War, death and destruction, rape and slavery...ethnic cleansing and all the attendant horrors as ancient conflicts, conflicts Jeremy and his men had tried to keep under control, restarted one final time. Entire planets collapsing into chaos, their populations going mad and tearing down the infrastructure that might—*might*—give them a chance of survival. Jeremy had seen the classified projections—he knew the specialists had predicted that twenty to thirty percent of the population would die in the first year, after Earthfall—but reality had somehow managed to be worse. Each successive wave of chaos claimed billions of lives.

Jeremy shook his head, slowly. Entire governments had declared independence, although it was pointless when there was no one left to declare independence *from*. Former Imperial Navy officers had declared themselves warlords, tearing the navy into a hundred feuding factions that would try to re-unite the human race under their rule, or die trying; garrisons that had once tried to protect ungrateful populations were turning on their hosts, throwing the rules of engagement to the winds and hammering insurgents who'd been protected by the laws of war...insurgents who were now being slaughtered, along with millions of innocents caught in the crossfire. And it was all so pointless! Jeremy suspected that half the warlords wouldn't survive the first year. Even if they kept themselves alive, would they be able to keep their ships functional? Jeremy doubted it.

He shuddered. Two days ago, a report had informed him that a fully-loaded bulk freighter had fallen out of orbit and crashed into a planetary biosphere. Hundreds of thousands of people had died in the first few seconds alone. Six weeks ago, it would have been a sensation. Ill-informed media pundits would have speculated on the cause—accident or terrorism, who knew? Grand Senators would have made pronouncements and promised new laws to prevent further such disasters, without ever knowing what had caused the disaster in the first place. There would have been protest marches and counter-marches and violence on the streets...six weeks ago. Now, it was barely noticeable. Hundreds of thousands dead? What were they, compared to the eighty *billion* people who'd died on Earth?

And the media is gone, he thought. *That probably makes things a little easier.*

He had to smile, even though he knew he shouldn't take any pleasure in the fall of the media empires who'd made his life hell. There would be no more journalists putting themselves in danger for a scoop, no more reporters taking his words out of context, no more editors making details up out of whole cloth, no more publishers insisting on articles being slanted to reflect political orthodoxy…whatever that happened to be at the time. The nasty part of his mind hoped the reporters were *enjoying* watching their world falling apart. The bastards had played a major role in undermining social trust. It was only *right* they would finally reap what they had sowed.

And you should take your pleasures where you can find them, he thought. *There's nothing you can do about it anyway.*

His wristcom buzzed. "Commandant? They're ready for you."

"I'm coming." Jeremy took one last look at the gathering storm, and eerie lightning flickering amongst the darkening clouds, then turned and walked to the door. "I'll be there in a moment."

There were no frills on Safehouse, nothing that might distract the base's staff from the awareness that the colony had only ever been intended as a temporary refuge. Even now, with the barracks crammed with evacuees from the Slaughterhouse and the training rooms steadily putting the final generation of recruits through their paces, Safehouse was about as welcoming as a prison. He made a mental note to do *something* to make the place more homely, although he wasn't sure what. The corps had a vast collection of paintings, some dating all the way back to semi-mythical organisations like the Royal Marines, the United States Marine Corps and the French Foreign Legion, but they were all in bunkers on the Slaughterhouse. It would be a long time before they were recovered, if ever. Jeremy knew there would always be something more important to do.

But a generation that has no past has no future, he reminded himself. It had been terrifying, once upon a time, to realise just how ignorant the average citizen was—and, worse, how ignorant they were of their own ignorance. *We have to make sure the newcomers know where we came from.*

The briefing room was larger than he would have preferred, he admitted to himself, but it was comfortably barren. A pair of folding tables sat in the centre, surrounded by a cluster of folding chairs. Someone had pulled them out of a MEU, he guessed. They'd been designed to allow marine officers to set up a command post at terrifying speed, with none of the frills their naval or army counterparts demanded as a matter of course. A holographic projector sat on one of the tables, displaying a star chart that had changed—politically speaking—sometime in the last two hours. It wasn't *easy* to keep track of political changes. Jeremy was uncomfortably aware that the chart might already be out of date—again.

He looked at the far wall, feeling a touch of wistfulness. The transparent metal overlooked one of the larger training rooms, where—he knew—new recruits would be being put through their paces. It had been fifty years, more or less, since he'd been a recruit, fifty years since he'd been so innocent that all that mattered was pleasing the Drill Instructors and mastering everything from unarmed combat and sharpshooting to tactics and logistics. He was tempted to stroll over to the window and watch, knowing it might be the *last* generation of recruits. Instead, he took his seat.

"Well," Jeremy said. "Shall we begin?"

He allowed his gaze to wander the room. Colonel Chung Myung-Hee, Marine Intelligence, sat beside the projector, her face grim. Beside her, Major-General Gerald Anderson, 1st Marine Division, looked uncomfortable. He was not the sort of man to *like* being trapped on Safehouse when he could be in command of his formation, heading out to crack some heads together. Jeremy understood that impulse. There were nine Major-Generals in the Marine Corps and seven of them had combat assignments. If Earthfall had waited a few days, Anderson and his men would have been on their way when the shit hit the fan.

"Sir," Chung said. "We have received word from Gamma Prime."

Jeremy studied her for a long moment. She was a short, heavy-set woman with dark hair and a sense of *age* that reminded him she'd actually been in the corps longer than he had. And yet, as an intelligence officer, she was permanently barred from the highest ranks. He might have worried about that, if he'd been in the navy. The corps, thankfully, allowed intelligence officers to qualify as line officers, if they wished. It kept resentments from building to dangerous peaks.

"What happened?"

"The operation itself was a success," Chung said. "The shipyard was seized. The personnel and decommissioned starships are being moved to secure locations. However, there was a curious incident. The planetary government intended to send its cadre of experienced personal to Hameau."

"Hameau," Jeremy repeated, slowly. "I seem to recall *something* about that world."

"It's a corporate settlement," Chung said. She indicated the planet on the display. "It belongs, through a series of shell companies, to the Onge Corporation. They were developing the planet as a centre of industry and space technology."

Jeremy's eyes narrowed. Grand Senator Stephen Onge had been an old sparring partner, always trying to bring the Marine Corps under the control of the Grand Senate. Jeremy had suspected the old bastard had had *some* form of contingency plan for Earthfall, even though he hadn't had any proof until the shit *really* hit the fan. But Onge himself had died when he'd attempted to flee Earth with the Childe Roland. It had probably been too much, Jeremy acknowledged privately, for the Grand Senator's conspiracy to die with him. The Onge Corporation had had more power, wealth and resources than most planetary governments. Power like that didn't simply...go away.

"And...they were willing to snatch the people *we* wanted to snatch," Jeremy commented.

"The people we were going to kidnap, kidnapped," Anderson said. "How *terrible*."

"It isn't as if we were going to use them as slaves," Jeremy said.

"We *were* going to take them—we *did* take them—without asking if they wanted to come," Anderson pointed out, dryly. "And not all of them are going to work for us willingly."

Jeremy nodded, as if he hadn't had any ethical or moral qualms at all. He had. He'd worried about it more than he cared to admit, certainly to any of his subordinates. There was something fundamentally wrong with kidnapping people and putting them to work. He'd liberated enough captives from pirate ships to believe that kidnapping was wrong. But he'd had no choice. The trained and experienced personnel—soldiers and spacers as well as mechanics and technicians—were all that stood between humanity and a new Dark Age. They had to be protected. They had to be *saved.*

"We'll give them the chance to survive, if nothing else," he said, sharply. "And if they refuse to work for us, they can go elsewhere."

Chung cleared her throat. "The intelligence staff on *Havoc* interrogated the captured officers," she continued. "They were basically promised homes and jobs on Hameau, presumably through the Onge Corporation, if they cooperated. Given that Hameau is actually quite heavily defended, for what is—on the surface—a stage-two colony world, the corporation should have had no trouble keeping those promises."

"No doubt," Jeremy said. The whole affair was an unexpected wrinkle. He didn't want to have to work with the Onge Corporation. He'd known its former CEO too well. The old bastard had always been genteel, but that hadn't stopped him from slipping in the knife as soon as the victim turned his back. "And now we have competition."

"Yes, sir," Chung said. "I've been studying the records. It's quite possible that the colony was further along than they claimed."

"I wouldn't be surprised," Jeremy said. "It's astonishing how many things get left off the official records."

"Such as the existence of this place." Anderson waved a hand at the nearest wall. "So...we know the bastards are up to something. What do we do about it?"

"Our projections always assumed there would be a power vacuum in that sector," Chung said. "If Hameau turns into a major power...it could be problematic."

"Perhaps," Anderson said.

"There's no *perhaps* about it," Chung said, grimly. "I've been running projections. They're going to get a *lot* of refugees, particularly once people realise that the Core Worlds are going to be really unsafe for just about *everyone...*"

"They've probably realised that by now," Jeremy said. He knew, better than most, how word spread amongst the stars. His most optimistic estimates suggested that everyone for a few hundred light years knew about Earthfall. "We have to assume the worst."

"Quite." Anderson shrugged. "The question remains, sir. What do we do about it?"

Chung tapped the display. "We get there first, sir. We take the world off them."

Anderson blinked. "You suggest we come out of hiding and...*invade*...a star system?"

"Yes, sir." Chung looked at him, evenly. Her voice was very calm. "That's *exactly* what I'm suggesting."

Jeremy kept his face under tight control. He'd never been comfortable with remaining underground, the finest military machine in the known galaxy lurking in the shadows while it refitted old starships and readied itself to return to the light. He'd seen the projections. He knew that any attempt to stem the chaos was likely to end badly. And yet, sitting on his ass and doing nothing seemed...*wrong*. Experience had told him that doing *something* was always the better option, if only because it kept the enemy from seizing the initiative. He'd certainly never been comfortable sitting around waiting to be hit.

There are times when you have no choice, he reminded himself. *And times when you have to throw caution to the winds and take the war to the enemy.*

"There are definite advantages to taking the system," Chung said. "The corporation has established a bunch of industrial nodes and such-like in orbit, all of which would come in handy if we took possession. The population is quite sensible, as many of them are first and second-gen immigrants...and probably very aware that the corporation will start to see them as cheap mass-produced tools, if it doesn't already. And...we can send our own new recruits there too."

She nodded to the display. "And sir, do we really *want* a corporation, one known for pushing the limits on just about everything, to turn itself into a government? A *real* government?"

Jeremy shook his head, slowly. Most corporate-dominated planets had maintained at least *some* pretence at democracy, although it was fairly clear that the corporate nominees were still in control. It helped that anyone who wanted to leave was generally allowed to go, urging corporations not to tighten their grip *too* much. But that had been with the Empire, enforcing—in its erratic manner—fair play. He dreaded to think what would happen if the Onge Family became *de facto* royalty. At the very least, they'd become a rival state…

And we might have to fight them later instead of now, Jeremy thought. The contingency plans would need to be updated, again. They'd assumed that most of the successor states would burn themselves out fairly quickly, either through war or simply running out of supplies. *This is definitely an unexpected surprise.*

He leaned forward. "Have the planning staff take a look at the details," he ordered. "Let them determine if it's *possible* to take the planet, with the ships and resources we have on hand. And then…if it's possible, we'll make the final decision then."

Anderson lifted an eyebrow. "You don't want to be decisive?"

Jeremy knew he was being teased. But there was a serious point behind it.

"We'll find out what we're facing, in every sense of the word, before we commit ourselves," he said. He'd seen too many people make that mistake, in the heyday of empire, to wish to make it himself. "And *then* we'll make up our minds."

But he knew, deep inside, that he'd already made a decision.

CHAPTER SEVEN

On the other, however, they lacked the ability to bootstrap themselves into a technological civilisation. The vast majority of their tech base was primitive, when it existed in the first place. They could produce tractors and primitive, gas-driven cars, but not shuttlecraft and spaceships. This ensured that any lingering off-world installations had to be rapidly shut down before the population starved, suffocated or simply died on the vine.

—PROFESSOR LEO CAESIUS

Earthfall and its Aftermath

KERRI GRITTED HER TEETH as the shuttle plunged through the storm.

She clung to her seat for dear life, cursing the commandant—and tradition—as another gust of wind hit the craft. She should have insisted on holding the discussion over the communications grid, damn it. If she'd realised just how unpleasant the flight would be, she would have insisted on it. She knew it was safe, relatively speaking, but...hell, she wasn't really *sure*. Shuttlecraft rarely had any problems landing on Earth-type worlds, even if they had to fly through a hurricane, but Safehouse? A tiny moon orbiting an immense gas giant, with tidal waves that reached up and kissed the skies? She would hardly have called it *safe*.

The craft shook again. She heard a giggle and felt the back of her neck burn, even though she was fairly certain the Pathfinders weren't laughing at her. Or perhaps they were. People who would make HALO entries through a full-fledged storm probably thought nothing of flying through heavy turbulence. They were welcome to it, Kerri considered, as the shuttle flew into a clear zone. The peace lasted just long enough for her to relax—slightly—before one final crash echoed through the shuttlecraft. The gravity field seemed to weaken a second later. They'd landed.

She unbuckled herself carefully and stood on wobbly legs. Safehouse was smaller than Earth, its gravity barely a third of the homeworld's. She was mildly surprised the corps hadn't installed a gravity generator to ensure the long-term residents didn't lose muscle tone, but it might be all too revealing if someone probed the system and picked up flickers of graviton particles. It would certainly attract attention if the wrong people noticed. Besides, the corps had probably made medical treatments mandatory for anyone who visited the planet. The treatments were expensive, but the corps had plenty of money.

Or had, she thought, as she stumbled through the hatch. *Who bankrolls us now?*

It was a sobering thought. She was devoted to the corps, but she hadn't intended to spend her entire life in its service. There would come a time—or there *would* have come a time—when she would want to go elsewhere. And then...what? Did her bank account still exist? Was her money worth anything? Did she have any legal existence at all? And...she frowned as she made her way down the corridor, following the handful of signs on the walls. Who was legally in charge, if Earth and the Empire were gone? Was she still bound by her oaths?

You have nowhere else to go, she told herself, dryly. *And you still have your duty.*

She walked down a flight of stairs, wondering at the mindset of whoever had decorated the place. There were no personal touches, no paintings or drawings...nothing to suggest that Safehouse was anything other than temporary—very temporary—accommodation for a handful of refugees. No, she'd been in makeshift refugee camps with more character. She heard a handful of voices behind her and stood to one side as a line of trainees ran past, chanting as they ran. She remembered her own days at Boot Camp, before she'd reluctantly admitted defeat and allowed herself to be streamlined into the Auxiliaries instead. It hadn't worked out too badly, but... part of her would always feel like she'd failed. She hadn't become a marine.

The Commandant's office was closer to the surface than she'd expected, although she supposed it shouldn't have been a surprise. His door was bare metal, without any decoration save for the single nametag. She was half-convinced she'd gone to the wrong place, despite the nametag. She tapped the door and waited, counting the seconds. It unlocked—no sliding doors on Safehouse, it seemed—bare seconds later. She stepped inside, looking around with interest. The office was large, but it was as bland and boring as the rest of the installation. It looked as if the occupant had only just moved in. He hadn't even set up an 'I Love Me' wall.

Which isn't always a bad sign, she reminded herself, dryly. *There's always* some *cock-sucking asskisser who will give the CO a memento of his service.*

"Captain," Major-General Jeremy Damiani said. His bluff appearance was almost reassuring. He didn't waste time with pointless power games. "Welcome to Safehouse. What do you make of the place?"

"Boring," Kerri said. She had the feeling that Damiani would prefer the truth over pretty words. "And very vulnerable, if the system is occupied."

"It's only the tip of the iceberg," Damiani said. He indicated a folding chair. "Tea? Coffee? Chocolate?"

Kerri relaxed, slightly. It was odd to have a senior officer serve the drinks...but she would have been a great deal more worried if the officer *hadn't* offered her something to drink. It would have been a sign that it was going to be a far from pleasant conversation. Her lips twitched, humourlessly. She might be about to be sent to do the impossible, or die trying, but at least she wasn't in trouble.

"Coffee, please," she said. "Milk, no sugar."

Damiani smiled. It was a surprisingly endearing expression. "A spacer's drink."

"Better to have something I can drink than something that stripes the enamel off my teeth," Kerri countered. She'd never cared for coffee so thick and strong that one could stand a spoon in it. "Or burn a hole in the deck, if I accidentally drop it."

"True." Damiani poured them both drinks, passed her a mug and sat down facing her. "I read your report. The operation was very well done."

"The Pathfinders did most of the work," Kerri acknowledged. "We would have been in some trouble without them."

"You handled your side of the operation very well," Damiani said. "Well done."

Kerri shrugged. She hadn't had to do much, beyond escorting the transports in and out of the system. She would have proved herself—or not—if the flotilla had actually been attacked. Or if she'd had to make a very hard call indeed. She kept that thought to herself. She was entirely sure Damiani knew it as well as herself.

Damiani took a sip of his coffee—black, she noted—and tapped a hidden switch, activating a holographic display. A starchart appeared in front of them, a lone star blinking red. Kerri leaned forward, silently running the calculations in her head. At flank speed, the mystery star would be around three weeks from Safehouse. She'd have to check her navcomp to be sure.

"Hameau," Damiani said. "I believe you've heard of it."

"Yes, sir," Kerri said. She'd read Specialist Green's report very carefully. "Those mystery ships might have come from Hameau."

"Might." Damiani leaned back in his chair. "We couldn't match their drive signatures against anything in the record books. They may simply have been retuned, sometime in the last few years, or they might have been deliberately kept off the books."

"They didn't come *that* close, sir," Kerri said. She knew the realities of naval life better than any groundpounder. "I wouldn't be confident that our long-range sensors were able to get an accurate reading on their drive fields. We certainly didn't get any *visuals* of their hulls. I wouldn't care to bet on the accuracy of *any* of our readings."

"True, Captain," Damiani said. "But it is something to bear in mind."

He met her eyes. "I'm detaching *Havoc* from the remainder of the flotilla, Captain. I want you to take your ship to Hameau, maintaining stealth at all times, and carry out a tactical survey of the system. Your formal orders will be forwarded to you before you depart, but basically we want you to pay close attention to defences, both fixed and mobile, and anything else that might... impede...operations within the system. If possible—and this I leave to your judgement—you are to land the Pathfinders on Hameau itself. I trust you to determine if the operation can be carried out without being detected."

Kerri nodded, slowly. She wouldn't have believed an Imperial Navy officer if he'd said *that* to her—everyone knew that he'd steal the credit if things went well, while leaving her holding the bag if things went badly—but Damiani? She believed him. It wouldn't be easy to convince the Pathfinders that things were too dangerous—she sometimes thought they had a death wish—but their ultimate superior would back her up. Besides, the corps didn't have enough active ships to risk losing one for little reward.

And we're not supposed to have any warships, she reminded herself. Officially, the corps was only allowed a handful of ships...none of which were *real* warships. *Havoc* and her sisters were thoroughly illegal, their existence known only to a handful of people before Earthfall. *And now we have a fleet, if we can get the decommissioned ships back into service.*

"Yes, sir," she said, finally. "Do you intend to invade the system?"

Damiani's lips twitched, as if she'd said something funny. "It depends. Bring back your report and we will see."

"Yes, sir." Kerri finished her coffee. "Sir...what are we going to do? I mean...everything's gone to hell."

If the sudden shift in the conversation surprised Damiani, he didn't show it. "We swore to uphold the Empire," Damiani said, simply. "We will do whatever it takes to reunite humanity and re-establish the society that, once upon a time, bound us all together."

"And also tore us apart," Kerri said. The Empire had been strong and domineering when it should have been weak and relaxed, weak and relaxed when it should have been strong and domineering...she understood, all too well, why so many factions sought independence. A sector, let alone the entire galaxy, could not be held together by force. "The future will not be peaceful."

"No." Damiani shook his head. "But we will do what we can to contain the damage."

Kerri nodded. It sounded like a dream, but it was more realistic—far more realistic—than anything she'd heard from their civilian superiors. Their *former* civilian superiors. They'd expected perfection, they'd expected peacekeeping missions to be carried out without a single casualty on either side...and they'd been bitterly disappointed when they'd discovered that it was impossible. Damiani had been serving for longer than she'd been alive. He knew what could and couldn't be done.

He met her eyes. "Do you have any other concerns?"

"Supply issues may be a concern, sooner or later," Kerri admitted. The corps had an excellent support system, one that had carefully been kept separate from the navy's, but Earthfall had placed a *lot* of strain on their logistics. "We may have trouble keeping the ships going."

"We should be able to overcome them, sooner or later," Damiani said. "But you're right. It will have to be watched."

"Yes, sir." Kerri finished her coffee. "When do you want me to depart?"

"This evening, if possible." Damiani's lips twitched. "But take as long as you need to make your final preparations."

"Yes, sir," Kerri said.

• • •

"I guess we're in trouble," Specialist Steven Phelps said, as the four Pathfinders made their way to the Commandant's office. "Which one of you bastards screwed the pooch?"

"It wasn't *me* who was caught in bed with the general and his wife," Specialist Michael Bonkowski countered. "What *were* you thinking?"

"Well, his wife *was* quite a looker and the general himself wasn't half-bad for someone who spent most of his time behind a desk, so I thought to myself..."

"I don't think you were *thinking* at all." Bonkowski sneered at him. "I think you were letting your small head do all the thinking for you."

"It *is* surprisingly qualified," Rachel teased. "It just can't resist the temptation to put itself in a convenient orifice."

"Hah fucking hah," Phelps snapped. He glared at the other three. "That was four years ago, you idiots. The Old Man isn't going to pound my ass about it *now*."

"Mental images, mental images," Specialist Tony Perkins moaned.

Bonkowski laughed. "You have a filthy mind."

"It wasn't *me* who took photos from the surveillance cameras and put them on the datanet," Perkins said. "It was you."

Rachel tuned them out as they reached the Commandant's office. There was no point in speculating, not when they'd find out why they'd been summoned in a few short minutes. She didn't *think* they were in trouble, if only because they hadn't had time to get *into* trouble. She couldn't imagine the Commandant hauling them in to give them grief about something that had happened years ago, particularly not now. It was more likely that another tempting opportunity to commit suicide was heading towards them at supersonic speed.

They stepped into the office and snapped to attention. The Commandant looked back at them evenly, then returned their salutes. He was shorter than Rachel remembered—it had been years since she'd last seen him in person—but that meant nothing. Some of the most vicious bastards she'd met, in and out of the corps, had been short. They'd always acted as though they were compensating for something. She supposed it made a certain kind of sense. A short man would look weak, compared to his taller contemporaries.

"You did well, on Gamma Prime," the Commandant said, curtly. "Green"—his eyes met Rachel's—"did very well. Your discovery that the evacuees were due to be transhipped elsewhere may have saved us some trouble."

Rachel nodded, stiffly. The Commandant *had* been surprised. He'd barely mentioned the rest of the operation, even though it could have failed spectacularly. But then, it hadn't come remotely close to disaster. And very little had been at stake...she shook her head, mentally. There was no point in woolgathering when the Commandant was talking.

"*Havoc* will be heading to Hameau this evening," the Commandant informed them. "The four of you will be accompanying her. If possible—and this is solely at the captain's discretion—you are to be landed on Hameau itself. Your orders, should you make it to the surface, are to scout out the political landscape and get an idea of how things work down there."

"Yes, sir," Phelps said. He was, technically, the team leader. "Will we be recovered?"

"No." The Commandant looked displeased. "If we proceed with operations within the system, you will be worked into our plans or eventually picked up after the operation goes ahead. If not...you are to extract yourself as quietly as possible."

"Ouch," Bonkowski muttered.

Rachel said nothing, although she agreed. Extracting oneself from a deployment into enemy held territory was never easy, not if the enemy was on the alert. Getting off a planetary surface and into deep space would be far harder, almost impossible. It had been done, she knew, but it had always relied on luck as well as judgement. They were among the best-trained soldiers in history, yet...if they were caught in transit, all the training in the world wouldn't save them from being blown to atoms.

"Yes, sir," Phelps said, again. "We won't let you down."

"I feel a bit of a sniffle coming on," Bonkowski said, mock-mournfully. "Can I take some sick leave? Or shore leave? I'm not fussy."

The Commandant gave him a droll look. "You can always take a walk out there," he said, indicating the view. Purple lightning flashed through dark and gloomy clouds. Droplets of snow brushed against the window and slid out of sight. "I'm sure it will do wonders for your attitude."

Rachel looked past him. The moon was eerie and alien and completely inhospitable, even to an enhanced and augmented human. She'd heard of people who augmented themselves to the point of being able to live in space without spacesuits, or survive on worlds that would otherwise have been lethal, but…she'd never wanted to be one of them. Safehouse was many things, yet…it would never be home. She'd certainly never considered retiring to such a desolate world.

"It's going to take at least two weeks to get there," Phelps said. "You'll have time for a nap or two."

"More like three," Rachel calculated. "Assuming we don't break any speed records…"

The Commandant nodded. "Report onboard *Havoc* before departure and *don't* give Captain Stumbaugh a hard time. If she feels she can't land you, put up and shut up."

"Yes, sir," Phelps said. "We'll see how things go."

Bonkowski let out an unconvincing cough. "I really need sick leave," he jested. "Really…"

"I'll have the doctors prescribe something painful, humiliating and absolutely unnecessary," Phelps said. "Sir, we'll do our best. And we won't let you down."

"Very good," the Commandant said. "Dismissed."

"I'll go see what I can find in the records," Rachel said, once they were out of the office. "It'll do us good to know what we might be facing."

"Three weeks of boredom, followed by an endless wait to see if we're getting the *go* order or not," Bonkowski said. "*That's* what we're facing."

"Three weeks of heavy-duty training," Phelps said, evilly. "Don't you know? A DI a day keeps the cough away."

Bonkowski snorted. "I hate you."

"And I'll bang your heads together, both of you," Perkins said. "Come on. Let's go get some chow before it's too late."

CHAPTER EIGHT

In one sense, this was simple practicality. A stage-one colony world could not support a modern tech base. Shipping vast amounts of advanced technology from Earth to the Rim was inefficient. It made a great deal more sense, to the colony planners, to install a very basic tech base, knowing that anything the colonies produced for themselves could be repaired on site.

—**Professor Leo Caesius**

Earthfall and its Aftermath

"COMMANDANT," CHRISTIE LOOMIS SAID. "Havoc just cleared the Phase Limit. She's gone."

"And out of touch for the next six weeks," Jeremy grunted. "Or seven, more likely."

"Yes, sir." Christie frowned. "Have you been getting enough sleep recently?"

"I don't think *anyone* has been getting enough sleep recently." Jeremy barely looked up from his datapad. "I'll rest when I'm dead."

"Which may not be that far in the future, if you keep pushing yourself too hard," Christie said, tartly. "Get some rest. Sir."

Jeremy snorted. "Let me know when Major-General Anderson arrives," he said. "I have too much paperwork to do."

His aide nodded and withdrew. Jeremy sighed and returned his attention to his datapad. It didn't seem fair, somehow, that galactic society had fallen into chaos and he *still* had to worry about paperwork. He'd been a serving officer long enough to understand the importance of keeping one's paperwork in order—and the dangers of allowing one's subordinates to write lies in the files—but it still ground on him. He wasn't cut out to spend the rest of his life driving a desk. He wanted to get back into action at least once before he was finally declared medically unfit and discharged...

And who, he asked himself, *is going to discharge me?*

He rubbed his eyes, tiredly. He'd never really imagined life without the chain of command, life without the Empire...a life where the corps were practically on their own, hiding in their boltholes as the galaxy collapsed. It had always seemed unthinkable, even as he'd made preparations for the day he dreaded...the day he knew would come. Who did they serve now? Themselves? Or some ideal of the galaxy? It wasn't as if the Imperial Family would ever retake the throne. The throne itself was nothing more than dust and ash on a heavily-polluted world.

On impulse, he reached forward and tapped his processor, bringing up the live feed from the training grounds. A team of men in black tunics were going through a series of exercises, readying themselves for yet another training exercise. He had no trouble spotting the former Child Roland amongst them, his body still flabby after nine weeks of intensive training. The Imperial Heir wasn't the sort of person he would have recruited, back when the galaxy had been sane, but...Jeremy had to admit Roland was starting to shape up nicely. It would be months, if not years, before he was ready to graduate...he was trying, at least. Jeremy had been impressed, despite himself, by how little complaining he'd heard from the former prince. Roland might even turn into a decent man.

If he completes Boot Camp, Jeremy thought. *And if we manage to put together a substitute for the Slaughterhouse.*

He sighed and turned off the display. He wasn't blind to the advantages of having the Imperial Heir under his wing, but he knew the advantages came with significant *disadvantages.* The Child Roland had never been popular, even—perhaps especially—amongst the people who had never known the real him. The tales of his debauchery -- and general unpleasantness -- had been firmly rooted in truth. And even if he'd been the sweetest, kindest man imaginable, there were plenty of worlds that resented the Imperial Family and had no intention of bowing the knee to them ever again. Roland was a knife that could turn in his hand, Jeremy knew. He could injure himself as easily as his enemies.

And Roland himself might want to slip into obscurity, Jeremy reminded himself. He'd seen the prince's psych report. Roland was ashamed of the man he'd been, before Earthfall. He didn't *want* to take the throne. *He might not want to let me use him.*

His intercom bleeped. "Commandant, Major-General Anderson is here."

Jeremy nodded. "Send him in."

The door opened, smoothly. Major-General Anderson strode in, eyes flickering to the rear window before resting on Jeremy. Jeremy waved a hand at the coffee pot, inviting his subordinate to help himself, and put the datapad aside. He should know better than to bury himself in the details, even though it gave him a sense of doing *something.* It was his job to keep an eye on the bigger picture. He had subordinates to handle the details.

"We just got word from Morrison," Anderson said, as he poured himself a mug of coffee. "He's evacuated Primark. He and his men will be on their way in a few days."

"I can't say I'm surprised," Jeremy said. Major-General Morrison had been given permission to pull his forces off Primark, if he felt the situation was beyond repair. Jeremy wasn't the man on the spot. He wouldn't judge the man who *was.* But…it still felt like a failure, one of far too many. "The cluster was heading into chaos well before Earthfall."

"Sins of the past return to haunt us," Anderson agreed. "If we'd been given a free hand…"

Jeremy shrugged. The Primark Cluster would have worked, he thought, if the colonisation department hadn't insisted on landing settlers from a dozen mutually-opposed cultures and then, instead of trying to forge a united society, wavering between repression and tolerance for the ethnic divisions and conflicts that had inevitably followed. Years later, the hatred between the cultures was so great that the only thing preventing mass slaughter, ethnic cleansing and outright genocide was a large and growing military presence. The Empire had tried to keep the peace, its leaders unaware there was no peace to keep. And now...

His imagination provided too many details for his peace of mind. The conflict would start small, but rapidly grow into a holocaust. Men would be tortured and killed, women would be raped and *then* killed, children—young children—would be taken away to be raised by the victors, their former culture beaten out of them...he shuddered. It would be horrific beyond words at any time, but now...? It was just another footnote in the bloodiest era of human existence.

"We can't worry about it now," he said, with more savagery than he'd intended. He wanted to tear Morrison a new asshole, even though he knew the poor bastard wouldn't have pulled out unless the situation was truly untenable. "As long as he got his men out..."

Sure, his thoughts mocked him. *They got out. And they left the world to burn.*

He tried not to remember his first deployment, on a world so savage that he'd almost despaired of humanity. Ethnic, racial and religious conflicts were the worst, the ones where both sides felt the other was utterly beyond the pale. He'd met *pirates* who were more civilised than fanatics. He could practically smell the blood, the burning flesh, the utter hopelessness of the handful of captives he'd rescued...he swallowed, hard. There would be no rescue for the captives on the cluster, not any longer. They'd have to make the best of it.

"I've been studying the files on Hameau," Anderson said. "It's a curious world and no mistake."

"Quite." Jeremy would never have admitted it, but he was privately glad Anderson had changed the subject. "Can we take it?"

"I think so." Anderson shrugged. "That said, the last survey was completed ten years ago. God alone knows how much got left *off* the survey. The researchers think the system was actually wealthier than the bastards ever admitted..."

"I'm not surprised," Jeremy commented. "It would have raised their tax liabilities."

Anderson grinned, humourlessly. "Did they ever *pay* taxes?"

"They paid them to themselves," Jeremy said. He'd once sat down with the researchers to determine why the Empire, with a tax base stretched across thousands of worlds, was permanently short of cash. It had taken him quite some time to realise that the Grand Senate used a financial sleight of hand to avoid paying any taxes at all. "And then they channelled the money everyone else paid to themselves too."

"Ouch," Anderson said. "From what I saw in the files, sir, we can take the world. But...we don't know what we don't know."

"Yeah." Jeremy keyed his processor, bringing up the planetary display. "What can we commit to the mission?"

"My division, of course," Anderson said. "And fifteen ships...twenty-one, if we're willing to recall units from other operations. We can probably pad them out with freighters, if necessary. The problem is that we're going to be committing ourselves to a ground campaign. Even with the gloves off, we may be engaged for longer than we'd prefer."

"Naturally." Jeremy took a moment to savour the irony. He'd spent his entire career begging for permission to take the gloves off and just give the wretched bastards the thrashing of a lifetime. One solid example of a terrorist-led insurgency being crushed would be worth a million threats from the Grand Senate, threats no one took seriously because they were never carried out. Now, when he was finally answerable to no one outside the corps, he might not have the *resources* to lay down the law. "How long do you think we'll be committed?"

Anderson shook his head. "It depends, sir. If there's no real resistance, the world will fall overnight. If they make a fight of it...we'll have to take or disable the Planetary Defence Centres by force. That could prolong the fighting indefinitely."

"And no way to know what we'll be facing," Jeremy mused.

He studied the display for a long moment. It had been *centuries* since the marines had carried out a landing on a hostile world. His entire career had been spent on worlds that had been unable, if not unwilling, to keep the marines from landing. A combination of orbital bombardment and rapid deployment had made them the masters of any situation, as long as they were not lured into engagements that played to their weaknesses. Indeed, there had only been a handful of engagements where they'd had to face serious opposition when they made the first landings. Most worlds understood that, when they lost control of the high orbitals, the game was up.

But now...he shook his head as he skimmed through the file. It was impossible to be sure, but it was fairly clear the Onge Corporation wouldn't have invested so much into the system unless they were sure they could take care of it. The Grand Senator—he wondered, sourly, who'd succeeded the man who'd died during Earthfall—hadn't been stupid. There would be a *lot* of hardware within the system, almost all of it off the books. Powerful corporations had been violating the rules on privately-held military hardware for longer than he'd been alive.

I probably shouldn't make too much of a fuss, he thought, dryly. *We've been violating the rules too.*

He leaned back in his chair, understanding—finally—why so many Grand Senators had been reluctant to commit everything to the field. The buck had stopped with them, once upon a time; now, it stopped with him. And yet...a Grand Senator could get a million soldiers and spacers killed and no one would give a damn. Jeremy knew the remainder of the Major-Generals wouldn't hesitate to remove him if they lost faith in his leadership. And yet...

They'd understand taking a gamble, he told himself. *And they'd be much more concerned about me doing nothing.*

"Start making the preparations," he ordered. "And keep me informed."

"Aye, sir." Anderson stood. "Get some rest, sir."

"You too?" Jeremy laughed. "Why does everyone want me to get a good night's sleep?"

"When the boss is asleep, everyone else can goof off," Anderson said. "And I've been waiting *years* to goof off."

"And you can wait a few years more," Jeremy said. "Your schedule is too full for goofing off."

Anderson chuckled, threw him a jaunty salute and hurried out. Jeremy sighed, then turned to the window and looked out over the darkening landscape. There were times when he was tempted to collect everything they'd built over the years, from the warships they weren't supposed to have to the giant transports and factory ships, and set course for the Rim. He'd seeded hundreds of marines and retired marines out there, most with sealed orders to maintain civilisation by any means necessary. He could join them, with enough firepower and technology to rebuild a formidable industrial base in a few short years. But it would mean giving up on the Core.

And giving too many others a chance to build up power bases of their own, he thought, grimly. He had no idea who'd inherit most of the Imperial Navy, but anyone who controlled a battle squadron and a handful of supplies would be in an excellent position to carve out a vest-pocket empire for himself. Jeremy had already authorised the assassination of one such officer, although it would be weeks before he knew if the operation had succeeded or failed. *And, one day, whoever comes out ahead will start expanding into the Rim.*

Shaking his head, he turned and headed for bed.

• • •

Haydn hadn't expected more than a day or so of rest when his company reached Safehouse. Indeed, he was a little surprised they'd been recalled to Safehouse in the first place. Their orders, filed before the raid on Gamma Prime, had been to remain on the concealed shipyard and provide security until the evacuees were processed, interrogated and shipped to their final destinations. Haydn hadn't expected trouble from their guests, save perhaps for the handful of evacuees who'd had to leave their families behind. He'd been morbidly amused to hear one man promising the stars, as long as he didn't have to go back to his estranged wife.

He walked into the briefing room and looked around with interest. The chamber was packed, with brass as far as the eye could see. Haydn himself was one of the lowest-ranking officers in the compartment, although that meant less amongst the marines than the regular army. His lips quirked at the thought. He'd be a coffee boy if he'd joined the regular army. An officer he'd met once—unfortunately—had thrown a fit when he'd discovered that he was expected to brief *mere* captains and even majors...

Haydn put the thought aside as he surveyed the other officers. Most of them were active-duty, but a handful looked to be reservists who'd been recalled to the corps when the shit hit the fan. Haydn guessed most of them had lived on the Slaughterhouse, evacuated ahead of the attack that had left the world a radioactive wasteland. The wags might joke that it was a vast improvement, but...rage simmered in his gut. There would be no mercy when they found out who was behind the attack. They'd pay for what they'd done.

That was part of our history, no matter how much we hated it when we were there, he thought. He didn't remember much about the Slaughterhouse, but pain...pain and a grim determination to never quit. *They had no right to take it from us.*

Major-General Anderson strode into the room, followed by a pair of grim-faced staffers. Haydn rose with the rest of the assembly, then sat down when Anderson waved them to their seats. He didn't stand on ceremony, unlike regular army officers. Marines knew their superiors had gone through the Slaughterhouse—and then served on the front lines—well before they'd been promoted. And they rotated in and out of the front lines for the rest of their careers, just to make sure they didn't lose their touch.

"We may be deploying, as a division-sized force, to a hostile world," Anderson said, without preamble. A rustle of anticipation ran around the room. "Our objective will be to land, capture the PDCs and convince the local population to work with us. As of *now*, we don't know how they're being treated or how they'll react to us."

Haydn nodded, curtly. Civilians were inherently unpredictable. Some loved the marines, some viewed them as trigger-happy Rambos—whatever a Rambo was—some viewed them as corrupt bastards like the Civil Guardsmen and some, the most heartbreaking of the bunch, saw the marines as people who restore order, then would go away and let the former government come back and punish anyone who welcomed the marines too openly. It was never easy to trust an outsider when that outsider might cut and run at any moment, leaving you to face the wrath of your former friends. Better not to commit yourself than run the risk of being abandoned.

"The staff will put together the deployment scenario, which will be updated when we obtain accurate information from the target," Anderson continued. "Your role will be to prepare your troops for deployment and poke holes in the plan, before the enemy puts bullet holes in it. I don't think I need to tell you that this mission is important. We cannot fail. We will *not* fail."

His eyes swept the room. "We haven't done anything like this for years. We're out of practice. And now...we have to get it right, first time. Failure is not an option."

Haydn let out a breath. A forced landing, an opposed landing...it would be a challenge. But he relished it. He'd joined the corps for the challenge. He would not fail. *They* would not fail.

"Now," Anderson said. "To work."

CHAPTER NINE

There was no point, they argued, in wasting time shipping broken devices or vehicles back to the Core Worlds. And indeed, they were right. Given the problems with interstellar shipping and trade, in the last century before the fall, there was no guarantee that anything sent back to Earth would ever be returned.

—PROFESSOR LEO CAESIUS

Earthfall and its Aftermath

IT WAS ALMOST A RELIEF, Kerri decided, when Havoc finally started her approach to the Hameau System. The trip itself had been so boring that she would have almost welcomed a pirate attack or an encounter with a hostile warship, even though she had strict orders to avoid enemy contact. The only real excitement had come from one of the marine pathfinders hitting on her, a courtship she'd shot down without hesitation. Technically, she wasn't in their chain of command, but as long as they were on her ship she was in charge. It would cause all sorts of problems, she thought, if it came down to a question of command. Both sides knew better than to put too much pressure on the relationship between spacers and groundpounders.

She took her command chair and watched as the timer steadily ticked down to zero. She'd given a great deal of thought to where and when to come out of Phase Space, but—in the end—she'd found herself balancing trade-offs between speed and security. It didn't help that she had no idea what sort of defences awaited her, or how many sensor platforms the Onge Corporation had scattered around the system. In the end, she'd made the decision to come out some distance from the Phase Limit. It would add several hours to their flight, once they headed into the system, but it would minimise the risk of detection. They'd have to get *very* unlucky to come out of FTL close enough to a ship that would note their presence and sound the alarm.

"Captain," Commander Joaquin said. "We will drop out of Phase Space in five minutes."

"Sound battlestations," Kerri ordered. "Set Condition One throughout the ship."

She smiled, grimly, as the drumbeat drove her crew to their combat stations. Cold logic told her there was no chance of detection, but she knew better than to take the risk of coming out of FTL fat and happy. Besides, it would underline the fact they were entering hostile territory. Her crew was as well-trained as any regular navy crew—she'd drawn half of them from the Imperial Navy, back when it had been a going concern—but all crewmen had a tendency to backslide when confronted with long weeks of boredom. It wasn't a problem in FTL—the odds of an engagement in Phase Space were very low indeed—but she couldn't tolerate it when they might find themselves going into battle at any moment. The slightest delay could prove fatal.

"All stations report combat-ready, Captain," Tomas said. "We are ready to engage the enemy."

"Keep all sensors passive only," Kerri ordered. "I say again, passive only."

"Aye, Captain," Tomas said.

Commander Joaquin was intently focused on his console. "Realspace in ten seconds," he said. "Nine...eight..."

Kerri braced herself as *Havoc* dropped back into normal space. It had been a long time since she'd had *any* reaction to FTL travel—people who didn't overcome their first nauseous reaction rarely served on starships—but she knew to take precautions, just in case. The display blanked, then started to fill with icons. Hameau's star—the locals hadn't bothered to give it a proper name, if the files were accurate—glowed in front of her. Hameau itself was on the other side of the primary. It would make it harder, she hoped, for anyone to notice their arrival.

"Transit complete, Captain," Joaquin reported.

"No enemy contacts detected," Tomas added. "Local space is clear."

"Deploy sensor platforms, then hold us here," Kerri said. The impulse to power up the drive and glide into the enemy-held system was almost overpowering, but training and experience held it at bay. She needed to wait and make sure of her ground before she put the ship at risk. "Put the live feed on the main display."

"Aye, Captain," Tomas said.

Kerri watched, grimly, as the display continued to fill with icons, natural and artificial. The system had two visible gas giants—the files claimed there was a third, which was presumably on the other side of the primary-each one surrounded by a host of artificial emissions. Artificial emissions *sources*, she knew; everything from cloudscoops to industrial nodes. A number of asteroids were clearly being mined, although—as far as she could tell—there wasn't a major asteroid-dwelling population. She supposed it wasn't really a surprise. It was uncommon for corporations to encourage asteroid settlements to develop, despite their advantages. They tended to be difficult for founder corporations to boss around after the first few years.

"I'd say this was more of a stage-three or stage-four colony, Captain," Tomas said, after the first hour. "There's more industry in this place than in a bunch of older worlds."

"It probably helps that they kept the colonial development bureaucrats out," Kerri commented. She'd yet to see a system the bureaucrats couldn't screw up, one way or the other. Malice, stupidity or ignorance…it hardly mattered. The bastards had given themselves a bad name, practically *guaranteeing* that hardly anyone outside the bureaucracy had a good word for them...or their masters. "Are you picking up any transmissions?"

"Not much," Tomas said. "It looks to be pointless chatter. Nothing obviously encrypted."

Kerri leaned back in her chair. "Tactical, put the ship on condition-two," she ordered. There was no point in keeping her crew at battle stations indefinitely, not when there was no immediate threat. "Helm, I think we'll go with Course-Delta. Take us into the system."

"Aye, Captain," Joaquin said.

Susan looked up. "We could be there a lot quicker..."

"Yes, we could." Kerri kept her face expressionless. Clearly, one lecture on not questioning superior officers on their bridge hadn't gone very far. She had to struggle to keep the sarcasm out of her voice. "If, of course, we wanted to be detected. Which we don't."

She understood the younger girl's impatience, though. It felt odd to be creeping around the system, but they had strict orders to avoid detection. She put the problem aside for later contemplation and forced herself to watch as a handful of new icons appeared on the display. It looked as if the cloudscoops were funnelling HE3 to the asteroids as well as the planet itself. Her analysts suggested that the corporation wasn't interested in making the asteroids self-sufficient.

Which would be par for the course, Kerri thought. *They'd sooner cut their own throats than risk having their people start dreaming of independence.*

Her lips quirked. There was literally no one more capable of improvising than RockRats, independence-minded asteroid dwellers. She would have been astonished if *someone* wasn't already thinking of ways to circumvent the corporation's dictates, probably by setting up fission reactors or even concealed fusion power plants. Who knew what would happen, if the system was left alone? Civil unrest? Civil war? Or a simple declaration of independence? She shrugged. It wasn't going to happen.

The hours ticked by, steadily wearing down the crew. Kerri sent her bridge crew to rest as they crawled through interplanetary space, then took a nap in her ready room. It felt odd to be sleeping when the ship was in danger, but she knew—through training and experience—that there was very little *actual* danger. If they were detected…theoretically, they'd have plenty of warning to reverse course and evade contact, or simply escape, before it was too late. It wouldn't be *easy* for the locals to set up an ambush without being detected themselves, although she knew it could be done. If that happened…

Nothing materialised as she slept, then returned to the bridge. Hameau itself was growing larger within the display, a slightly oversized world surrounded by a single moon and thousands of pieces of space junk. She sucked in her breath as she saw the impossible sight, her experience telling her that her passive sensors *had* to be having flights of fancy. Earth's halo of industrialised asteroids and space habitats had been huge, but Hameau was an order of magnitude bigger. It took her several seconds to realise that most of the rocky asteroids had been utterly untouched by mankind.

"My God," Susan said. "What happened here?"

Tomas looked up. "Well, Ensign, there were some very angry aliens who blew up a moon and the debris…"

"Please," Kerri said. She'd read the files. No one had been able to give any *real* explanation for why Hameau was surrounded by a halo of asteroids, but she doubted the truth included aliens. No traces of alien life had ever been discovered. It was far more likely that the double-system—more like a triad system, really—had been unstable until gravity had torn one of the worlds apart. "We don't need to waste time on a snipe hunt."

She felt her expression darken as she studied the sensor feed. Dozens of asteroids were being mined, or converted into industrial facilities, or… the scale of the program was astonishing, the vision quite beyond anything she would have expected from a latter-day interstellar corporation. She silently saluted whoever had come up with the plan, even though it *was* inconvenient. They were well on their way to establishing a formidable industrial base. She tapped her console, making a handful of projections. It was hard to be sure, but it looked as if Hameau was well on the way to becoming the most efficient industrial base in the sector.

"Captain," Tomas said. He sounded hesitant, as if he expected her to refuse him without thinking. "I'd like to deploy a pair of stealthed drones."

Kerri hesitated, silently weighing up the pros and cons. The drones were tiny, compared to the ship. The odds of them being detected were very low, even in an empty system. Here, with so much space junk orbiting the planet—her sensors tracked a handful of chunks of debris falling out of orbit and burning up in the atmosphere—it was hard to believe that the drones would be detected, let alone identified. The system had to be a nightmare to secure. The sensor grid must either be stepped down or… her lips quirked in amusement. The alarms would be going off every day. The defenders must be sick and tired of the sensors crying wolf.

And when a real wolf comes along, no one believes in him until it is far too late, she thought, dryly. *And then everyone starves to death.*

"Launch the drones, ballistic-only," she ordered. There was no point in wool gathering. The corps needed the information only drones could provide. "Steer one of them into the planet's atmosphere."

"Aye, Captain." Tomas sounded surprised. He knew as well as she did that they had orders to minimise risk…but he also knew, he should know, that some risks had to be taken. "Drones launching…now."

Kerri smiled—normally, the beancounters would have thrown a fit at her sending a drone to certain destruction—and then sobered as more and more data flowed into the display. The planet was heavily defended, although most of the defences appeared to be automated weapons platforms rather than giant battlestations. She wasn't sure if that was a good sign or not. Battlestations were formidable opponents, but they were also easy targets. They couldn't hide from incoming missiles or move to evade them. Their only real advantage came in soaking up hits, and even *that* wouldn't last. Sooner or later, their defences would be ground down.

"I'm picking up twelve warships, holding station just above the halo," Tomas said, slowly. "None of them are within engagement range, none appear to be powering up. The largest appears to be a battlecruiser."

"Interesting," Kerri said. The Imperial Navy was the *only* force authorised to deploy battleships and battlecruisers...or it had been, before Earthfall. There should have been no way in hell the Onge Corporation could have gotten its hands on a battlecruiser—or the trained and experienced crews to keep her functioning. "Can you get an ID?"

"No, Captain," Tomas said. "She's not emitting anything beyond basic navigational beacons. No IFF, no nothing. I can tell you her class, but not her name."

"Curious." Kerri considered it for a moment. The battlecruiser CO could have been working for the corporation all along, or been bribed, or... or simply offered a safe port in the storm tearing the galaxy apart. "Is she in working order?"

"Impossible to say," Tomas said. "Her sensors are stepped down and her drive nodes are offline. She could be ready to depart at a few hours' notice, or in desperate need of a refit before she risks bringing her drives online."

We'll have to assume she's in full working order, Kerri thought. The Imperial Navy had taken a relaxed attitude to maintenance, but...she dared not assume the battlecruiser was anything other than a deadly threat. She'd have to take it seriously. Hopefully, they could get into engagement range before the battlecruiser's crew brought her weapons and drives online. *And if we can't force her to surrender, we'll have to destroy her.*

She put the battlecruiser out of her mind as the lead drone neared the planet, relaying its impressions back to the mothership through a pinpoint laser link. Hameau was...odd, although perhaps it should be expected. The planet was a strange mixture of pitted airless rock, scarred by generations of meteor strikes, and perfectly habitable world. The atmosphere was Earth-normal, more or less; there was no reason to think that humans needed rebreathers or genetic modification to live on the surface. It was clear that the corporation had established hundreds of settlements, from tiny hamlets and farms to mid-sized towns and cities. She felt an odd little twinge as she surveyed the images, flicking through pictures of people at work and children at play. Had her homeworld looked so...so *decent*, once upon a time? Had *Earth* looked so decent? So...so *free*.

You can't see the details, she thought, coldly. *You have no idea what it's really like down there.*

She slowly shook her head. Earth had looked like one giant city from orbit. In reality, the planet's land surface had been covered with endless cities and the ocean had been so heavily polluted that no one in their right mind would swim in it without protective armour and breathing mask. She hated to think of what the planet looked like now. And she'd seen idyllic towns and villages ruled by religious fanatics, places where the slightest mistake could get someone whipped, mutilated or brutally killed. They'd looked nice, on the surface. So did the planet in front of her. It was what lay beneath the surface that worried her.

"They've planted a number of Planetary Defence Centres on the surface," Tomas said. He was still working his console, parsing his way through the torrent of incoming data. "A *lot* of them."

"Good thinking on their part," Kerri said. There was no way to capture the orbital industry without taking the planet's surface first. The defenders could blow the hell out of any industrial node that fell into enemy hands. "We wouldn't find it easy to take the high orbitals."

She scowled, remembering the private briefing notes the Commandant had forwarded to her. The Onge Corporation had *definitely* been making preparations for Earthfall. And they'd done well, too. She wondered if there was any point in asking for cooperation, in trying to make an alliance, before dismissing the thought in annoyance. She'd met too many corporate managers to have any doubts about the world they'd create, if they had a chance. Better to nip it in the bud before it was too late.

"Keep us here," she ordered. They should be reasonably safe from detection, as long as they didn't go too close to the planet. She keyed her intercom. "Specialist Phelps?"

"Yes, Captain?" The Pathfinder sounded surprisingly respectful. "What can I do for you?"

"I trust you've been monitoring the live feed," Kerri said. "Do you think you can make it down to the surface?"

"I think so." Phelps sounded utterly confident. Kerri hoped he had the common sense to be careful. "It might be easier than we thought. There's a *lot* of junk orbiting the planet."

"You'd still be dropping through the planet's atmosphere," Kerri warned. "And if they think you're a potential threat, they'll blow you out of space without ever having the slightest idea what you actually *are*."

"We are aware of the dangers," Phelps said. He sounded like he was stating a simple fact, rather than bragging. But then, she knew Pathfinders had carried out *far* more dangerous missions. To them, it was probably just another day in the office. "We're ready."

Kerri nodded, even though she knew he couldn't see her. "We'll take a few more hours to complete the survey," she said. They'd have to survey the gas giants too, but they could do that after they'd inserted the Pathfinders. "You have that long to plan your deployment. And then we'll deploy the communications platforms and drop you."

"Understood," Phelps said. He still sounded confident, even though he was about to throw himself into an uncertain future. "We won't let you down."

"Don't worry about me," Kerri said. "Worry about yourself."

CHAPTER TEN

The colonials themselves accepted the logic, although with certain caveats. They did not want to find themselves in (any more) hock to interstellar corporations, who would have to do the repair work (one of the problems with the late-stage imperial tech base was that on-site repairs were effectively forbidden) and they were quite happy to build and maintain a reasonably small tech base. If nothing else, it provided an outlet for colonists who didn't want to settle the land and set up farms.

—PROFESSOR LEO CAESIUS

Earthfall and its Aftermath

"REMIND ME," RACHEL SAID as the landing pod disengaged from Havoc, "which one of you bastards came up with this idea?"

"This from the person who put herself at risk walking into a high-security zone," Bonkowski said. "You could have been caught and killed at any moment."

"That wasn't *quite* so dangerous," Rachel said. "And I was in *control*."

That wasn't entirely accurate, she acknowledged as she felt a low shudder running through the landing pod. She could have been killed at any moment, if the defenders had realised she was a deadly threat. But she was good at reading people. She would have known as soon as *they* knew that they had orders to arrest or execute her. She could have fought her way out or, at the very least, died with her boots on. A plasma pulse from an orbiting weapons platform wouldn't care if she tried to fight or not. It would just blow her to dust before she even knew their cover had been blown.

She shifted uncomfortably within the suit, feeling oddly confined even though she wasn't claustrophobic. The suits would be no protection whatsoever if the planetary defences opened fire, but...they might provide *some* protection if there was a hull breach or something else went wrong. She wasn't sure it was worth it. The suits were cumbersome, weighing her down if she had to move in a hurry. Her imagination kept suggesting that they'd be trapped, the moment they hit the ground. She cursed herself under her breath for simply going along with the plan, when it had been suggested. A stealth shuttle would have been a great deal more comfortable.

But riskier, too, she told herself. *Put up and shut up.*

She watched through the pod's passive sensors as it fell towards the planet, mimicking the course and speed of a meteor shower. She had to admit there was no real *reason* for the planetary defences to pay attention to them, not when there were thousands of pieces of space junk falling into the atmosphere every day. Most of the pieces were tiny, unlikely to survive long enough to reach the surface. She hoped the defenders would assume the pod would burn up well before it landed. If they thought otherwise, they'd be dead before they knew it. She told herself, firmly, that they'd done all they could. All they could do now was wait and let the automated systems handed it.

The shaking grew worse as the pod hit the planetary atmosphere and started to fall. Rachel gritted her teeth, wishing—again—that she was in control. They *might* have been able to sneak onto one of the orbital facilities and get down from there...she shook her head. Corporate assholes *always* knew who should and who shouldn't be on their platforms. The odds of being caught in transit were just too high. She heard Perkins mutter a prayer as the pod spun madly, a gust of wind blowing it off course. Beside him, Bonkowski started a loud and involved story about a crewwoman he'd met on *Havoc*. It was torrid and filthy and Rachel would have been astonished if there was *any* truth whatsoever in it, but it kept her distracted from the prospect of imminent death. She wouldn't feel any better until she hit the ground.

"We're going slightly off course," Perkins said. "We'll be coming down a few extra miles from the target."

"Better than the alternative," Phelps commented. "We don't want to look like a threat."

"They'll probably die laughing when they see us," Bonkowski said. The pod rattled, violently. "Impact in ten..."

"Stasis field active," Perkins said. "Ready for..."

The world sneezed. Rachel blinked. The hull was torn and broken, bright sunlight beaming in. She reminded herself that they'd been in stasis for a few seconds, the field protecting them from the impact. Her suit felt heavy, so cumbersome she had to struggle to move; she opened the breastplate and crawled out, one hand grasping her pistol. If the enemy suspected something, they'd have troops on the way already. She had no idea how quickly they could respond, but she dared not assume they'd be slow. The corporations didn't *always* hire incompetents.

She took the lead as the three men joined her, Bonkowski marching along in his suit while the other two disengaged themselves. They'd crashed down in the middle of a forest, the force of the impact smashing a number of trees into firewood and sawdust. Rachel kept herself low, hoping the enemy wasn't watching from high orbit. They'd aimed themselves at the woods deliberately, but the treeline wouldn't provide much cover if the enemy suspected something. She looked around, listening carefully. She couldn't hear any engines or helicopter blades. The coast appeared to be clear.

"Here." Phelps passed Rachel her pack as Bonkowski struggled out of his suit and dumped it in the pod. "Ready to march?"

"Yes, sir," Rachel said. She checked her internal compass. They'd only added a few short miles to their journey. "You?"

"As ready as I'll ever be," Phelps said. He checked the other two had their equipment, then triggered the pod's disintegrator. Anyone who stumbled across the wreckage would be hard-pressed to realise it had been more than a simple metallic rock that had practically melted on re-entry. "Let's move."

Rachel fell into position as the four marines walked through the forest, looking around with interest. It was clear that someone had dumped a terraforming package on Hameau—and, afterwards, left most of the undeveloped land strictly alone. She spotted a handful of plants and lichen that were clearly native, utterly alien to the flora and fauna from Old Earth. They had to be tough, she guessed. Hameau had been savagely bombarded by asteroids sometime in the distant past. The local biosphere had been lucky to survive. *That* was rare. Normally, Old Earth's plants and animals rapidly displaced their alien counterparts.

And no one has been here for years, if at all, she thought. There were no signs of human settlement, nothing to suggest that they weren't the first people to set eyes on the forest. *I wonder why they never bothered to develop it.*

She considered the question as they kept moving, finding their way through a mountain range that looked decidedly odd to her experienced eyes. It took her longer than it should to realise that they'd walked into a blast crater, one left behind after something had hit the planet thousands of years ago. The impact had practically liquefied the ground below her feet, once upon a time. She had to admit it looked striking. The different ecosystems were practically isolated from one another. The terraforming package might not have changed *that* very much.

They rested up in a cave as darkness fell, taking the moment to test the communications link to the stealthed platform. *Havoc* was probably already on her way to the gas giants, unless her CO had decided—for whatever reason—to change her plans. Rachel felt a little isolated, although she was used to that. She took first watch as the sun started to set, the stars overhead coming out in force. There were so *many* stars in the sky...she frowned, then realised that she was looking at the asteroids and other junk orbiting the planet. Her enhanced eyes had no trouble picking out a handful of industrial nodes and starships moving from place to place. The industrial tempo was quite frightening. It was clear that the corporation had no intention of hiding from the chaos and waiting for things to settle down.

So they're just like us, she thought, dryly. *But we can't let them shape the future.*

Perkins relieved her, three hours into the watch. Rachel slipped into the cave, lay down next to Phelps and closed her eyes. She'd grown used to sleeping next to the men long ago, although it helped that she'd learnt to fall asleep and catch some rest whenever she had the opportunity. There was no way she could predict when—if—she'd have a chance to sleep again. It felt as if she hadn't slept at all when she heard Phelps clearing his throat, a few seconds later. She was surprised, deep inside, to see the sun rising outside. Phelps offered her a ration bar, then went to relieve himself at the back of the cave. She politely ignored him as she chewed. It tasted like cardboard.

They checked the cave carefully, just to make sure there were no traces of their presence, then resumed their march. The land was starting to look more cultivated. Their ears picked up hints of engines in the distance. It was almost a surprise when they stumbled across a road—more of a muddy track, really—leading westward. They looked up and down the road, then continued their march towards the nearest hamlet. They'd discussed what they intended to do, when they reached civilisation, but they'd come up with no real answers. It would depend on what they found.

"Nearly there," Phelps announced, cheerfully. "We should be able to see the town from the other side of this hill."

"Killing...you...with...mind," Bonkowski grumbled. "I haven't been so tired since I serviced the entire..."

"Oh, shut up," Perkins said. "We're nearly there."

Rachel took point as they climbed the hill and, staying down, crawled towards a cliff. The drop was awesome, the land scarred and pitted by ancient impacts that had carved a channel for a twisting river leading down to the town. The town itself was like something out of a dream, at least at first. It was almost idyllic, the kind of place someone could raise a family without being too worried about their neighbours. Rachel felt an odd twinge of envy, mingled with an awareness that something was wrong. It took her a long moment to place it. The town was *planned.* Someone had designed it, piece by piece. The more she looked at it, the more she was convinced of it. There was something oddly inhuman about its sheer perfection.

"The shops should be close to the houses," she said. "But instead, they're on the other side of the town."

Bonkowski gave her an odd look. "I don't understand."

"You can just walk to the shops," Rachel pointed out. "But an old man—or woman—wouldn't be able to get there so easily. Or..."

She shook her head. It wasn't the first time she'd seen planners place neatness and organisation over simple common sense. They should have put the shops closer to the homes...in fact, the more she surveyed the town, the more she was convinced the population didn't have access to cars, aircars or any other form of personal transport. There were only a handful of vehicles on the roads and they looked to be designed for the farm. Beyond them...her eyes narrowed. The people looked prosperous, certainly when compared to Earth's teeming billions, but they didn't look *happy.* She wondered if they knew how lucky they were. They could have been on Earth!

And if they had been living on Earth, she thought grimly, *they'd be dead.*

"They're all women," Bonkowski said. "I..."

Phelps glared at him. "This is no time to be thinking with your dick!"

"I'm serious." Bonkowski sounded serious too. "*Look* at them. Pretty much everyone within sight is a woman or a child. There aren't many men within eyeshot."

Rachel frowned as she scanned the town. Bonkowski was right. There weren't *many* people on the streets and almost all of them were women. Adult women. There weren't many children, male or female; there weren't many *men* at all. A shiver ran down her spine. It was normally the other way 'round. The only place she'd visited where women outnumbered men so strikingly had been a colony that flatly refused to allow men to visit. Ever.

"It's mid-morning," Perkins pointed out. "The menfolk could be in the fields, harvesting corn."

"Perhaps." Phelps didn't sound convinced. "I think we'd better keep our eyes open."

He took charge effortlessly. "Rachel, set up the passive sensor array. Michel, find us somewhere we can hide. Tony, keep an eye on the town. Watch for any traces of military activity."

"Yes, sir," Rachel said.

She slipped back until she was hidden under the trees and dug into her pack. The passive sensor array was—for once—*almost* as useful as the techs claimed, although it was so expensive that most marine recon teams were denied permission to take them into the field. She wondered, as she powered the device up, if that would change. They didn't have to answer to the beancounters every time they spent an extra credit over their budget, not now. She smiled, then set the limits as wide as possible. She'd narrow them down later.

Her eyes narrowed as the sensor array started producing results. There were a handful of radio transmitters within the town, but...surprisingly few database nodes. It was possible they were using wires rather than relying on wireless systems, yet...it was odd. She hadn't seen such a hardened system outside Safehouse. Unless...she frowned as she studied the results. What if there *wasn't* a datanet? She could easily imagine the corporation restricting—or even banning—their development. They were useful, but they also made life far too easy for dissidents.

Particularly the dissidents smart enough to realise that nothing *is completely secure on the datanet*, she mused. She'd known worlds that basked in the semblance of free speech and communications while ruthlessly undercutting the reality. By the time the population had realised their freedoms had been sharply circumscribed, it had been too late. *And the ones cunning enough to find ways to work around it.*

She stroked her chin. It wasn't going to be easy to hack a solid-state system, assuming it existed in the first place. They'd have to find an access point...she contemplated the possibilities as an alert popped up on the display, warning her of a short-range broadcast. She connected her earpiece to the sensor array and watched a local news program, most of which was completely uninformative. There was no mention of *anything* outside the local system, not even Earthfall. The locals couldn't be *that* ignorant, could they?

"I doubt it," Phelps said, when she explained the problem. "This isn't some low-tech world. They don't think the primary revolves around the planet."

"No," Rachel agreed. She'd been on worlds where the population truly was that ignorant. They'd been hellholes. "We're going to have to get up close and personal with someone. Someone snotty."

"If we can *find* someone snotty," Phelps said. "And if we can figure out what *snotty* means in this context."

"There will be someone," Rachel said. Bureaucratic worlds tended to *breed* snotty bureaucrats. It was funny how few people bothered to complain when tax assessors and collectors went missing, somewhere in the hinterlands. There was never any *proof* they'd been murdered, even if everyone knew what had happened. "We just have to find him."

"We'll spend the rest of the day studying the town," Phelps said. "And if we can't find a place to get into the network...well, we'll just have to look elsewhere."

"Yes, sir," Rachel said. She frowned. The town was going to be a nightmare. If everyone knew everyone else, a stranger would stick out like a sore thumb. It would be a great deal easier to infiltrate a large city. "Getting out of here might be a bit tricky."

"We knew the job was dangerous when we took it," Phelps said. "If nothing else, there's an army garrison and a small PDC not too far away. We can try and get some answers there."

Rachel nodded. They had time, thankfully. They could take a few days to survey the local region before deciding what to do next. But if they couldn't learn anything useful...she shook her head. They'd have to do a *lot* of research before deciding what to do next. A corporate-dominated world could be hell, if one didn't have the right travel permits. It was quite possible they'd be caught because they didn't have permission to leave town and go elsewhere.

She shuddered. *Whoever controls the government and bureaucracy can keep the rest of the population in a vice.*

There would be dissidents, of course. She was sure of it. The terraforming package included hundreds of plants humans could eat. Someone could survive, beyond the edge of civilisation. But they would be difficult to find and they probably wouldn't be very well organised. Any large insurgency on a corporate world would be crushed before it took on shape and form. Leaderless resistance worked well, under the right circumstances, but it wouldn't be enough to break the corporation's grip on power.

"We should probably start with the farms," she said. Farmers tended to be very practical, with little tolerance for corporate bullshit. They also tended to have covert links with the underground, if there *was* an underground. "They can fill us in on what's *really* going on."

"Yeah," Phelps said. He grinned at her. "And if we can do them a favour, perhaps they'll do us one in return."

CHAPTER ELEVEN

However, it also ensured that—when contact with Earth was finally lost—the colonies lost a great deal of technology. On one hand, things that did come from Earth were suddenly irreplaceable. On the other, the colonials lacked the time and resources—and, in some cases, the knowledge—to rebuild the lost tech base.

—PROFESSOR LEO CAESIUS

Earthfall and its Aftermath

"THEY'VE IMPROVED THE CLOUDSCOOP DESIGN," Tomas commented. "The Jupiter Corp is not going to be pleased about that."

"If the Jupiter Corp still exists," Kerri pointed out, dryly. "I would be surprised if whoever's left has any reason to worry about illicit cloudscoops."

She smiled, rather nastily. The Jupiter Corp's cloudscoop design was inefficient, to say the least. It was designed for a full-fledged stage-five system, not a stage-one or two colony world that didn't need so much fuel and couldn't afford to buy or maintain a Jupiter Corp cloudscoop in any case. And yet, the corporation had made a deal with the Grand Senate and ensured that *their* design was the only *legal* design. They'd earned vast sums of money and stored up great quantities of hatred. If there were any corporate executives alive, after Earthfall, they'd wake up to discover that *no one* was paying them any longer.

Particularly as no one has the power to keep colony worlds from building whatever manner of cloudscoops they like, Kerri thought, coldly. It would power an economic boom, if the remnants of galactic civilisation hung on long enough. *No one's going to care about laws from a dead world...*

Havoc hung over the gas giant, her passive sensors tracking enemy activity. There were no less than *three* cloudscoops, all looking strikingly flimsy compared to the approved design...but, if her analysts were correct, more efficient. It probably wouldn't matter if they *weren't* so efficient, they'd pointed out. They'd lose some gas, as they transhipped it to orbit, but there was so *much* of it that the loss hardly mattered. Gas giants were so large than even a tiny percentage of their atmosphere was more fuel than humanity could use in a millennium. It was just another excuse to slow economic activity outside the Core Worlds.

She put the thought aside as she watched a small fleet of enemy craft moving to and from the cloudscoops. The gas giant's moons had already been settled—it looked as if each of them had a small, but growing colony—and they'd set up a mass driver to launch frozen chunks of fuel towards the planet itself. It was clear they had big plans. They'd invested in far more facilities then they needed, if her estimates were correct. They were laying the groundwork for more expansion in the very near future.

Her eyes narrowed, picking out the handful of orbital weapons platforms floating near the cloudscoops. The defences looked flimsy, although she knew they'd have no trouble standing off a pirate ship or two. She was surprised they hadn't been strengthened in the last few weeks. The Imperial Navy wouldn't come riding to the rescue if the corporation got into trouble, no matter how much they'd paid in bribes over the last few decades. Her lips quirked. They *must* have shelled out *trillions* of credits so inspectors would look the other way. There was no way anyone could miss the non-standard cloudscoops unless they'd been insulted with a fairly considerable bribe.

Or maybe they cut a sweetheart deal, she reminded herself. *The Onge Corporation was so far up the Grand Senate's ass they were practically crawling out of their mouth.*

"I don't think there's much more to see here, Captain," Tomas commented. "Do you want to slip closer."

"No." Kerri didn't have to think about it. The gas giant's orbitals were surprisingly free of debris. The locals would have more reason to be alarmed at any unexpected—and unidentified—sensor contact. She doubted there was any point in taking the risk. "Pull us back to Point Alpha, then hold us there."

"Aye, Captain."

Kerri settled back in her chair as a dull vibration echoed through the hull, her ship picking up speed as she moved away. They'd done all they could, over the last three days. They'd surveyed the system, eavesdropped on transmissions between the planet and the various off-world colonies and generally built up a detailed picture of enemy operations. But she knew it was frighteningly incomplete. There was a great deal they didn't know, a great deal they couldn't find out without risking exposure. Kerri had given some thought to snatching an asteroid miner, or planting a recon device on a habitat, but both options were risky. She had strict orders to evade detection, if possible. Thankfully, the person who'd given her those orders knew the score. She wouldn't be penalised for failing to do the impossible.

Two more days, she thought. *And then we have to go home.*

She felt a twinge of guilt. She'd never been *comfortable* with the idea of landing the Pathfinders on a world they couldn't escape, not until the shit *really* hit the fan. Her survey had made it clear the Pathfinders wouldn't be leaving, not even on a stealth shuttle. They'd known the risks, when they'd accepted the mission, but...she couldn't help feeling terrible, as if she'd deliberately abandoned them. The poor bastards might wind up stuck forever if their superiors decided the invasion plan was unfeasible.

"Captain," Tomas said. "We'll be at Point Alpha in four hours."

"Very good." Kerri rose. "You have the conn. Inform me if we hear anything from the away team."

"Aye, Captain."

• • •

The farm, Rachel decided as the land slowly fell into darkness, had seen better days. She was mildly surprised it was allowed to exist. It was decaying, crumbling into rubble; the wooden farmhouse and barns looked as if they would collapse at any moment. The other farms, the ones they'd noted as they surveyed the land surrounding the town, looked prim and proper, as if the farmers were afraid to look uncaring. They were like something out of a picture book, too nice to be real. The farmhouse in front of her was much more realistic.

And that says something about the locals, Rachel thought. She'd met too many senior officers—and government bureaucrats—who prized appearance over reality. *They want the place to look good first...*

She took point as the Pathfinders made their way towards the farmhouse, lurking in the shadows. They'd watched the building for the last two days, spotting only one man and a handful of dogs in the area. She knew that proved nothing. She'd been on worlds where women were kept firmly inside at all times, with beatings—or worse—for anyone who dared defy the law. Hameau didn't seem to be one of those shitholes—she'd seen plenty of women on the streets—but it was still worrying. She'd been told that a farmer could get away with a hell of a lot, if he was careful. His unfortunate wife and kids were a long way from help.

They reached the door and waited, listening intently. There was a faint scuffling sound inside, right on the other side of the door. The dogs, probably. The Pathfinders had been treated to reduce their scent—and trained to move silently—but it was harder to fool dogs than humans. Rachel glanced at Phelps, then took her multitool from her belt and opened the door. A pair of large dogs snarled at them. Phelps stunned them both before they could start barking. Rachel was surprised they hadn't been barking right from the start. She didn't think it was a good sign.

The interior of the farmhouse was dark and gloomy. Rachel moved through it quickly, Phelps bringing up the rear. The air smelt foul. Empty bottles lay everywhere, a handful lying smashed against the far wall. She kept moving, clambering up the ladder into the loft. A man lay on a rumpled mattress, wearing a farmer's outfit. Rachel knew better than to relax, just because things seemed harmless, but she allowed herself a moment of relief anyway. He was so drunk—she could smell the alcohol from halfway across the room—that he wouldn't have noticed if a bunch of naked women had danced into his room singing loudly. She grabbed his hands, tied them behind his back with a zip-tie and rolled him over. He groaned, loudly, then went back to sleep. Rachel had to smile.

"The rest of the house is empty," Perkins muttered. "He's alone."

"I'm not surprised," Rachel said. "Give me a moment."

She searched the man roughly, then carried out a medical inspection. He was probably in his late thirties or early forties, she decided, but he looked older. It looked as if he'd drunk enough to float a battleship. She glanced around the wretched room, wondering how anyone could willingly live in such squalor. She'd been in worse places, but the poor bastards who'd lived there hadn't had a choice. The man on the bed could have done far better for himself.

"I've found a terminal," Bonkowski said. "Rachel? You want to handle it?"

"Coming," Rachel said.

She passed the prisoner to Phelps, then clambered down the ladder. The rest of the farmhouse was just as bad, save for a bookshelf with a handful of well-thumbed books. She made a mental note of the titles and frowned. They didn't seem to fit with her impression of their prisoner. But there was no sign that anyone *else* lived in the farmhouse. She glanced into a wardrobe and nodded to herself. No female clothes, no children's clothes…nothing that couldn't fit their prisoner. The drunkard looked to be completely alone.

The terminal was the only piece of electronic equipment in the farmhouse, as far as she could tell. She inspected it carefully before booting it up, noting that it was a piece of solid-state machinery that would break if someone opened the casing and tried to look inside. *That* wasn't uncommon, on the Core Worlds, but quite rare on the colonies. The locals couldn't afford to wait months for a technician or a replacement, not when they needed the device repaired immediately. There'd been a big scandal, if she recalled correctly, when pieces of farming equipment had been remotely disabled and a colony had nearly starved to death. It had been so horrific that—for once—even the Grand Senate had taken note.

She pushed the switch and watched as the terminal lit up. She'd expected to have to use her hacking tools to get into the system, or force the password out of their prisoner, but the network opened up in front of her. She leaned forward, biting her lip as she realised the entire datanet was a self-contained system. It was quite possible that monitoring software was already sounding the alert, if it had noticed the midnight log-in. If something was out of character, for the terminal's owner...

There's nothing I can do about it, she thought, as she started to browse the datanet. *If they come, they come.*

She worked her way through the system carefully, noting what was—and what wasn't—on the datanet. The news sites weren't *precisely* censored, as far as she could tell, but they were intensely focused on local news. There was very little about Earthfall, even though it was the biggest news story in decades. The writer made it sound no more significant than an apple falling off the tree. She shook her head in amused disbelief, then continued her search. There was something almost disturbingly *clean* about the datanet. No political forums, moderated or not; no place for independent discussion. And no porn. There weren't even any R-rated flicks. It looked as if someone had sanitized the datanet before allowing the civilians to use it.

"I'd bet good money there's a whole host of monitors embedded into the terminal," she muttered. She'd have to take the terminal apart to be sure—and that might trigger an alarm, given that it was hardwired to the datanet—but she was morbidly certain of it. "And if there is a dark web, it will be very hard to find."

She felt a flicker of sympathy for the planet's residents as she searched for information on how the planet was actually run. *Earth's* datanet was so full of holes—and archives that dated back so far they predated the Empire itself—that anyone, with a little training, could find just about anything. There were whole *armies* of WebHeads and hackers who made—who *had* made, she supposed—the datanet their playground. But here, the system was so tightly controlled that anyone who *tried* was more likely to attract attention than set up a hidden system. She could see the advantages, but she could also see the weaknesses. It would be impossible to use the datanet for political action without being detected, arrested and...and what? She had no idea, but she doubted it would be pleasant.

The sound of retching echoed through the house. Rachel winced. Phelps had given their captive a sober-up pill. She'd used them herself, back when she'd been young and wild. The captive would be sober, afterwards, but he wouldn't be grateful. Rachel hadn't been happy when she'd been given a tab either. The experience certainly wasn't one she wanted to repeat. She would almost sooner have risked the Sergeant's anger for returning to post drunk.

She turned back to the terminal, carefully reading through the files. There was little enough, as if the locals expected everyone to share the same understanding of the world. The files talked about the government, but... they didn't really go into detail. And yet, reading between the lines, it was clear Hameau was no democracy. There were no references to elections, no suggestion that the people had a say in government...the only reference she found to a politician was in a news story that detailed a mayor being *appointed* to a town.

Which means that this is a corporate state on a terrifying scale, Rachel thought, grimly. It was rare for a planet to be *openly* dominated by a single corporation—most corporations gave themselves a figleaf of respectability, even if real power remained firmly vested in their hands—but...she supposed it didn't matter. The original settlers would have known the score, when they landed; their children or grandchildren wouldn't know any better. *And if there is a resistance movement, it's probably powerless.*

She kept skimming through the files, wishing she dared use one of the hacker tools loaded into her implants. It would be simple enough to hack the system and download the entire datanet—it was so *small*—but that would set off alarms. She briefly considered leaving their captive to take the rap, yet...she shook her head. That would be immoral and, worse, futile. There was no reason for their captive to download so much overnight, certainly none that would stand up to scrutiny. Any halfway decent investigator would suspect a trick.

Her eyes narrowed as she downloaded a map. It was as sanitised as the rest of the network, but she could make guesses about what the locals were trying to hide. There was an entire section, only a few short miles from the town, that was completely blanked out. And it was too close to the settlement to be undeveloped land. She smiled, grimly. If that wasn't some kind of military installation, she'd eat her socks.

We have to go there, she thought. She started putting the plan together in her mind. *And quickly.*

Perkins entered the room, his face grim. "The poor bastard has an ID implant."

Rachel looked up. "A tracking implant?"

"It doesn't look like it," Perkins said. "It doesn't appear to be emitting anything. It might be waiting until it receives a query. But it's very definitely an ID implant."

"Shit." Rachel glanced at the terminal, wondering if she dared search for information on implants. If everyone was implanted...at the very least, it would be hard to pass as locals. And if the implants *were* tracking devices... she shuddered. The world might be so tightly controlled that resistance was impossible. No wonder the civvies had looked so stressed. They could be watched at any moment. "Can we duplicate the ID codes?"

"Yeah, once we track them," Perkins said. "And if it does start emitting something..."

Rachel nodded. The local surveillance system might not notice people who didn't have tracking implants. They might as well not exist, as far as the system could tell. Or...it might notice people who didn't *have* tracking implants. The potential of modern technology for people-control was terrifying. The planetary government would have to break a number of imperial laws, but...no one was enforcing the laws any longer.

Perkins was having similar thoughts. "What the fuck is this place?"

"A corporate paradise," Rachel said. She felt sick. She'd once beaten the crap out of someone who'd spied on her in the shower, but...this was different. There was no way anyone could beat up a government. They wouldn't even be aware of when and where they were being watched. And *that* type of government tended to attract—or create—the worst kind of monsters. "And anyone who lives here is just another interchangeable widget in their machine."

CHAPTER TWELVE

This was not always a problem. Stage-one colonies could feed themselves. Given time, they could and did ensure their survival. But it also limited their ability to influence events outside their gravity well. A single corvette, controlling the high orbitals, could bombard any stage-one colony world into submission.

—PROFESSOR LEO CAESIUS

Earthfall and its Aftermath

"YOU'RE RUNNING TOO FAST," Phelps muttered, as they made their way down the dusty road. "You're meant to be a young girl out for a jog, not a speedster trying to win a race."

"Sorry, sir," Rachel muttered.

She scowled, then schooled her face into a mask. She'd learnt too much about the planet in the last day, first from searching the datanet and then from interrogating their captive, to feel comfortable. The corporation had the entire world sewn up, as far as they could tell. There was no way to be *sure* they weren't being watched, no way to be entirely *certain* they'd escaped notice. Rachel knew that maintaining a world-sized surveillance network wasn't easy, but with computers monitoring the citizens it would be fairly simple to keep tabs on *all* of them. There would certainly be fewer false alarms to put the human supervisors off their guard. It was all too easy to fear that their captive missing a day of work would set off an alarm *somewhere.*

There are always cracks in the system, she told herself, as she concentrated on keeping her speed down. *You just have to find them before you take advantage of them.*

She followed Phelps, silently cursing the dust under her breath. The road ran around the forbidden zone—an army base, according to their former captive—and they needed to survey the area, if only to discover what—if anything—the locals might be able to throw at an invasion force. The datanet had said nothing about the planetary defences, as far as she'd been able to tell. Such information was probably on a strict need-to-know basis. She would have been surprised if asking pointed questions about such matters *didn't* set off alarms.

Her implants flashed an alert as the dust billowed higher. They could hear someone approaching, from the rear. The sound was too low to be heard by human ears, but...Rachel resisted the urge to glance back as it grew louder. The hummer was growing closer...she heard a crackle behind her, loud enough for *anyone* to hear, and glanced back. A small police car was pulling up behind them. The officers looked competent, if unwary. Their uniforms were just a little *too* fancy for her peace of mind, designed for appearance rather than practicality. It looked as if they hadn't faced any *real* challenges in a long time, if ever.

She stopped and turned to face the police car as one of the officers clambered out of the vehicle. He looked fit enough, she supposed, but it was clear he wasn't expecting any real trouble. His eyes lingered on her breasts, rather than assessing her as a potential threat. She silently assessed *him* and his companion, the one who'd remained in the car. It was standard procedure to have someone hang back, to sound the alert if something went wrong, but he didn't have his hand on his console. Rachel silently calculated how long it would take her to subdue both cops if they turned nasty. She was fairly sure they could take them both out before they could raise the alarm.

Phelps stepped forward, playing the concerned boyfriend. "Is there a problem, officer?"

The policeman looked at him, reluctantly. "Your ID. Now."

Rachel shuddered, inwardly, as Phelps held out his right hand. The ID chips were buried deep under the skin. Anyone who wanted to remove his chip—and didn't have access to an autodoc—would practically have to cut off his hand. She tensed, readying herself as the policeman touched Phelps with his scanner. They'd rigged their implants to fool the scanners, keying them to hack the system and return a positive response, but...if they were wrong, the shit would hit the fan very quickly. The cop seemed almost disappointed. Idiot. A *smart* cop would know just how quickly a seemingly-innocuous traffic stop could turn to screaming violence.

Maybe he thinks he'll get promoted if he catches a spy, Rachel thought. *And the hell of it is that he's probably right.*

She forced herself to stay still as the cop tested her implant, his eyes leaving trails of slime over her breasts. She knew she should be grateful that he wasn't more alert, but...she shuddered to think about the innocent and defenceless civilians who were unlucky enough to wind up in his clutches. Corporate security forces tended to turn nasty very quickly, she knew from grim experience. They were more interested in pleasing their paymasters than upholding the law. Even so.... they were still better than Earth's cops. *They* were just another gang.

"Clear," the cop said. He *definitely* sounded disappointed. "You may proceed, if you stay on the road."

"Yes, sir," Phelps said.

The cop nodded, took one final look at Rachel and returned to his hummer. The police car drove past them and headed into the distance. Rachel was too professional to exchange glances with Phelps, but she knew from experience what he was thinking. It was unlikely to be a coincidence that they'd been stopped *now*, when they were so close to the base. They'd been spotted. But when? And how?

They resumed their jog, following the road as it bent around the forest and passed a large sign indicating the military base. Another road—properly paved, this time—led down to the base itself. Rachel glanced down the road, then hurried onwards, silently replaying the scene in her mind. A guardpost, with four guards and an armoured car clearly visible. It looked like overkill, suggesting the defenders were excessively paranoid. But did they have *reason* to be paranoid? It was rare for anyone to waste so much firepower guarding a base when there was no reason to expect attack.

She considered it as they kept moving, the road growing narrower as it headed down towards a farm. They role-played slipping under the trees, straightening up as soon as they were under the canopy. Rachel wanted to keep moving, but she knew she had to wait to see if the cops came back. Better they stumbled across a young couple making out under the trees than a pair of commandos sneaking towards the base. The cop hadn't struck her as particularly bright or experienced, but even a moron would be suspicious if he caught them in a place they had no reason to be. And then they'd have to fight their way out...

If we can, she thought, as they waited. *They'd send everything they had after us.*

It was nearly an hour before they stood and walked towards the base. The forest was rough, yet...there were hints that people regularly patrolled it. Or simply went on exercise. She rather suspected the terrain was used to train soldiers. It wouldn't pose a major challenge, not like the Slaughterhouse, but it would give them experience they desperately needed. She wondered, sourly, just how the corporation organised its troops. They might have copied the Imperial Army or...they might have come up with something new. There was no way to know.

They slowed as they reached the edge of the fence and peered through the foliage. The base itself definitely *looked* like something the Imperial Army would have built and maintained, although there was a permanence about the setting that surprised her. The base certainly *wasn't* hundreds of years old. Hell, it might be shut down at any moment. And yet...there were no prefabricated buildings, no tent cities, nothing that could be moved in a hurry. The barracks looked solid, the defences looked concrete...literally. The base was designed to repel attack.

Phelps nudged her. "Training base?"

Rachel considered it. "Possibly."

She frowned. The base was a little *too* close to civilisation for comfort, although she supposed it didn't matter so much when someone could hardly cough without having a note made of it in his file. Deserters probably couldn't evade capture unless they headed into the wildlands, where they'd be no one's problem. And they had implants...she shuddered, again. Marine recruits had tracking implants too, but they were removed when the candidate graduated or quit. Here...the implants appeared permanent.

Her eyes swept over the base. There were a handful of tanks in the middle of a field, surrounded by armed soldiers. She didn't recognise the design. That could be good or bad, she knew. The old designs had their flaws, but they wouldn't have lasted so long if their advantages hadn't outweighed their disadvantages. A new design would be an unknown factor, at least until she saw it in action. And if it had flaws, they might be a nasty surprise to the operators as well as everyone else. She hated the thought of driving onto the battlefield in a tank that might have an unexpected—and undiscovered—weakness. Who knew when it would blow up in her face?

"It looks as if they're expecting trouble," Phelps muttered. "Or...or what?"

"I don't know," Rachel said. The defenders looked alert, although it still wasn't clear if they had any *reason* to be alert. Maybe it was good practice, maybe it was steadily wearing down their edge. "You want to try to get *onto* the base?"

Phelps shook his head. "No point in pressing our luck."

Rachel was almost disappointed, but she didn't push the issue. It was his call. Instead, she silently catalogued everything she saw. Twenty large barracks, each one...she considered for a moment, then decided the absolute maximum would be two hundred soldiers per barracks. It didn't look as if they'd be hotbunking. Twelve tanks, five armoured cars…she had no idea why the tanks were on the base, unless they were training vehicles. It made a certain kind of sense. Soldiers needed to learn how to operate alongside tanks, even if they weren't intending to drive them. And they'd be on alert if anything happened that required heavy firepower.

They'd have to get to the landing site first, Rachel thought. *And that will be tricky.*

She studied the soldiers as a handful ran past the fence, their sergeant leading them in a marching song. They looked surprisingly competent, for corporate troops. There was none of the misplaced arrogance, mingled with incompetence, of the Civil Guard. Their weapons were simple assault rifles, their webbing crammed with grenades, ration bars and other things that might be useful. There were no antitank weapons or portable artillery. She wondered if they were actually allowed to carry loaded weapons on base. Marines did, once they qualified; regular soldiers weren't allowed to carry weapons or draw ammunition unless they were going on deployment or the base came under attack. It had ensured hundreds of needless deaths during the waning years, when terrorists attacked unarmed soldiers.

"We'd better go," Phelps muttered. "We're not going to learn anything else here."

"Probably not," Rachel agreed.

She followed him back through the trees, careful to ensure that they returned to the road at the point they'd left. She rumpled her clothes just before stepping back into the light, hoping it was enough to fool any watching eyes. There were no cops as they made their way down the road, but that didn't mean they were being watched. She tensed every time she heard an aircar or helicopter in the distance. Someone could already be vectoring troops and security forces towards them.

Her implants sounded the alert as the hummer returned, driving towards them. This time, the policemen didn't stop. Rachel wondered if they'd decided there was no point in checking IDs again or if they had other problems, elsewhere. It didn't seem likely. Crime was low, almost non-existent. The world was almost a paradise, if one didn't mind sacrificing freedom and privacy for security. She wouldn't have made that trade-off herself, but she knew people who would.

They saw little else as they slipped off the road and made their way back to the hideout. The remainder of the team was waiting for them, having concealed their appearance at the farm before returning to the hide themselves. Rachel allowed herself a moment of relief as they rested, even though she knew they might have led unseen watchers to the base. They should be able to get their report back to the ship, before they went undercover. And then...

Getting off this world is going to be a real nightmare, she thought, as she uploaded her observations to the transmitter. *We might have to steal a shuttle, then hijack a starship.*

She sat down and ate her ration bar, thinking hard. She'd been in worse places. She'd been in places where men were butchered, women were raped and children were brainwashed and abused for being the wrong skin colour, or religion, or simply being the closest target for angry drug-addicted monsters in human form. And she'd been in places where a handful of men and women were on top, with everyone else firmly under them...they'd looked worse, on the surface, but at least there'd been a chance for the poor bastards to fight back. Here, on the other hand, a political campaign or violent insurgency would have no time to take root before it was mercilessly destroyed. The population was caught in a vice. She wondered, darkly, how long it would be before the vice started to tighten.

And I wouldn't live here if you paid me, she thought. *There simply isn't enough money in the entire universe.*

• • •

Kerri reviewed the away team report with a profound feeling of dissatisfaction, mingled with cold anticipation. She wasn't too surprised to hear that the entire planet was under firm control, with resistance utterly futile.

She'd grown up on a world where the political system was so firmly sewn up that there was little hope of reform, despite a vast and growing underclass. And she was pleased, in her own way, that the system was so vile. It would be harder to justify aggression against a democratic system that operated with the consent of its population.

And if it was a democratic system, we could work with it, she thought, as she finished the report. It wasn't as detailed as she would have liked—the Pathfinders hadn't managed to get close to one of the PDCs—but it contained enough for the planners to go to work. Combined with her survey, it should be enough to let the Commandant decide if the invasion should go ahead or not. *There's no reason to feel guilt about anything that happens to these people.*

She studied the map for a moment, silently comparing the report to what her probes had reported. They knew more about how the system functioned, in broad terms, but few details. They *thought* they knew which city was the capital...she shook her head in droll amusement. It was astonishing just how much had been left off the official files. She wondered how the Onge Corporation had intended to hide what they'd done, when the inspectors finally came calling. The bribes would be through the roof. Or... had they thought Earthfall would come before someone started asking awkward questions? Kerri had heard some of her friends speculating that someone had been working, behind the scenes, to ensure the Empire fell...

And that's tempting, because it tells us that someone is to blame, she thought, sourly. She could see the appeal, even if she'd been a serving officer long enough to know the danger of self-delusion. *We don't have to take responsibility for ourselves if someone did it to us.*

She put the thought to one side and thought, hard. She had permission to stay in the system for another week, if necessary, but it seemed pointless. There was no hope of learning anything else unless they risked exposure, which would be disastrous. The system was strongly defended. It would be hard enough to invade the system if the defenders *weren't* on alert. And if they were, the cost might be more than they could bear.

"Communications, inform the Pathfinders that we will be departing the system in an hour," she ordered. "Helm, plot us a least-time course to the Phase Limit. I want to be on the way home as quickly as possible."

Susan glanced at her. "Captain…"

"They knew the job was dangerous when they took it," Kerri said, a little more sharply than she'd intended. She didn't like the thought of abandoning anyone, even though there was no choice. The Pathfinders had volunteered, damn them. Somehow, the thought didn't soothe her conscience. "And we will be coming back for them."

"… Aye, Captain," Susan said.

Kerri nodded, stiffly. They *would* be back, sooner or later. Hameau posed a significant threat to the galaxy…maybe not a short-term threat, but a long-term one. Better to nip it in the bud before it could turn into a hydra and start raising hell. The Pathfinders had made it clear the locals were in hell. It wouldn't be long before their world turned into a *de facto* aristocracy and started exporting its system to the stars. It had happened before and it would happen again.

Three weeks to get home, she thought, as she settled back in her chair. She'd run the figures so often she could practically *taste* them. She knew them as well as she knew the oath. *And another month, perhaps, before we can come back.*

She sighed, inwardly. They'd be back. And then they would see.

CHAPTER THIRTEEN

And indeed, many colony worlds were often absorbed into vest-pocket empires as pirates, warlords and various rebel factions took advantage of Earthfall. Their empires were often weak, unable to support themselves, but—by the time they fell apart—they did a great deal of damage.

—PROFESSOR LEO CAESIUS

Earthfall and its Aftermath

"COMMANDANT, WE JUST GOT A COURIER BOAT from Huxley's Haven," Christie Loomis reported, through the intercom. "The extraction mission went off without a hitch. The targets have been remanded to Base Theta until they can be processed."

"That's good," Jeremy said. He didn't look away from the window. "What about Huxley's Haven itself?"

"The planetary government is desperately trying to pretend that nothing is wrong," Christie said. "The report makes it clear that their balancing act is about to fail."

"Understood," Jeremy said. "Inform me if anything changes."

He stood by the window, watching the ever-darkening sky. The news was good, but it was only a drop in the bucket of *bad* news. Mass pogroms on a dozen worlds, mass deportations on a dozen others...all pointless, as if removing hundreds of thousands of undesirables would fix the underlying problems threatening to bring hundreds of planets to the brink of collapse. And war, pestilence, famine and death…if anything, Jeremy considered, the projections had been optimistic. The Empire was tearing itself apart, and there was nothing he could do about it. There was no way he could tell himself otherwise. He was condemned to bear witness as galactic society fell into hell.

His intercom bleeped, again. "Sir, *Havoc* just cleared the limit," Christie said. "She's transmitted her full report."

"Summon the working group," Jeremy ordered. "Meeting in my office, one hour from now. And have coffee and sandwiches sent in. It's going to be a long day."

"Aye, sir."

An hour later, he sat at the head of the table and studied the holographic images from Hameau. *Havoc*—and the Pathfinders—had done a good job. The planet—and its halo of space debris—was surrounded by hundreds of icons, ranging from space habitats and industrial nodes to orbital weapons platforms and sensor satellites. The Pathfinders had been lucky to get down to the surface without being detected. The analysts had made it clear that the locals had the system sewn up tight. There was no way they could land an entire company, let alone a division, without being detected.

Which wasn't entirely unexpected, Jeremy thought, coldly. *We knew we'd have to fight for the world.*

"The good news is that the orbital defences are thinner than we anticipated," Colonel Chung Myung-Hee said. "The bad news is that the ground-based defences are staggering. We will be unable to take control of the world, let alone put it to use, unless we first knock-out or seize the ground-based defences. It's quite an unusual problem."

"Yeah." Jeremy was more used to orbital platforms than ground-based defences. "Can we get troops to the surface?"

"I believe so." Anderson leaned forward. "We could land our advance elements here"—he tapped a spot on the map—"and fight our way towards the capital city and the surrounding PDCs. They couldn't call down orbital fire without exposing their platforms to *our* fire. It would be costly, but doable."

"I don't want costly," Jeremy said, tartly. "We don't have *that* much manpower."

"The planetary government might come to terms, once we get down on the ground," Chung said. "They won't want to fight it out."

"And let them get away with everything?" Anderson shot her a sharp look. "They're monsters. They have an entire world in their grip and..."

Chung looked back at him, evenly. "And how many lives do you want to spend, sir, to bring them to justice?"

Jeremy held up his hand. He saw both points of view. Anderson was right for wanting to hang the corporate executives who'd turned a world into a prison camp, even if—in many ways—it was a very *nice* prison camp. But, at the same time, the corprats would fight to the death if they thought they'd be executed the moment they surrendered. Better to make a deal that let them keep their lives, as distasteful as it was, than devastate the planet in the course of bringing them to justice. Besides, the PDCs could make a terrible mess of the orbital industries. If they thought they had nothing to lose, why not? It wasn't as if they could be stopped.

"We can promise them their lives, at least," he said, curtly. "Can we take the orbitals?"

"That battlecruiser is a bit of a surprise," Chung said. "Captain Stumbaugh is confident she can be taken out, though. She didn't power up once in the time *Havoc* was in-system. It doesn't prove she's worthless—Stumbaugh was very clear on that, in her report—but as long as she's powered down, she's an easy target. We might even be able to land troops on her hull and take her for ourselves."

Jeremy scowled. Landing troops on an enemy ship was always a gamble. The enemy CO might hit the self-destruct, rather than allow his vessel to be captured. And that would cost the lives of however many marines were committed to the operation. He silently weighed the pros and cons for a moment, then shook his head. They were going to be making enough gambles in the coming months. There was no point in taking an unnecessary gamble.

"Mark her down for destruction," he said. "If she doesn't surrender, when she comes under fire, kill her."

"Yes, sir." Chung made a note on her datapad. "If she's powered down, she will be an easy target."

"You said," Anderson commented. "Who are you trying to convince?"

He adjusted the display. "The Pathfinders may or may not be able to carry out diversionary operations. We're planning on the assumption they won't be able to influence events in any way. We'll drop lead elements here, on the edge of the settled zone"—he altered the map—"and move at once to secure the closest army garrison and nearby settlements. We don't expect much resistance, if we have the advantage of surprise. They won't have time to react before we get them by the neck."

"And as long as we stay away from the PDCs, they'll have problems bringing their weapons to bear on us," Jeremy said. He couldn't help a thrill of excitement. This was *real* war. "And then?"

"We'll move against the first PDC, securing our supply lines." Anderson's finger traced points on the map. "The locals appear to be largely disarmed, according to the Pathfinders. There's a few farmers with hunting rifles, but apparently ammunition is in short supply. We don't expect civilian resistance to be a major factor, at least at first. Civil Affairs teams will keep them under control and out of the firing line, as much as possible. Given time"—he shrugged—"we don't expect them to switch sides at once. They'll be afraid of us and afraid of what their government will do to them, if it manages to drive us back into space. I think wary neutrality is the best we can expect."

"I know." Jeremy sighed. It was unlikely in the extreme that no civilians would be killed during the fighting—only a Grand Senator could be so ignorant as to believe it was possible to wage war without killing innocents—but they'd do everything in their power to keep the death toll as low as possible. "And then…?"

"If they don't surrender, we'll have to punch our way up to their capital city, isolating or destroying the PDCs along the way," Anderson said, flatly. "It's possible, sir, but it may become costly. Given time to prepare, distribute weapons, organise stay-behind teams…it could get sticky. Our troops are experienced vets, sir, but there will be a *lot* of enemy soldiers."

"And they might have heavier tanks and shit," Chung warned. "Most of *our* tanks were lightened for transport decades ago."

Which was rarely a problem, when we ruled the skies, Jeremy thought. *Anyone stupid enough to drive a tank at us didn't last long enough to realise his mistake.*

"We'll distribute antitank weapons and plasma cannons as well as self-propelled guns," Anderson said. "It shouldn't be a problem."

He nodded to the map. "The real problem, sir, lies in supply lines. Even with mobile factories and suchlike, we frequently ran into trouble when our ammunition started to run dry. Here…the operational tempo will be higher. Supply and distribution problems will be a great deal worse."

"And little hope of scrounging supplies from the locals," Jeremy said.

"No, sir," Anderson said. "Even if they wanted to give them to us, even if we were prepared to *take* them, they simply don't have much we can use for military purposes. Food and drink, sure. Weapons and ammunition? Not so much."

"And if we start losing supply shuttles in large numbers," Chung warned, "the campaign will be on the verge of being lost with them."

Jeremy nodded. A shuttle that flew too close to a PDC would probably not survive the mistake. The locals would have no trouble blowing an unwary shuttle out of the sky. But that wasn't the real problem. It would be easy to hide from the PDCs, but harder—much harder—to hide from roving HVM teams. A lone soldier with an HVM launcher could catch a shuttle by surprise and kill it before the crew could take evasive action. And a smart team of defence planners would prepare to do just that.

"We can plan for losses," Anderson said. "But there are limits."

"Yes." Chung looked at Jeremy. "Do we proceed?"

Jeremy raised his eyes to the display. The invasion had been purely theoretical, even when he'd dispatched *Havoc* and the Pathfinders to Hameau. He'd sent them with the full awareness that the invasion might not go ahead, that the former might have a wasted journey and the latter have to find their own way off the enemy world. They knew he might not be able to come for them. And yet…

Now, the invasion *wasn't* theoretical. If he gave the word, it would go ahead. The Major-Generals, those who could be consulted, knew the score. They'd all approved the plan, at least when it had been a concept. They wouldn't say no if he approved the invasion himself, not now. Things hadn't changed *that* much. But…the buck stopped with him. He could say no now, himself, and stop everything. Or he could say yes and commit the corps to a campaign that could easily go wrong. He understood, now, why so many politicians had been reluctant to make a final decision and stick to it. Whatever happened, afterwards, would haunt them for the rest of their lives.

He took a breath. "We proceed."

"Yes, sir," Anderson said. He sounded pleased, but also concerned. He'd be in command of the operation. Jeremy couldn't have micromanaged from Safehouse, even if he'd *wanted* to. "I took the liberty of issuing warning orders. The units can be gathered over the next five days."

Jeremy nodded, stiffly. Everyone would be very busy over the next week. The planning staff would take the vague concept Anderson had outlined and turn it into reality, sorting out the precise details of who would do what when the operation was finally launched. Civilians never understood just how much planning went into military operations, although Jeremy had been a marine long enough to know that plans *never* went perfectly. Something would go wrong, normally at the worst possible time. It was then, he reminded himself, that trained and experienced marines would have the edge.

War is a democracy, he thought. His training had drilled it into his head, time and time again, before he'd ever seen an enemy soldier on the field. *The enemy, that dirty dog, gets a vote too.*

"Put the fleet together," he ordered, quietly. "We'll aim to leave in a week."

"Aye, sir," Anderson said.

Jeremy glanced at Chung. "I want a full intelligence-gathering unit to accompany them," he added. "If there are any other surprises waiting for us on Hameau, I want to know about them."

"Yes, sir," Chung said. She frowned. "We do have reason to think that many of our original projections are wrong."

"An intelligence officer admits she might be wrong?" Anderson smirked. "Who are you and what have you done with the colonel?"

Chung smiled, but it didn't touch her eyes. "*Havoc* reported a *lot* of details that were never included in the files," she said. "I'm not talking about under-reporting their income to fool the taxman or keeping quiet about a mineral strike until they're ready to exploit it, but leaving entire cities and installations off the reports. The cloudscoops alone are quite surprising. If they'd been caught..."

"Grand Senator Onge would have brought pressure to bear on the Jupiter Corp," Jeremy said, shortly. Onge had been a ruthless bastard, in his day. "And there would have been a nominal fine or two, but nothing else."

"There would still have been a scandal," Chung said. "Once the first cracks appeared in the monopoly, the edifice would have collapsed with astonishing speed."

"There are cracks in the monopoly along the Rim," Anderson pointed out. "Cloudskimmers harvest gas and sell it to colonies who can't afford a cloudscoop. It's not the safest of occupations, but it pays well and helps circumvent the monopoly."

"They're not flying fixed installations," Chung said. "They were a headache, as far as the Jupiter Corp was concerned, but hardly life-threatening. I'd be surprised if they were ever considered more than a minor nuisance.

A working cloudscoop design that was cheaper and more efficient than theirs...oh yes, that would be a threat. The customers would be demanding to know why they couldn't have one and there would be no good answer the corprats could give."

"Quite," Jeremy said. "What's your point?"

"My point is that there's a great deal we don't *know* about the system," Chung said. "And we don't know what we might encounter on the ground."

"They can't have something *really* new," Anderson pointed out. "They'd have kicked everyone's ass by now if they did."

"I don't know," Chung said. "I merely advise caution."

"There's a time for caution and a time for taking action," Anderson said. "Fortune favours the bold."

Jeremy looked from one to the other. "We will be careful," he said. "But our window of opportunity is closing. They know we took people from Gamma Prime. Even if they don't know who we are, they cannot have found that very reassuring. Someone *else* is making preparations for the gathering storm. If we don't nip them in the bud, they'll come looking for us. And we dare not assume they won't *find* us."

"They won't look *here*," Anderson predicted. "Safehouse isn't the normal sort of place to house a major colony."

"We can't take that chance," Jeremy said. "And someone is already gunning for us. The Slaughterhouse is gone."

He switched off the display. "Keep me informed, both of you. Dismissed."

They left, leaving Jeremy alone. He picked up a sandwich and slowly chewed it, barely tasting the processed cheese and ham. Someone *was* gunning for the remnants of empire, although he wasn't sure if they were targeting the marines in general or just whatever was left of the once-great galactic civilisation. They'd taken out the Slaughterhouse, plunged Terra Nova into chaos and triggered off a series of wars that threatened to destroy the remnants of the Core Worlds. All hope for peace had died with Terra Nova.

And we don't know who they are, Jeremy thought. He'd assigned Belinda Lawson and her lover to find the unknowns, but—in truth—he wasn't expecting miracles. *The Nihilists, intent on wiping out the rest of the human race, or someone with more sinister ambitions of their own?*

He finished the sandwich and took another one, his mind elsewhere. There were more ways to kill a cat than stuffing it with cream, more ways to accomplish one's objective than merely brute force. He'd seen the great and the good manipulate their enemies so they fought each other, expending their strength uselessly before the *real* enemy showed its hand. And... he'd watched tribes be pushed into war, weakening themselves until they could be slaughtered with ease. If someone was attacking the remnants of the empire, pitting the warlords against each other...

The Grand Senator wouldn't have hesitated to throw half the galaxy into the flames, if it meant he could take control of the other half, he thought. *And yet, he was trying to take power on Earth, not save what he could for the post-Earthfall era. He didn't seem to know that Earthfall was coming.*

He stood and paced over to the window, peering out over the desolate landscape. There was no way to know. Certainly, a man as power-hungry—and smart—as Grand Senator Onge would have had several strings to his bow. Jeremy did it too, in the hopes that one plan would succeed even if the others failed. But Onge had failed completely. He couldn't have planned for his own death. No, he *wouldn't* have planned for his own death. He'd known he was riding a tiger, but...he would have assumed he couldn't possibly fall off.

Which doesn't mean he couldn't have laid the groundwork for his heirs, Jeremy thought. The Grand Senator had known the limits of power. He had never missed a step until his final days. His heirs might not be so careful, more given to rash moves. *The sooner we nip whatever they're doing in the bud, the better.*

CHAPTER FOURTEEN

The Rim, therefore, survived...but interstellar communications and trade were lost. Most of us joked they didn't feel the lack. Given what happened in the Core, the joke stopped being funny.

—PROFESSOR LEO CAESIUS

Earthfall and its Aftermath

IF THERE WAS ONE DOWNSIDE to being a Marine Auxiliary, Kerri had discovered years ago, it was that she wasn't always taken seriously.

It wasn't that they didn't *respect* her. She was seen as a competent professional in her field. But she wasn't a *marine*, she never *would* be a marine... and the marines themselves, particularly the officers who'd paid their dues, tended to look down on her. Survivors of the toughest training ground in the galaxy, experienced officers who'd tested themselves against the worst of the worst and emerged victorious...they didn't quite grasp matters that were out of their sphere. Kerri admired them for their strengths, but she wasn't blind to their weaknesses. And, perhaps more importantly, to their blind spots.

She studied the assault plan, wondering just who'd come up with it and just how many hours he'd spent on the bridge of a starship. None, she thought. Travelling on a MEU didn't make someone an instant expert in starship tactics, even if they were high-ranking enough to have their own office and attached staff. She would have bet half her pay packet—if she was still being paid, these days—that the planner hadn't even spent a few hours playing *Imperial Combat, Service to the Empire* or one of the other commercial tactical simulators. They'd been designed by actual naval personnel and paid attention to technological realities. Anyone who played them would be much better prepared for naval combat than a groundpounder who'd never served in space.

"The plan is deeply flawed," she said, shortly. Marines, at least, knew how to take criticism. They'd heard worse from their Drill Instructors. "And it will probably get a lot of us killed for nothing."

Marine Captain Pete Buckland eyed her sourly. "How so, Commodore?"

Kerri scowled. The corps believed in brevet promotions and makeshift command structures, rather than an established chain of command. A captain could jump up to being a colonel and assume command of a combat group that had been thrown together in a hurry, then go back down to being a captain when the emergency came to an end. It worked for them, but it was harder to run a naval unit like a marine company. A fixed chain of command worked better for starships and their crews. The Imperial Navy had been riddled with corruption—she knew an officer who'd been promoted after selling two cruisers to planetary governments—but there had been little doubt of who was in command at any given time. A dispute over who was calling the shots, in the middle of combat, could be utterly disastrous.

And they made me a Commodore and gave me the task of commanding the squadron, because I was the one who probed the enemy system, she thought, dryly. She didn't mind the promotion, even though it wouldn't last, but...it had its problems. At least she was still in command of her ship. *And yet... will they listen to my comments?*

She keyed the terminal. "Your plan assumes the enemy will sit still and wait to be attacked," she said. "We would have to get very lucky to sneak the fleet into the high orbitals without being detected."

"We have to get the troops on the ground as quickly as possible," Buckland pointed out. "They're no good to anyone in deep space."

"Yes, but we have to punch a hole in the orbital defences *first*," Kerri countered. "Or the troops will either be blown out of space when they try to land or simply smashed from orbit when they're on the ground."

She sighed, inwardly. There were no currently serving officers, as far as she knew, who'd commanded operations without control of the high orbitals. They'd always been able to call down KEW strikes from high orbit, if the enemy stood and fought. They'd never fought a battle where the enemy controlled the high orbitals, never had to hide from very unfriendly skies... it was an easy thing to miss. But it could prove fatal.

"We have to split the fleet into two detachments," she said. "The first detachment takes control of the high orbitals, killing or capturing the handful of enemy ships. The second actually lands the troops."

She altered the map. "And yes, we actually *are* going to have to land them on the edge of the settled zone. There's no way we can drop marines straight into their capital."

"Unfortunately," Buckland agreed. "If we knew more about the planet..."

His voice trailed off. Kerri nodded in agreement. The analysts had tagged every file they'd forwarded with stern warnings that *nothing* could be taken for granted. Kerri was inclined to agree. Either though incompetence or malice, the Onge Corporation had managed to hide a great deal of information from the Empire. She wondered, idly, how they'd planned to *keep* hiding the information. Perhaps they'd just intended to shell out billions of credits in bribes.

Unless they really were pushing the Empire towards Earthfall, she mused. She'd heard the theories. She just didn't believe them. Years of experience had taught her the importance of following the KISS principle. A complex plan with dozens of moving parts—and an unspoken assumption that the enemy would react as planned—was doomed. *They probably thought they could get away with it.*

She moved the display away from the planet. "If the battlecruiser is powered down when we arrived, we'll sneak into missile range and demand her surrender. She won't have time to power up if she wants to fight, so... we won't waste troops trying to take her. We'll just blow her away. The remaining ships won't pose a problem if we manage to trap them against the planet. I'm more concerned about the ground-based defences."

"The planet is rather odd," Buckland agreed.

Kerri nodded. "They have a battlecruiser and a handful of destroyers," she said. "That's odd, yes."

She stroked her chin, ignoring the perplexed look he shot her. It *was* odd. Hameau was hardly a stage-one colony, but...it looked as if they'd made no attempt to build a balanced force. The destroyers made sense. The battlecruiser didn't. She felt her frown deepen as she studied the enemy ship. Hameau shouldn't have been able to man the ship, let alone provide the infrastructure a battlecruiser required to remain operational. Maybe they were improvising. Or maybe she was missing something. It *was* quite possible that Hameau had scooped up the battlecruiser by accident.

It wouldn't be the first time a planetary government opted for prestige over practicality, she mused. The battlecruiser was tough, but she could only be in one place at a time. A dozen or so destroyers would be far more effective. *It would be odd for corprats to make such a mistake.*

"We can insert the troops over the ocean," she said. Her probes had noticed a handful of tiny colonies on the other continents, but none of them were large enough to merit concern. "And then get them down to the ground."

"That's all we ask," Buckland said. "Can you clear the other PDCs?"

"Probably not, unless we use nukes." Kerri shook her head. A blast that would pass unnoticed in interplanetary space would be devastating on a planetary surface. They could throw nuclear-tipped missiles at the PDCs until one of them got through, but the collateral damage would be appalling. Millions of people would be killed. Hell, they'd have to be careful not to *accidentally* hit the planet. "The Commandant would never go for it."

She studied the display for a long moment. Major-General Anderson was smart enough to leave naval operations in her hands. She—and her new subordinates—would have broad authority to take the high orbitals and land the troops. No one would complain, as long as they won. She doubted she'd be alive to worry about recriminations if they lost. And once the troops were on the ground, they could do what they did best. There was no way the planetary army could stand in their way.

Particularly if we catch the bastards by surprise and never give them time to recover, she thought, grimly. *It might be as simple as marching up to the PDCs and demanding surrender.*

She scratched her head. It would be nice, but she didn't dare count on it. Terrain wouldn't pose a problem if no one was going to fight them on it—not *much* of a problem, she conceded—yet it would be tricky to get to the PDCs quickly if there was *any* resistance. A handful of infantrymen with HVMs could shoot Raptors and Prowlers out of the sky, if they had time to set up. And delays tended to lead to more delays. A blitzkrieg could easily devolve into a slogging match if it ran into fixed defences, manned by capable soldiers. And they knew nothing about the defenders. Would they cut and run? Or would they stand and fight?

That's not my problem, she told herself, dryly. *My job is to get the troops on the ground.*

"We should be able to do it," she said. If nothing else, she and her staff would have three weeks to play around with the plan. Major-General Anderson wouldn't object if they came up with a completely new concept. "Now, the practicalities…"

• • •

"There's some grumbling amongst the men," Command Sergeant Mark Mayberry said, as they filed towards the giant shuttle. "Shore leave facilities are a joke."

"Tell me about it," Haydn said, dryly. "There isn't much to do here, is there?"

He snorted. Safehouse was a bunker on a planetary scale, not an Intercourse and Intoxication centre. The Corps was generally very good about providing shore leave facilities, from brothels to flights back home if possible, but...that had been in the days before Earthfall. Safehouse was ruthlessly practical. There was nothing to *do* on the planet, save watching flicks and sleeping in. A handful of marines had probably formed relationships with the support staff—he would turn a blind eye, as long as it didn't get out of hand—but there were no prostitutes, VR centres or even somewhere *different* for a few hours. He didn't blame the men for being pissed.

"It's terrible," Mayberry said, deadpan. "And no football on the MEU either."

"Disaster," Haydn said. "We're doomed."

"Yes, sir," Mayberry said. He sobered. "You think we ran through everything?"

Haydn knew the question was more pointed than it sounded. Mayberry had two jobs, looking after the men and looking after their commanding officer. The Sergeant wasn't asking because he wanted reassurance. He was asking to make sure that *Haydn* had run through everything. Haydn didn't mind. He wasn't so insecure that he had qualms about someone checking his work. Besides, it was quite possible that he'd overlooked something. Better to be embarrassed before deployment then killed in action.

"I think we ran through all the known knowns," he said. "And we took a few guesses at the known unknowns. But the unknown unknowns?"

He sighed. They'd run through a dozen exercises in the last four days, ranging from a simple landing with no opposition to a full-scale assault on a heavily-defended LZ. The results changed, depending on what assumptions were programmed into the simulator; they'd pulled off the operation in a few hours, in one exercise, and been brutally slaughtered in another. There was no way to know what contingency plans the enemy had, or what they'd do if—no, *when*—they realised the high orbitals were under attack. No matter how they gamed it, the enemy would have at least half an hour of warning before the marines hit the ground. And *that* was dangerously optimistic.

"We'll have to improvise," he said. Major-General Anderson had made sure that everyone knew the plan of campaign. He'd pointed out that they *might* be able to take the world overnight, if they risked everything on one throw of the dice, but if they tried and failed...it would shorten the campaign. Disastrously. "And hope the locals don't offer much resistance."

"There will be resistance, sir," Mayberry warned. "They do have an army down there."

"Yes," Haydn agreed. "But how *tough* is their army?"

He shrugged as the line started to inch forward. Planetary armies were a mixed bag. The Empire had never really discouraged them, on the assumption that any planetary army could be smashed from orbit if their homeworld had to be brought to heel, but they tended to be unpredictable. Some were tough enough to give the marines a real fight, armed with modern weapons and led by experienced officers. Others were comic-opera outfits, with fancy uniforms, little actual training and officers in brown pants. One hint of danger and they'd evaporate like snowflakes in hell. There was no way to know what they'd be facing until the shit hit the fan.

Particularly as there's no way to know how someone will cope until the bullets really start flying, he thought. He'd pissed himself, the first time he'd gone into combat. It had been a simple little engagement, far easier than anything he'd faced at the Slaughterhouse, but...it had been real. *They might fight or they might run, and the only way to find out is to put ourselves in harm's way.*

He forced himself to relax. They'd have three weeks onboard ship, three weeks to evaluate the recon reports and finalise their plans. And get some rest, before the shit hit the fan. A MEU wasn't a fancy cruise liner, with swimming pools and other entertainments for the rich, powerful and politically-connected, but they did have some facilities. The troops wouldn't lose too much of their edge. If nothing else, being on a MEU on her way to a battleground had a tendency to concentrate the mind.

Mayberry frowned as they stepped into the shuttle. "Harris isn't coping too well with the news from Terra Nova, sir," he said. "It might be good to keep an eye on him."

"I would have expected trouble from Brittanie," Haydn said. Brittanie was the sole rifleman in the company to hail from Old Earth. He'd had parents on Earth, before Earthfall. The poor bastards hadn't had a chance to leave the homeworld. "But Harris?"

"His family are on Terra Nova," Mayberry said. "Not *knowing* is worse than being certain."

"True." Haydn winced in sympathy. "Keep an eye on him, offer counselling if he wants it."

"Aye, sir," Mayberry said. "But I wouldn't bet on him taking it."

"I know," Haydn said. The poor bastard would have to be kept busy, if only to keep him from having time to brood. "He'll be better when we hit the ground."

"Yes, sir," Mayberry said. "But I'll keep an eye on him, anyway."

• • •

"The plan is as solid as we can make it," Anderson said. His hologram turned to follow Jeremy as he paced his office. "So it has the consistency of jelly."

"Naturally." Jeremy put his doubts to one side. "Don't be afraid to throw the plan out the airlock if you come up with something better. Or if it turns out to be unworkable."

"I will, don't worry." Anderson leaned forward. "We'll be back before you know it."

"I hope not," Jeremy said. The plan called for a six-month deployment. He suspected that was optimistic. "I want you to succeed. I want that world in our hands."

He walked back to his desk and sat down. They'd done everything they could to give the operation a fighting chance. It was so *good* to be able to put together an operation without political interference, without untrained and ill-educated politicians micromanaging from thousands of light years away. And yet...he wished Anderson had more firepower under his command. If the squadron ran into trouble, they might not be able to handle it.

And we won't be able to blame the Grand Senate if this operation goes off the rails, he thought, wryly. This time, he'd planned things from start to finish. *The fingers will be pointed at us.*

"Good luck," he said. "Keep me informed."

"Yes, sir." Anderson nodded. He sounded confident, at least. "We've covered all the bases we can. We're as close to ready as we'll ever be."

"Then expect the unexpected," Jeremy said. He raised a hand in salute. "Goodbye."

Anderson returned the salute. His image blinked out a moment later. Jeremy sat back in his chair, feeling...grim. Expect the unexpected...his instructors had said that, at OCS, but they'd also made it clear there were limits. There was no point in expecting an alien battleship from a galaxy humans had never visited to turn up tomorrow, armed with weapons that rendered the entire navy obsolete overnight. Even if someone did...how did they prepare for *that*? It was impossible.

And if we'd proposed spending trillions of credits on a battle fleet that might not even be necessary, he thought, *the Grand Senate would have had a collective heart attack.*

His intercom bleeped. "Sir, the fleet is leaving orbit," Christie said. "They'll cross the Phase Limit in twelve hours."

"And then they truly *will* be gone," Jeremy said. Twelve hours...it wasn't long at all, on a galactic scale. "I wish I was going with them."

"Sir?"

"Never mind." Jeremy shook his head. He knew his duty. He had to stay where he was and wait for news. "You'd better send in the next round of paperwork. I have an urge to drown my sorrows."

"Yes, sir."

CHAPTER FIFTEEN

Towards the Core, matters were different. The middle-worlds often possessed tech bases, private navies and governments that—in theory—were capable of establishing themselves as major powers. Many of them certainly tried to make a go of it for themselves, often after making a purely symbolic declaration of independence...

—PROFESSOR LEO CAESIUS

Earthfall and its Aftermath

"YOU KNOW," BONKOWSKI MUTTERED, "I think I'll choose Han for my holidays next year. It was so much nicer. More honest."

Rachel nodded in agreement as they walked through the forest, towards the giant Planetary Defence Centre. They'd spent the last two weeks building up a picture of the planetary society, and what they'd found wasn't pretty. The entire planet was under tight control, a control that wasn't obvious unless one knew what to look for. The locals weren't just implanted. Their every move was dictated by the ruling class. They worked in local subsidies of the planetary corporation, their kids were educated at corporate schools and they shopped in corporate-owned stores. There was even a company scrip system! It didn't look as bad as some of the systems she'd seen, on the Rim, but only because it was universal. There was no system for converting scrip into credits or any other off-world currency.

But that might actually be a blessing in disguise, she mused. *If there's no link to the other currencies, the scrip shouldn't lose value when the economic shockwave arrives.*

"And yet, everyone who lives on Han wants to get off," Perkins pointed out. "Here…not so much."

"As far as we can tell," Rachel reminded him.

She slowly shook her head. There didn't seem to be any push for off-world emigration, although that didn't mean it didn't exist. She supposed a lot of the locals preferred safety and security to privacy and freedom. She could see the attraction, but…it meant putting a hell of a lot of power in the corporation's hands. Who could trust that the corprats would always be benevolent? Their self-interest would override common decency any day of the week.

Phelps glanced back at him. "Why would anyone choose to live here?"

"Back when I was on leave, I met someone who tried to convince me to move to a religious colony along the Rim," Rachel said. "It was one of those very traditionalist worlds. Women are protected, true, but they're also second-class citizens. They're effectively children. They have fewer rights than children on the Core Worlds."

"Which might not be a bad thing," Bonkowski muttered. "You know how many of the little bastards get into trouble because no one's allowed to punish them before they *really* go off the rails?"

Rachel shrugged. "Point is, there were a *lot* of women who wanted to go there. They were practically selling themselves into slavery, I thought, but they saw appeal. I suppose I can understand it. I just couldn't go along with it."

"I'd be surprised if you did," Phelps said.

"Yes." Rachel nodded in the direction of the town. "There are no thugs on the street, no threats of random violence. There are no corrupt policemen or bureaucrats. Supplies of food and suchlike are not rationed, nor given to being contaminated or simply cut off because someone too high up to understand reality thinks it would be better for the proles if they didn't get any food. Compared to Earth, that town is paradise. And all they have to do is serve the corprats and give up pretty much all of their freedom and security."

"Which is a dumb bargain to make," Bonkowski insisted.

"Yes," Rachel agreed. "But it looks pretty good to someone who grew up on Earth."

"And they probably wouldn't have any freedom or security either," Perkins commented.

"Or lives, now," Phelps agreed.

"Yes," Rachel said. "Either way, they're screwed. It's just that the screwing here is gentler."

"Hah," Bonkowski said. "And what happens to those who don't conform?"

"Use your imagination," Perkins said.

"They probably just buy them a starship ticket and tell them to fuck off," Phelps said. "No point in being gratuitously nasty when you can just kick them out of paradise instead."

They slowed as they approached the outer fence. Rachel felt her eyes narrow. It was nothing more than a simple chain-link fence—it didn't even look to be electrified—but it was an effective barrier. There was no way for someone to claim they wandered into the security perimeter by accident. Beyond the fence, the trees had been cut down and the land treated to prevent anything else from growing in their place. She could see a handful of bunkers, so clearly visible that she wondered if they were decoys. Or, perhaps, if whoever had planned the complex had intended to make it clear that anyone who risked approaching without the proper permissions would be shot.

And the guards probably won't get in trouble if they shoot someone, she thought. The soldiers within view looked alert, even though there was no hint the base could come under attack at any moment. *They probably have authority to kill anyone who strays into their field of fire.*

She looked up, towards the PDC itself. The designers had worked the complex into the mountain, relying on rock and earth to shield the underlying structures from enemy fire. She guessed the visible complex was nothing more than the tip of an iceberg, with power plants, supply dumps and barracks concealed beneath the ground. Getting inside wouldn't be easy. If the corprats had copied the standard design, there would only be two or three entrances, all heavily guarded. The air vents would be sealed so tightly there would be no hope of using them to gain access. If, of course, they existed at all. A *properly* sealed complex would use recyclers and starship-grade life support systems instead.

"Impressive," Bonkowski muttered. "How do we get up there?"

Rachel followed his gaze. A giant pair of mass drivers sat on a formidable mount, sweeping the skies constantly. Below them, railguns and plasma cannons rotated, tracking targets Rachel didn't think existed. It was far too early for the fleet to arrive and there were no signs that anyone *else* was attacking the system. She wondered if they were running an exercise, doing everything short of actually firing the guns, or if they kept their systems moving constantly. The wear and tear on the guns and gunners would be staggering, but she could see some advantages. If nothing else, they'd have plenty of experience for when the shit *really* hit the fan.

"I don't think we can," she said. There probably *were* ways to get closer, but they all involved unacceptable levels of risk. A sealed system was always harder to access without triggering the alarms. "We'll have to find a way to disable the complex from the outside."

She scowled as she eyed the system. The PDC would pose a threat to any ships in orbit, particularly as the space junk would make it harder for them to shoot back. They'd have to take it out, somehow...she considered a handful of possibilities, then dismissed them. They couldn't destroy the complex with what they had on hand. Even disabling the weapons would be beyond them. They might have to wait for the landing force to deal the death blow.

"Rachel, stay here," Phelps ordered. "The rest of us will slip around the fence and see what we find."

"Have a good one," Rachel said, automatically. "I'll be here."

She lay on the ground concealed within a bush and watched the enemy defenders as they went through their routine. It didn't look like an exercise, as far as she could tell. There was something *casual* about it that suggested they weren't putting on a dog-and-pony show for any important visitors. No, they were careful and thorough all the time. It would have been impressive if it wasn't so...*inconvenient.* They'd pose a *real* threat if the Pathfinders had to take out the PDC. Her implants bleeped as they recorded a handful of local transmissions, all tightly encrypted. There was no such thing as an unbreakable code, but it might take *years* to get anything readable from the recorded messages. The messages looked like handshakes, routine security checks. It would be difficult to fool them without access to enemy records...

And we can't get the access without getting into the system, she thought. Her lips twitched, humourlessly. *And without being in the system, we can't get the access.*

She heard someone moving behind her and froze, hugging the ground. Ice ran down her spine. Someone was coming. Someone was coming and he *wasn't* one of her comrades. None of them would have blundered through the woods like an overgrown animal, confident there was nothing to fear. She heard sticks cracking under their feet and silently counted, as best as she could. It sounded like three or four men heading towards her.

Shit, she thought. *What are they doing here?*

She stepped up her implants, readying herself. Her ears grew sharper. She could hear chatter, careless inconsequential chatter. A man bragging about his girlfriend and how she'd do anything for him...typical male bombast, so extreme that she doubted the girlfriend existed outside her boyfriend's mind. And besides, she'd have to be a contortionist to live up to his boasts. She smiled to herself, but stayed alert as the voices came closer. The situation could still turn dangerous, if they spotted her. How well did they know the area? How many civilians came close to the fence? They were so far from the nearest settlement that she assumed few civilians ever came near the PDC. Besides, if the system *did* come under attack, the PDC would be amongst the first targets. Better to stay well away.

Her body felt primed, ready to act, as she saw shapes moving amongst the trees. The forest played tricks on her eyes, but...she tensed as the men came into view. There were five of them, all young. They moved by rote, rather than experience...she had the impression they'd been thoroughly trained, but they hadn't actually seen the elephant. There was an air of... *unconcern* about their movements, even as they did their level best to appear ready for anything. They didn't think they could die at any moment.

Which isn't too far wrong, she thought. *They have no reason to think they're so close to me.*

She allowed herself a moment of relief, but didn't relax. She didn't dare. The men were joking together, chatting so loudly she didn't need her implants to pick out the words, but they were watching each other's backs too. She wondered if their rifles were loaded. Swinging them around like that was asking for trouble, if someone had a negligent discharge at the worst possible time. Hameau seemed to be a little more trusting of its fighting men than the Imperial Army. She frowned as they stopped, not too far from her position. A trap? Were they the beaters, trying to drive her into someone's arms? Or...or what?

Wait, Rachel told herself. *They're not looking for you.*

She watched one of the men unzip his fly and take a piss, the liquid splashing on the ground. His comrades laughed and made rude remarks, mostly concerning the size of his manhood and questioning his masculinity. They *really* didn't sound like men who'd seen the elephant, she noted. Crude jokes were epidemic in the military, but experienced men knew better than to jest when they were on patrol. Her lips quirked as she waited. Someone might use the poor bastard's manhood for target practice. They couldn't possibly miss.

The men continued their patrol, laughing and joking. Rachel stayed still, listening carefully. If they were the distraction, someone a little more experienced could be creeping up on her from the rear. But there was nothing, save for a faint hum in the distance. The giant turrets were revolving, tracking targets only their operators could see. Rachel glanced up into the clear blue sky and shrugged. There were lights clearly visible, but they looked like pieces of space junk. The PDC would have fired on anything else.

Just a random patrol, she decided, finally. *They never knew how close they were to me.*

She waited for nearly an hour before she heard a rustle. The remainder of the team was returning. She turned to greet them, muttering a quick explanation. Phelps decided to withdraw at once, once she'd finished. She didn't blame him. They were too close to the PDC for their peace of mind. They'd have to sneak back to the hideout.

"They didn't know we were there," Phelps said, once they were on their way. "But it doesn't matter."

Rachel looked at him. "No way in?"

"Not that we found," Phelps said. "We *could* try to bluff our way through the security guards..."

Rachel shook her head. There were plenty of *stories* about Pathfinders who'd done just that, and she knew most of them were true, but they'd tended to rely on the enemy not being particularly alert. If they ran into someone who *knew* the officer they were impersonating, or had the sense to check with head office...they *might* be able to force their way through, but it would be a gamble. No *sensible* military would penalise someone for checking credentials before letting a stranger walk onto a heavily-guarded base.

Which didn't stop the navy from doing just that, Rachel thought. *How many people got killed because someone was too dumb to let his subordinates do their job?*

"We could attack in force," Perkins pointed out. "The four of us are fast..."

"They'd have a chance to seal the bunker before we reached the entrance," Phelps countered, shortly. "And then we'd be fucked."

"And not in a good way," Bonkowski agreed.

"Get bent," Perkins said. "Do you have a better idea?"

"We need a nuke," Rachel said. "Or an aircar. We could turn it into a modified cruise missile..."

"If we could override the control system," Bonkowski said. "You want to bet the locals aren't allowed to fly their own aircars?"

Rachel refused to even *think* about taking the bet. The locals weren't allowed to drive, unless they were farmers. Their cars were self-driving, controlled by the local datanet...they could be shut down with the press of a button, if the network controllers willed it. She remembered their earlier conversation and shuddered. How could anyone stand to live in a world, as pleasant as it seemed, when their freedom could be taken away in a heartbeat? On *her* homeworld, learning to drive had been a mark of maturity. There would have been riots in the streets if anyone had suggested banning manual cars.

"And the aircar would be shot down if it entered the no-fly zone," Perkins said. "You saw those plasma cannons."

"Yeah." Phelps shook his head. "We should have brought a nuke with us."

"Or a penetrator warhead," Bonkowski agreed. "Can we *steal* a nuke?"

"Where from?" Rachel snorted, rudely. "Where do they keep their nukes?"

Phelps pointed upwards. "In space, where they belong."

"Probably," Perkins said. "What sort of nut keeps *nukes* on a planetary surface?"

"Right now, it doesn't matter." Phelps picked up speed. "We have orders to keep an eye on the enemy. And we'll carry them out."

"We can plan an operation," Bonkowski insisted. "We could make them miserable, if nothing else."

"And nothing else," Perkins said. "That's the point, isn't it?"

"We can try and come up with something," Phelps said, before the argument could turn nasty. "But we're not going to throw our lives away for nothing."

Rachel allowed her mind to wander as they made their slow way back to the hideout. There *had* to be a way to do it. There were plenty of ways to do it, but they all involved weapons and equipment they didn't have. She could come up with a handful of ideas, yet…she shook her head. They were wishful thinking, at best. She had no qualms about risking her life, but she had no intention of throwing it away. Phelps was right. They weren't going to surrender their lives for nothing.

"So we wait," Bonkowski said.

"Yes," Phelps said. His voice was firm. He'd made up his mind. The time for debate was over. "And when the fleet arrives, we see what their CO has to say."

"It'll be Anderson," Perkins predicted. "I served under him on Han. Good man. Solid too."

"He'll make the final call," Phelps said. "Until then…we'll do our duty."

And hope we can remain hidden for the next three weeks, Rachel thought. It wasn't her first long deployment to an unfriendly world, but *this* world was unique. The risk of being detected was quite high. *Perhaps we should go look for a bigger city.*

She shrugged. It was too risky. Their orders were strict. They were to remain near the LZ and recon the surrounding area. They hadn't been told anything explicit, but it didn't take a genius to guess where the troops would be landing. And if the enemy was placed on alert…

Her implants bleeped an alarm. She glanced up, one hand reaching for her pistol, as a flight of aircars roared overhead. There were a pair of escorts—they looked like modified Raptors, bristling with weapons—but their sensors didn't seem to be active. They certainly weren't doing anything that suggested they thought they might come under attack. The small convoy raced into the distance, heading east. Her mind raced as she relaxed, slightly. The flyers weren't looking for them. Where were they going? The town? Or the army base? Or…a complex they didn't know existed?

She shrugged. They'd probably never know.

CHAPTER SIXTEEN

It says a great deal about the delusions that affected the elites, in the last few years before Earthfall, that they believed there was any point in making a declaration of independence. Earth was gone! The Imperial Navy was in ruins. There was no one trying—not then—to hold the Empire together. Why would they bother to declare independence when—practically speaking—they were already independent?

—PROFESSOR LEO CAESIUS

Earthfall and its Aftermath

"WE'LL BE THERE IN TEN MINUTES, Your Excellency," his secretary said. "Will you be requiring anything else?"

More time to read these bloody reports, Governor Simon Morgan thought, barely looking up from his datapad. His personal secretary had been *very* attentive since Earthfall, as if it had finally dawned on her that the only reason she'd been given the job was because her family had powerful connections. The *real* work was done by staffers who'd been with him since he'd started climbing the corporate totem pole. *But you can't give me that, can you?*

"No, Sandra," he said. She wasn't a bad person—and she was easy on the eye, with long dark hair and a face that spoke of centuries of genetic tailoring—but she was useless. "Just wait until we arrive."

Simon sighed, not bothering to hide his unease. He was ninety years old, although—thanks to the corporate health plan—looked to be somewhere in his early forties. He'd spent seventy of those years working for the Onge Corporation, climbing the ladder until he'd been rewarded with a succession of planetary governorships. The corporation had been good to him, even though he wasn't related to the Grand Senator. He'd made sure to return the favour. He'd been as loyal as any corporate official could have wished.

And there are some things I wish I hadn't known, he thought. He hadn't been briefed on the corporation's *real* plan until he'd been posted to Hameau. Even then...he hadn't thought the worst could happen until Earthfall. The contingency plan that had struck him as insane, if not absurd, had turned out to be a serious underestimate. *And now I'm playing for keeps.*

He shook his head slowly as the aircar banked, heading towards the military base. Hameau was an order of magnitude more complex than any of the stage-one and stage-two colony worlds he'd ruled in his earlier days. It belonged to the corporation, as completely as *any* world could belong to the corporation, yet...he sighed, inwardly. He knew, better than most, that an absence of open rebellion didn't mean there wasn't any bad feeling. Or resentments that could become rebellion, given time. And now...he knew the plan. He knew his role in it. And he knew there would be worse fates than losing his stock options if he failed now. The entire galaxy had turned upside down.

His eyes sought out a handful of people in the field, turning their heads to peer up as his convoy flew overhead. Their lives were so *simple.* Simon almost envied them. They didn't have to worry about paperwork, or making the right call...the one that pleased his corporate superiors as much as his subordinates. Simon sometimes felt as if he was drowning in paperwork, from loan applications and proposals for asteroid mining stations to law and order, matters that would normally be handled by an elected government. But here...he was judge and jury, just as he'd be on a stage-one world. It was very far from normal.

The aircar started to descend, his escorts falling into a protective pattern as his vehicle landed on the base. Simon was sure it was pointless—the only real threat was a handful of runaways living in the undeveloped parts of the continent—but rules were rules. He wondered, sourly, who'd be impressed by his escorts. The people who might be impressed didn't matter, the people who *did* knew too much to be impressed. They knew his bodyguards were intended to display his power and position, rather than actually *protect* him. He pasted a calm expression on his face as the hatch opened. It was time to pretend he was interested.

"Your Excellency," the military officer said. His green uniform was so crisp it practically shone, the gold braid glittering in the light. "Welcome to Eddisford Garrison."

"Thank you, General," Simon said. He couldn't remember the man's name. "It is a pleasure to visit."

He stepped out of the hatch and looked around. A row of soldiers stood there, so stiff and still that they might as well have been statues. Simon wondered, sourly, if they were as bored and unimpressed as himself. He'd been a governor too long to be impressed with pageantry, military or civilian. He understood the importance of having well-trained police, security and military forces—he'd faced an uprising during his second governorship—but he'd never been a military officer himself. He'd had subordinates for it. He didn't mind if they wanted to play soldier, as long as the troops were on call when trouble started to get out of hand.

And they're greeting me when they could be training or doing something useful, he mused, as he inspected the platoon. Half the men wore medals, but the decorations meant nothing to him. They could be for anything from sharpshooting to excessive KP. He resisted the urge to glare at the General... what *was* the man's name again? *Are you trying to impress me or snowball me?*

He nodded his approval when he reached the end of the line, then allowed the general to lead him and Sandra into the nearest building. It would have passed for a low-rent office block if it hadn't been surrounded by soldiers, security barriers and a handful of fixed weapons. It looked like overkill to him, but Head Office had been *very* concerned about security. Better to invest millions in defence than lose *billions* of credits in infrastructure if there *was* an uprising. He snorted to himself. They'd taken all the precautions they needed to take. Anything else was excessive.

Empire-building, more like, he thought. It was the corporate plague. *The General wants a nice little empire of his very own.*

Simon put the thought aside as the General showed him into a mid-sized office. It looked to have been put together by a bunch of propaganda specialists, rather than someone who actually had to *work* for a living. The desk was solid oak, a large portrait of Grand Senator Onge rested against one wall…he kept his thoughts to himself as he realised the painting was tinged in black. Hardly anyone on Hameau knew the Grand Senator was dead. He wondered, as he sat down on the sofa without waiting for an invitation, how the General knew. He probably had contacts within the capital.

"Wine?" The General sat facing him. Sandra stayed by the wall. "Or whiskey?"

"A Scotch with extra Scotch sounds very good right now," Simon said. General…*Taggard. That* was the man's name. He felt a flash of almost child-like glee at remembering. "But I don't have long to stay and chat."

"I quite understand." General Taggard rose and walked over to a large drinks' cabinet. "You'll be pleased to hear that we're on schedule."

"I'm very pleased to hear it," Simon confirmed. He took the glass and sipped it, carefully. He'd never really had a taste for expensive alcohol, but pretending an interest was a must in polite society. "When will the first units be assembled for departure?"

Taggard didn't bother to pretend to consult a datapad. "We've identified several hundred possible candidates in Eddisford's conscript force alone. Most of them are the right personality type to be attracted to off-world deployments. The remainder can probably be convinced, with a large infusion of cash. If there are any stragglers"—he shrugged—"they can go back to their homes. It won't be a major issue unless there are a *lot* of stragglers."

Simon frowned. "Will there be?"

"It's hard to say, Your Excellency." Taggard shrugged, again. "The personality type we're looking for will *not* be happy in little Eddisford. They won't *want* to farm or take up entry-grade corporate work. The ones who are interested in spacer work have already had a chance to signal it. Realistically, we think most of the possibilities will take us up on the offer. It's better than staying at home."

"If they say so," Simon said. Adventure was someone else in deep shit, far away. There was something to be said for the comforts of home. Personally, he'd never served on a world that didn't have proper facilities for him. "You don't expect resistance?"

"There will be no compulsion, Your Excellency." Taggard sounded shocked by the very idea. "We're interested in volunteers only."

"As long as we meet our targets," Simon said. Head Office's demands had been sharp, with little room for disagreement. It was more than his job was worth to put up more than minor *pro forma* resistance. "When will they be ready?"

"I'm planning to make the offer at the end of the month, a month before the current group's conscript period actually terminates," Taggard said. "At that point, we'll split the group into two and start preparing the volunteers for departure."

His eyes widened. "Do you have any idea where they'll be sent?"

"No." Simon shook his head. "I wasn't told."

"It might be important to find out," Taggard said. "This place, sir, is a reasonably mild climate. The lads will be in trouble if they have to travel to a different clime. And our equipment might just break."

Simon's eyes narrowed. "Explain."

"We use oil in the rifles," Taggard said. "If it gets too cold, the oil freezes and the rifle refuses to fire. There's ways around it, sir, but they have to be implemented. And planned for."

"I see your point," Simon said.

"And then the lads themselves are not braced for extreme heat or cold," Taggard added. "We really need to expand our facilities into different climes."

"Something to discuss at the next budget meeting," Simon said. Head Office hadn't been clear, when the issue had been raised, but the budget *was* going to be a problem. They couldn't draw money from corporate funds any longer. "Have your staff put forward a proposal."

"Yes, sir," Taggard said. "I was surprised it wasn't raised already."

"Just one of the little details that got overlooked," Simon said. He finished his glass and put it to one side. "Based on your experience, how are things going?"

Taggard frowned, as if he suspected there was a knife glinting in the darkness. "As well as can be expected. They start out well, thanks to school fitness programs. Weapons training is expensive, as we shoot off hundreds of thousands of rounds on the shooting grounds, but it makes sure they know what they're doing on the battlefield. And there's a lot of healthy competition between groups, ensuring they're all committed to victory. That said..."

He met Simon's eyes. "There are gaps in our training. Quite apart from the climate issues, we haven't held any large-scale exercises. The lads know the theory, but not the reality. I had to relieve a couple of officers for glossing over the issue during training. Really, we need to let them make the mistakes on the training field so they don't make them on the *battlefield.* The first *real* exercise will be a fuck up—pardon my language—from start to finish, but at least we'll learn something from it."

"I see, I think." Simon frowned. "You think we should hold one before the troops leave?"

"Yes." Taggard nodded, curtly. "Really, we should hold one *now.*"

"The budget wouldn't cover it," Simon said. He sensed the younger man's disappointment, but ignored it. "I'll take your words under advertisement."

He leaned forward. "Now, about the long-term plans..."

• • •

"You know," Corporal Loomis whispered, "that girl was a stunner. Who do you think she is?"

"Probably some corporate secretary," Corporal Derek Frazer whispered back. The girl really had been stunning, completely perfect in every way. He couldn't name a single girl in Eddisford who was as perfect. Only the certainty of Lieutenant Hobbs noticing and bawling him out—or worse—had kept his eyes from following the girl as she walked away. "Beyond that…I have no idea."

"Maybe I could ask her out," Loomis muttered. "And…"

Derek rolled his eyes. "You know what they say about whiskey tastes, beer income? Well, she's got *really* expensive tastes and you can barely afford water. Just like Jenny, only worse…"

Loomis snickered. "But I'm in love," he protested. "I…"

He broke off as Lieutenant Hobbs marched up to him. "If you two clowns are finished *clowning*…

"Yes, sir," Loomis said. "Sorry, sir."

"You can go clean the barracks afterwards, both of you," Hobbs snarled. He dismissed the rest of the platoon with a wave of his hand. "And don't let me see you for the rest of the day."

"Yes, sir," Derek said. There was no point in arguing with an officious LT. It was one of the first lessons he'd learnt, when the sergeants had grudgingly declared him and his class ready to move to the next level. "We'll go there now."

Hobbs glared at them, then stomped off to find someone else to bully. Derek watched him go, resisting the urge to make a rude gesture at Hobbs's back. Someone would see, someone would report him…and then he'd be in real trouble. Hobbs wasn't normally so bad, he supposed. It was just the pressure of the governor's visit…

Loomis wasn't feeling so charitable. "What crawled up his ass?"

"Everyone dumps on everyone else," Derek said. "And you'd better shut up before they hear you."

He turned and led the way to the barracks. They'd been promised the afternoon off, after greeting the governor, but…there was no point in arguing *that* with Hobbs either. They should have known better. They'd grown up in an environment where *everything* they said or did was recorded, even if it wasn't made public. Derek had had enough proof of *that*, at school, to make certain he went to the toilet with the lights turned off. Sure, the principal *claimed* there were no pick-ups in the toilets and changing rooms, but only an idiot would believe him. The principal might be telling the truth as he knew it—Derek had to admit it was possible—yet someone else could have lied to him. What was the point of wrapping the entire world in a surveillance blanket and, at the same time, making sure everyone knew there was a safe place?

"Maybe she's like Jenny," Loomis said. "Hard on the outside, soft on the inside."

"If anyone manages to get that close," Derek said. Jenny was corporate royalty. Her father was the town's director. Low on the corporate pole, he thought, but still higher than anyone else Derek was ever likely to meet. "Didn't Bryan's family get reassigned to a lunar colony after he asked her to the dance?"

He nudged his friend. "Face it. You're just scum beneath her feet. No, you're something beneath the scum."

"Hah," Loomis said. "I will not be forestalled."

Derek shrugged as they ambled into the barracks. The cramped chamber had become home—somehow—over the last few months. It wasn't the lack of privacy that bothered him, but the simple fact of sharing a barracks with a hundred other young men. He liked most of the conscript life, to the point he would be almost disappointed when demobilisation came in two months, but…he shrugged. He didn't think his stats were good enough to warrant transfer to Corporate Security. His connections certainly weren't.

"I heard a rumour," Loomis said. "We're going to be kept in uniform for a year."

"I doubt it," Derek said. The law was clear. Conscripts could only be kept in uniform for seven months, unless there was an emergency. "Why us?"

"Maybe they want to get rid of us," Loomis said. "Or something. I'm just repeating what I've heard."

"And you know what someone else will hear," Derek said, warningly. He picked up a broom and started to sweep the barracks. "Better to keep your mouth firmly shut."

"You know me," Loomis said. "I talk like a…very talkative thing."

"Far be it from me to dispute with you," Derek said. He shook his head as he picked up a pile of old linen. It said something about the panic to make everything ready for the governor that they hadn't had the time to rush the old bedding to the washhouse. Hobbs had been too busy to notice when he'd inspected the barracks. "Look on the bright side. Tomorrow we'll be on guard duty."

"Boring, and you know it," Loomis said. "Don't you want to play a nice wargame instead?"

"Oh, yes." Derek shrugged. "But there can be more entertainment on guard and you know it."

He shrugged. Two more months…perhaps he *would* try to apply for Corporate Security. He wasn't completely qualified—he wasn't an asshole who made normal assholes look bland by comparison—but perhaps the surprise would get him over the first hurdle. What else was he going to do with his life? The thought of becoming a mid-level corporate stooge like his dad was appalling. If his father hadn't moved the entire family to Hameau…

Perhaps you should be grateful, he told himself. He'd been too young to remember much about Earth—he'd been two years old when his father had accepted the post on Hameau—but he'd heard his sisters talking in hushed whispers. They'd made Earth sound hellish. *You could have grown up on Earth instead.*

CHAPTER SEVENTEEN

The answer lay, at least in part, by just how thoroughly the Empire had slid into the public mindset. Practically speaking, Earth could not impose direct rule on the Core Worlds. Even if there had been no resistance, it took time for the men on the spot to request instructions and receive a reply... by which time, the situation would almost certainly have moved on.

—**Professor Leo Caesius**

Earthfall and its Aftermath

THE BRIDGE FELL SILENT the moment Havoc and the squadron dropped out of FTL.

Kerri felt it too, even though cold logic insisted they couldn't have flown right into a trap. This time, they weren't alone. This time, everything rested on them. This time, everything had to go perfectly. She tensed, despite herself, as the display rapidly filled with icons. There didn't *seem* to be a welcoming committee waiting for them.

"Local space is clear, Captain." Tomas sounded calm, but she could hear the underlying tension in his voice. "No enemy contacts detected."

"Order the squadron to remain here, on the other side of the limit," Kerri said. "We'll proceed as planned."

"Aye, Captain," Susan said.

Kerri nodded. "Helm, take us into the system."

"Aye, Captain."

She settled back in her command chair as *Havoc* slipped into the system, heading directly towards the planet. The display continued to update, revealing countless asteroid mining ships and industrial nodes in the asteroid belt. A pair of ships—freighters, judging by their speed—were heading out of the system, going…somewhere. Kerri wondered, idly, just *where* they were going. Interstellar trade was grinding to a halt everywhere. But then, Hameau had plenty to offer the rest of the sector. They might have already started re-establishing trade links.

But it'll take them a while to repair the damage and rebuild the economy, she thought. She'd seen those projections too, although the analysts had been at pains to make it clear that most of them were guesswork. *We might have been knocked all the way back to barter.*

Her lips quirked at the thought. Countless planets, in hock to off-world corporations, were probably relieved the interstellar economy had evaporated. Their creditors had probably evaporated too. Even if they wanted to repay their debts, how could they? She supposed it might work in their favour, in the long run. Successive governments had made noise about debt forgiveness, but nothing had actually been done. The debts had held back planetary development right across the galaxy. Now…the debts were gone. Who knew what the colonies could do now that they didn't have to worry about paying off the founding companies?

She frowned as they made contact with the stealthed recon platforms they'd left behind and downloaded the messages from the Pathfinders. It didn't look encouraging, although there was one bright spot. If society was as tightly controlled as the Pathfinders suggested, the landing forces should have no trouble finding people willing to collaborate. Merely knocking down the surveillance system should do wonders for encouraging resistance. But…she forwarded the data to the analysts, who'd have to add it to their projections. She didn't *think* there was anything that would force Major-General Anderson to cancel the operation.

And he's probably watching right now, she mused. She was surprised Anderson hadn't insisted on being on the bridge when they returned to Hameau. Instead, he and his staff were sitting in the CIC. It wasn't as if they could have done anything—Anderson might outrank her, but she was in command—yet...she shrugged. Anderson was smart enough to know his limits. *I just hope he isn't so keen to get on with it that he ignores the danger signs.*

"Captain," Tomas said. "We may have a problem."

Kerri looked up, sharply. "Explain."

"I can't find the battlecruiser," Tomas said. "She's gone."

"... Shit," Kerri said. It was hardly a dignified response, but...she leaned forward. "What about the other ships?"

"I'm picking up four cruisers, all mid-range designs, and nine destroyers." Tomas's frown deepened. "Two of the destroyers were *not* catalogued during our earlier visit."

Kerri studied the console for a long moment. "Do we have any ID on them?"

"Four of the ships were registered to the Onge Corporation, according to the files," Tomas said. "I mean...they were registered to the corporation's planets and..."

"I know." Kerri waved her hand impatiently. The corporation had managed to find a loophole in the law. It would have astonished her if she hadn't known about it already. Really, it would have been more surprising if they *hadn't* found a loophole. It wasn't as if they couldn't hire the best lawyers in the business. "And the other ships are unknown?"

"Yes, Captain," Tomas said. "They *could* simply be refits..."

"Or they dropped off the records at some point," Kerri said. She knew from bitter experience that the records were incomplete. Someone was always cooking the books, to hide everything from incompetence to criminal activity. The navy's clerks were poorly paid and *easy* to subvert. "Check with the platforms. Find that battlecruiser."

There was a pause as Tomas queried the nearest platform. "She left orbit, four days ago, on a least-time course to the Phase Limit. Destination unknown. The platform lost track of her shortly afterwards."

"Destination unknown," Kerri repeated. She wasn't surprised—experienced spacers knew that tracking a ship through FTL was difficult, almost impossible—but she was worried. She'd assumed they'd be fighting the battlecruiser, either catching her with her guard down or taking her down in a straight fight. Instead...she scowled. A rogue battlecruiser could be a serious threat. "And she could have gone anywhere."

"Yes, Captain."

Kerri keyed her console. "General Anderson?"

Anderson's image appeared in front of her. "Yes, Captain?"

"The enemy battlecruiser has departed," Kerri said, shortly. "We don't know where she's gone and we don't know when she'll be back. How do you intend to proceed?"

She glanced at the display as Anderson considered. There was no sign of the battlecruiser, but that meant nothing. The enemy ship could be a hundred light years away by now, if she'd remained in FTL for the last few days, or trying to sneak up on *Havoc* while *Havoc* tried to sneak up on the planet. It didn't seem likely—there was nothing in the enemy dispositions that suggested they expected attack—but she couldn't rule it out either. And yet...cold logic told her the enemy was utterly unaware of her approach. There was no way they could have figured it out. The Pathfinders could have been captured, she supposed, but they couldn't tell their captors something they didn't know.

Anderson stroked his chin. "Do you think you can take the battlecruiser, if she returns?"

"I believe so," Kerri said. He already knew that, damn him. She wondered, sourly, if he was checking to see if her opinion had changed...or if he was playing CYA games. It was unusual for a marine, but no one reached high rank without *some* awareness of the political realities underpinning military operations. "We do not, of course, have any idea of *when* she will return."

She glanced at the downloaded datapackets, already knowing it was futile. The platforms had recorded hundreds of encrypted messages, messages that probably wouldn't be decoded in a hurry. They might already have the answer in their hands, an answer that would be completely useless as long as they couldn't read it. She shrugged, dismissing the thought in a flicker of irritation. She'd known they would be operating from incomplete information almost as soon as the operation had been proposed.

"And if she catches us in the disembarking stage, we might be in some trouble," Anderson mused. "Afterwards..."

"If she's alone, we can take her," Kerri said. "If not...we either wait until she returns and jump her or give up now and go home."

Anderson smiled. "I don't think *that* would look good in my personnel file."

"No, probably not," Kerri agreed, dryly. It *was* within Anderson's power to simply cancel the operation, but the Commandant and the other Major-Generals would be *very* sarcastic about it. They'd argue that the missing battlecruiser was a good sign. And there would be no way to prove them wrong. "The buck stops with you. Sir."

"Yes." Anderson let out a long breath. "Call the ships. Tell them...tell them, we will proceed as planned."

"Yes, sir," Kerri said. If everything went as planned, the operation would commence just before dawn, local time. The defenders would be at their lowest ebb. "Should we alert the Pathfinders?"

"Yes," Anderson said. "Tell them to proceed as they see fit. If they can do anything to keep the enemy from mobilising, when the shit hits the fan, they are to do it."

"Yes, sir," Kerri said. "The ships will be here in twenty-one hours."

"'Time enough to finish the game and beat the Spanish too'," Anderson quoted.

His image vanished from the display. Kerri felt her lips tighten as she contemplated the display. Her instructors had quoted Francis Drake—an almost-forgotten man from an almost-forgotten country in an era most people considered to be mythical—but they'd made it clear that Drake *couldn't* take his ships out to sea. The tides were against him. Kerri had only the faintest idea of how tides had impeded sailing ships, but she understood their point. It was easy to sit back, relax and do nothing when one could *only* do nothing. She—and Anderson—had too much to do. They couldn't relax.

"Susan, signal the squadron," she ordered. "They are to move to the RV point immediately."

"Aye, Captain," Susan said.

• • •

Rachel had always liked sleeping under the stars, even as a young girl. There was *something* about watching the stars twinkling overhead that soothed her, although she was very aware she was on an enemy world. Hameau's night sky was a constant reminder of just how odd Hameau was, by galactic standards. There were so many lights overhead that she could deceive herself into thinking they were *very* close to the galactic core. In many ways, it made her feel small. She was utterly insignificant on a galactic scale. The stars would burn long after she was dust.

She felt the communicator vibrate and sat up, hastily. The others were asleep, leaving her on watch. She rolled over, one hand reaching for the pistol on her belt. If someone had tripped the warning sensors, she might have bare seconds before the intruders came into view. She let out a sigh of relief as she saw the message on the screen. The fleet had returned. They were safe.

Well, maybe not safe, she thought, sardonically. They'd discussed contingency plans for getting off Hameau without assistance, but none of them had seemed practical. The system was just too tightly sewn up to be easy to fool. *But at least we won't have to get home on our own again.*

She keyed the terminal, bringing up the message. The fleet had arrived. Active military operations would commence in twenty-seven hours. That meant...she calculated it quickly, then nodded to herself. Local dawn. The capital city, several hundred miles to the west, would still be in darkness. Night wasn't a barrier to modern military operations, but...the defenders would be half-asleep. She wondered if the planetary defenders would think to remain alert during the night. The marines knew to expect attack at dawn, but...they'd had plenty of experience. As far as she could tell, none of the locals had any *real* experience.

They're just playing at war, she thought, as she read the rest of the message. *They don't know what's coming their way.*

She frowned. The orders were vague, almost useless. If practical, they were to launch delay and disruption operations. If it was *not* practical, they were to hide and link up with the landing force when it arrived. Rachel hated the second idea on principle. The idea of doing nothing while others fought, bled and died was horrific. Besides, there was no shortage of marines who thought the Pathfinders were overrated. They'd suggest abandoning the program altogether if the Pathfinders sat out the invasion altogether.

At least we have freedom to plan and act as we see fit, she told herself. She nudged Phelps, gently. *They're not trying to tell us what to do.*

Phelps jerked awake. "Rachel?"

"The fleet is here." Rachel passed him the terminal. The message might be sparse on detail, but it had told them the important thing. "And we have a mission."

"Yeah." Phelps returned the terminal and sat up. "You think we have to take out the garrison?"

"Not with what we have on hand," Rachel said. She ran through a mental checklist of what they could do with their supplies. Taking out the entire garrison wasn't likely, even if the enemy screwed up by the numbers. She doubted they would. Their emergency training might have left out the emergency, a common problem, but they couldn't be *that* incompetent. "We can give them a fright, but..."

“Yeah,” Phelps said, again. He opened a ration bar and chewed it, slowly. “We can give them a fright.”

He woke the others and briefed them as Rachel brewed coffee and sorted out their maps. They hadn’t been able to get their hands on local maps—apparently, maps were considered classified information—but they’d been updating the vague maps they’d downloaded from the records before landing. They’d marked out quite a number of potential targets, from military garrisons to the giant PDC. Rachel scowled as she contemplated *that* note on the map. They’d brainstormed for days, but they hadn’t been able to think of a way to take out the PDC that might actually *work.*

They’ll have to drop a missile on it from high orbit, she thought. *And if that doesn’t work, the landing force will have to take it out.*

“Well,” Perkins said. “What do we do *first*?”

“We hit the garrison,” Phelps said. “Give them a fright.”

“And then fall back to…where?” Rachel leaned forward. “There are a few *other* things we can do.”

“Take out the datanode,” Perkins offered. “And the nearest bridge. If we can cut this region off from the rest of the continent…”

Rachel shrugged. “We should prepare to take down the bridge,” she said. “But General Anderson won’t thank us if we deny it to his forces. He might intend to use it to move troops towards the PDC.”

“True.” Phelps grinned, his teeth white in the darkness. “But whoever gets there first with the most will win.”

“Yes, sir,” Bonkowski said. “I believe we all know that. Sir.”

“Of course,” Phelps agreed, dryly. “It depends on how quickly they can react, doesn’t it?”

Rachel nodded. They’d traced out the road network as far north as they could. It was quite impressive, for such a young world. The defenders *could* rush tanks and troops to the landing zone at speed, if they wished… if they managed to react in time. Taking out the bridge would slow them, although probably not for very long. Modern tanks and APCs were sealed vehicles, designed to be driven across river beds. And hovertanks could simply float *above* the water.

Although it's easy to take them out, Rachel thought. Hovertanks had never really caught on, simply because they were dangerously vulnerable. *A single plasma burst would turn them into a pile of flaming debris.*

"Bonkowski, you're to target the datanode," Phelps ordered. "You blend in best with the locals."

"That's because he's an ugly bastard," Perkins said.

Bonkowski made a rude gesture. "And yet I get all the girls."

Phelps cleared his throat, loudly. "Take out the node and its support staff, if you can get inside without trapping yourself, then get out. Don't worry about the rest of the town. Just get your ass back here. If we don't come back, link up with the landing force and mourn us afterwards."

"Yes, sir," Bonkowski said. He sounded serious. They all knew the time for joking was over. "I'll see you back here."

"The rest of us will target the garrison," Phelps said. He nodded to the sketch maps they'd drawn up. "We get in, hit them as hard as we can and then withdraw before they have a chance to get reorganised."

"Sounds like a plan," Rachel said. She sipped her dark coffee, savouring the sour taste. "Specifics?"

"We'll go back to our old friend," Phelps said. "And...*borrow*...his lorry."

"We'd better make sure he's taken somewhere safe," Rachel said. "If he gets the blame..."

"If he gets the blame, and they're in a position to do something about it, the entire operation has failed anyway," Phelps said. "And that would be pretty bad."

"Yes," Bonkowski said, dryly.

"Still," Rachel said. "We should do what we can for him."

"Idealist," Bonkowski said.

"Isn't that why we joined?" Rachel met his eyes. "We're not the bad guys, here."

"I think you'll find that depends on someone's point of view," Perkins said, flatly. "A civilian who loses their partner or parents or siblings or kids to the invasion isn't going to see us as heroes."

"No," Rachel agreed. She couldn't disagree with him. A lot of people were going to die in the next few days, people whose only real crime had been being in the wrong place at the wrong time. Or people who thought they were repelling an invasion, rather than serving a fascist regime. "But we should at least *try* not to be the bad guys."

"We'll do our best for him," Phelps said. He glanced at his watch. "Now, we have a day to make preparations so...this is what we're going to do."

CHAPTER EIGHTEEN

The Empire, therefore, was seen as the ultimate power, without being able to wield ultimate power. It loomed so large in the public mindset that it was difficult to believe that it was gone, that a distance of a few short light-years was now an impassable gulf. Indeed, so many people refused to believe it that they declined to take steps to protect themselves from the economic shockwaves radiating out from Earth.

—PROFESSOR LEO CAESIUS

Earthfall and its Aftermath

BRIDGE EXPERIENCE, Lieutenant Wesley Jacobson thought, wasn't quite what he'd been promised. Captain Jiang had made it quite clear that, while Wesley was in command of Nocturne while her captain and XO were asleep or planetside respectively, he was to do nothing beyond badgering the junior officers for status reports. If there was the slightest hint of an emergency, Jiang had said, Wesley was to call Jiang at once. There was little hope of gaining the experience that might put him on the shortlist for a command of his own.

Wesley shifted in the chair, bored. The thrill of sitting in the command chair had long-since palled when everyone knew he wasn't allowed to do anything. The display showed nothing, nothing save for hundreds of freighters, asteroid miners and worker bees humming around the planet or heading out to deep space. Wesley had run a pair of tracking exercises on the freighters, but even *that* had proved more tedious than exciting. He cursed his CO under his breath as he waited for his shift to end. Jiang was obliged to offer his junior officers command experience, but he didn't *have* to make it meaningful. Wesley would have no chance to prove himself as long as nothing happened, yet…if it did happen, Jiang would retake command. He glared at a freighter as she headed out of orbit. He really should have gone into the merchant marine. He might just have seen something of the universe if he had.

"Captain," Ensign Han said. "I'm picking up *something* on the active sensors."

Captain. That was a joke. Wesley was in command, so he was entitled to be addressed as *Captain*…but he was a Captain without authority. He glowered at Han's back, wondering just how long it would be before she was promoted past him. She was younger, but she had relatives in high places. They'd smooth her path to command rank while Wesley remained stuck as a lieutenant. She would probably be giving *him* orders in a year or two.

"Something," he repeated. Was it worth calling Jiang? The Captain *had* given orders that he was to be awakened if anything happened, but… would he be pleased he'd been called or pissed? "What *sort* of something?"

Han sounded puzzled, not angry. "I'm not sure," she said. "There's something fuzzy…it could be a sensor glitch, sir, or it could be a stealthed ship."

Wesley stood and walked over to her console. A stealthed ship? *That* wasn't too likely. The system was heavily defended. Most pirates and warlords would probably prefer to try their luck elsewhere, if they bothered to do more than glance at Hameau. And yet…he peered at the sensor readings. There *was* something there. It could be a glitch, or an energy fluctuation caused by the constant activity in orbit, or…or what? Whatever it was, it was far too close for comfort.

He knew he should call Jiang. But…he didn't *know* the contact, whatever it was, was dangerous. And…he didn't *want* to give up command, not yet. It was his first, perhaps his only, chance to shine. He couldn't really believe the contact was dangerous, not this close to the planetary defences. It was probably nothing.

"Do a sensor focus," he ordered.

"Yes, sir," Han said. Her fingers worked her console. "I..."

The display cleared. Wesley blanched. A cruiser, a *heavy* cruiser, was coming right at his ship. No, *nine* heavy cruisers in tight formation. He barely heard Han gasp in shock. His head spun. The images couldn't be real. They just couldn't. But they were there...

Training took over. "Red alert," he snapped. The sirens began to howl. Jiang wouldn't need to be summoned personally. The alarms would get him out of bed more effectively than an emergency call. "All hands to battle stations!"

But it was already too late.

• • •

"They made us, Captain," Tomas said.

"Open fire," Kerri said, shortly.

She gritted her teeth as *Havoc* fired the first salvo of the campaign. She'd managed to get closer to the enemy destroyer than she'd expected, although they weren't *quite* in point-blank range. The enemy ship was desperately trying to bring its drives and weapons online, but it was already too late. Their ECM was weak, almost pitiful. Kerri watched, dispassionately, as four laser warheads slammed into the enemy ship. The hullmetal melted like a snowflake in hell. The crew, suited or not, didn't stand a chance. If there were any survivors, and she was fairly sure there were none, they were no longer important.

"Target destroyed, Captain," Tomas said.

Kerri nodded. The remainder of the squadron had opened fire at the same time, taking out their targets before they could return fire. A lone ship managed to evade the first salvo of missiles—Kerri silently saluted her commanding officer, who'd managed to react despite being taken by surprise—but the second salvo killed her before she could orient herself and open fire. There was no time to mourn the dead and dying. Her squadron altered course, launching a hail of missiles, railgun pellets and plasma bursts towards the orbital defences. The defenders were barely starting to react...

"Captain, I'm picking up an additional layer of scansats," Tomas reported. "They're going live now."

"Take them out," Kerri ordered. The enemy wouldn't have any trouble tracking her ships, not now they were firing on the planetary defences, but there was no point in letting them have a free shot at the shuttles. "And target any platform that opens fire."

"Aye, Captain," Tomas said.

"Susan, transmit the surrender demand," Kerri added. "And repeat it on all frequencies."

"Aye, Captain."

• • •

Commodore Jeanette Lang hadn't been expecting trouble, when she'd taken command of the planetary defences for the night. Nothing much ever happened in high orbit, even after Earthfall. She'd planned to sit in the CIC and do her paperwork, leaving the staff to do the majority of the work. There wasn't much to do. The vast majority of activity in and around the high orbitals didn't have to be cleared through the planetary defences.

She threw her datapad to one side and jumped to her feet as alarms howled and the display lit up with red icons. An entire fleet—hundreds of ships, *thousands* of ships—was approaching Hameau, launching so many missiles at the planetary defences that it seemed unlikely *anything* would survive long enough to fire back. Panic yammered at her mind as icons started to vanish, the entire mobile force wiped out in less than two minutes. Training and cold logic took over seconds later, pointing out the immense fleet simply could *not* exist. The Imperial Navy, at the height of its power, could not have deployed thousands of ships to Hameau. And while her defences were taking damage, they weren't taking *that* much damage. Her sensors were being spoofed.

"Bring all the active sensors online," she snapped. The situation was bad—the damage was mounting rapidly—but it wasn't disastrous. Not yet. "Track enemy targets, fire on my command."

She studied the display, muttering a calming manta under her breath. The enemy ships were firing...*all* of the enemy ships were firing. The vast majority of them had to be sensor ghosts, but...which ones? She tapped a command into the system, trying to track the real missiles back to the ships that had launched them, but it wasn't easy. The enemy—whoever he was—had done an excellent job of messing with her sensors. She couldn't fire on the enemy ships if she didn't know which ones were real.

"Commodore, we're losing missile pods in..."

"If they're targeting the missile pods, launch the damned missiles," Jeanette snapped. A number of icons vanished, enemy ships popping out of existence. It would have been good news, if she hadn't *known* they were fakes being wiped from the display. "Target the most likely contacts and *fire*!"

She glanced at the planetary display and swore, again. The PDC network was coming online, but it wasn't going to be able to offer much help. They could keep the enemy from getting too close, once they opened fire, yet...her orbital structures were vulnerable. A low rumble ran through the CIC as an enemy missile found its target. She supposed they should be grateful the base was surrounded by layers of rock. A lighter target would have been vaporised by the nuclear blast.

"Who are they?" An operator was freaking out, she noted dispassionately "What do they want?"

"Be quiet," Jeanette snapped, one hand resting on her pistol. Half the staff had been in their bunks when the attack began. The attackers had timed it perfectly. "Concentrate on your job."

Another shudder ran through the asteroid. The attackers were pushing harder...they knew she was in command. She tapped a command into the network, preparing the system for a sudden switch in command. If she lost contact, her second would have to take over immediately. They didn't have time for a succession crisis. Better to lay the groundwork now than hope her subordinates would handle it when she was gone.

"They're broadcasting a surrender demand," another operator said. "They're demanding immediate surrender."

"Forward it to the governor," Jeanette ordered. Her sensor platforms were being targeted and destroyed, but so were the enemy sensor decoys. The enemy fleet was *much* smaller than she'd thought. Still a problem, given how much damage they'd inflicted in the first few seconds, but... *manageable*. Perhaps. "Do we have an ID?"

"No, Commodore," the operator said. "They're not identifying themselves."

Jeanette nodded. A warlord, perhaps. God knew there were hundreds of Imperial Navy squadrons that had been left in the cold by Earthfall. Head Office believed they wouldn't pose a serious problem, but...Head Office was definitely wrong. It wouldn't be the first time, either. Hameau would be a very tempting target to any warlord who saw the infrastructure and realised how it could be turned to his advantage. And he would do a hell of a lot of damage even if he was beaten off.

She frowned as the enemy bombardment refused to abate. They were spending missiles like water, tearing great holes in her defences. Her sensor coverage was pitiful, barely a shadow of what it had been an hour ago. She had no trouble tracking the enemy ships on passive sensors, but still...she had no idea what *else* might be sneaking through. An asteroid had already been struck by a missile and smashed, pieces of debris flying in all directions. Large chunks were falling towards the surface. The PDCs were doing what they could, but they couldn't get everything...

Murderers, she thought, coldly. *Whoever you are, you're murderers.*

"They're coming closer," a third operator reported. "They're sweeping space for targets."

"And they'll be coming here," Jeanette grunted. "Prepare to reroute the remainder of command through the ground-based network."

She looked at the live feed from the surface. The PDCs had isolated themselves from the orbital defences, as planned. It was good to know that *something* was working, amidst the chaos. The governor hadn't said anything to her or to the invaders, whoever they were. He wouldn't surrender. Head Office would have his head. No, they'd have his pension. He was too well connected to be executed for his failure.

And he's not bothering me while I try to do my job, she thought. On the display, another salvo of missiles was roaring towards the asteroid platform. *That's one thing, at least.*

She took a breath. Two of the incoming missiles fell to point defence fire, but the remainder kept coming. They were unstoppable…

"I'm sorry," she said, quietly. She wasn't sure who she was talking to. The governor? Her staffers? Or herself. "I…"

The asteroid rocked violently, then shattered. Jeanette saw space, an endless array of whirling stars and lights; she found herself struggling, hopelessly, for breath. She tried to scrabble for her breath mask, but her fingers refused to work. The world was quiet, so quiet…

... And then it all faded.

• • •

Governor Simon Morgan had made it clear, when he'd taken up residence in Government House, that he was *not* to be disturbed unless it was a *real* emergency. In his experience, anything less than a life-or-death emergency could wait until he woke at seven in the morning. Indeed, the vast majority of emergencies could be handled by his staff. He'd made sure to give them a great deal of discretion. They didn't need him to rubberstamp orders they had the authority to give on their own.

It was a surprise, therefore, when someone burst into his room in the middle of the night.

Simon jerked awake, half-convinced he was having a nightmare. He slept alone—he'd slept alone since his marriage became more of a match of convenience than love—and no one should have disturbed him. He was really too old to fill his bed with beauties, even though he knew there was nothing like power for making an ugly old man strikingly desirable. Jokes aside, it had always struck him as a little pointless. Power was so much more rewarding than sex.

"Your Excellency!" It took Simon a moment to recognise Captain Allan, his close protection team leader. "The planet is under attack!"

"What?" Simon thought, for a second, that it was an exercise. But he would have been warned in advance. "What do you mean?"

Allan caught his arm and hauled him out of bed. "Sir, the planet is under attack! We have to get you to the bunker!"

Simon spluttered in astonishment as Allen half-carried, half-dragged him to the door. The planet was under attack? Absurd! Who would dare? And yet…he heard alarms howling in the distance as he was hurried down the stairs to the emergency shaft. Allan typed a code into a keypad, then hurled Simon into the shaft. Simon fell, opening his mouth to scream an instant before he hit the counter-gravity field at the bottom. Allan landed next to him a second later. He didn't seem remotely put out by the experience.

"Your Excellency," a uniformed officer Simon didn't recognise said. "Welcome to the bunker."

"Thank you," Simon grunted. He stumbled to his feet and brushed himself down, silently grateful he hadn't slept naked. Dignity could go hang when one slept alone. "What's happening?"

"Five minutes ago, the orbital defences came under attack," the officer said. His nametag read KENDRICK. "Every ship we had in orbit was wiped out very quickly, along with most of the sensor and weapons platforms. The remaining facilities are still under fire."

Simon pinched himself. It was a nightmare. It *had* to be a nightmare. He'd seen all the simulations, back when they'd been planning the defences. The planners had been *certain* they could stand off any *reasonable* attack, up to and including the Imperial Navy itself. But if the defences were already crumbling…he pinched himself again, harder this time. It didn't work.

"Fetch me some coffee," he ordered, finally. He couldn't cope without *something* to wake him up. The stimulants he'd used as a younger man would probably give him a heart attack now. "Who are they?"

"We don't know," Kendrick admitted. "They're broadcasting a message..."

"Show me," Simon growled.

There was no visual, just a simple audio recording. Simon listened in increasing disbelief as the speaker promised that surrender would be rewarded, that anyone who just gave in would be free to go wherever they wanted...he shook his head. Surrender would mean the end of the world, *his* world. He'd be a marked man the moment his superiors heard what had happened. And he was too old to change his ways, have a genetic transplant and flee to the other side of the galaxy.

He took a chair and watched as the remainder of the orbital defences disintegrated. The attackers, whoever they were, were good. Damn them. They were tearing holes in defences he'd been told were practically invulnerable, all the while carefully avoiding the orbital industries that had been built up over the last few years. And yet, they'd barely touched the PDCs. The handful of missiles that had entered the planet's atmosphere had been killed before they'd hit the surface.

This isn't a raid, he thought. Pirates didn't fight when the odds weren't firmly in their favour. A warlord, on the other hand, would have more than simple vandalism in mind. *This is an invasion. They're not going to destroy facilities they want to take intact.*

"No response," he ordered, finally. He was no military officer, but he'd seen the simulations. The attackers would have to come a lot closer if they wanted to take the orbital installations, bringing them far too close to the PDCs. They'd be blown out of space if they tried. And they'd be in for a nasty surprise if they tried to land. "Order the defences to engage the enemy where possible."

"Aye, sir."

"And put all the garrisons on alert," Simon added. The alert would have already gone out, but he had to issue the order anyway. For the record, if nothing else. "If they try to land, I want to be ready for them."

CHAPTER NINETEEN

This was not, unfortunately, without precedent. There are many examples, throughout history, of governments and bureaucrats being unable or unwilling to believe the worst even though the truth was staring them right in the face. The disaster at the Falcone Shipyards, for example, was made considerably worse by corporate bureaucrats who insisted that the yards could be returned to service within a few short weeks...when, as the people on the spot were all too aware, the yards were nothing more than debris and radioactive dust.

—PROFESSOR LEO CAESIUS

Earthfall and its Aftermath

"THIS PROBABLY SOUNDED LIKE A BETTER IDEA before we actually put it into practice," Rachel muttered, as she drove the farmer's lorry towards the garrison. The lorry itself was primitive—they hadn't found a governor within the engine, something that would have let the government turn it off remotely—but she was grimly aware she could be spotted at any moment. "If this goes wrong..."

She pushed the thought aside as she drove onwards, silently counting down the seconds. The briefing notes had told her when the fleet intended to launch the invasion, but she knew better than to assume everything would run like clockwork. Something would go wrong—a delay, an enemy sentry in the worst possible place—and all hell would break loose, off schedule. The defenders up ahead had no reason to be alert, as far as she knew, but that could change in a moment. Standard practice in the marines was to sound a general alert first and worry later about the consequences. She'd seen nothing to suggest the locals disagreed.

The lorry twitched under her as she turned the corner. The police hadn't shown up again, much to her relief. There was no way she could talk her way out of being arrested, not when she was driving a stolen lorry. She would have had to fight, which would have cost them the mission even if she'd successfully extracted herself from the situation. And yet...she glanced upwards as her implants sounded an alert. There were explosions in high orbit. They looked almost pretty to her, flashes of light amidst the twinkling stars...it was hard to remember that each of those flashes marked a missile finding its target. She put the thought aside as her target came into view. The gatehouse looked as formidable as ever, the guards armed to the teeth...

She activated the makeshift autopilot, setting the lorry on a collision course towards the gatehouse, then scrambled out of the chair, clambered into the rear of the vehicle and jumped to the ground. Her implants triggered a second later, boosting her speed. She ran as if the hounds of hell were after her, ignoring the shouts from the guards. They hadn't realised—yet—that she'd jumped out of the lorry. Her lips twitched. The guards were definitely inexperienced. Anyone guarding a post in a war zone learnt very quickly to watch for leapers. It was a pretty clear sign that the unmanned truck was a VBIED.

The timer reached zero. She threw herself to the muddy road, hugging the ground as the lorry exploded behind her. They'd put the explosive together from farming supplies—she'd been surprised they weren't more restricted, although they all had commercial uses—but she hadn't been confident the results would be worth the effort. She rolled over and peered towards the remains of the gatehouse as the other two started firing, tracking the handful of visible guards within the base. The gatehouse itself still stood—they'd built it out of concrete and hullmetal—but it was apparently empty. Beyond it, the blast had shattered windows and smashed defences.

Good, she thought, coldly. *By the time you realise this is a diversion, it will be already too late.*

• • •

Corporal Derek Frazer and the rest of the platoon had been sitting in the guardhouse, drinking coffee and sharing lies about the girls they knew back home, when the entire complex shook violently. The sound of the blast swept over them seconds later, the impact shattering windows and sending lights crashing to the floor. Derek hit the floor himself, grabbing his rifle with one hand as he climbed under the table. The others followed him, readying themselves for...for what? A drill? This was no drill.

Lieutenant Hobbs stumbled into the room, blood pouring down his face. Derek stared, realising—to the very core of his being—this was *real*. They'd taken mandatory courses in medicine, from first aid in school to battlefield treatment during basic training, but...he told himself, sharply, that face wounds often looked worse than they were. Hobbs had probably taken a piece of glass to the jaw. God knew there was enough of it scattered on the floor. He could feel it crunching under his feet as he clambered out from under the table and stood to attention. Hobbs, to his credit, was holding himself upright despite the pain.

"The base is under attack," he said. He sounded as if he didn't believe his own words. The sound of gunfire echoed in the distance. "Get out there and fight."

The alarms started to sound, too late. Derek exchanged glances with Loomis, then hefted his rifle and headed for the door. The sound of shooting grew louder, much louder. He glanced at the rifle in his hand, his blood running cold as he realised his platoon might be the only ones ready and able to defend themselves. There were hundreds of soldiers in the barracks, none of whom had weapons and ammunition. Their weapons were all locked up in the armoury. There was no way they could be armed in a hurry...

He pushed the door open and peered outside. The gatehouse was a blackened mass. It looked intact, but he could see flames licking inside the structure. The gate itself was gone, leaving behind a smoking crater. And...a bullet whistled over his head, hitting a soldier he'd known since childhood. He threw himself to the ground, firing a pair of rounds back into the forest. His instructors had taught him to look for muzzle flare, a flash that would mark the enemy's position, but he couldn't see any. The bullets seemed to be coming out of nowhere, somewhere within the gloom. He saw a shimmering wave of...*something*...passing through the air, striking the rearward barracks. A second later, the entire structure burst into flame.

"Get closer," Hobbs snapped. "Hurry."

Derek gritted his teeth, then nodded for Loomis and the others to lay down covering fire. They couldn't see their targets, but...he kept low as their bullets tore through the trees, hopefully forcing the enemy to duck. He reached the remnants of the bunker and peered inside. A pair of blackened bodies lay on the floor. He took a breath and nearly threw up at the roast pork stench of burning flesh. He'd been told about it, but...actually smelling it was very different. He glanced back as Loomis joined him, then led the way into the bunker. The weapons locker was still intact, thankfully. They'd been warned never to open it without permission...

He laughed, suddenly. They didn't need permission *now*, did they?

The lock was jammed. He swore at it, then tore the multitool off his belt and pried the locker open. A court martial offence, his mind noted; they'd been warned against deliberately damaging government property. He snorted as he dug out plasma grenades and their launchers, then machine guns and extra rifle ammunition. They'd already expended far too much. Their opponents, whoever they were, seemed to have far too much ammunition at their disposal.

Loomis took half the grenades. "You want to hit the trees?"

"Yes." Derek glanced back, but there was no sign of Hobbs. The LT wasn't a coward, so where *was* he? He hadn't been wounded *that* badly. "Get ready to fire on my signal?"

"Got it." Loomis didn't argue, not now that everything had gone to hell. "Ready."

Derek glanced at the rest of the platoon—seven men, all angry and scared at their first taste of combat—then directed them to ready themselves. "Now!"

Loomis opened fire, directing a hail of HE and plasma grenades into the trees. A series of explosions tore through the forest, ripping the enemy cover away. Flames followed in their wake, creating a threat Derek hadn't anticipated. Forest fires weren't much of a threat in Eddisford—it rained too often—but no one had bombarded the trees with plasma grenades either. The flames would burn themselves out, he was sure, yet...he allowed himself a moment of relief as the enemy fire stopped abruptly. He hoped the attackers, whoever they were, had been killed.

He felt his legs start to shake as he swept the burning trees for targets. They'd been attacked. They'd been attacked...but by whom? It wasn't as if there was *anyone* who could have attacked them. The entire planet belonged to the corporation. Sure, there were whispered stories of hidden colonies and barbarians beyond the settled zone, but...he'd never believed them. They were just too far-out to be true...

Loomis touched his arm. "Look up."

Derek followed his gaze. Dawn was breaking, the sun already glimmering on the horizon, but he could still see the halo. The sky was full of shooting stars, of trails of fire burning through the atmosphere. He could hear a faint popping sound in the distance, a sound he couldn't place... ice settled in his gut as he realised the entire planet was under attack. The halo had been destroyed and the debris was falling into the gravity well...

"Fuck," he breathed. He heard a clattering sound behind him and glanced back, breathing a sigh of relief when he saw reinforcements. "What's happening?"

A whistle blew. Someone had taken command. He turned and hurried out of the bunker, cursing again as he saw the bodies on the ground. Someone had lost most of their head...he felt his gorge rise as he realised

Hobbs was dead. The lieutenant had been shot down in the midst of his run. Half his head had been shot away. Derek forced himself to keep running. He'd never liked the LT, but...he would have preferred to know the chain of command had remained intact. Right now, he had no idea who was in command.

And, worst of all, he had no idea what was coming next.

• • •

That was clever, Rachel reflected, as she forced herself to run through the forest. Whoever had taken command after the gatehouse had been destroyed was a quick thinker. The forest had concealed the Pathfinders, so burn down the forest...her lips twitched at the thought. It was the kind of solution no one would authorise until the shit had *definitely* hit the fan. *I hope we killed you, whoever you are.*

She wished, not for the first time, that they'd brought heavier weapons. The plasma pulsar and the grenades had done a lot of damage, but not enough. There was still a formidable enemy force in the garrison, if it had time to rally, distribute ammunition and fight back. She had no idea when the landing force would actually arrive. There was no way to tell—yet—if they'd struck a major blow or merely put the enemy on alert.

We'll find out, she told herself. They reached the road. In the distance, she could hear the sound of shooting. She had no idea who was being shot at. There were no other Pathfinders on the planet, as far as she knew. Her senior officers wouldn't keep that from her, would they? There were dangers in too much secrecy...and in trying to be clever. *Maybe they're just firing at shadows.*

Her lips quirked into a smile. She hoped that was true.

• • •

Hannah Weston knew perfectly well that most of her acquaintances considered her a no-good busybody, someone who was always interfering in their lives even when her involvement was decidedly not welcome. Hannah knew it and didn't care. As Eddisford's Chief Morale Officer, it was her job to monitor public opinion and smooth out problems before they became dangerous. Better to quietly pressure—or remove—someone than risk discontent spreading out of control. And besides, she *liked* knowing the intimate details of their private lives. It was so much better than wasting away in front of the viewscreen.

She sat in her office, thumbing through the latest surveillance reports. There were safeguards in place to prevent them from being abused, safeguards she'd sworn to uphold when she'd been given the job, but she'd long-since rationalised her way around her oaths. It was easy enough to subvert the safeguards, with a little effort. It was how she'd come to realise just how many people hated her guts. And, more importantly, when they were lying to her. The surveillance was so omnipresent that most people tended to forget just how intrusive it really was.

Or how much of it I have to view personally, she thought. The computers assessed most of the reports, but anything they couldn't understand had to be passed to their human supervisors. No matter how well they were programmed, there were subtle aspects to human behaviour they simply couldn't follow. *It's my duty.*

She blinked in surprise as she heard a knock on the door. Someone was outside, someone who'd evaded the security sensors. Her eyes narrowed. The only people who could do *that* were inspectors from the capital, men who came out every year to check that the system was still working. She scowled as she hastily blanked her screen, triggering a macro her programmer son had written to conceal how *badly* the safeguards had been subverted. She was surprised she hadn't heard any hint of an inspection from her friends in the capital. It was rare for one to be launched without *some* warning.

"Coming," she said, as the newcomer knocked again. She checked the macro had finished its work and erased all trace of its existence, then stood and hurried to the door. "I'm here..."

A young man stood there, his hands held behind his back. Hannah frowned. She wouldn't have got the job if she hadn't been a good observer of human nature and there was something faintly *off* about the unexpected visitor. He was tall and lanky, yet…there was a sense of power and control that worried her. Hannah felt a flicker of concern, mingled with a hint of fear. There was no doubt in his mind that he could handle anything. She was morbidly sure of it.

"Please," she said. If he was an inspector, turning up at this decidedly early hour, she'd better be nice to him. Happy inspectors didn't ask awkward questions. "Come on in."

The newcomer followed her into the building, closed the door behind him and cleared his throat. Hannah turned…and had the shock of her life. The newcomer had a gun in his hand, a gun he was pointing at her. She nearly fainted. She'd never *seen* a gun, not outside the ridiculously stupid flicks her son had loved to watch. The pistol seemed to gleam under the light. It was small and deadly and…it could kill her.

"Keep your hands where I can see them," the newcomer said. Inspector? He was no inspector. She couldn't place his accent, but she was sure he hadn't spent more than a few weeks planetside. An offworlder? "Is there anyone else in this building?"

"...No," Hannah stammered. She was too scared to lie. "I…"

"Good," the newcomer said. "Lie down on the ground."

Hannah shuddered as the man, whoever he was, trussed her up like a chicken, searched her with surprising gentleness and then left her lying on the floor as he checked the rest of the building. Who *was* he? What was he doing? He was going down to the datanode below the building…she smiled, despite her growing fear. There was no way to get into the chamber without the right code. She didn't know it. She just hoped he'd believe her when she told him.

She heard the door opening. She nearly fainted, again. He'd gotten into the datanode chamber. The most important chamber in Eddisford, so secure that even the Town Director couldn't enter without special permission, and he'd just walked in. Who *was* he? That node handled communications for the entire district. She heard a smashing sound, followed by an explosion. Horror gripped her. She was going to be blamed. She just knew it. And if the node was down…

The surveillance network will be down too, she thought. She didn't know the technical details, but she understood the importance of the node. *No one will be being watched any longer.*

He reappeared. She glared at him. "What have you done?"

"Freed the people," he said. "And, if you'll take my advice, you'll go straight home and stay there."

Hannah glared at his retreating back. His advice? He'd left her tied up and yet he advised her to run? What sort of idiot *was* he? Or was it a trick? She wanted to shout at him, but she didn't quite dare. If one of her enemies found her…

She shuddered, helplessly. All of a sudden, the future looked very bleak.

• • •

"General," Kerri said, formally. The enemy fire was slacking as the final orbital defences were wiped out. Her ships had taken some fire, but damage had been minimal. "We have completed Stage One."

"Very good," Anderson said, with equal formality. "Begin Stage Two." He raised his voice. "Deploy the landing force."

CHAPTER TWENTY

But a greater truth is that no one wanted to believe the news because that would have forced them to come to terms with the disaster, gird their loins and do whatever it took to preserve their lives, their worlds and some semblance of civilisation.
—PROFESSOR LEO CAESIUS
Earthfall and its Aftermath

MANY—MANY—YEARS AGO, Haydn had read a book in which the main character had always gotten the shakes before a drop. The book had been required reading at OCS, but he'd never really understood it. Haydn had made countless parachute and suborbital HALO drops in his career and...he considered himself to be used to them. It helped, he supposed, that he'd never really made a proper combat drop. The days of forced landings on planetary surfaces were long gone. Or so everyone had thought.

He gritted his teeth, feeling his stomach churning as the assault shuttle raced towards the planet, zigzagging from side to side to avoid enemy fire. The pilot kept up a stream of chatter that might have been meant to be reassuring, but left Haydn with a powerful and almost irresistible urge to unstrap himself, climb out of his armour, march to the cockpit and brutally strangle the bastard. He didn't want to know how close they'd come to a missile that would have smashed them to atoms if it had struck them. He just wanted to get down on the ground before it was too late.

The shuttle rocked violently, the gravity field twisting under their feet. A timer appeared in his helmet HUD, counting down the seconds to deployment. They'd hit the atmosphere, then. He'd been through the simulators, and he'd flown such missions during live-fire exercises, but this was different. This time, there were people down there who wanted to kill him. Something slapped the shuttle, a casual backhand that sent the craft tumbling through the air before the pilot regained control. Haydn guessed someone down there had set their missiles to proximity detonation. It was probably their best chance at scoring a hit.

"Whoops, that was a close one," the pilot said. He sounded inordinately cheerful for someone who would have to fly the wretched craft back to the MEU. "Getting a little nasty up here, folks."

"Someone kill that fucker," a marine muttered. "Please."

"Be quiet," Mayberry barked. "Get ready to drop."

Haydn carefully resisted the urge to find out who'd made that remark as the last few seconds ticked away. Instead, he accessed the live feed from the invasion coordinator. The picture was a mess, as always, but it was clear they were on target. Resistance was surprisingly light...he snorted, rudely. A handful of PDCs were engaging the invasion fleet, trying to kill the shuttles before they disgorged their targets. The invaders had deployed hundreds of decoys, creating a sensor haze that made it difficult to pick the *real* shuttles out of the swarm, but...the PDCs would hit a handful of shuttles by the laws of averages alone. So far, his company seemed to be intact. He knew that could change at any second. He wondered, sourly, how many of his friends and comrades were already dead.

The map updated again as the drones mapped the landscape, picking out more and more potential targets. The Pathfinders had done a good job, but it never hurt to have confirmation. Besides, they'd missed a handful of defence facilities. There was a giant blind spot over the PDC, a gap in coverage caused by the loss of a handful of drones. Haydn gritted his teeth in annoyance. It was rare to lose a drone...or, rather, it *had* been rare. They normally floated too high for the average insurgent to see, let alone bring down, but the PDCs were relatively modern. They'd had little trouble in tracking and shooting down the drones.

We'll just have to get used to it, he thought, coldly. *In the old days, they didn't have any drones either.*

"Ten seconds." The pilot sounded more focused now. A puff of smoke exploded far too close to the shuttle for anyone's peace of mind. "Nine...eight..."

Haydn winced as the gravity field picked him up, hurling him out of the shuttle. The world spun around him—he had a crazed series of impressions, from a fleet of shuttles to enemy missiles coming right at him—as he plunged towards the ground. Hameau had looked small, on the display, but now...it was an illusion. Hameau was only fractionally smaller than Earth. On a human scale, the planet was still gigantic. He felt himself pick up speed as he plummeted down. The skies were full of explosions. He said a silent prayer for his lost comrades as he prepared for landing. God alone knew how many marines had died...

The ground came up and hit him. The gravity field lurched again, the antigravity pods cutting in a second before he slammed into the ground with terrifying force. He felt the gravity field fade away a moment later, the planet's natural gravity taking a firm grip on him. It felt no different from Earth, as far as he could tell. Hameau wasn't small enough for him to leap tall buildings in a single bound. In truth, he was relieved. Fighting in low-gravity environments tended to be dangerously unpredictable.

"Bucker bought the farm," Mayberry said. "His suit failed."

Haydn nodded, shortly. There would be time to mourn later, if there *was* a later. He snapped orders, forming up his platoons as the map stabilised in his HUD. They were a single mile from the enemy garrison, hardly any distance at all. Judging by the updates, they could probably have landed on top of them...he shook his head. There had been no way to know what would happen until it was too late to change plans. There was always *someone* who didn't get the update, and then the shit would *really* hit the fan.

"Forward," he ordered.

They made their way through the forest, armoured strength smashing trees like paper when they got in the way. It was impossible to be stealthy, but it hardly mattered. It was more important to get to the enemy garrison before someone managed to organise resistance or command the troops to hurry to a fallback position. The corps had plans and procedures for everything, including surprise attacks on bases that should have remained unmolested. He dared not assume the locals were any less determined to prepare for anything. They'd certainly invested trillions of credits in their defences.

A handful of updates flashed up in front of his eyes. The second assault echelon was already landing, unloading hovertanks, assault gunships and heavy combat suits. General Anderson would probably have his forward command post set up shortly, if the post wasn't online already. There would be heavy support on the way, if they needed it. The Pathfinders had suggested the garrison was heavily defended, but they couldn't have expected an all-out assault. Could they?

They punched through the trees. The garrison lay ahead of them.

• • •

"All right," General Taggard snapped. "Listen up!"

Derek clutched his rifle in one hand, feeling uncomfortably out of place. General Taggard had never spoken to him, not directly. They'd been warned that being noticed by the general would be tantamount to a dishonourable discharge…if they were lucky. Better to take non-judicial punishment from the instructors and lower-ranking officers than risk appealing to the general. But now…

His eyes swept the scene. The normal command structure was broken beyond repair. A pair of colonels, two of the most bombastic men he'd ever known, were gibbering silently to themselves; a third was sitting on a rickety chair, staring at nothing. Lieutenant Hobbs was dead; Captain Hafiz was missing, presumed dead. Derek had found himself in command of what remained of the training company, seemingly by default. He wasn't the only inexperienced officer to gain a battlefield promotion. The attackers, whoever they were, had killed a *lot* of commanding officers.

"The planet is under attack," General Taggard said. "We don't know who they are and we don't know what they want. We've lost contact with the government. We *do* know that they're landing to the east, that they're coming here. We're going to give them a bloody nose."

Derek felt his stomach clench. A handful of conscripts had fled into the trees, even though they'd be tracked down and punished for desertion in the face of the enemy. God alone knew what would happen to them, but it *would* happen. Derek had no doubt of it. And yet, part of him was tempted to run too. Their world had shrunk to the garrison and the surrounding trees. He could hear explosions in the distance, see smoke rising from targets that had been hit from orbit. They had no way to know what was happening outside their little bubble, but the general was right. It was only a matter of time until they came under attack.

General Taggard continued to bark orders, outlining emergency procedures no one had seriously thought they'd ever have to use. Derek allowed himself a moment of relief that he'd spent so long exploring the countryside outside Eddisford, even though it had brought him attention from the town busybodies. He could navigate back to the river and over the bridge if there was no other choice. It would be a long walk, but...probably better than being taken prisoner. He'd heard hundreds of horror stories. People who fell into enemy hands rarely came out again.

He glanced up as he heard another explosion, closer this time. The enemy troops were approaching. General Taggard gave his final orders, then dismissed them to their posts. The men had already built a defence line, but Derek had no illusions. He and his company could have overrun it in a few minutes, if they didn't simply outflank it. Hell, the bastards could simply starve the garrison into submission. They might not know it, but they'd hit the kitchens. The garrison's food supplies were buried under a pile of rubble.

A crashing noise echoed through the forest, coming closer. Derek hefted his rifle, then barked a handful of orders of his own. There was no point spending their lives uselessly, not when they were out on a limb. The enemy would take what remained of the garrison. Derek and his men would fire a handful of shots for the honour of the flag, then turn and run for their lives. Better to regroup, as the general had ordered, than die for nothing...

Shapes appeared in the treeline: tall men, wearing black armour. Their faces were hidden behind featureless helms. Derek blanched. He'd heard about combat armour, about battlesuits, but he'd never worn one. They carried weapons, pointed at his men...he threw himself to the ground as *something* passed over his head, streaks of light striking the remaining buildings. Explosions tore them apart, collapsing the barracks and office blocks into piles of rubble. The defenders returned fire, but it was useless. The attackers didn't seem to be deterred. Derek couldn't tell if their armour was protecting them or if his men were just missing, but it hardly seemed to matter. They advanced swiftly, moving with the ease of men who'd done it a hundred times before. Derek would have been impressed if he hadn't been on the receiving end. They'd crippled the entire garrison in less than a minute.

Loomis lifted a grenade launcher and fired at the nearest attacker. The explosion picked the attacker up and threw him through the air, his body landing in a crumpled heap. Dead? Derek couldn't tell. It hardly mattered. The attackers were zeroing in on them, bullets and plasma bursts crackling through the air. He heard an officer shouting, an instant before he was silenced forever. The attackers were almost on them.

Derek blew his whistle. The defenders rose and ran towards the rear of the garrison, towards the holes their peers had cut in the fence. He half-expected the attackers to mow them down as they fled, shooting his men in the back, but instead...they let them go. Derek blinked in surprise, then set the timer before running himself. The assault had been so savage that they'd barely had time to prepare any booby traps, but they'd done what they could. It might just slow the bastards down.

He heard a rumbling sound as a tank moved into view, its main gun turning with terrifying speed to engage the enemy. Derek covered his ears and glanced back as the gun fired, hurling a HE round into the armoured figures. Fast, but not fast enough. The attackers scattered, jumping aside like giant grasshoppers. They fired back a second later, hurling a set of plasma pulses into the tank. The vehicle exploded in a massive fireball. There was no time for the crew to bail out before it was too late. Derek hoped, as he resumed his run, that they'd died quickly. Death by fire was not a good way to go.

It could be worse, he told himself. *If they take us alive.*

A handful of junior officers were waiting by the fence, directing the fleeing men to the paths that would take them through the forest and down to the river. There was no sign of General Taggard or the officers who simply hadn't been able to take their first taste of combat. Derek felt sick, wondering just what he'd do if those officers were put in command in the future. They were cowards, but...he shook his head. They'd boasted of their military skills and yet...he knew, deep in his heart, they'd lied. He wished he knew why.

"We got one of the bastards," Loomis said, as they hurried down the track. "Didn't we?"

"Yeah," Derek said. He wasn't sure it was true, but...no matter. It was important they believed they *could* hit back. Besides, armour or no, anyone who got thrown around like that was probably badly hurt at the very least. "I think we got him."

"And we probably made them mad." Loomis paused. "Wasn't there supposed to be a giant *BANG*?"

Derek nodded, shortly. The charges hadn't detonated...he scowled, wondering just what had gone wrong. He'd set the timer personally. They hadn't been *encouraged* to learn how to set booby traps, but...they'd known what they were doing. Perhaps an enemy round had cut the detonator or they'd simply disarmed the charges. They shouldn't have had *time* to cut the charges, but...they shouldn't have been able to attack the garrison at all. He glanced at the sun, still rising in the distance. Was it really only nine o'clock? It felt like hours had passed since the world turned upside down.

He frowned as he saw a swarm of aircraft in the east. They couldn't be *friendly*, not if they were there. The enemy landing site, he guessed. They could move like greased lightning, whoever they were. They'd be coming after the refugees in no time at all. He wasn't sure they'd make it across the bridge before the attackers either planted themselves on top of it or dropped it into the water. If that happened, they'd be trapped.

We'll find a way to hit back, he promised himself. It was personal now. He'd seen too many men die in the last hour to feel anything but horror and rage. *And we'll be back.*

• • •

Haydn smiled as the enemy defences crumbled. The enemy had made a dreadful mistake when they'd chosen to make a fight of it, instead of scattering or falling back to the inner defence lines. But then, it was never *easy* to explain to one's superiors why one had issued the order to retreat... Haydn felt his smile grow wider. Whoever had been in command probably hadn't realised just *what* was coming his way. The conscripts had fought bravely—he gave them that much—but they hadn't stood a chance.

A handful of prisoners stood in the middle of the garrison, some badly wounded. One, wearing an officer's uniform, looked to be completely out of it. Probably a staff officer, Haydn guessed. Marine officers were expected to rotate between front-line and staff positions, but the Imperial Army preferred to keep them separate. Their staff officers had been routinely unprepared for actual *violence*. It looked as if the locals had made the same mistake.

And they'll tell us what we need to know, he thought. POWs would be treated decently—they weren't fighting terroristic insurgents, who could be put in front of a wall and shot after they'd been interrogated—but they *would* be questioned. *We can start putting some hard numbers to the enemy order of battle.*

His intercom bleeped. "Captain?"

"General." Haydn had no trouble recognising General Anderson's voice. "I beg leave to report that the enemy garrison has been secured. We took nineteen prisoners. The remainder were either killed in the fighting or fled into the forest."

"Very good," General Anderson said. He'd clearly managed to set up his command post. "Tanks and reinforcements are on their way. Link up with them, then proceed to Target Alpha. It is imperative Target Alpha is secured as soon as possible."

The PDC, Haydn said. He could *see* the structure in the distance, firing missiles and railgun pellets into orbit. It wasn't designed to fire on targets on the ground…he frowned, wondering if that was actually true. It might not be. The locals had been paranoid, astonishingly paranoid. Who was to say they *hadn't* designed the PDC to fire on ground-based targets? *We need to capture or take it out before they start getting any ideas.*

"Yes, sir," he said. "We'll be on our way once the armour arrives."

CHAPTER TWENTY-ONE

The economic shockwave, therefore, hit worlds that were utterly unprepared for the sudden—effective—collapse of interstellar civilisation. Theoretically, most of the middle-rank worlds could have survived the crash; in practice, tumbling dominos—the remnants of interstellar corporations—brought down the planetary economies in their wake.

—PROFESSOR LEO CAESIUS

Earthfall and its Aftermath

THE BRIDGE, RACHEL CONCEDED as she sat in their perch and watched from a distance, was an impressive structure for such a young world. It wasn't the most impressive bridge she'd seen in her career, but it was easily big and strong enough to allow a whole armoured division to cross without collapsing. Now, hundreds of refugees—soldiers from the garrison, she guessed—were hurrying across the bridge, a handful taking up positions at the eastern side as if they hoped they could slow pursuit enough to give their fellows a chance to escape. They were brave, she noted as she kept them in her scopes. But bravery wouldn't be enough.

Her enhanced ears detected the light tanks before she saw them, rushing down the road. The locals were probably cursing the colony planners for working so hard to build useful roads, although she had to admit the road network was better than it had any right to be. It would always have been a two-edged sword. The roads allowed the planetary government to control the towns and farms on the edge of the settled zone, but they also provided ready-made highways for any invader. But then, they probably hadn't taken the prospect of invasion seriously. Very few had since the Unification Wars.

She watched from her perch as the hovertanks came into view, readying herself to open fire if necessary. The defenders seemed to hesitate, then fired off a handful of shots before throwing their rifles away and raising their hands. *Someone* seemed to have realised the marines were taking prisoners. She didn't blame them for surrendering. They didn't have heavy weapons, nor did they have anything that could take down the bridge. A single burst from the machine guns would wipe out the defenders, for nothing. She'd feared that someone *would* try to rig the bridge for demolition, and readied herself to intervene if they'd tried, but no one had. She guessed their contingency plans hadn't included the wholesale destruction of corporate property.

Which was a mistake, she thought, as the tanks swept across the bridge. *They could have slowed us down if they'd blown up the bridge.*

Rachel waited until the western side of the bridge was secure, then tapped her communicator to signal her presence. After everything she'd done, after everything she'd survived, it would be the height of irony to be killed in a blue-on-blue incident. The tankers were likely to be jumpy, at least until they encountered enemy antitank weapons. It went against the grain to reveal herself so openly, but there was little choice. She didn't want to be shot down by her own side.

She kept her hands where they could see them as she stepped into view. The riflemen eyed her nervously, their weapons not *quite* pointed at her. Rachel waited, patiently, as they called the CP to verify her identity. She didn't blame them. Marines had died when someone young, female and apparently harmless had approached them. It was funny how concerns about strip-searching the locals faded when it was clear the only other option was giving the enemy a free shot at one's troops.

The riflemen relaxed as soon as her identity was concerned. "Glad to have you with us, Specialist."

Rachel concealed a smile. The word *specialist* concealed a great many sins. "Glad to be with you, LT," she said. The lieutenant was newly-promoted, at a guess. He'd probably been one of the last officers to go through OCS before the Slaughterhouse was destroyed. "Are you heading to the PDC?"

"Target Alpha," the LT said. He nodded to the tank. "Coming?"

"Coming." Rachel scrambled onto the tank, silently reminding herself how to jump off if they ran into enemy troops. It had been a long time since she'd been a rifleman herself. "The others are closer to the base."

The tank glided into life, crossing the bridge and heading west. The sound of explosions grew louder, streaks of light flashing through the air. It looked as if General Anderson's forces had set up their self-propelled artillery, calling down strikes on the PDC and any enemy forces foolish enough to show themselves. She tried to log into the command datanet, but the net seemed weak and insecure. The drones were having problems getting closer to the PDC, she noted. There was little recon imagery to light the way.

"Specialist," the LT said. "Do you know where the enemy are going?"

"We don't know what contingency plans they had," Rachel said. She had no doubt they *existed*, but...were the enemy in any state to put them into operation? And what *were* they? She considered a handful of possibilities, then shrugged. "I guess they'll be trying to rally the troops."

They drove past a handful of civilians, staring in astonishment and disbelief as the convoy roared past. Rachel was surprised they were on the roads, although...she supposed she shouldn't have been. The local datanet had been crippled. If the planetary government had issued any orders to its civilians, they probably hadn't gotten through. She hoped the Civil Affairs teams would be smart enough to issue orders soon, once they were in position. The last thing they needed was hundreds of thousands of refugees clogging the roads. It would be much better if the civilians stayed home, out of danger.

She put the thought out of her mind as the tanks turned and headed up the road towards the PDC. The defenders would know they were coming; she was sure. Even if they hadn't had the time or the imagination to put spotters on duty, they'd have to know they'd be attacked sooner rather than later. The PDC was the largest target in the region and, as long as it remained in enemy hands, it could hamper the rapid offloading from the MEUs. They had to know that too. The sound of railguns and mass drivers firing grew louder as they approached the structure. The ships in orbit were taking a pounding.

And they're having to waste time defending themselves, she thought. The PDC's point defences were doing a good job, shooting down shells as they came over the horizon. *But that won't last when we hit their defence line*.

She jumped off and landed on the muddy track as bullets started to ping off the tank's armour. The tank returned fire, its heavy gun taking out the guardposts one by one; the other tanks spread out, an antitank missile slamming into one and punching through its heavy armour. The crew managed to bail out an instant before the tank exploded, pieces of molten debris scattering everywhere. She ducked and kept watching, cursing under her breath. The PDC was going to be a nightmare to take.

And we're going to have to kill everyone inside the structure if they refuse to surrender, she thought, grimly. *There's no other way to take it out*.

• • •

"This is the Terran Marine Corps," Haydn said. The Pathfinders had recorded enough enemy emissions that they could be fairly sure which channels the enemy used, even if they weren't broadcasting anything at the moment. He had men looking for their underground datalinks, in the hopes of cutting the PDC out of the planetary network, but he was fairly sure they wouldn't be successful. "Your base is surrounded. We have the power to destroy it. If you surrender, we promise good treatment and eventual repatriation in line with the laws of war…"

He waited, but there was no answer. Were the enemy even *listening*? They *should* be able to hear his message…were they asking their superiors for permission to surrender or were they preparing to fight to the death? They had to know their position was hopeless, but they *could* force him to either risk his men by storming the fortress or simply reduce the entire structure to a puddle of molten rock. Either way, the enemy would hamper future operations.

Sure, he mused. *At the cost of hundreds of lives.*

He repeated the message as the assault force prepared to storm the fortress. There was no way they could punch their way through the lower doors, not without taking heavy casualties, but they *could* climb to the guns and punch their way through *there*. Would the enemy *know* it? No one had stormed a PDC for hundreds of years, as far as anyone outside the Grand Senate and the Marine Corps knew. And yet…there was no reason the defenders couldn't have figured it out for themselves. They could have offered a reward to anyone who poked a hole in their defences. Better a little embarrassment during an exercise than death and destruction during a real battle.

No answer, he thought. *Shit.*

He monitored the enemy channels as he snapped orders, setting the assault force in motion. The tanks and self-propelled guns readied themselves, preparing to launch a hail of fire at the fortress to keep the defenders from noticing the *real* threat. It was almost a shame they couldn't simply destroy the guns and move on, but PDCs were built to be fortresses. There could be an entire army in the bunkers under the PDC, ready to emerge after the front lines had moved on and wreak havoc in the rear. It couldn't be allowed.

"Go," he ordered.

The self-propelled guns opened fire. He looked up, just in time to see the enemy fortress wreathed in a blaze of fire. It looked like a forcefield, an invisible bubble protecting the fortress from attack…the kind of technology that scientists had been promising for hundreds of years, if only they were granted unlimited budgets for research and development. Haydn had been told, when he'd been briefed on Safehouse, that the marines had been carrying out their own private research projects into newer and better technology, but nothing had been developed. It was possible they'd reached the limits what tech could do.

He shook his head and snapped orders to his troops. The company formed up by platoons, then charged at the fortress. The PDC would pose a difficult problem to any mountain climber, but his men had been trained at the Slaughterhouse. They laughed at mountains that deterred experienced climbers. And their suits were designed to assist them in ways hardcore climbers would deem cheating. Haydn's lips quirked at the thought as he began the ascent to the guns. He didn't care if they were cheating. All that mattered was *winning*.

The sound of gunfire and explosions grew louder. It would have been unbearable if he hadn't been wearing his earplugs and helmet. Even with protection, he could feel the vibrations in his bones. A handful of shells broke through the point defence, exploding harmlessly against the fortress's armour. He cursed the enemy gunners under his breath, wondering how they'd managed to let *those* shells through the defences. They couldn't harm the fortress, not really, but they *could* blow his men off the rock. The inquest on *that* disaster would be a circus. He supposed he should be grateful he wouldn't be around to see it.

There was no opposition as they reached the giant guns, even though the enemy had to know they were there. They couldn't come out to fight, not without the snipers picking them off as soon as they showed themselves. Haydn watched the guns moving constantly, quickly calculating where was safe for him and his men to stand. Armour or no armour, they would be crushed to a bloody pulp if they got caught in the gears. The incoming fire started to dwindle as they placed the charges on the guns. The enemy would be desperately suiting up, if they had armoured suits on hand. They'd know what he was doing too.

"Charges in place," Lieutenant Hammond called.

"Get back, then detonate them," Haydn ordered. He'd never had a chance to use tactical laser-head warheads in combat, not outside simulations. They were so rare that even the marines only had a handful in their stockpiles. "Hurry!"

The ground shook below his feet. There was a second, violent explosion—he saw tongues of flame pouring out of the gun barrels—before the remainder of the guns stopped moving. One of his men tumbled back, falling off the rock. His antigravity pods would ensure he survived the fall, but the ribbing from his comrades would be merciless. Haydn's HUD blinked up alerts as he stumbled towards the guns. The metal beneath his feet was uncomfortably warm.

It must be hell in there, he thought, feeling a flicker of pity—and guilt. He had no qualms about making someone die for his cause, if *someone* had to die, but...he'd unleashed an utter holocaust on the fortress. The smoke pouring out of the gun mounts was grim proof that the warheads had done their work. *How many people did we just kill?*

He enhanced his helmet's sensors as he lowered himself into the gun mount. The chamber below the guns was unrecognisable. The gun barrels themselves were made of hullmetal, but even *they* were scorched and pitted beyond repair. The remainder of the chamber was a molten mess. Cooling rapidly, but...he shuddered, silently glad his helmet had a built-in air supply. The stench would be appalling. There was no sign of anyone, living or dead, at all.

"The uppermost layers are nothing but debris." His voice sounded shaky, even to him. "I don't think there's anyone alive."

He peered towards the gash in the floor. A low rumbling sound echoed through the complex...an explosion? A generator on the verge of giving up the ghost? Or...his environmental sensors bleeped a warning as he lowered himself to the next level. The air was poisonous, utterly lethal. Anyone below him would choke to death, unless they'd had the presence of mind to grab a rebreather and a protective suit. He doubted they'd had time. They couldn't have expected his company to scale the heights so quickly.

And if the rest of the PDCs know what happened to this one, he thought, *they'll make sure we can't do it again.*

Mayberry caught his eye. "Sir? Do we continue searching the complex?"

"Yeah." Haydn didn't want to, but he knew his duty. "We have to be sure there's no one left alive."

• • •

The radio transmission was clear, straight to the point. "There is a combined military and civil emergency in progress," a voice said. "All civilians are ordered to remain indoors and stay off the roads for the duration of the emergency. I say again, stay in your homes. Follow orders from uniformed personnel. Listen to this channel for further instructions. There is a combined military..."

"Sounds like a plan," Phelps said, as they drove through the enemy town. It was silent, utterly unmoving. The crowds they'd seen two days ago were gone. "What do you think they'll do when they realise the truth?"

Rachel shrugged. She thought she could see someone peeking out from behind the curtains. The locals knew *something* was going on, even if they didn't know *what.* It wasn't as if anyone could hide the battle in orbit, or the explosions on and around the garrisons, or the unpleasant-looking smoke billowing from the PDC. They'd realise their homeworld was being invaded even if they didn't know who was doing the invading. And who knew what they'd do then? They didn't have many—if any—weapons, but that didn't make them harmless. Someone with a little ingenuity could do a great deal of damage if he had the chance.

"I think we have to keep them out of the way as much as possible," she said. Civvies would be a major headache, at least while the war was going on. Afterwards...she had the feeling that most civilians would welcome the marines. It couldn't be easy growing up in a goldfish bowl. Earth had been bad enough, but Hameau was worse. "Our first priority is winning the war."

She leaned forward as the car powered its way towards the CP. General Anderson would have orders for them, probably. Anderson had worked with Pathfinders before. She smiled in anticipation. They'd be watching the enemy from the shadows or hitting their command posts or even trying to sneak into their command bunker...wherever it was. Or something. She didn't care, as long as it meant she had a chance to get stuck into the enemy. She was sick of sneaking around.

A pair of Raptors roared overhead, their weapons moving constantly as they searched for targets on the ground. She felt her expression tighten. The locals would *definitely* see the Raptors and then...would they see the markings? Or...or what? She had no idea. What *would* they believe? A government crackdown? She dismissed the thought a second later. The planetary government would hardly start a crackdown by blowing up its own orbital facilities. The very thought was absurd.

And there are still enemy troops out there, she reminded herself. A drone flew over them, probably making sure of their identity before they were allowed any closer to the command post. *All it takes is for one of them to have an HVM launcher and some nerve for him to blow the Raptors out of the sky.*

She shrugged. Right now, it wasn't her problem.

CHAPTER TWENTY-TWO

The effects were immediate—and disastrous. Entire economies simply ceased to exist. Billions of jobs were lost, throwing uncounted numbers of people out of work at the worst possible time. The Empire's social security network, already straining under the pressure of budget cuts combined with steadily-increasing demands, collapsed in its wake. It is impossible to estimate just how many people starved to death in the first few weeks following Earthfall.

—**Professor Leo Caesius**

Earthfall and its Aftermath

"HALT," A VOICE BARKED. A sentry stepped out of nowhere, rifle aimed at Derek's chest. "Identify yourself!"

"Corporal Derek Frazer," Derek said. The sentry had taken him by surprise. He was tired, too tired. Really, he was too tired to care that the asshole was pointing a gun at him. "3rd Training Company, Eddisford Garrison."

"Advance and be recognised," the sentry snapped. Two more sentries appeared, one holding a portable scanner. "Put your hand against the sensor."

"Yes, sir," Derek said. He really *was* too tired to care. It was late afternoon and it felt like evening. "Where do we go now?"

"They're setting up a food kitchen up the road," the sentry said, as the remainder of the platoon were tested. "Colonel McIntyre is in command."

"Good." Derek had never met Colonel McIntyre, but at least he wasn't one of the officers who'd frozen when all hell had broken loose. "We really need something to eat."

"It's just ration shit and water." The sentry sounded friendlier, now they'd passed the test. "I heard it was rough up there."

"It was," Derek said, shortly. "And the storm is coming here."

He felt his tiredness start to lift as they made their way into a makeshift army base. It had once been a factory complex, but now...hundreds of soldiers ran around, desperately trying to ready a defence before the enemy started breathing down their necks. Military policemen and sergeants were everywhere, barking orders and trying to get everyone organised. He spotted a handful of men who'd clearly escaped from Eddisford and others who seemed to have fled from bases all over the region. It was a droll reminder that Eddisford was far from the only town in the world. Perhaps one of the others would be more interesting.

A pair of tanks sat by their road, escorted by a mobile air defence system. The guards standing next to them looked nervous, as if they expected to come under fire at any moment. Perhaps they were right. The AD unit had powerful active sensors, according to his instructors, but the moment they were switched on the enemy would know where they were. He glanced back, seeing a plume of smoke in the distance. The enemy would probably fire on the vehicles the moment they saw them. Derek just hoped the vehicles would have a chance to fire back.

He passed a pair of lorries, soldiers springing out of their backs with weapons in hand. It looked organised, but...the young men hurrying to their posts were no older than himself. Not physically, yet...he'd grown up a lot in the last few hours. He felt old, older than the youngsters passing him. He tried to tell himself that he was being silly, but the impression refused to leave him. He'd turned into a man overnight.

A grim-faced woman in an ill-fitting military uniform greeted them as they came up to the command post. "Welcome to hell. You were there when the shit hit the fan?"

"Yes..." Derek had to hesitate. How did one address a female officer? He'd never met one before. "Yes, sir."

The woman didn't seem to care. "What happened?"

Derek braced himself, feeling his legs starting to totter. He forced himself to stand up, then went through the whole story from the first explosion to the attack on the garrison and the final headlong retreat. The woman listened, sometimes asking questions to bring out details he hadn't known he knew. She seemed to be building a case, but...a case for *what*? Did she intend to blame him for the garrison's fall? Or for following orders and retreating when their position became untenable? Or...?

"There's food in the kitchen," she said, when she'd sucked every last scrap of information from him. "Go get yourself something to eat and a quick rest. The MPs will put you in a company soon enough."

"Yes, sir." Derek leaned forward. "Who *are* they?"

"They claim to be the Terran Marines," the woman said. She barked a harsh laugh. "But that doesn't seem very likely, does it?"

Derek shrugged. He honestly had no idea.

• • •

Simon was more familiar with the concept of 'fog of war' than his military subordinates would probably have realised. He'd spent enough time on stage-one colony worlds to know that information tended to arrive late and, when it finally arrived, to be more than a little outdated or inaccurate. It wasn't that the people on the spot were liars, although he'd *also* spent enough time in corporate headquarters to know just how many people massaged the data to make themselves look good or cover their asses. It was the simple fact that communications tended to be primitive. But it shouldn't have been a problem on Hameau.

We spent billions of credits on crafting a first-rate datanet, he thought angrily. *And now it fails us when we need it.*

He scowled at the holographic map, wondering just how many of the units displayed still existed. The enemy—the Terran Marines, they claimed—had established a solid foothold in less than a day. Simon wasn't a military man by any stretch of the imagination, but he understood the implications. By taking out a PDC, they'd reduced his ability to keep reinforcements from pouring onto the surface. If they managed to take out *all* of them…

Simon felt old, for the first time in decades. The attackers had expended weapons and supplies at a terrifying rate, practically drenching his forces in missiles and sensor decoys. Simon knew there was no way Head Office would *ever* sign off on such expenditure—lives were cheaper—but he had to admit it had paid off for the attackers, whoever they truly were. They had a foothold, one that couldn't be smashed from orbit. The issue would have to be settled on the ground.

Unless help arrives, Simon thought. He'd sent an emergency message as soon as the full scale of the disaster had dawned on him, but there was no way to know if it had reached its destination. The asteroid miners were unreliable and the cloudscoop operators permanently on the verge of mutiny. *We might be on our own.*

He started to pace the bunker, cursing the designers under his breath. The bunker felt like a last refuge, a place a mad dictator would spend his final hours moving imaginary units around a map before his time finally ran out. He wished someone had made it more home-like, he wished someone had installed more defences…he reached for his coffee and took a long swig. He wanted to go back to bed, but he didn't dare. Who knew *what* would happen while he was asleep?

The door opened. Sandra stepped in. "Your Excellency, the conference is ready to begin."

Simon scowled at her and had the satisfaction of watching the brainless twit take a step backwards. The conference had been due to start an hour ago...he supposed the delay wasn't Sandra's fault, but she could take the blame anyway. God knew there would be enough of it to go around. Any hope of collecting his corporate pension and retiring to a quiet life on a recreational world had evaporated with the orbital defences. He put the thought aside as he followed her into the conference room and took a seat at the head of the table. The other three attendees were holograms. They didn't dare assemble the remnants of their ruling council in one place. A single KEW could put an end to all organised resistance.

"Lady and gentlemen," Simon said. He glanced from face to face. "Heather?"

Heather MacDonald, Deputy Governor, leaned forward. "Right now, there's a great deal of confusion on the streets. The people are scared and official information bulletins aren't cutting it. They can look out their windows and see the debris falling from orbit. So far, we haven't seen many refugees from the occupied zone, but we think that will change shortly. And then all hell will break loose."

Simon frowned. "Can we keep it under control?"

"Perhaps." Heather's lips thinned in disapproval. "So far, the human resources system remains intact...outside the occupied zone, at least. I've activated all the monitors and given orders to arrest the known dissidents, the ones who might try to make hay out of our misfortunes. There are police on the streets and food in the shops, so...really, Your Excellency, we just don't know. It's unprecedented."

General Atherton snickered. "You mean they'll behave themselves until they see us weakened, at which point they'll throw themselves wholly into the enemy's arms."

"Unfortunately so," Heather said, stiffly. "We cannot let this go on."

"We may not have a choice." General Atherton sounded serious, now. "The vast majority of our orbital defences, and all of our starships, have been destroyed. Our ability to influence events outside the planetary atmosphere has been sharply curtailed."

"Jesus, General," Heather snapped. "What the fuck were we spending our money on again?"

Simon held up a hand. "It doesn't matter right now," he said, calmly. He knew there would be recriminations, when Head Office got involved, but they could wait until they drove the invaders off their world. "General. Continue."

General Atherton nodded. "Yes, Your Excellency. PDC Nineteen has been destroyed. PDC Thirteen and PDC Nine both took minor damage, but their commanders assure me that they will be back in full working order within the week. We can kill anything that shows itself within range of our guns. The attackers...we assume they can spoof our sensors again, but we have enough firepower to kill real ships and decoys alike. This ensures they cannot simply batter us into submission from orbit."

A holographic map appeared on the table. "The enemy appears to have secured Eddisford District, including capturing or destroying every military establishment on the eastern side of the Dunn River. They have advance elements on the western side, but so far they appear to have concentrated on destroying PDC Nineteen and securing the approaches. We assume they will resume their drive westwards as soon as they feel ready. So far, we only have guesses as to when they will begin."

"I see," Simon said. "And what's your best guess?"

"They claim to be the Terran Marines." General Atherton looked uncomfortable. "If that's true, and they *fight* like the marines, they'll resume their advance in a day or so. We've tracked literally *hundreds* of shuttles landing within the occupied zone. There will be some friction, we assume, but they know how to overcome it."

He took a breath. "General Taggard has assumed command of the defence lines. He's concentrating his armour at key points while assembling his troops and readying himself..."

"I don't care about the details," Simon said. He knew they were important, but he didn't have time to worry about them. "Can he *stop* the attackers?"

"I don't know, Your Excellency." General Atherton met Simon's eyes, evenly. "Logically, we should have a significant edge in firepower and troop numbers. Practically, we will have...problems...getting the troops where we need them to go. They also have a significant edge over us in mobility, at least at the moment. We were preparing troops for off-world deployment; they've been *doing* it for years. On the other hand, we can bleed them white if we draw them into engagements that play to their weaknesses..."

Heather rubbed her forehead. "It sounds like you believe we *are* facing the marines."

"They have marine-grade equipment," General Atherton said. "And they fight like marines. And...if it was some Imperial Navy Admiral who'd declared himself Grand High Lord of All He Surveys, wouldn't he have said so? What's the *point* of claiming to be the marines if you're not the marines? Or if you couldn't keep up the pretence for very long? We are well past the point of stolen valour. This is...someone claiming to be a marine who'd been through Boot Camp and the Slaughterhouse and seen active service. It's odd."

"It doesn't matter," Commissioner Hoyt said. "From an economic point of view, this is utterly disastrous. The program will be set back decades!"

"It isn't as if we can do anything about that," Simon pointed out. "We cannot sweep the invaders away with a wave of our hands."

"We have to roll with it," General Atherton agreed.

"Perhaps we should consider opening discussions," Commissioner Hoyt said. "If nothing else, it would buy time..."

"Head Office would have our heads. Literally." Heather didn't sound impressed. "You're talking about surrender."

"I'm talking about coming to terms," Commissioner Hoyt said. "If this goes on..."

General Atherton shook his head. "Their first demand, as part of a general settlement, will be for the PDCs and population control systems..."

"Human resources systems," Heather corrected.

"... To be shut down," General Atherton finished. "And then…that will be the end."

"So we have to drive them back into space," Simon said. He had no illusions. The human resources system came with a price. When it fell, their control would fall too. "Can we?"

"Perhaps," General Atherton said. "But right now, our main control is keeping them from breaking out. If they reach the capital…game over. We're doomed."

"Help will arrive," Heather said.

"Yes," General Atherton said. "But will it arrive in time?"

"Continue to concentrate your forces," Simon ordered. "And if you see a chance to take the offensive, take it."

"Aye, sir," General Atherton said. "We would be better, however, to remain on the defensive. Let them bleed themselves white against us."

"Do it how you see fit, General," Simon said. "But do it."

• • •

Derek lay on his back, staring up at the night sky.

He was surprised he hadn't been woken earlier, not when the general needed all the manpower he could get. It was odd for the military to let him have a full night's sleep…of course, it hadn't really *been* a full night's sleep. By his estimate, it was late evening. He'd slept five hours, at most. He rubbed his head, reaching for his rifle to check it was still there. He was damned if he was putting it back in the armoury now.

Someone moved, beside him. "Jock?"

"You were expecting Jenny?" Loomis sounded tired and worn. "What do you think is happening to her? Or everyone else back home?"

"I don't know," Derek said. They'd been told all sorts of horror stories about what would happen if they failed in their duties, everything from mass looting and rape to outright genocide, but…he wasn't sure he believed it. The enemy *could* have slaughtered him and his men without difficulty, if they'd wished. "I hope they're safe."

"Yeah," Loomis said. "I hope Betty has the sense to stay out of sight."

Derek winced. Betty was Loomis's sister, four years their younger. "I'm sure your parents will keep her safe," he said. "They're smart people."

"I hope so," Loomis said. "But you know Betty. She's always pushing lines."

"She'll be fine," Derek said. He didn't know what else to say. Eddisford could be a smoking ruin by now. The handful of men who'd escaped the garrison and fled west might be the only survivors. "I think..."

He broke off as an MP walked towards him. "Captain Derek Frazier?"

"*Corporal* Frazier," Derek corrected. They'd got his rank wrong, unless they'd mixed him up with a *Captain* Derek Frazier. He'd never heard of anyone sharing his name, but the army was big enough that it was quite possible. "If you're looking for me..."

"The Colonel wants to see you," the MP said. He turned, as if he could hardly wait to get away. "Tent Seven, on the double."

Loomis sniggered as the MP walked away. "You think they promoted you and forgot to *tell* you? Should I genuflect? Prostrate myself?"

"No," Derek said. "And if an MP hears you say that, you'll be in deep shit."

"Hah," Loomis said. "The planet is being invaded. How much *more* shit can I get dumped on me?"

Derek shrugged and hurried off towards the tent. The guards outside didn't show any surprise when he gave them his rank, so he assumed the MP had simply been mistaken. He loathed the military police, like every other junior soldier, but he had to admit they'd been very busy over the past few hours. It must have been a shock to their system.

"Corporal Frazier, reporting as ordered," he said, as he stepped inside the tent. Colonel McIntyre was a heavyset man with dark skin and a reassuring air of competence. "Sir?"

"You got your men out when others would have failed," Colonel McIntyre said, without preamble. "General Taggard's report made it clear that you helped beat off the first attackers too."

"Yes, sir," Derek said. He had the feeling he was in trouble, but for what? "I had no choice."

"Quite," Colonel McIntyre said. "You are promoted to lieutenant, Frazier. Normally, we wouldn't promote you so quickly, but…these times are far from normal. I can't guarantee the rank will stick, after the war ends, yet…you *will* be paid for it."

"Yes, sir," Derek said. It was hard to speak. "I…thank you, sir."

"You have command of the remainder of your detachment," Colonel McIntyre said. "And we have a little job for you."

Derek felt his heart sink. "Yes, sir.

CHAPTER TWENTY-THREE

Where there was strong leadership, the effects were mitigated. In theory, middle-rank worlds could feed themselves without importing food. In some places, disaster relief structures went to work and saved millions from starving to death. In others, it proved impossible to save more than a bare minimum.

—PROFESSOR LEO CAESIUS

Earthfall and its Aftermath

THERE WAS SOMETHING EERIE about the enemy town.

Haydn felt it as he patrolled the streets of Eddisford, rifle at the ready, yet…he found it hard to put his finger on it. Most of the local population was staying firmly off the streets, rather than loudly protesting the marines, throwing rocks or shooting at them. The streets were almost completely empty, the houses dark and silent. He swept his gaze from side to side as they walked past a pair of grounded aircars, the perfect site for an ambush—or an IED—if the citizens had been intent on fighting. But there was nothing.

You should be grateful, he told himself, sternly. *You've been in places where the locals were willing to die, if they could take you with them.*

His gaze alighted on a house, almost exactly the same as every other house. He shivered as he realised what bothered him about Eddisford. The entire town had been carefully planned, as neatly as if it had been laid out on a grid. It *had* been laid out on a grid. The houses and apartments were in one sector, the shops, businesses and factories were in another…it was perfect, with little hint of individuality. The houses were nice, he supposed, but…there was little variation between them. A particularly daring household had a handful of roses growing up their walls. Otherwise, they looked dull, boring and lifeless. He wondered, morbidly, what happened to people who dared step out of line.

He felt a flicker of pity for the locals as he kept walking. He'd been on a dozen worlds in his career, but none of them—even Earth—had been so *uniform*. The social pressure to conform had never been so intense. He remembered what he'd been told about the surveillance system and shuddered in disgust. The locals could never take their privacy for granted. Everything they did was recorded, somewhere. Haydn was used to a lack of privacy, but he'd volunteered for it when he'd joined the corps. The locals had grown up in goldfish bowls.

A pair of young men caught his eye, hurrying down the street. They seemed to flinch when they saw the marines, torn between the urge to keep going and the urge to turn and run for their lives. Haydn eyed him for a moment, wondering if they'd do anything stupid. Young men were almost always the footsoldiers, when an insurgency got going. Their leaders kept to the shadows and sent the young fools out to die. But these men didn't look to have the guts to fight, even if victory was certain. They turned and scurried away with their tails between their legs.

"They've been beaten down, sir," Mayberry said. "They're going to have problems if we can't get the power back on."

Haydn nodded, shortly. The defenders had shut down the local power grid before withdrawing from the town, leaving the civilians in the shit. It had been getting hotter, apparently, *before* the infrastructure had started to shut down. It wouldn't be long before the effects *really* started to sink in. The locals would starve when their food started to go bad.

Which will be unpleasant, unless we can get the power back online or start bringing in food from outside, Hayden thought. The locals might have been beaten into submission, but that wouldn't last if they started to starve. They'd try to flee the town or take food from the marines or even start eating each other. *We might have to divert shipping to ration bars.*

He gritted his teeth as they reached the end of the residency section and crossed the road into the factory section. It was as dark and cold as the rest of the town, although a handful of technical specialists from the landing force were crawling through the buildings, trying to figure out what they'd been doing. Haydn wondered, wryly, if they'd be smart enough to scoop up a handful of locals and *ask*. It wouldn't be the first time the analysts had overlooked the obvious answer in a bid to prove how smart they were. General Anderson would not be pleased if they wasted time. He smiled at the thought, then sobered. The factories were big gloomy buildings, casting long shadows over the platoon. Anything could be hidden within the darkness...

"We can probably get the factories back online pretty quickly," Mayberry said. "That'll help offset the demand for supplies."

"Perhaps," Haydn agreed. He'd seen the projections. The landing force had expended over sixty percent of its ammunition and supplies in just over a day. Thankfully, the locals hadn't mounted an immediate counterattack. They might have been outmatched by the invaders, but that wouldn't have mattered if the invaders had run out of ammunition. "We'd have to trust the locals to man the factories."

He kept the rest of his thoughts to himself as they crossed another big road, then marched towards the CP. General Anderson and his staff had commandeered a school and turned it into a base, much to the delight of the local schoolchildren. They wouldn't be returning to lessons until the war was over, one way or the other. Haydn's lips twitched at the thought. If their schooling had been anything like his, the kids were probably praying for a missile strike…unaware, like he would have been, that a missile strike would devastate the town and kill most of the locals. He walked past a pair of air-defence units, their laser cannons ready to shoot down any missiles or shells headed in their direction, and stopped by the checkpoint.

"Take the platoon to the barracks," he ordered Mayberry. "I'll join you there once the general has finished with me."

"Good luck, sir." Mayberry saluted, then turned away. "This way, you lot."

Haydn smiled as he hurried into the school. He shouldn't have been on patrol at all, but if there was one thing he'd learnt in *years* of service it was the importance of gaining and maintaining a sense of the local environment. He'd seen too many officers misled by inaccurate maps or overly-optimistic reports to want to fall into the same trap himself. Besides, he needed to keep his skills sharp. There was no way to know when he'd find himself back in the midst of the action.

The school itself was just as uniform as the rest of the town. He felt a shiver running down his spine as he saw dozens of paintings pinned to the walls, none showing any flair or imagination. The classrooms looked designed for teenagers, but…he shook his head in dismay. Any trouble causers or rabble-rousers would probably have been expelled long ago, if they hadn't been beaten down by the system. A photo on the wall showed students in matching uniforms, matching hairstyles, matching everything. There was no individuality at all.

It could have been worse, he thought. He'd heard enough horror stories about schooling on Earth to know he never wanted to send his kids there. *But it could be better too.*

The command post itself had been set up in the middle of a large classroom. Haydn hid his amusement as he saw staff officers sitting at desks, working on portable terminals or subvocalising into microphones. It looked funny, more like a corporate office than a military base, but he knew staff work was important. Someone had pinned a large map of the surrounding area to the wall and covered it in notations; black for the marines, red for enemy forces. A defence line was taking shape to the west, Haydn noted.

The enemy would be digging trenches, siting heavy weapons and planning a counteroffensive. The marines would have to punch through the enemy lines before it was too late.

General Anderson himself stood in front of a table, stroking his chin and making a show of studying a map. Haydn had no idea why he bothered. There were no reporters or bureaucrats to impress, not here. Every last member of the invasion force was a marine or an auxiliary. They *knew* the score. They wouldn't be impressed by someone pretending to study a map. But...he shrugged. Good leadership was sometimes a matter of pretending you were calm, even if you wanted to panic. Panic was infectious.

"General." Haydn saluted. "You wanted to see me after the patrol?"

"Yes," Anderson said. He didn't look up. "What's your impression of the locals?"

"Unlikely to trouble us, now," Haydn said. "That will change if they start to starve."

"True." Anderson glanced at him. "Is your company ready for redeployment?"

"Yes, sir." Haydn didn't have to look at his terminal or log into the command network to know the answer. The platoons that hadn't gone out on patrol had rearmed as soon as they reached the base. "We can move at your command."

"Good." Anderson tapped the map. "This is what we're going to do..."

• • •

If there was one lesson that had been hammered into Rachel's head, time and time again, it was that first impressions could be misleading. Someone who looked deadly might be nothing more than a poser, someone who looked harmless might be waiting for her to drop her guard, someone who looked useless might be quite useful indeed if approached properly. Her very *career* relied on people looking at her and not taking her seriously. And yet, the more she looked at the woman in the chair, the more she disliked her. It wasn't something she could put into words. It was just an impression that refused to go away.

She scowled as she studied the woman, who was clearly terrified and just as clearly trying to hide it. She was in her late forties, according to the file, but looked older. Her gray hair was in a tight bun, giving her a severe appearance that probably terrified the children, her gimlet eyes dared anyone to challenge her power. Rachel felt a flicker of disgust, followed by an urge to reach out and crush the woman's neck. She knew what the woman had done. It was hard to convince herself that the captive deserved mercy.

"You spied on the entire town," she said, keeping her voice calm. "And when someone did something wrong, you reported them."

The woman—Hannah Weston, according to her file—put a stern expression on her face. "I was merely doing my job..."

"Spying on everyone?" Rachel raised her eyebrows. "What kind of job is that?"

Hannah couldn't quite meet her eyes. "My job."

"Tell me something," Rachel said. "If we handed you over to the townspeople, what do you think they'd do to you?"

"... I was just doing my duty," Hannah said, unconvincingly. "I'm sure they'd understand."

"Really?" Rachel allowed herself a smirk. "I rather doubt that, you know? Should we put it to the test?"

Hannah flinched. Rachel didn't blame her. The townspeople had *known* she monitored every aspect of their lives. No one, no matter how obsessive, could see everything...but it hardly mattered. If someone caught Hannah's eye, or did something that triggered a monitoring program, she could parse through the records until she had a complete picture of what her subject had done. The very thought made Rachel queasy. Earlier generations of busybodies had never had such complete insight into people's lives.

"And you're not the worst," she said. She picked up a datapad, silently wishing she was somewhere—anywhere—else. "Did you know about Chandler?"

"Chandler?" Hannah sounded confused, as if she scented the trap without quite understanding it. "What do you mean?"

"This is his private collection of images and video recordings." Rachel held up the datapad so Hannah could see it, then started to flick through the files. "Stop me when you get to the one who looks eighteen."

Hannah retched. "No…"

"Yes." Rachel glanced at a picture. It was hard not to retch herself. She'd seen horrors, but…this was different. "I'd say this one looks *eight*, not *eighteen*. Or do you want to argue otherwise?"

"No." Hannah looked very pale. "I…I didn't know…"

"Who watches the watchers?" Rachel met her eyes. "Didn't you *notice* he was abusing your system? That he was spying on *children*? That he was…"

She shook her head, unwilling to continue. "Chandler will be handed over to the townspeople for trial, when this war is finished. You…? You have a choice. You can cooperate completely, in which case we'll ship you elsewhere when the war is over, or you can join Chandler in the dock. Somehow, I don't think they'll find you innocent."

"I was only doing my job," Hannah protested. "I…"

"An excellent excuse," Rachel said, dryly. "What's the old joke? How lucky for you that your job is also your hobby? Except…you have to answer for your crimes. And I don't think your victims will be very forgiving."

She watched the older woman, refusing to feel even a twinge of pity. Hannah had spied on the entire town, spied on them and used what she'd learnt to keep them in line. And she'd either overlooked Chandler or turned a blind eye to his activities. The system was tailor-made for abuse and… somehow, it had never occurred to her to keep an eye on the people who might abuse it. Or…Chandler had known where the blind spots were. He'd certainly managed to hide his activities from his supervisor.

And he won't be getting out of this alive, Rachel vowed, silently. If there was any crime worse than abusing children, even if the children didn't *know* they were being abused…she shook her head. There was *no* worse crime. She would sooner have forgiven a genocidal dictator than a child molester. *I'll see to it personally.*

Hannah swallowed, hard. "What do you want me to do?"

"It's very simple," Rachel said. She turned off the datapad and put it on her belt. "I have questions. My friends outside have questions. You're going to answer them. And if we think you're lying, we'll throw you to the mob. Do you understand me?"

"Yes," Hannah managed. She looked broken. "I understand."

"Good." Rachel met her eyes, silently daring the older woman to lie. "First question..."

She supposed she shouldn't have been surprised to discover, she reflected an hour later, that Hannah knew a *lot* about Hameau. She'd spent a good third of her time playing politics, trying to convince her superiors that she should be promoted to a higher-ranking position before she reached mandatory retirement age. She knew who was in command of the planet, she knew who was in his cabinet...she knew a great deal about life in Haverford, the capital city. She'd even *been* there. She knew little about the planetary military, or what might be waiting for the marines between Eddisford and Haverford, but she knew enough to confuse her audience. Why had the locals been running a full-scale planetary draft when there was no one to fight?

"You look ghastly," Phelps said, when Rachel left the interrogation chamber. He was standing outside, watching through the monitors. "Did she put up a fight?"

"No." Rachel rubbed her scalp. It itched. She felt unclean. "It would have been better if she *had*."

"I imagine clobbering her a few times would have made you feel better, even if it *is* against regulations," Phelps agreed. He fell into step beside her as they walked down the corridor. "Did she say anything useful?"

"Too much." Rachel understood the urge to dominate, however it was expressed, but...busybodies had always annoyed her. What sort of person took pleasure in micromanaging someone else's life? Or in harassing them over the smallest little detail? She understood people who wanted power, but…somehow, she'd always found sanctimony more irritating than a simple lust for power. "What sort of place *is* this?"

"It could be worse," Phelps said. "Remember Gilead? Or Medina? Or even Draka?"

"It's no consolation," Rachel said, dryly. "Even on Draka, the locals had *some* freedoms. Here they have none. They gave up their liberty for a little security and they didn't even get *that*."

"It's easy to make those kinds of judgements when you're not *there*," Phelps commented, after a moment. "I was born on Earth. And if I'd been offered a chance to live here, as a kid, I would have taken it."

"Even with…" Rachel tapped the datapad at her belt. "You'd still live here?"

"Now? No." Phelps shook his head. "But back then…yes? I'm ashamed to admit it, but I would have given up my privacy to live here. Because it's still better than Earth."

"Sickening," Rachel said. "I find it hard to believe."

"Earth." Phelps laughed, humourlessly. "The wretched hive of scum and villainy that makes all other wretched hives of scum and villainy look like wonderful places."

"Hah," Rachel said. She knew it was true. "What about Han?"

"Grab some sleep," Phelps ordered, ignoring her question. "We'll be off again soon. The General has a few ideas for how we might be employed on the battlefield…"

"Unless we put together a plan to go to Haverford instead," Rachel said. She felt tired, too tired to sleep. Her head ached. "It might be possible, if… *she*…cooperates."

"We'll see," Phelps said. "But, for the moment, grab some sleep."

CHAPTER TWENTY-FOUR

Indeed, in some places, the economic shockwave took down entire governments. Police and military forces fragmented, individuals looking to protect their families and friends instead of upholding the law. The result was absolute chaos. Riots tore through the streets, people fighting desperately for scraps of food that—a few short weeks ago—they would have scorned.

—PROFESSOR LEO CAESIUS

Earthfall and its Aftermath

THE ENEMY FREIGHTER CAME IN FAT AND HAPPY.

Kerri watched, dispassionately, as the freighter glided towards her position. She'd had ample time for her crew to plot an intercept course, ample time to put her ship in the perfect position to catch the freighter before she could turn and run if someone on the planet managed to transmit a warning or if her commander smelled a rat. The ship probably didn't have military-grade sensors or communications gear, but the missing orbital defences and the jamming field surrounding the planet *should* have alerted anyone that *something* was wrong. But it hardly mattered. The freighter came into engagement range with nary a hint that her crew was having second thoughts.

"Drop the stealth," she ordered, curtly. The freighter couldn't avoid engagement, not now. Even if she turned and fled, *Havoc* could catch up with her well before she crossed the Phase Limit. The only real danger was that she might be a Q-Ship, her hull crammed with weapons to blow away anyone who stumbled into point-blank range, but Kerri had no intention of going so close. "Susan, transmit the surrender demand."

"Aye, Captain," Susan said.

Kerri watched, wondering what decision the freighter CO would make. His only rational choice was to surrender, but the galaxy was full of people who were far from rational. A freighter CO might fear losing his ship, his career or even his *life* if he surrendered, if his corprat superiors thought he'd done it deliberately. The galaxy was *also* full of REMFs who spent their days making life miserable for those who made mistakes with their paperwork in the hopes it would justify their salaries. She'd heard enough stories of starship crews deserting, taking their starships with them, to make her hope that most of those corprat REMFs were realising that their ships were never coming home.

The freighter shut down her drives. Kerri breathed a sigh of relief.

"Launch the assault shuttle," she ordered. "And prepare to dispatch a tech team."

She leaned back in her chair and waited as the assault shuttle sped towards the freighter. If she was armed, she'd never have a better chance to harm the marine corps. A single plasma pulse would turn the shuttle into an expanding ball of fire. Kerri would blow the freighter into dust, a second later, but it would be too late to save eleven marines from certain death. Eleven *irreplaceable* marines. The Slaughterhouse was gone. God alone knew how long it would take to set up a replacement.

The shuttle docked, without incident. Kerri breathed a sigh of relief, then listened to the channel as the marines hurried through the giant ship. Bulk freighters were huge, but their crew quarters—unsurprisingly—were small. The marines wouldn't need long to secure the bridge, the engineering section and verify that the cargo holds were sealed. Unless...

Her console bleeped. "Captain, this is Lieutenant Park," a grim voice said. "This ship was rigged to carry passengers. We've got upwards of twenty thousand souls crammed into the hold."

Kerri blinked. Twenty *thousand*? It was possible, theoretically, but they would have to cram people in like sardines. The life support pods would have to be pushed right to the limit. She shuddered at the thought. Who *were* they? And why were they on the ship?

"Get a manifest," she ordered. The freighter would have to be unloaded as soon as possible. The life support systems would probably be close to collapse. "And get some answers from the captain. I want to know who the passengers are and why they're on the ship."

"Aye, Captain," Park said. "We'll get right on it."

Kerri keyed her console, sending an update to the system command net and forwarding the precise question of what to do with the newcomers to General Anderson. Some of them could be transferred to the MEUs, if necessary, but it would be a little awkward if they had to pull the landing force back into space. Others...she frowned. They *could* be moved down to the occupied zone, but feeding them would be a problem. They'd have to eat ration bars, MREs and slop until the local farms could be put back into production. The marines on the ground would have riots on their hands.

"Captain," Susan said. "Lieutenant Park is escorting Captain Grissom back to the ship."

"Very good." Kerri stood. "Have him brought to my ready room when he arrives."

Captain Grissom turned out to be surprisingly old and grizzled for a corprat, although Kerri supposed that standards had been slipping badly even *before* Earthfall. She rather suspected he had some strong connections *somewhere*, as worrying about appearance over reality was practically universal amongst REMFs. The starship could be on the verge of total drive failure, she thought, and the corprats would be trying to slap on a new coat of paint.

"Captain," he said, when he saw her. "What is the meaning of this?"

"We have taken control of this system," Kerri said, curtly. "Who are the people on your ship, and why are they there?"

Grissom studied her for a long moment. "I was ordered to collect them from Hangchow and bring them here. The local authorities wanted to be rid of them, I believe. We stepped in to take them."

"The majority of them are women and children," Lieutenant Park put in. "Only ten percent of them are men."

"That's who the locals let us take," Grissom said. "My superiors accepted it. I believe they intended to continue negotiating for the remainder."

Kerri frowned. "And who *are* your superiors?"

"Interstellar Transport and Logistics, a fully-owned subsidy of the Onge Corporation," Grissom said. "Believe me, I've worked for worse people."

"Really?" Kerri thought he was probably right. "My intelligence staff have some questions for you. Answer them and...we will take it into account when we consider your future."

"My future," Grissom repeated. "What the hell are you doing here?"

"Taking the system," Kerri said. She had the odd feeling she was missing something. But what? "For what it's worth, I don't believe we'll hang on to you."

"No," Grissom agreed. "But you'll hang on to my ship."

Kerri didn't bother to deny it. He wouldn't have believed her.

"Take him to the brig," she ordered. "The intelligence staff can talk to him there."

"Aye, Captain," Lieutenant Park said.

Kerri keyed her wristcom as the marine escorted his captive out the hatch. "Tomas? Put a prize crew on the freighter and tell them to check the life support thoroughly, then have her follow us back to the planet."

"Aye, Captain."

"Good," Kerri said. "And update General Anderson on the situation."

She sat back in her chair and keyed her terminal, bringing up the report from the boarding party. Captain Grissom hadn't kept a good manifest, not particularly to her surprise. If he'd been transporting people who'd been kicked out by the planetary government, he probably hadn't had time to collect names and faces for the record books. She gritted her teeth at the thought. Some REMF was probably going to complain about *that*. She wondered if the locals would fit in on the planet below, then decided it didn't matter. The planetary government had every reason to think it could keep the newcomers under control.

Or it did, before we invaded, Kerri thought. *Now, the refugees are our problem.*

• • •

Her intercom bleeped. "Captain, this is Terrace," a voice said. "The life support systems on the freighter *should* hold for another few days, but I wouldn't push them much further. We can't do more than basic maintenance without either shutting the system down completely or putting too much strain on the sections we leave running. I'd suggest setting up inflatable tents on the moon if the refugees can't be dropped on the planet."

"Understood," Kerri said. "We'll set the tents up when we get back to orbit."

She closed the connection, then rubbed her eyes. It spoke well of the locals, she supposed, that they'd agreed to take refugees, although she wasn't blind to the demographics. Women and children were *always* easier to integrate than military-age males. She wouldn't be surprised to hear that the men had been rerouted somewhere else, if they hadn't mysteriously gone missing in transit. And if they caused trouble...she shook her head. They probably wouldn't. They'd be too grateful for being rescued from detention camps—and probable ethnic cleansing—to cause trouble.

Havoc shuddered as she reversed course and headed towards the planet. Kerri smiled, then checked the in-system display. She'd dispatched a handful of ships to seize the cloudscoops and a couple of orbital facilities, but she'd left the remainder strictly alone. They'd fall into her hands once the fighting on the ground was decided. She would have ignored the cloudscoops if she hadn't needed to secure a source of fuel for the invasion force. The marine replenishment ships were already starting to run short of raw materials.

And the local miners will need some encouragement to sell to us before the matter is decided on the ground, she thought. *It's never easy to time the exact moment one should switch sides.*

"Captain." The intercom bleeped, again. "I have General Anderson on the line for you."

"Thank you, Susan," Kerri said. "Put him through, please."

She straightened as General Anderson's image appeared in front of her. "General."

"Captain," General Anderson said. "I hear you've had some excitement."

"Unfortunately not, sir," Kerri said. "I was on duty."

General Anderson chuckled at the old—and weak—joke, then sobered. "What do you make of it?"

"It's odd, sir," Kerri said. "I'd say the locals were trying to boost their population."

"And Hangchow is trying to reduce theirs," General Anderson added. "Interesting. And really quite worrying."

He shrugged. "And it isn't our problem at the moment. Right now, we have a war to win."

"Yes, sir." Kerri met his eyes, evenly. "There's still no way we can provide fire support."

"Unfortunately so." General Anderson grimaced. "We got too used to it, didn't we?"

"Yes, sir." Kerri couldn't disagree. "But as long as those PDCs are active, we cannot provide fire support."

General Anderson looked down, at something outside the pickup's range. "Right now, the enemy appears to be trying to form a fairly strong defensive line," he said. "We've had a number of tiny skirmishes over the last few hours, but...no concentrated attempt to push us out or interfere with our supply chain. Maybe we caught them by surprise, Captain. They should still be doing *more*."

"They're probably up to something," Kerri said. "Did they have any contingency plans for invasion?"

"We're not sure," General Anderson said. "But we won't catch them by surprise again."

"No," Kerri agreed. "What do you intend to do?"

"Launch a full-scale offensive, aimed up towards Haverford," General Anderson said. He smiled, humourlessly. "If we can force them to surrender, we can take the planet with most of the defences intact. If not, we'll have to take out enough of the PDCs to clear space for you and your ships to operate."

"Which would give them room to devastate the orbital industries," Kerri finished. "Was there no response to your demand for surrender?"

"None." General Anderson looked perturbed. "You'd think corprats would start cutting deals by now."

Kerri nodded, slowly. The planetary government had something to bargain with, now. That wouldn't last. If the marines had to fight their way to Haverford, taking out a number of PDCs in the process, the planetary government would have *nothing* it could use as a bargaining chip. It might even lose all power well before the capital city actually fell. Kerri had expected them to open communications, to *try* to come to a deal. But instead...they said nothing. It was odd.

"That battlecruiser is still out there somewhere," she said. "And Captain Grissom implied there were more ships and corprats out there too."

"Yeah." General Anderson scowled. "Get what you can out of Grissom. And his crew. And his datacores. *Someone* will talk."

"Yes, sir." Kerri had no doubt of it. "And then...what?"

"It depends on what they have to say," General Anderson said. "Maybe we caught them by surprise. Maybe they're still stunned. But I don't like counting on my enemy doing something stupid. I think they're up to something."

"Maybe they're giving you time to land your entire force before they kill it," Kerri said. "If they can't go after the MEUs, they can go after the shuttles..."

"But they're not," General Anderson said. "They haven't made any attempt to impede our shuttles. Or our resupply efforts."

Kerri frowned. Basic military doctrine called for cutting an attacker's supply lines as quickly as possible. Even a handful of shuttles going down would put a serious crimp in operations, particularly given the tempo of modern war. The marines were dependent on imported supplies and if they ran out, the invasion was doomed.

And a single nuclear-tipped warhead would wipe out most of the lodgement, she thought, coldly. *But they'd have to be insane to use such weapons on a planetary surface.*

"I think the final call is in your hands, General," she said, giving him a sweet—and completely fake—smile. "My ships and I will do whatever we can to support you..."

"Thanks," General Anderson said, with equal insincerity. "Fortune *does* favour the bold."

"And if we can keep them away from our supply lines, we can bury them," Kerri added. "Good luck."

"And to you," General Anderson said. "See you on the flip side."

• • •

The night was quiet, suspiciously quiet.

Rachel kept her enhanced sensors jacked up as the team walked through the outer edge of the forward line, the tripwire the marines had established to warn them of a major counterattack, and strode bravely into enemy territory. She could detect faint hints of animal life all around her, from nocturnal birds to rodents and insects within the undergrowth, but most seemed determined to remain in hiding. If there were any humans around, they were in hiding too. She couldn't even hear gunshots in the distance.

She kept her thoughts to herself as they kept walking, heading alongside the road to the nearest major town. The enemy had set up a base there, according to the drones, although *they* hadn't lasted very long once the enemy had gone on alert. Rachel was morbidly unsurprised to hear that the fog of war had draped itself over the battlefield. The planetary army was nowhere near as capable or experienced as the marines, but they'd trained hard and they had access to modern equipment. The drones hadn't stood a chance once they'd started transmitting.

Phelps held up a hand, an hour later. The team froze, remaining very still. They were barely visible within the gloom, but...she knew, all too well, just how easy it would be for the Mark-I eyeball to spot them if they fucked up. The human eye was attracted to motion, even motion within the shadows. And, if the enemy commanders had any sense, they would have issued orders for the sentries to sound the alert if they had the merest *hint* there was anyone out there. Better to wake the garrison for nothing than have their throats slit while they slept.

Her eyes probed the darkness. A line of makeshift defences, trenches and barricades, hastily thrown together. Not very tough, by her standards, but they'd only had a couple of days to get their defences emplaced. The guards looked alert, sweeping the ground constantly for threats. Beyond them, she could see a handful of armoured vehicles and aircars. They looked still and unmoving, but that didn't make them harmless. A skilled crew could get a tank underway in seconds.

"This way," Phelps hissed. "We need to be on the other side of town."

Rachel nodded, staying low as they circumvented the town. It was larger than Eddisford, but...the lights they'd seen, the last time they'd passed this way, were gone. The defenders had turned off the power, probably to keep news from spreading from place to place. She wondered just what they'd told the locals, when the military had taken over the town. Perhaps they hadn't bothered to tell them anything. They were just...civilians. They hadn't even tried to *evacuate* the local population.

They probably don't want the locals jamming up the roads, she thought. She knew how badly roads could be impeded by fleeing citizens. *And they can't rely on their troops firing on unarmed civilians if the shit hits the fan.*

She put the thought aside as they reached the other side of the town. The defences were weaker, but the terrain was worse. It wouldn't slow the riflemen, she was sure, but it would make life harder for the tanks and APCs. She considered a handful of possible options, then shrugged. It was someone else's problem right now. She had concerns of her own.

"And now we wait," Phelps said, as they slipped back into the undergrowth. "H-Hour is at 0700."

"Dawn," Perkins muttered. He sat down, resting his rifle on his lap. "Don't you think they'll know it?"

"Probably," Phelps said. "But knowing the attack is coming and being ready for it are two separate things."

"True," Rachel agreed. "And we'll find out in five hours."

CHAPTER TWENTY-FIVE

Unsurprisingly, class warfare played a major role in the chaos. The rich had always been envied, particularly in the final years before Earthfall. Now, the rich had no money to pay their hired guards. Some managed to flee into space, or take up residence in space platforms that were effectively self-supporting; others, less paranoid about the future, were hunted down by the mob.

—PROFESSOR LEO CAESIUS

Earthfall and its Aftermath

"ARE WE SUPPOSED TO GENUFLECT to you now," Loomis asked, "or will a simple bow and scrape do?"

"Right now, I'd be happy with you keeping your mouth shut," Derek said. He'd never really expected to be promoted, much less placed in a position of power over his former equals. It felt odd to be giving orders, real orders, to Loomis in the knowledge his superiors would back him if push came to shove. "They're coming."

He glanced up at the lightening sky, then back along the road. There was no sign of the enemy, but he was morbidly certain they were coming. A handful of enemy positions were under observation, from what little he'd garnered through the grapevine; the observers had reported the enemy troops gearing up for operations shortly before going off the air. He heard a faint hum in the air and glanced up, trying to spot the drone even though he knew it was futile. The last few hours had included a crash course in military matters that, previously, had been deemed none of his concern. They'd included a warning that drones flew so high they couldn't be spotted by the naked eye.

Loomis caught his eye. "How long do you think it'll be before they get here?"

Derek shrugged. How the hell was *he* supposed to know? It wasn't like the enemy commander had sent him a personal message, promising to meet him at high noon like two gunfighters from an old storybook. The enemy would be on him when they were on him and then...Derek knew he'd be wishing the enemy had stayed far, far away. He could die today, like so many others. He could die or...

He shivered, suddenly. His parents, and his sisters, were behind the lines. He'd asked the colonel if something—anything—could be done for them, but the colonel hadn't been too interested. The civilians weren't important, as far as he was concerned. The only thing that mattered was keeping the enemy from breaking out of their lodgement and driving on Haverford. Derek hadn't liked that argument, but he'd known better than to argue. A handful of men had already been shot for insubordination and desertion.

Something *flickered* in the sky. A moment later, he heard the dull booming sound of artillery fire. The enemy offensive had begun. He glanced back, just in time to see flashes of light and billowing plumes of smoke to the east. There didn't seem to be anyone shooting back, as far as he could tell. He felt his heart sink. The enemy would be on them in seconds if their movements weren't being impeded.

Loomis cleared his throat. "All of a sudden, I'm feeling very exposed out here."

"Me too," Derek said. An officer wasn't supposed to confess weakness, was he? Perhaps that was taught at Officer Training School. *He* felt terrified. "And they're coming."

His heart started to race as he saw the enemy hovertanks whooshing along the road. He'd seen tanks before, tracked tanks and hovertanks, but these were a different kettle of fish. Their gun barrels moved constantly, tracking threats only they could see; their escorting infantry moved in their wake, allowing the tanks to take the lead. Derek wondered if the enemy commander was intent on pushing his lines as far forward as possible before he encountered resistance. He'd been taught not to let the tanks get too far ahead of the infantry.

"Target the tanks," he ordered. They'd been *promised* their single-shot antitank weapons would be effective, if they had a chance to hit their targets. "Fire on my command."

The seconds ticked away as the tanks moved closer. Their infantry escorts were catching up...Derek gritted his teeth. They *had* to know they were nearing the perfect place for an ambush, they had to know...

"Fire," he snapped.

Four antitank missiles flew towards their targets. One ploughed itself into the ground and exploded harmlessly, some distance from the tank; the remainder slammed into their targets with terrifying force. One tank was lucky enough to take the blow on its frontal armour, leaving it scarred but effectively undamaged; the other two exploded into colossal fireballs. Derek stared, heedless of the danger as the remaining tanks brought their weapons to bear on him. Loomis grabbed his arm and yanked him down, a second before machine gun bullets slashed through the trees. Branches and sawdust crashed down all around them. Derek felt the insane urge to curl up in a ball and shake helplessly, but instead forced himself to stumble up and start running. They'd been warned not to make a stand. It would only get them killed.

An explosion shook the ground, far too close for comfort. He glanced back, just in time to see a fireball rising from where they'd been. A shell?

A grenade? A missile? It didn't matter. They'd escaped. The enemy would know it too, if they bothered to check. There were no bodies there, nothing to suggest they'd been killed. Derek turned, put his head down and ran for his life. They had to get back to the town before it was too late. If they didn't get back...

Loomis punched his arm. "We got the bastards!"

"Two of the bastards," Derek agreed. The colonel would be pleased. "Now, move it!"

• • •

Haydn bit down a curse as the lead platoon swept the enemy position, the *former* enemy position. The tank commander had been a fool, utterly convinced of his unit's invincibility, utterly convinced...elsewhere, perhaps, he would have been right. But here, the enemy had modern weapons. Two tanks were now burning piles of debris, a third damaged even if still in fighting trim...and, to cap it all, the enemy antitank team had escaped unharmed. They'd taken a standard tactic, a tactic the dead commander should have known to expect, and made it work.

And if you hadn't died in your tank, Haydn thought savagely, *I would have strangled you myself.*

He put the thought aside as he assumed tactical command and started to bark orders. General Anderson wanted the enemy town, a pleasant little hellhole called Alphan, enveloped as quickly as possible...but not, Haydn assumed, at the cost of half his force. The riflemen would have to go forward, ready to trip any further antitank positions before they got into firing range. It wasn't much, but it would have to do.

"Get the microdrones in the air," he snapped. "Call down fire on any suspicious targets."

A flight of Raptors hummed overhead, searching out targets on the ground. Haydn watched them go, noting how the pilots constantly kept their craft moving in evasive patterns, surrounded by decoys. They knew there might be HVM teams hidden in the undergrowth...Haydn wondered, suddenly, if there was something to be gained by knocking down the forest. The land beyond Alphan was surprisingly level, at least until they reached the mountains...he dismissed the thought. They had to win the engagement first.

He and his men followed the tanks as they moved east, watching for further ambushes. A couple revealed themselves too soon, only to be shot down before they could repeat their early success. The marines took prisoners, zipcuffed their hands behind their backs and left them to be collected by the follow-on forces. Haydn found it hard to care if the prisoners managed to escape. They couldn't do much harm without their weapons, not immediately.

The sound of firing grew louder as they pushed out of the forest, down towards the town itself. Alphan looked nicer than he'd expected, from the recon reports, although it hardly mattered. The barricades in front of them wouldn't slow the tanks for long, but they'd slow them enough...Haydn cursed under his breath. They'd have to clear the nearby houses first, just to make sure the tanks couldn't come under fire. And there were civilians in the area too.

He gritted his teeth. This wasn't going to be pleasant.

"Target the barricades," he ordered. They didn't have time to lay siege to the city. "Fire on my command."

"Aye, sir."

• • •

General Anderson surveyed the steadily-updating map with a profound feeling of dissatisfaction. The Marine Corps had invested billions of credits and hundreds of years of experience in battlespace management systems, a buzzword that boiled down to clearing the fog of war as much as possible, but—faced with an enemy that fought on nearly even terms, the fog of war remained as prevalent as ever. Drones got shot down, communications channels got disrupted or jammed...it was frustrating, in more ways than he cared to admit. The outcome of the battle rested in the hands of subordinates who couldn't see the overall picture…

He felt his scowl deepen as the pattern started to emerge. The enemy weren't making a stand. They weren't lining up their troops to be blasted down, nor were they mounting suicide attacks that got hundreds of their own people killed for a handful of marines. Instead, they were mounting spoiling attacks and brief ambushes that were—briefly, so briefly—slowing his troops. Individually, none of them were a problem. Collectively, they were a major headache. The advance was slowing down.

"General, the lead elements are approaching Alphan," Lieutenant Hammond reported. "They're requesting fire support."

"Give them whatever they need," Anderson ordered. He disliked the idea of civilians being killed in the crossfire—the locals had clamped down hard on civilians who wanted to flee their homes—but there was no choice. He didn't have time to waste. "And repeat our demand for the enemy to surrender."

"Aye, sir."

Anderson glanced around the chamber, then turned back to the old-fashioned paper map. A computer display would have been so much better, but they came with their own problems. Instead…he shrugged as another set of lines were drawn. The enemy defence line was taking a pounding. Forward reports made it clear that it was only a matter of time before Alphan itself fell to his forces. And then there would be a clear route to Bouchon.

He wasn't looking forward to *that* at all.

"Tell the rear elements to increase speed," he ordered, curtly. There would be time to sweep the rear and pick up prisoners later. Right now, all that mattered was smashing the enemy resistance. "We have *got* to take that town!"

• • •

Derek kept his head low as he led the platoon through the defences and into Alphan. They hadn't lost anyone during the march back to the town itself, but it had been a very close thing indeed. A shell had landed far too close, badly injuring two of his men. Cold logic had insisted he leave the wounded behind, but he'd refused to listen. Instead, they'd carried the wounded back to the town.

The sound of shooting grew louder as the enemy pressed towards the town. Derek heard bullets zinging through the air, far too close for comfort. There was no one in the streets, not out in the open. Flames and smoke drifted up from the distant yards, where enemy shells had crashed down… seemingly at random. The medics took the wounded as soon as they saw them, leaving Derek and his platoon at a loose end. It was hard to tell who was in charge. The defenders seemed to be completely on their own.

He caught a passing staff officer and yanked his arm. "Where's Colonel Macintyre?"

"In the command post," the officer said, pulling his arm free. His eyes were wide and staring. "It's over there!"

Derek blinked as the officer waved vaguely into the distance, then hurried away. *That* was odd. The officer had outranked him, hadn't he? And yet, he'd just run away instead of issuing orders or chewing him out or doing…anything.

"That was a captain," Loomis said, bemused. "What was *wrong* with him?"

"Shellshock, perhaps," Derek said. He'd heard that combat did odd things to people, although the briefers hadn't gone into details. They'd spent more time insisting it was impossible to fake shellshock than actually teaching the soldiers how to cope. "This way."

The scene seemed to grow more chaotic as they made their way further into the town. The streets were filled with people. Officers barked orders, never quite seeming to notice that they were constantly contradicting themselves. Soldiers ran around, carrying piles of rifles and boxes of grenades to the barricades; a pair of tanks inched their way to the front, their horns bleeping loudly whenever the crowds got in the way. A handful of civilians, their eyes wide with fear, were helping to carry supplies—and the wounded—all over the town. Derek caught sight of a girl who looked to be the same age as his sister and felt his heart skip a beat. She wasn't his, but…she *looked* like her.

Loomis had the same thought. "That's not Abby, is it?"

"No." Derek felt his cheeks heat as the girl looked at him. Up close, she didn't look *much* like his sister. He tried not to notice she was wearing a very tight shirt. His mother would have thrown a fit if his sister had dressed like *that* in public. "She's not."

"You could always ask her out," Loomis said. He wasn't trying to hide his stare. "She seems to be interested in you."

"Oh, fuck off." Derek rolled his eyes. "She's staring at me in horror."

"Ah, she's seen your face," Loomis said. The girl hurried off. "Poor bitch. You probably struck her blind."

"I say again my last," Derek said. What would happen to the girl, when the town was stormed? Caught in the crossfire and killed? Forced to flee? Captured by the enemy and…he didn't want to think about it. He didn't want to think about Abby either. "We're in trouble, aren't we?"

Loomis leaned close to whisper in his ear. "We don't have to stay here…*sir*."

Derek glanced at him. If they'd been alone, if they'd been the only ones involved, he might just have walked out of the town and left the defenders to do or die without him. It was hard to believe the surveillance system was still working. There were people pilfering from military supplies and civilians carrying weapons, for crying out loud! But he wasn't alone, not any longer. The men behind him were under his command. He couldn't leave them behind.

He shook his head, choosing to ignore Loomis's snide remark. If he wanted to go on his own…

Derek couldn't say it. Not out loud. But he wouldn't fault Loomis for leaving.

Colonel Macintyre was standing outside the tent, snapping orders to a pair of staff officers. A team of civilians and soldiers were folding up the tents, either packing them away or dumping them in a massive pile. Others were dropping computer terminals and other pieces of equipment on the pile. Derek felt his eyes narrow. What the hell were they doing? He'd been warned, in no uncertain terms, that missing or damaged equipment would come out of his salary. The record keeping was so good there was little hope of covering up a single spent shell casing. But now…

"Sir," he said, putting his doubts aside. "We destroyed two enemy tanks."

"And damaged a third," Loomis put in.

"Good, good." Colonel Macintyre looked harassed. "They're right on top of us. The town is no longer safe. We have orders to leave."

Derek heard a dull roar and turned, one hand dropping to the pistol at his belt. Behind him, the pile of tents and computer terminals had caught fire…no, it had been set alight. The flames spread rapidly, the heat beating against his skin. He saw a pair of soldiers grinning like loons, one of them holding an empty can of gasoline in his hands. The flames were already threatening to spread out of control.

"Sir," he protested. "The civilians…"

"Don't matter right now," Colonel Macintyre snapped. "Get your people together, Lieutenant. Bleed the attackers, then turn and run. We'll be making our stand at Bouchon."

Derek blinked. "But sir!"

"Those are your orders!" The colonel's voice rose, sharply. "Will you carry them out? Or do I have to find someone else who *will*?"

Derek found his voice. "No sir," he said, as the flames licked higher. The staff officers were forming up by the numbers, MPs pointing them towards the rear. "I'll carry them out."

"Good man." Colonel Macintyre clapped his shoulder. "I'll see you on the far side."

He turned and hurried off. Derek watched him go, unsure what had just happened. The staff officers were buggering off, leaving Derek and his men alone…no, not alone. There were hundreds of soldiers in the city. He took a breath, feeling torn between his duty and an overpowering urge to run.

The fires were spreading now, flames licking at the grass and threatening to set fire to the town hall. There was no one left to fight them.

"Come on," he ordered. One of his men seemed to have vanished. The remainder seemed ready to do their duty. He almost wished the rest had gone too. "We have work to do."

Behind him, the flames spread further.

CHAPTER TWENTY-SIX

They were not the only targets. The remnants of the imperial bureaucracy were particularly detested by the mob, not least because of how they treated people who applied for much-needed help. This was understandable, but dangerous. The bureaucrats were needed to help rebuild the local economies.

—PROFESSOR LEO CAESIUS

Earthfall and its Aftermath

"THE GUNS ARE OPENING FIRE, SIR," Mayberry said. "Impact in ten, nine..."

Haydn watched as the enemy barricade disintegrated in a single tearing explosion. It hadn't been a particularly *strong* barricade, the sort of thing that might be thrown up by a rebel faction in a tearing hurry, but he'd no intention of risking his men by clearing the barrier manually. Instead, he'd called down shellfire. He snapped out orders, directing his men into firing positions as the smoke rapidly cleared. A pair of enemy tanks appeared, spitting fire in all directions; a hail of plasma bolts punched through their armour, destroying both vehicles so quickly the crews had no time to bail. Haydn felt a stab of pity, mingled with contempt and hatred for their commanders. Those tanks hadn't been designed for urban warfare.

He barked orders, directing his men forward. They scrambled over the debris, firing at enemy targets when they presented themselves. The enemy seemed to be in retreat, but Haydn wasn't fooled. The enemy was smart enough to know they couldn't take the marines in open combat. Instead, they were trying to lead the marines into an environment where their advantages would be reduced, if not eliminated entirely. His eyes narrowed as he saw a handful of enemy soldiers running into a house, gun barrels clearly visible in the upper windows. The enemy hadn't had *long* to prepare—he'd fought his way through cities where every room had been turned into a death trap—but they'd still had enough time to make life very unpleasant. And there might be civilians in there…

The company split up into platoons as it pushed further into the town. Gunners directed missiles and shells into buildings that spat fire, explosions knocking them down or burning them out from the inside. Haydn kept his head down as he ran towards an enemy-held building, three men on his tail. He threw a grenade into the building, waited for the explosion and then charged inside. The four defenders were lying on the floor, dead. There might have been more than four. He couldn't tell. The damage was just too extensive. They searched the rest of the house—he thought it had been a family home, once upon a time—but found nothing. Whoever had lived in the house had moved out long ago.

Poor bastards, he thought, relieved the enemy hadn't thought to use human shields. The old rules were in abeyance now, but…he didn't *want* to kill civilians, not if it could be avoided. He understood the logic, he understood why ransoms weren't paid and human shields put at risk, yet it didn't make it any easier to bear. Cold logic told him the enemy was responsible for their deaths, but his heart told a different story. *I wonder what happened to them.*

The ground shook, violently. He stumbled out of the house, just in time to see another building collapse into rubble. The secondary elements had arrived and were moving forward, pushing into uncleared terrain. A flight of missiles soared overhead, coming down in the distance. He heard the explosions, but saw nothing in the rising clouds of smoke. It looked as if the entire town had caught fire.

Mayberry caught his attention. "This way, sir."

The company reformed, then resumed the advance. There seemed to be no rhyme or reason to the enemy fortifications, not now that they were inside the town. It was impossible to tell, from the outside, which buildings might be housing defenders and which had been left empty...he scowled as he saw a trio of defenders emerge from a cleared building, firing into the marine rear. That building had been cleared. He cursed as the platoon shot the soldiers, realising there was a tunnel underneath the building. The bastards had used the sewers to sneak up on the marines.

Clever bastards, he thought, grudgingly. *They have balls, I'll give them that much.*

Haydn kicked down another door and hurled a grenade into a small house, then charged inside as soon as the explosion shook the building to its core. There was no one inside, as far as he could tell. He felt a pang of guilt at smashing a wooden table and a bunch of chairs, two of them so small they were clearly for children. Something smashed in the distance and he jumped, hastily bringing his rifle to bear. There was nothing there... he realised, dully, that a painting had fallen from the wall. It had hit the ground and smashed. And yet, he could hear *something...*

He braced himself, then inched down the corridor. The house was bigger than he'd realised, bigger than the tiny boxes on Earth or the small apartments he'd rented during shore leave. A bedroom—he felt another pang as he realised it belonged to a child, probably a girl—another bedroom...the scuffling sound was growing louder. He held up his hand, warning the other two to keep back. General Anderson would chew him a new asshole for daring to put himself in danger when there were riflemen handy, but he was damned if he was leaving the young men to carry the burden themselves. Besides, he had to keep his skills sharp. Too many good officers let their skills atrophy and found themselves in trouble when they had to go back into the field.

Something moved, beside him. Haydn spun, too late. A man crashed into him, knocking him to the floor. Haydn pulled the trigger, the shot going wide in the confined space. He cursed his mistake a second later, then started to struggle with his attacker. The man was unskilled, but strong. And he was too close to Haydn, in the semi-darkness, for anyone to assist him. Haydn gritted his teeth, grabbed the knife from his belt and stabbed up. His attacker grunted in pain, blood pouring from his chest. Haydn wondered, as he pushed the man away, if he was hopped up on something. It was quite possible, although he had to admit it was unlikely. Drugged-up men tended to be utterly uncontrollable.

"Fuck," he said. His body armour was covered in blood, none of it his. He wished he'd been able to wear proper armour, but it was a hindrance in house-to-house fighting. "You got him?"

"I got him," Rifleman Harms said. He pushed a bandage against the attacker's chest. "He needs medical attention."

Haydn studied the man in the dim light. A young man, young and brave and foolish...he shook his head. The same could easily be said of *him*, when he'd been a young man. The poor bastard had done his duty, which was more than could be said of some of his superiors. The reports had made it clear that hundreds of people were fleeing the town and heading west...

"Get him to a medic," he ordered, shortly. He checked the rest of the house, then keyed his throatmike. "Report?"

"Pushing west, sir," Sergeant Mayberry said. "We're encountering a stronger line of defences, backed up by mortars."

"I'm on my way," Haydn said.

• • •

"We've been thrown into the sausage machine," Loomis muttered. "And they're about to make mincemeat of us."

"Be quiet," Derek hissed. "If someone hears you..."

He scowled. He'd been given a couple of dozen more men, a scratch force consisting of stragglers from other units that had either been largely wiped out or shattered under enemy fire. He didn't know *any* of them, save for the handful he'd brought from Eddisford. There was no way to know who could be trusted to keep his mouth shut or who might curry favour by reporting seditious talk to his superiors. And even if the *men* were completely trustworthy, who knew about the technology? Anyone could be bugged, anything could be spying on them for their superiors. There might be a war on, but who cared?

Sweat trickled down his back as he lay in wait, the heat almost overpowering. The flames had spread to the rear of the city, hundreds of buildings catching fire...smoke and fumes wafted towards them every time the wind changed, reminding them that they were literally caught between the fires and the advancing enemy. He saw a mortar team rushing towards their position and angrily waved them away before they could set up and start lobbing shells towards the enemy troops. The enemy was *good*, damn them. Every time a mortar fired, answering shells smashed down seconds later. He'd seen it happen often enough to know he didn't want the mortar crew anywhere near his men.

And half of them don't manage to break down the mortar and run before they get blown to bits, he thought. They were brave, he supposed, but they were going to call attention to his position. *Do they even know what they're shooting at?*

He felt his heart start to pound as the sound of shooting grew louder, a handful of stragglers running past their positions and picking their way through the flames. The last update, before the forward posts had gone off the air, had been grim. The enemy were clearing the buildings ruthlessly, using grenades to smash the defenders before overrunning whatever was left of them. It wasn't clear if they were taking prisoners or not, but it hardly mattered. There wouldn't be many people left to take prisoner...

And the colonel went and left us, Derek thought. It was hard not to resent the colonel for just...leaving. It was...his heart twisted as he felt a surge of bitter anger. *If this town cannot be held, we should all leave.*

He heard a pair of mortars firing, the enemy guns returning fire a second later. The sound of shooting was growing louder, approaching from the east...he peered into the smoke, wondering just what was happening. The command network seemed to have broken down completely. He felt alone, even though he had twenty-five men under his command. The other defences might already have broken. They might already have been outflanked. He shuddered in horror at the thought of what might be happening to the civilians. If they'd been allowed to flee...

"They're coming," Loomis said. "I can *smell* them."

Derek gave him a sharp look, then tensed as he saw the enemy soldiers in the distance. They'd abandoned their armour, but they still looked formidable as they advanced through the remains of the town. They moved with a rough elegance he had to admire, a tactic born of real experience instead of exercises on the parade ground. Derek had heard, from a couple of other survivors, that working by the book was a good way to get killed... he gritted his teeth, remembering how many lessons *he'd* learnt in the last few days. He dreaded to think what would have happened if the enemy troops had landed right on top of the garrison.

"Don't fire until I give the command," he ordered. The advancing troops had too much cover. "And then be prepared to run."

"I'm always prepared to run." Loomis tossed him a smirk. "Request permission, sir, to take my sick leave."

Derek had to smile. "Request denied."

He waited for the enemy to come a little closer, then raised his rifle. "Fire!"

The troops opened fire. The enemy troops scattered with terrifying speed. Derek grabbed his radio and babbled coordinates into it, just as his men—as planned—turned and started running for their lives. If someone was listening, if someone had a mortar ready to fire, they might just get some real payback for everything they'd lost since the war began. If not... he ran too, as fast as he possibly could, as he heard shells whistling through the air. The force of the explosion picked him up and tossed him through the air, as casually as a child might discard a ragdoll. He landed badly, grunting in pain as he rolled over. Nothing seemed broken, but he felt as though he'd been in a bare-knuckle fight with a drill instructor. Loomis grabbed his arm and helped him to his feet, ignoring the bullets zipping through the air.

"Shit," Derek grunted.

"Go in the potty," Loomis said. "We have to move."

Derek glanced behind them. The trench was little more than flaming debris. A pair of bodies were clearly visible, men caught in the open when the shells hit. He tried to tell himself they were enemy soldiers, that they'd been hit by their own guns, but he couldn't even *begin* to convince himself. He'd lost two men, perhaps more…he allowed Loomis to help him run to the east, into the flames. It was crazy, but he thought it was the only way to get out. There was no point in fighting in a burning town.

His entire body ached as they stumbled into the flames. The heat grew stronger, but…thankfully, the roads remained clear. He shuddered as he saw rivers of fire moving across the ground, then reached for his rebreather as the stench of smoke grew stronger. Breathing in smoke *couldn't* be good for him. There'd been a man from Earth who'd gone crazy when he discovered he couldn't get tobacco for love or money. It was banned on the grounds it was a health risk.

The rest of the platoon, as per orders, had gathered at the rear of the town. Derek straightened up and silently counted them, trying not to wince as he realised that only twelve men had made it out alive. Two were dead… had the others deserted? Or were they lying dead too, somewhere within the flames? He didn't know. He was tempted to wait, in hopes of finding the others, but he knew they didn't have time. The flames hadn't stopped them; they wouldn't stop the enemy. He could still hear shooting, echoing over the roar of the flames. The enemy was in pursuit.

Damn them, he thought. *What do we do now?*

"There's no point in staying here," he said, stiffly. It was true. They'd shot off most of their ammunition in the brief engagement. He had no idea where they could get more, if indeed there *was* more. The flames had consumed the former supply dumps as well as everything else. "We'll follow the road west until we reach the next defence line."

Loomis nudged him. "Or we could circle around and go back east…?"

Derek shook his head. They'd been told that anyone who was taken prisoner by the invaders, whoever they were, went straight into a POW camp. Derek had no faith in their ability to sneak back into Eddisford, nor to remain undetected once the invaders booted up the surveillance network. Jenny's father had *known*, the moment boys started sniffing around her. The invaders could put the wretched system to a far more dangerous use. He considered trying to remain in the countryside, before dismissing the idea. They couldn't hope to hide without help from the farmers and he didn't know if the farmers could be trusted. They might side with the invaders, if the invaders let them raise their prices…

"No," he said. "We have to keep going."

"Aye, sir," Loomis said. "I just hope it doesn't get us killed."

"Me too," Derek said. He wiped sweat off his brow as they started to walk. There were no trucks waiting for them, let alone armoured vehicles. And if there had been, he wouldn't have trusted them. They would have attracted unfriendly attention. "Me too."

• • •

"And we made a desert called peace," Sergeant Mayberry said. "They practically destroyed their whole town to keep it from us."

Haydn nodded as the marines slowly transitioned into occupation and peacekeeping mode. There was very little of the town left, particularly on the western side. The fires had burnt themselves out after consuming hundreds of homes, businesses and factories. Even the seemingly-intact buildings on the eastern side were badly damaged, after the marines had cleared them of enemy soldiers. The battle had been futile, right from the start, but the enemy troops had fought bravely. Only a tiny handful had chosen to surrender.

"But we broke their defence line," he said. Advance elements were already roaming ahead, harassing the enemy troops as they retreated. "And we can proceed with the next offensive as planned."

"Yes, sir," Mayberry said. "But what do we do with the civilians?"

"God knows," Haydn said. "General Anderson will have to make the call. Probably have them billeted on homes and farms to the east."

"And fed, somehow," Mayberry said. "Or we'll have a real crisis on our hands."

Haydn nodded, then dismissed the thought. "Did we recover the bodies?"

"Ours, yes." Mayberry looked grim. "We lost ten men."

"Rats." Haydn kicked a charred stone. The defenders had lost far more, but...he shook his head. Marines weren't expendable. The replacements had never kept up with the demand, even before Earthfall. Now...it would be a long time before the company saw *any* replacements. "We'll bury them after the campaign is over."

"Yes, sir," Mayberry said. "We also lost two tanks and a self-propelled gun."

"The problems of victory," Haydn said. "They must be feeling worse."

"Yes, sir," Mayberry said.

And that's true, Haydn thought, as he reached for his terminal. *But it doesn't make me feel any better, does it?*

CHAPTER TWENTY-SEVEN

The most dangerous—and, ironically, the most stable—places fell into two categories. First, a number of Imperial Navy officers—the ones lucky enough to find themselves in command of fleets and supply bases—set themselves up as warlords. Like their counterparts along the Rim, they started setting up small empires of their own... bringing a certain degree of security to worlds under their control.

—PROFESSOR LEO CAESIUS

Earthfall and its Aftermath

"THEY'RE SAYING THE TOWN IS FINALLY FALLING," Perkins commented.

Rachel nodded from where she was watching the enemy leaders—and civilians—flee the town. They'd had MPs on duty at the rear, keeping the roads clear of refugee traffic, but now order was beginning to break down. She'd watched a handful of civilians attack MPs, knocking them down before hurrying their families out of the burning town. The floodgates had opened, civilians—and soldiers—heading in all directions. She hoped most of them knew how to survive in the countryside.

And that they don't get caught by the MPs, she thought, grimly. She understood why people wanted to run, but...the local government wouldn't be happy. They couldn't let the roads be blocked with refugees and they couldn't trust their own troops to massacre civilians who might well be their own friends and families. Most repressive governments had bully-boy units to do the particularly nasty jobs, but did the locals? *They might not have thought it necessary.*

"Got something interesting coming," Perkins said. "Look."

Rachel followed his gaze. A small convoy was nosing its way out of the town; a pair of motorcycle outriders, an armoured car, an armoured transport, another armoured car...unless she missed her guess, it was transporting someone—or something—the locals considered important. A commanding officer? It was hard to think of anything *else* that might be worth the risk of attracting unfriendly attention. General Anderson had kept the Raptors back, deploying them to support the troops as they pushed into the town, but that would change. A single pass would leave the convoy, and whatever it was carrying, little more than flaming debris.

She glanced at Phelps. "A valid target?"

"Looks that way," Phelps agreed. Below them, the motorcycles were pressing forward, scattering the refugees. "There has to be someone important in that vehicle."

He snapped orders as the team prepared, moving forward into ambush position. Rachel found herself next to Perkins, readying herself for the charge as Phelps and Bonkowski stood by to lay down covering fire. She wished, suddenly, that they had a little support, but they'd have to make do with what they had. Besides, there was a certain degree of freedom in knowing they were the only friendly forces in the area. They could lay down covering fire without worrying about accidentally hitting their allies.

"Shit," Phelps said, as the convoy escorts opened fire. "Bastards!"

Rachel shuddered. The escorts weren't firing on the Pathfinders, but on the civilian refugees. Machine guns tore through bodies like hot knives through butter, practically disintegrating *things* that had once been living men, women and children. Blood flew everywhere, staining the ground and the vehicles as the rest of the refugees ran for their lives. The road was clear, at a terrible price. Rachel cursed the enemy troops under her breath as their vehicles picked up speed. They *did* have bully-boys ready to do the dirty work.

"Now," Phelps ordered.

Bonkowski opened fire. A streak of plasma fire shot towards the first armoured car, blowing it into a fireball. The plasma cannon was designed to take out tanks. The armoured car and its crew never stood a chance. Phelps opened fire a moment later, taking out the second armoured car. This time, the crew were halfway through deploying their troops as the plasma burst struck the vehicle. They were good, but not good enough. Sniper fire took them all out before they could deploy.

Rachel triggered her enhancements, picking herself up and practically *flying* towards the lead motorcyclist. He was grabbing for a pistol when she grabbed him, her hand catching his neck and squeezing with enhanced strength. She felt a flicker of cold pleasure as she crushed his throat, hurling his body off the motorcycle and tossing it into a ditch as soon as he was dead. Perkins took out the second motorcyclist, then turned to face the armoured transport. A pair of guards were stumbling out of the vehicle, clearly unaware of the mistake they were making. Rachel could have hit them both before they brought their weapons to bear, but she didn't have to. Bonkowski and Phelps killed them both before they realised they'd exposed themselves to the snipers.

Not used to ultra-violence, Rachel thought, as she ran towards the transports. *But then, so few bully-boys are actually prepared for anyone who wants to fight back.*

She yanked open the hatch and hurled a stun grenade into the confined space. Blue light flared, tingles running down her skin even at a distance. The transport ground to a halt, the wheels screeching in angry protest. The poor bastards inside would need to be wearing body armour, if they didn't want to be jangled into helplessness. She glanced at Perkins as the light faded, then led the way into the transport. The driver was bent over the wheel, moaning. She paid him no heed as she checked the rear. Two middle-ranking men, a young woman in civilian clothes and a general. She smiled, coldly, as she hurled the stunned bodies out of the transport. They didn't know it, not yet, but—for them—the war was over.

"Got them," Perkins said. The woman cried out as she hit the ground, but the others were too stunned to notice. "Who do you think they are?"

"Rats leaving the sinking ship," Rachel said. She understood that senior officers needed to keep their distance from the combat zone, and the risk of being taken prisoner, but it still struck her as cowardly. "Three senior officers and...*someone*."

She searched the vehicle quickly, collecting anything that might be of value to the intelligence staff. A briefcase, a handful of maps, a dozen and two datachips...they'd be encrypted, probably, but the intelligence hackers were amongst the best in the business. And besides, the prisoners could probably be induced to hand over their passcodes and suchlike if there was no other choice. She eyed the driver for a moment, wondering if she should take him prisoner too, then decided it was probably a good idea. She had no qualms about slitting someone's throat if she had to, but she drew the line at cold-blooded murder. And it would be murder. The man posed no threat.

She heard voices outside as she picked up the driver and tossed him out of the hatch, then took one final look around the transport before following him. Perkins had the four prisoners lying on the ground, their hands and feet bound with zip-ties. They were in no state to walk to the pickup point, even if Rachel and the others had been inclined to trust them. She nodded to Phelps as he and Bonkowski joined them, their faces grim. They couldn't stay where they were for long.

"I've got their crap," she said, dumping the briefcase and its contents into her knapsack. "Shall we go?"

"I think we've outstayed our welcome," Phelps agreed. "Search them, then let's go."

Rachel nodded and hastily patted down the woman, taking care to check for signs of genetic or mechanical enhancement. Hardly anyone would take *her* seriously, when they laid eyes on her out of uniform. She knew better than to let someone else work the same trick on her. But the woman appeared to be baseline human...probably someone who'd worked in the town's administration before the war. Her dress was professional, rather than sexy; her underwear was ruthlessly practical, concealed under her trousers. She dressed as someone who wanted to be taken seriously, rather than a general's whore. Rachel's lips thinned in disgust. She'd met too many officers who'd paid more attention to their sexual conquests than ongoing operations.

She pulled her knapsack on, then hefted the woman over her shoulders and started to march to the pickup point. The woman groaned as the effects of the stun grenade started to wear off. Rachel allowed herself a moment of pity. The woman's clothes wouldn't have provided *any* protection from the stun grenade. Rachel knew *she* would have recovered quicker, but *she* was enhanced. A normal civilian, without any training, might take hours to return to normal. Bonkowski picked up the general and one of his aides, then followed her. The remaining two brought up the rear.

It felt like hours before they finally reached the pickup point. Phelps had called in, requesting a Raptor to extract them. Rachel had worried about that. There had been no guarantee that a bird would be on hand to pick them up, nor that they'd be able to evade prowling HVM teams. She would have preferred to circumvent the fighting and walk back to Eddisford, but they couldn't have transported the prisoners that far. It would have been very inconvenient. She tossed the woman into the aircraft and secured her to a railing, then sat down next to her. The Raptor climbed for the sky as soon as everyone was onboard.

"We'll have you there in two shakes of a lamb's tail," the pilot called. "Pretty harrowing down there, what?"

"Pretty much," Phelps agreed, as Bonkowski made a rude gesture at the pilot's back. "You seen any action?"

"Bunch of dumb bastards stalking the fields with HVMs," the pilot said. "Nearly got fucked by one of them...and not in a good way."

Rachel leaned back against the bulkhead and closed her eyes, just for a second. The pilots were amongst the bravest men in the corps, even though they weren't riflemen or combat medics. She'd seen pilots land in the middle of a storm of bullets, their airframes soaking up damage as wounded and dead troops were hastily loaded onboard so the aircraft could take off again. It took real courage to fly through unfriendly skies. The pilot was right. A single HVM could fuck up everything, *definitely* not in a good way.

The craft hit the ground hard enough to jar her back to reality. "Off you hop," the pilot called. "Give them hell from me."

"Yeah." Rachel helped the woman to her feet, then passed her to a pair of marines outside the craft. "We'll see what they have to say."

She jumped down, keeping her head low. The propellers were still turning, whipping the air. A pair of intelligence officers greeted her, pointing towards the nearest tent. Rachel sighed inwardly—she disliked post-mission debriefings intensely—but followed their lead. They'd probably have coffee in a pot, ready for their victims. She would forgive them anything for coffee and a few hours of sleep.

"Catch up afterwards," Phelps said. "We'll be going back out there shortly."

"Tell me about it," Rachel said. "I can't wait."

The intelligence officers seemed distracted as they fired questions at her, as if they weren't interested in her answers. Rachel found herself torn between amusement and grim understanding. *She* wasn't the important one, not now. The general and his aides were the *really* important ones. She wondered if the general had been conditioned, to keep him from blabbering everything to his captors. There was no way a man could resist the combination of truth drugs and lie detectors if he hadn't been treated in *some* way. They'd have to find a way to make him willingly spill the beans if he *had* been conditioned.

And that is never easy, Rachel thought, as she was dismissed. *The bastards have to be talked into doing the right thing.*

• • •

Intelligence Lieutenant Sally Heming knew, without false modesty, that men tended to underestimate her. They certainly didn't realise, until it was far too late, that her genetically-tailored appearance concealed a razor-sharp mind, one that was perfectly capable of seeing through most lies and deceits. Sally's own *mother* had never realised what she'd brought into the world, never thought that her perfect daughter would turn her back on her family and join the marine corps. But then, she'd never thought of her children as anything other than an accessory.

She studied the enemy officer through the one-way mirror, silently considering everything they'd learnt about him. The POWs had been quite talkative, once they'd realised they weren't going to be killed for daring to exist. General Taggard had been in command of Eddisford Garrison when the invasion had begun, they'd claimed; he'd planned the defence before fleeing with the rest of the survivors. The POWs hadn't been able to tell their captors much *else* about the man, but it hardly mattered. It was somewhere to start.

Sally smiled to herself, then pasted a calm expression on her face as she opened the door and stepped into the room. General Taggard sat on a chair, his hands and feet firmly cuffed to the metal bars. Judging by his expression, he was nerving himself up for pain and suffering. Sally already knew it would be pointless. The medics had done a workup and concluded the general had been conditioned. There was no way they could *make* him talk.

Which is a good thing, Sally thought. *Torture is not always reliable.*

She took a chair facing him and met his eyes, evenly. His eyes flickered over her shirt, two sizes too tight, but didn't linger. Gay? It was possible, she supposed. The locals didn't seem to have any taboo against homosexuality. Or maybe he was too aware that he was a prisoner to feel anything beyond fear. Or to suspect her motives…

"General Taggard," she said, calmly. "Welcome to our base."

The general glared at her, but said nothing. That was smart, she knew. A person who became talkative, perhaps in a bid to taunt his captors, could be induced into saying something a little more useful. The other prisoners had been quite talkative, but they hadn't been very *informative*. They simply hadn't known anything useful. Their world had ended just outside their hometown. They knew almost nothing of the greater world, let alone the universe itself. Some of them hadn't even known about Earthfall!

"Let me outline our position," Sally said, calmly. "We have beaten your troops whenever we have met them. Given time, we will finish off the remaining PDCs and take your capital city. At that point, we will have won the war. Your future will depend, General Taggard, on just how informative you plan to be."

She saw an expression cross his face, just for a second. A lie...not his lie, but *hers.* He thought she'd lied to him. Why? She kept her expression artfully blank as she quickly reviewed everything she'd said. It was all true, wasn't it? She certainly hadn't set *out* to lie.

"If you cooperate, we will treat you well," she continued. "There are places you can spend the rest of your life in relative comfort, far from anyone who might want to hurt you. Or you can stay here, if you feel you will be safe. Your wife and children will be welcome to join you."

She allowed her voice to harden. "If you refuse to cooperate, we'll take you to our labs instead. There, we will try to break your conditioning. You might be the lucky one who survives, but...well, the odds aren't in your favour. None of the people who went into the labs ever came out again."

His face darkened. She knew she'd hit a nerve.

"There's no way you'll be traded back to your superiors," she added. "And..."

General Taggard let out a bitter laugh. "When will you take me off-world?"

Sally concealed her delight. He was starting to break. "As soon as you've told us everything."

"Really?" General Taggard eyed her, suspiciously. "And how do I know you'll keep your word?"

"You don't." Sally knew there was no point in trying to lie. "However, you really have no alternative."

"Hah." General Taggard chuckled, humourlessly. "You don't know what you've started, do you?"

Sally felt a prickle of excitement running down her spine. "What do you mean?"

"Well, that would be telling," General Taggard said. His voice was heavy with grim satisfaction. "You take me off-world tomorrow, young lady, and I'll tell you everything I know. Oh, and I want a sizable cash bonus as well. At least a million credits. Make it two million."

"Of course." Sally was tempted to point out that credits were practically worthless these days. Taggard might not have realised. The local currency hadn't collapsed. "We'll make it three million if you are very cooperative."

She allowed her voice to harden, again. Whatever he had to say had better be worth it. "Why do you want to leave this world so quickly?"

General Taggard looked back at her. He knew she had to dicker with him. "Do we have a deal?"

"We do." Sally had no doubt of it. A cash reward was well within her authority. General Taggard hadn't done anything, as far as she knew, that would require amnesty. There would be no need to convince her superiors to hold their noses as they dealt with him. The locals might have different ideas, but there was no need to tell them that the general had been taken alive, let alone given a chance to start a new life somewhere else. "Now, what do you have to tell us?"

"It's like this." General Taggard lowered his voice. "This planet is not alone..."

CHAPTER TWENTY-EIGHT

However, many of the warlords had severe problems. They were, as a group, more interested in their own ambition than maintaining civilisation. They were certainly disinclined to put themselves (back) under anyone else's authority. And, as they rarely controlled enough shipyards and industrial nodes to keep their fleets operating, they often found their ships decaying away from the inside.

—**Professor Leo Caesius**

Earthfall and its Aftermath

"**GENERAL TAGGARD IS OVERDUE**, Your Excellency," General Atherton said, his holographic image flickering as he spoke. "We have to assume the worst."

Governor Simon Morgan gritted his teeth. "You're *sure* he's lost?"

"He never reached Bouchon." General Atherton's voice was grim. "He may have been killed or he may have been captured. His convoy was apparently attacked. We haven't been able to recover any bodies."

"Because that's behind enemy lines," Simon finished. "What do we do if they *do* have him?"

"We don't know they *do* have him," Heather pointed out. The Deputy Governor sounded bemused. "Wouldn't they be trying to use him if they *did*?"

"In theory, they wouldn't be able to get anything out of him." General Atherton spoke with a grim certainty that could not be denied. "In practice, there are always...*holes*...in conditioning. His captors *could* have convinced him to talk."

"He *knows* time is on our side," Simon said. "He wouldn't talk."

"But time wouldn't be on *his* side," General Atherton said. He smiled, humourlessly. "It's astonishing what someone will do if you put a gun to their head and threaten to pull the trigger."

"You think he might betray us," Simon said, flatly. "What if he does?"

"Taggard knew a *lot*," General Atherton said. "Not everything, true, but enough to make their attacks more effective if they get him to talk."

"If they have him in the first place," Heather reminded him.

"We have to assume the worst," General Atherton said. "For a start, we should probably consider evacuating this bunker. Taggard knows where it is."

Simon stared at his hands. "If they knew...what could they do about it?"

"Right now, the war in space has stalemated," General Atherton said. "Neither side controls the high orbitals. They couldn't drop a KEW on the bunker, but they *could* lob a cruise missile at it. Or something else... realistically, if they take out the bunker, it will be impossible to coordinate our defences."

"They're already picking at our network," Heather said, darkly. "We're repelling round-the-clock hacking attempts."

"I thought that was supposed to be impossible," Simon protested. "It's a closed system!"

"They've overrun a handful of datanodes," Heather countered. "And locking them out of the system is proving difficult. Right now, we've managed to keep them from doing any *real* damage, but it's only a matter of time before they do *something*."

"I've already started setting up duplicate command nets," General Atherton said. "If we lose the datanet, we won't lose *everything*."

"Good," Simon said. "So, militarily speaking, where do we stand?"

General Atherton took a long breath. "There's no point in trying to sugar-coat it, Your Excellency. We have effectively lost control of the entire eastern region. The enemy hasn't occupied *everywhere*, but they've smashed our military and police forces. They've also enveloped PDCs seventeen and eighteen, although—so far—they haven't tried to launch any frontal assaults. They may be trying to starve the PDCs out."

He smiled, rather coldly. "That will take quite some time," he added. "There's enough food and drink in the PDCs to keep them going for at least a year or so."

"By then, it will be over," Simon said. "Head Office will dispatch help."

"Precisely." General Atherton displayed a map. "I believe their shortest route to Haverford is through Bouchon, a city resting in the Craggy Mountains. The mountains themselves will pose a formidable obstacle if they try to circumvent Bouchon, while their logistics would get...*problematic*...if they try to go north or south in a bid to avoid Bouchon entirely. If we cannot meet them in open battle, and it looks as if they have a clear advantage in such engagements, we can force them to meet us on our terms. I propose to turn Bouchon into an insurmountable barrier."

"Really?" Heather's voice was arctic. "What about the refugees?"

Simon winced, inwardly. He'd issued orders for civilians to stay in their homes, to stay off the roads...but word was spreading, even though the local datanets had been shut down. Thousands, perhaps hundreds of thousands, of people were on the move, jamming roads and draining supplies as they searched for a safety they probably wouldn't be able to find. The cities were already starting to feel the pressure. They simply hadn't had time to stockpile food and bedding for thousands of extra people.

"I've had some of them pressed into service," General Atherton said, flatly. "The remainder are being ordered to leave Bouchon. The enemy... hasn't shown any desire to slaughter civilians. They should be safe enough."

Simon cocked his head. "Will they take over the care and feeding of the refugees?"

“We don’t know,” General Atherton said. “Our spy networks in the east have gone silent.”

“They can’t get in touch with us without the datanet,” Heather pointed out. “In hindsight, we should have issued them with portable coms.”

“They would have been harder to control,” Simon said. The datanet had been designed for control, not efficiency. The inefficiencies that anyone with half a brain could spot were a small price to pay for keeping the planet under control. “And people would have started to ask questions.”

“They’ll be asking them soon enough anyway, Simon,” Heather said. “The first wave of refugees is already reaching Haverford.”

“Keep them away,” Simon snapped. “We don’t need them *here*...”

“We may not be able to keep them away,” General Atherton said. “Your Excellency, we don’t have the manpower to secure Bouchon—and the approaches to Haverford—while, at the same time, providing the normal level of internal security. We’ve already had reports of police and security officers being assaulted...frankly, sir, there were always tensions in our society. Now, some people feel free to express them.”

Simon rubbed his forehead. “We didn’t plan for this, did we?”

“No, Your Excellency,” General Atherton said. “Prior to Earthfall, a full-scale invasion would have been unthinkable.”

“Someone obviously *did* think of it,” Simon said, dryly. “How long do we have?”

“Until help arrives?” General Atherton shrugged. “I don’t know. It depends on how quickly Head Office dispatches a relief fleet. Until they reach here...? If they hit Bouchon and bounce, we can wear them down. We can stall for time until help arrives. Even if they get through Bouchon, they’d still have to get here...”

Simon glared at him. “How long?”

“Roughly?” General Atherton shrugged, again. “I’d say somewhere between three to six weeks. It depends on resistance as well as terrain. They could be here in a few days if there was no resistance at all, but...

they're going to have to fight their way through Bouchon and as many strongpoints as we can throw in their way first."

"Fuck." Simon rarely swore, but the word felt good in his mouth. "Haverford might fall before help arrives."

"Perhaps, sir," General Atherton said. "We need to start planning for the worst."

"Then do it, General," Simon said. He jabbed a finger at the console. "Dismissed."

The images vanished, leaving him alone. In truth, he'd always been alone. He glared at the projector, then rose and started to pace the bunker. He'd always been more of a bureaucrat than a military man and he found it hard to maintain any optimism, no matter how competent he believed his military subordinates to be. Whatever happened, even if the invaders were defeated, the program had been smashed beyond repair. It would take years to fix the damage, years he knew he didn't have. *Someone* was going to be the scapegoat for the whole affair.

And no one could have predicted a full-scale invasion, he thought, sourly. He'd seen the projections. No one could get through the defences, no one could establish a bridgehead, no one could march on Haverford...the invaders had done it, somehow. They'd made a mockery of all the defence plans, all the concepts he'd approved when he'd taken office. *And I will bear the blame.*

He looked at his datapad, wondering what he should do. The invaders didn't know it, but they'd put their head in a vice. If Head Office responded in time...Simon shook his head. It would be too late for him, but not for the program. The planet was just too important to write off. He briefly considered surrender, only to dismiss the thought. The invaders were screwed. They didn't have a hope of success. And if he threw his lot in with them, he'd be screwed too.

There was a knock at the door. "Come!"

Sandra poked her head into the room, looking frazzled. Simon allowed himself a tight, nasty smile. Doing actual *work* had taken a toll on her. It hadn't taken long for the other secretaries and glorified personal assistants to realise that Sandra's relatives were either dead or out of commission for the foreseeable future. And when they'd worked out that she *wasn't* Simon's mistress...he felt his smile widen. Sandra didn't know it, but the experience was actually doing her good. She'd have some *genuine* skills when Simon's replacement took office.

"Your Excellency," Sandra said. "I have the profit-loss reports from the eastern region..."

"Total loss," Simon said. There was no point in trying to deny it. "They won't be sending anything west, will they?"

"No, Your Excellency." Sandra took a breath. "Councillor Bunco suggested assessing the refugees and redirecting the workers to factories in *his* neighbourhood..."

"A power play," Simon said. "The entire world is burning down and he's making a power play..."

"Sir?"

Simon scowled. On paper, he had no doubt the scheme looked good. Bunco had always been good—more accurately, his *staff* had always been good—at making a dreadful idea sound perfectly feasible. On the surface, it *was* a good idea. But, practically speaking, it would be disastrous. Bunco wouldn't prosper at everyone else's expense. He'd take himself down with them.

But it would look good on paper, he thought. *And if I reject it out of hand, he can cite it when he puts in a bid for the governorship. Proof he can have good ideas...*

"Tell him the plan will have to wait," Simon said. Registering the refugees was going to be a pain in the butt. The datanet's problems were making it harder to keep track of people. If *that* got out...Simon had few illusions. The original settlers had been happy to trade a surveillance state for safety, *real* safety. Their descendants, the ones who had never seen Earth, weren't so inclined to accept social controls and a complete lack of privacy. "We can tackle it after the war."

"Yes, sir," Sandra said.

• • •

"Is this for real?"

Sally braced herself. She had expected disbelief, even though she'd verified everything General Taggard had told her. He believed what he was saying...she knew it was quite possible that someone had lied to him, that he was repeating their lies in the firm belief he was telling the truth, but... it explained too many of the puzzles that had confronted the intelligence team when they'd landed on Hameau. The planet was not alone.

"I believe so, sir," she said. "General Taggard is not *trying* to mislead us."

General Anderson studied her report. "Hameau is one of several worlds," he said. "And we've just declared war on a vest-pocket corporate empire."

"Yes, sir," Sally said. "And they're expecting help to arrive soon."

"I see." General Anderson sounded as if he wanted to say something sharper. "We may be in some trouble."

He met her eyes. "Do *you* believe him?"

Sally hesitated. Intelligence work rarely admitted of simple answers. It was often a matter of putting together jigsaw puzzles without being certain they all belonged to the *same* puzzle, without even knowing they had *all* the pieces. There were so many problems with intelligence work, from gaps in coverage to outright misleading information, that a goodly percentage of her reports were composed of guesswork. *Informed* guesswork, true, but guesswork nonetheless. It was quite possible that *someone* had lied to General Taggard and he'd fallen for it hook, line and sinker.

"I do," she said, finally. "There are a lot of puzzles here, sir. This may explain them."

"Like where that wretched battlecruiser went," General Anderson grunted. His lips moved soundlessly for a long chilling moment. "If they have other worlds...if Hameau is only a small part of a greater plan..."

He snorted. "The Commandant thought we weren't the only ones preparing for life after Earthfall," he said. "I guess he was right."

"Yes, sir," Sally said.

General Anderson keyed his wristcom. "Council of War, twenty minutes."

Sally felt the bottom drop out of her heart. A council of war was only summoned when the shit had well and truly hit the fan. Normally, a commanding officer would make decisions on his own; he might invite comments and ideas from his subordinates, but the final call would be his and his alone. But when a council of war was summoned...General Anderson had just surrendered a little of his authority, something that would *not* please his superiors. He wouldn't have called a council unless he'd felt there was no other choice.

He met her eyes. "How long do we have?"

"I don't know," Sally said. "It depends on factors outside our control."

"And our awareness," General Anderson grunted. "Forward your report to the council, then wait. They will have questions."

"Yes, sir." Sally worked her datapad for a moment, then looked up. "What are we going to do?"

The general said nothing as he studied his terminal, drawing up everything from troop readiness reports to MEU updates. Sally frowned as she realised the timing couldn't be worse. One of the MEUs was crammed with refugees, another had been dispatched back to Safehouse...it wouldn't be *easy* to evacuate the entire landing force, if the general gave the command. She shuddered as she realised they could *lose*. If the enemy regained control of the high orbitals, the marines would have to go underground until...

She didn't want to think about it. But she had no choice.

General Anderson said nothing as the holographic projector sparkled to life. The tent was suddenly populated by holographic images, blurring slightly as they intersected. Sally sat back, feeling suddenly intimidated by the high-ranking officers. They would not *want* to believe what she had to tell them. She didn't want to believe it either.

"As you can see, matters have taken a turn that is not entirely to our advantage," General Anderson said. The understatement made Sally smile. "We may be on the verge of running out of time."

"If this is true, we may be in some trouble," Captain Kerri Stumbaugh agreed. Sally reminded herself that Kerri was also—technically—a Commodore. "Do *you* believe it?"

"The Onge Corporation does not appear to have moved its headquarters here," General Anderson said. "I always thought that was a little odd, particularly as they *did* have plans to evacuate their people from Earth. If this is just one of several worlds…we may be out on a limb."

"Quite," Kerri said. "I ran the projections. Assuming they have a major base orbiting the nearest G2 star, they could have a fleet of ships on us tomorrow. Hell, they should have a fleet of ships on us *now*. We simply don't know what they *do* have."

"Apart from that battlecruiser," General Anderson said. "We have no clue where they might have based themselves."

"Or what forces they have on hand," Kerri said. "Yes, they *could* have subverted an entire fleet. The Imperial Navy was so corrupt that they'd sell their own grandmothers for a handful of credits. But, General, they might also have only a handful of ships. We simply don't know."

"Obviously, there was a major intelligence failure at some point," General Anderson said, flatly. "But there's no point in crying over spilt milk."

Sally felt her cheeks redden, even though she knew it wasn't her fault. Intelligence failures were a dime a dozen, but…she kept her face as expressionless as possible. *This* failure was likely to turn into an utter disaster. And thousands of marines might be about to die.

"We have two options," General Anderson said. "We can continue the offensive, sharpening our sword and plunging into Bouchon and Haverford, with the objective of forcing the planetary government to surrender and hand over the PDCs before relief arrives. Or we can fall back and evacuate the planet, conceding defeat. What do you say?"

The debate raged backwards and forwards as the senior officers thrashed out the details. Neither option looked *good*, as far as Sally could tell. Abandoning the planet—and the system—wouldn't be easy, even if the enemy didn't interfere with the evacuation. But pressing the offensive would be difficult too. They could get caught in the open and then they'd be really screwed. They'd face the worst defeat in the Marine Corps' history.

"We seem to have no choice," Anderson said. "We must press the offensive, as hard as possible. And we must get to Haverford before time runs out."

It might already have run out, Sally thought.

She didn't dare say it out loud, but she could tell that the officers were having similar thoughts. Time was no longer on their side. And things had been going so well…

No, we thought they were going well, she corrected herself. *And we would have been caught by surprise when they went to hell.*

CHAPTER TWENTY-NINE

Worse, they had axes of their own to grind. Far too many officers had watched, helplessly, as insurgents, terrorists and renegades defied the Empire and, owing to politically-expedient orders from Earth, were allowed to get away with it. Those officers knew that each display of weakness guaranteed more trouble, more atrocities, more attacks on military personnel that weren't allowed to so much as defend themselves.

—PROFESSOR LEO CAESIUS

Earthfall and its Aftermath

"I FEEL NAKED," Derek muttered, as the lorry rattled down the darkening road. "I feel..."

Loomis glanced at him, his pale face oddly bright in the gloom. "I assure you you're not naked, sir," he said. "And if you were, we would all have been struck blind."

"Hah," Derek said. "Get some rest. You need it."

He closed his eyes, but sleep refused to come. He was tired, too tired to sleep. They'd walked for hours, after fleeing the town; they'd barely had a chance to sleep before they'd resumed their march, grimly aware that the enemy might be right behind them. If they hadn't encountered the truck, and convinced the driver to give them a lift to Bouchon, he knew they'd still be somewhere on the road. Or, perhaps, being herded into a POW camp. God knew what the enemy would do to them if they were caught.

The lorry rattled, again. He jerked awake, looking around in shock. His men snored loudly, the handful who remained. The others had vanished, somewhere along the road. They'd taken their rifles and deserted. Derek hadn't tried to stop them. He wasn't sure why he'd stayed himself. It was growing harder to believe the state would win, that the old system would be re-established. He didn't want to admit it, but there was a part of him that was tempted to jump out of the lorry and walk back to Eddisford. The only thing that kept him from doing just that was the grim awareness he didn't know the way.

He sat upright and peered into the gloom. They were rattling past a handful of houses, all as dark and silent as the grave. It was hard to be sure, but it looked as if they'd been abandoned in a hurry. Everyone knew the enemy would be using the motorways to move their troops. Everyone knew the civilians weren't safe. Everyone knew...Derek shook his head. He couldn't blame the civilians for fleeing. He hoped his family had had the sense to flee Eddisford before it was too late.

They drove past a handful of refugees, struggling along the road. He opened his mouth to order the driver to stop, to take the refugees onboard, but they were lost in the darkness before he could find the words. They'd been ordered not to have anything to do with refugees, to leave them to the tender mercies of the MPs...he shuddered. The poor bastards were unlikely to find any succour in Bouchon. The MPs had had plenty of time to set up barricades and direct the refugee flows away from the city.

"Nearly there," the driver called. "Get your papers ready, please."

Derek shifted, uncomfortably aware that he'd fallen asleep again. It felt as if bare seconds had passed between seeing the refugees and reaching Bouchon. He could hear the faint sound of helicopter blades in the distance, echoing gunfire...he shivered. Were the enemy troops really that close? He didn't know. They hadn't come under fire, but that proved nothing. They'd passed enough burnt-out wrecks to know the enemy aircraft were on the prowl. If they hadn't been so desperate, he would have forbidden his troops to climb onto the lorry.

"Well," Loomis said. "Here we are."

The lorry rattled to a halt. Derek stood, slipping between the slumbering forms of his troops and jumped down to the ground. A large roadblock stood in their way, manned by MPs and security troops. The night air was warm, but...he shivered anyway. It was hard to keep his face under tight control. He'd never seen the green-tabbed security troops before, but he knew their reputation. They were the ones the government sent when someone *really* needed a thrashing. He looked at the man ambling towards him and frowned, caught between fear and an odd sense the man hadn't seen the elephant. His uniform was so clean and pressed that it was hard to escape the impression his mother had washed it for him. Derek almost snickered. He told himself, sharply, that he was too tired for his own good.

Up close, the man looked sallow...and unpleasant. "Identify yourself."

"Corporal...ah, *Lieutenant* Derek Frazer," Derek said. "Eddisford Garrison..."

"Palm." The man held out a scanner. "Now."

Derek obeyed, wondering if Colonel Macintyre had had a chance to enter his promotion into the system before he'd been forced to abandon the town. The security trooper eyed the scanner for a long moment, then scowled. Derek tensed, bracing himself. If something was wrong...the trooper looked irked, not angry. It slowly dawned on Derek that the trooper had been *expecting* something to go wrong.

"Your men will go into the personnel pool," the trooper said, once he'd checked the rest of the soldiers and the driver. "You can report directly to Colonel Macintyre."

Derek frowned. "I should go with them..."

"You have your orders, *Lieutenant*," the trooper said. "You'll find the colonel in the southern school. Your men can make their own way to the barracks."

Loomis glanced at Derek. "I'll take care of them," he said. "Good luck."

Derek nodded, feeling as if he was abandoning the people who had been placed in his charge. He felt like a heel for turning his back and walking away, and yet...he knew he had no choice. Gritting his teeth, he forced himself to walk through the barricades and into the city itself. Bouchon was huge, easily the largest city he'd seen in his life. Towering skyscrapers, giant apartment blocks...he shivered as he saw hundreds of refugees sitting or sleeping on the streets. They had nowhere else to go.

The sense of being trapped grew stronger as he made his way down the street. The apartment blocks were being converted into strongpoints, their doors lined with barbed wire and windows broken to keep them from shattering when the first enemy shells fell on the city. Armed men were everywhere, digging trenches and siting weapons; he shuddered, despite himself, as he saw civilians press-ganged into fortifying their city. A handful of mobile sensor platforms and air defence weapons were scattered around, waiting for the enemy aircraft to fly over the city. Behind them, he saw a handful of soldiers goofing off, passing a bottle of wine around as they waited for orders. He wondered, sourly, just what they thought they were doing.

He forced himself to keep going, stopping an MP long enough to ask for directions. The southern school was a large building, surrounded by tents, armoured vehicles and armed guards. His identity was checked twice before he was allowed to enter the compound, a pair of security troopers escorting him to Colonel Macintyre's tent. It looked as if the colonel himself wasn't allowed to enter the school. Perhaps it was a good thing. The enemy would—eventually—realise where the command post was and do something about it. The building looked tough, but a single antitank missile would be enough to bring it crashing down in ruins.

And plenty of schoolchildren would probably cheer, he thought, nastily. He'd hated school, himself. Most of it had been as impractical as teaching men how to get pregnant. *I wonder what happened to them.*

Colonel Macintyre looked up as he entered. He looked to have aged a decade in the last two nights, dark circles clearly visible around his eyes.

Derek felt a pang of sympathy, despite his belief the colonel had abandoned him and his men to fight while he fled. Maintaining the chain of command was important, but Colonel Macintyre wasn't *that* important. It wasn't as if he was General Taggard. Derek wouldn't have blamed the general for fleeing before he could be killed or captured.

"Lieutenant," Colonel Macintyre said. He sounded tired too. "What happened?"

"We gave the enemy a bloody nose, then retreated." Derek was too tired to give a proper report. Besides, he wasn't sure how many enemy soldiers they'd actually killed. The squad's estimates had always struck him as way too high. "And then we made our way here."

"Good, good." Colonel Macintyre looked down at the map. "Did you see General Taggard?"

Derek blinked. "No, sir."

"He's missing, somewhere between here and there." Colonel Macintyre ran a finger along the map. "Do you have any idea where he might be?"

"No, sir," Derek said. Why on Earth was *he* being asked? "I don't recall seeing the general since we abandoned the garrison."

Colonel Macintyre said nothing for a long moment. Derek tried to force himself to think, despite the dull ache in his temple. Something had happened to General Taggard? What? And what did it have to do with him? He certainly hadn't been assigned to General Taggard's staff. He was too low-ranked to be the coffee boy, let alone a bodyguard or an advisor. He wasn't sure Colonel Macintyre was high-ranking enough to have a place on the general's staff, under normal circumstances…

His mind was wandering. He dragged it back to reality.

"Unfortunate," Colonel Macintyre said. He sounded as though he was looking for someone to blame. "However, not our problem at the moment. You will assume command of one of the defence teams."

"Yes, sir." Derek couldn't keep himself from yawning. "I…I'd like to keep the rest of my original team with me, sir, if you don't mind."

"As long as they're not snapped up by someone else, I don't mind," Colonel Macintyre said, stiffly. "First, however, go check out the refugee camp in the park. There are some people from Eddisford there."

Derek straightened up. "Yes, sir!"

Colonel Macintyre smiled, tiredly. "Dismissed."

"Yes, sir," Derek said. He wanted to ask if the colonel was planning to leave them holding the bag again, but he didn't quite dare. "And thank you, sir."

He stepped out of the tent. Someone was smoking outside, the scent hanging in the air. That was against regulations...he snorted. Under the circumstances, no one was likely to give much of a damn. Besides, it was probably a senior officer. He hurried away, passing through the security cordon as he made his way towards the park. It had probably been a nice place, a few short days ago. Now, the grass was covered with tents and the trees had been chopped down for firewood. A large fire burned merrily at the edge of the park, the sight sending shivers down his spine. It would be a long time before he stopped seeing fire as a threat.

A tired-looking woman pointed him towards a tent. "We only have a handful of refugees from Eddisford," she said. "They all went in there."

"Thank you." Derek felt his heart sink. If only a handful of people had escaped, the odds of his family being amongst them were low. "I'll just take a peek."

"Don't wake them," the woman snapped. "They need their sleep."

Derek nodded—he needed his sleep too—and hurried towards the tent. The flap was open, revealing a handful of blankets. He peered into the gloom, trying to pick out a handful of faces. He thought he'd known everyone in Eddisford...

"Derek?" A voice. A *female* voice. "Is that you?"

"Yeah." Derek found himself caught between hope and fear. It didn't *sound* like his sister, but...could it be? "Come out, please."

A figure emerged from the shadows and stepped into the half-light. Derek stared, feeling a mixture of surprise and a dull awareness that he probably *shouldn't* be surprised. If there had been an evacuation list for Eddisford, the Town Controller and his family would probably have been right at the top. Jenny...his heart skipped a beat. Jenny had escaped, while his family were trapped behind enemy lines...

"We don't want to wake my parents," Jenny said. She took his hand and led him away from the tent. "What happened to you?"

"What happened to *you*?" Derek found himself staring at Jenny. She was as pretty as he remembered, but her clothes were practically rags and her hair...he smiled, despite himself. He probably didn't look as *she* remembered either. How long had it been since he'd changed his uniform? "Jenny?"

"Dad grabbed the car and told us to run," Jenny said. "We got out barely ahead of *them*."

"You got out," Derek said, slowly. "What happened to *my* family?"

Jenny looked down. "I don't know. I'm sorry."

Derek felt a hot flash of anger. "You did nothing to get them out?"

"How could we?" Jenny's voice rose. "One moment, everything was peaceful; the next, enemy troops were storming the town!"

She was right. Derek knew she was right. But it didn't make it any easier to bear. Jenny's father had been all-powerful, as far as the townspeople were concerned. His merest whim was law. And yet, he was now as helpless as the rest of the townsfolk. Derek glanced towards the tent. Surely, a Town Controller and his family rated better lodgings. The tent looked as if it had come out of a military surplus dump on the other side of the world.

"Yeah," he said. "It wasn't fun and games where we were either."

Jenny squeezed his hand. "What happened?"

"They kicked our asses, twice," Derek said, curtly. "How did *you* get here?"

"Dad drove," Jenny said. "We ran into a checkpoint on the far side of Chelmsford. The MPs told us to drive to Bouchon. Dad...Dad thought he had friends here, but they declined to put us up. I...they decided it was better to put us in a tent."

"I'm sure it won't last," Derek said. It had only been a few days, after all. Jenny's father was probably already in high demand. "Did anyone else make it out?"

"Uncle Johan left us shortly after we departed Eddisford," Jenny said. "He owns a farm. He thought he'd be safe there. Dad wasn't convinced. Everyone else...as far as I know, we're the only ones who made it out."

"And my family are back there," Derek said. "Probably being tortured to death."

"They're not," Jenny said, earnestly. "I overheard a pair of officers talking. They said they were spreading horror stories to convince the troops not to surrender. They..."

Derek looked at her. "Where *were* you...?"

"I was trying to find work," Jenny said. There was an edge in her voice that bothered him. "Dad promises that his friends will come through, but...I don't know. What good is a Town Controller when the town is *gone*?"

"I don't know," Derek said, quietly. He was surprised at her. Jenny had never struck him as someone who intended to *work*. She'd always made it clear she wanted to find a good husband and spend the rest of her days as a society wife. "I'm sure they'll find something for him to do."

"Digging ditches, probably," Jenny said, bitterly. "That's what most of the refugees are doing. Digging ditches and hauling cargo."

"No doubt." Derek's mind was elsewhere. If the officers were lying to the men, what *else* were they lying about? Colonel Macintyre had left him and his men in the shit, General Taggard had vanished...had he deserted? Or surrendered? It would be a lot easier for someone to surrender if he *knew* the horror stories were just stories. "Jenny..."

"And you're going to go back to the front lines," Jenny said. "You could get killed..."

"I know." Derek looked down at his hands. The prospect of getting killed was bad enough. The prospect of dying for a bunch of liars was worse. "You should get out of here."

"I wish I could," Jenny said. "I should have gone with Uncle Johan. A farm would be better than this..."

She met his eyes. "I'm sorry about your family," she said. "I'm sure they'll be fine."

"I hope so," Derek said. "And yours too."

"You'd better come back," Jenny said. She sounded almost as if she were pleading with him. "I don't know *anyone* else here. Just my parents and you. Being alone..."

"There are other refugees," Derek said, although he knew it wasn't the same. How could it be? Jenny and he had known everyone in their town, once upon a time. Now, they were among strangers. "Jock and I may be the only survivors from Eddisford Garrison."

"Come back," Jenny said. "And..."

She leaned forward and kissed him, hard. Derek hesitated, just for a second, then returned the kiss. Her body felt warm and soft in his arms, her breasts pressing against his chest. He felt his heart start to race as the kiss deepened, his hands stroking her back and slipping into her pants. She moaned as she ground herself against him. Her father would kill him if he ever found out...it crossed his mind, suddenly, that Jenny's father no longer had the power to do anything. Derek was more powerful than him, now. And he didn't want to die a virgin. Perhaps...

"I know a place we can go," Jenny whispered. She pulled back, taking his hand. Her eyes shone in the semi-darkness. "You want to come?"

"Yeah." Derek could not have said no, even if someone had pointed a gun at his head. He wanted her, wanted her so badly it was almost painful. "I'm coming."

CHAPTER THIRTY

It was no surprise, therefore, that many of the warlords resorted to naked planetary bombardment in the wake of Earthfall, casually slaughtering the guilty and innocent alike. It was as clear a declaration that the old days were over as one could have wished.

—PROFESSOR LEO CAESIUS

Earthfall and its Aftermath

"I CAN'T GET YOU ANY CLOSER TO THE CITY," the pilot said, as the Raptor flew west. "They've got some pretty good air defence systems around the city itself and we're too close to the PDCs for comfort."

"We understand," Phelps said. "Put us down as close as you can."

But not too close, Rachel said, as she checked her outfit. She looked like a refugee, like an upper-class woman who'd been forced to flee her home. She felt naked without her rifle and body armour, even though she was far from defenceless. *We don't want them to see the aircraft land and start asking awkward questions.*

She braced herself as the Raptor dropped towards the ground, readying herself to jump out the minute the hatch snapped open. They really *were* too close to Bouchon and the PDCs for comfort. Ideally, she would have preferred to walk all the way from the front lines to the enemy city. But *something* had lit a fire under General Anderson's ass. He'd ordered them to forgo tradecraft and focus on speed, despite the risk. Rachel didn't know what, but she had a feeling it had something to do with General Taggard. He'd probably sung like a canary under sentence of death.

The Raptor hit the ground. Rachel jumped up and threw herself through the hatch, landing neatly on the damp grass. It had been raining overnight, unfortunately for the refugees who'd been caught on the roads. Rachel had slept in the open since she was a child, well before she'd had the idea of joining the corps, but she knew *most* people preferred to sleep with a roof over their heads. She felt a stab of sympathy for the refugees, mingled with an odd kind of contempt. They should have known that their world could go to hell in a heartbeat, without the slightest hint of warning. *Her* homeworld had taught her to prepare for the worst, even as she hoped for the best. It was a lesson the civilians really should have remembered.

She glanced at the others, silently running through their cover stories. They were farmers, three brothers and a wife. They'd taken ID cards from one of the farms they'd overrun, then modified them to match their biometrics. She was uncomfortably aware that they might not be able to fool the system, but…who dared, won. Or so she'd been told. Hopefully, they'd be able to break free and escape if the shit hit the fan. That part of the plan didn't faze her. The only real awkwardness was pretending to be husband and wife.

It could be worse, she thought. She considered posing as a sister, but that might draw more attention. *And we really didn't have time to be picky.*

They walked through the woods, then down to the motorway. There were no cars or other vehicles, save for a burnt-out ruin by the side of the road. She guessed a Raptor had spotted an enemy tank or armoured car and taken the opportunity to kill it before it could set an ambush. The enemy were in disarray, but that hadn't stopped them from doing their best to impede the marines as they pushed towards Bouchon. She frowned as she saw the clumps of refugees, shuffling west. They probably wouldn't notice a few more, but…

She allowed herself a sigh of relief as they stepped onto the motorway and joined the throng heading west. The refugees were too shocked to realise that they'd been joined by newcomers...if, of course, there was anything odd about newcomers stumbling out of the forest. There were a handful of abandoned farms, only a few short miles away. The refugees looked as if they were out of their minds, unable to believe what had happened. Their nice, safe world had been torn asunder...the hell of it, Rachel knew, was that the worst was yet to come. Refugees never had an easy time of it. It wouldn't be long before they started selling themselves for scraps of bread.

And we did this to them, she thought. It was a new feeling, and not one she liked. Everywhere else, the marines had been outsiders. They'd never borne the blame for whatever had started the exodus. But here...it was their fault. She knew they'd had to intervene, but...they'd have to bear the burden of what they'd done. *Our cross to bear.*

She kept her thoughts to herself as Bouchon steadily came into view. Unsurprisingly, the maps had failed to convey the full immensity of the city. It rested between two mountain peaks, within an impact crater that reminded her of a long-dead volcano. A giant PDC was clearly visible in the distance, its guns dominating the horizon. Dozens of helicopters flew overhead, bringing in supplies and lifting out—she hoped—civilians. She could see defence lines being built, refugee labour being pressed into service to get the lines emplaced before the marines arrived. She shivered. The city would be a bitch to take, even without reinforcements. A frontal assault across a limited field...it was going to be bloody. The marines would find their advantages cut to a nub.

Particularly as we cannot destroy the entire city, she told herself. *Even if we put morality aside, we couldn't afford to wreck the motorway.*

The sense of looming oppression grew stronger as they made their way towards the checkpoint. Soldiers were everywhere, swaggering around with the unspoken confidence that marked them as bully-boys, rather than men who'd seen real fighting. She wasn't remotely surprised to see the green tabs on their shoulders. They'd be used to pushing unarmed civilians about—she winced as she spotted neural whips and shockrods on their belts—but there was no way to know how well they'd perform against marines. She suspected they wouldn't last long enough to run. If they were aware of the juggernaut bearing down on them, they hid it well.

She tensed, watching as refugees passed through the checkpoint. The security troops were directing most of them into the city, separating men from women and children. She hoped that meant men were being conscripted into building defences, rather than something more sinister. The planet had taken a beating, but civilisation shouldn't have broken down completely. Not yet. A handful of refugees sat on the ground, their hands cuffed behind their backs. She studied them for a long moment, wondering what they'd done. Protested their treatment? Or…were they deserters? It was clear that hundreds of enemy soldiers had fled into the undergrowth, rather than continue the war.

"Here we go," Phelps said. "Get ready…"

Rachel nodded as the security trooper pressed his scanner to Phelps's palm. His implants went to work, trying to fool the enemy system. The techs had sworn blind that they should be able to override whatever response the trooper got from the datanet, but there was no way to be *sure* until they tested it. If the trooper sounded the alert, they'd have bare seconds to kill him and run before the rest of the garrison came after them…

"You're a farmer?" The trooper sounded impressed. "Report to Section Nine."

Rachel kept her expression under tight control as the trooper ran the rest of the group through the scanner. The trooper seemed astonishingly respectful, under the circumstances. He'd leered at other women, but not at her. She puzzled over it as her implants tricked the scanner, then followed the rest of the team into the city. It was odd, to say the least. Perhaps they were desperate for farmers…

She looked around with interest as they made their way through the defence lines. Bouchon had a certain elegance that was conspicuously missing from Eddisford and the other towns she'd seen on Hameau, but it was steadily falling into darkness. Entire buildings were being turned into strongpoints, their inhabitants evacuated...she watched a handful of families being forced to leave their homes, feeling cold. The defenders intended to force the marines to come to them on their terms. And they might succeed too. She recorded everything she saw, grimly aware that it was just the tip of the iceberg. The defenders couldn't turn the city into an impregnable fortress, but they could make the marines pay a blood price for taking it.

"Look," Bonkowski said. "The prostitutes are already out in force."

Rachel followed his gaze. A handful of women were standing on the roadside, calling out to anyone who looked wealthy or powerful enough to give them a crust of bread. She shuddered, unable to keep from feeling sorry for the women. They weren't career prostitutes, she thought. They didn't have the right attitude for women who'd made a career out of sex work. Instead, they were refugees. They were so desperate that they'd forced themselves to sell their bodies for food. She felt sick, sick and guilty. The poor wrenches didn't deserve to be turned into prostitutes.

They could evacuate them along with the rest of the civilians, she thought, grimly. *Why are they keeping them here?*

She put the thought aside as they reached Section Nine. A harassed-looked official sat at a portable terminal, typing pieces of data into a keyboard. The local datanet must be in worse state than she'd thought. Or perhaps it had been reserved for military use. A modern datanet could handle the demands of an entire *planet* without crashing, but—if she were in command of the defences—she wouldn't have taken the chance. Better to lock the civilians out than risk a crash at the worst possible moment.

The official examined their ID cards, then frowned. "You're farmers. You're on the list for evacuation as soon as possible."

"That's good," Phelps said. His accent was flawless. "Can you tell us where we'll be going?"

"I don't know," the official said. He was typing as he spoke, copying elements from the ID cards into his terminal. Rachel rather thought it looked like make-work. "It depends on your orders from Haverford."

He waved a hand at the barracks. "You are free to explore the city, as long as you check in here every hour on the hour," he said. "Once you get your orders, you'll be on your way."

"My wife needs a rest," Phelps said. "I'll stay with her, if you don't mind."

"Sure thing." The official sounded as if he didn't care. "I'll be out here if you need me."

The interior of the barracks was surprisingly roomy. A handful of men lay on bunks, dead to the world. Farmers, Rachel guessed. Someone in Haverford was thinking ahead. The planet would need farmers, particularly now the government had lost control of the eastern region. She took a bunk as close to the door as possible, then activated her implants and carefully, very carefully, started searching for access nodes. If the enemy had a working ECM routine, she might be in some trouble…

A handful of nodes blinked up in front of her, all locked. She grinned at Phelps, then closed her eyes and went to work. The nodes might be encrypted, but they were basically civilian…her implants had no trouble hacking through the firewalls and slipping into the city's datanet. It was smaller than she'd thought, practically closed down…she grinned again as she realised the tracking and monitoring systems were completely offline. The local population hadn't realised it, not yet. She'd have to find a way to make sure they found out before it was too late.

She felt her smile widen as she skimmed the official's terminal, then rode its link to the planetary datanet. The official had requested files on all four of them—or, rather, on the four identities they'd stolen. There was no reason to think that anyone had realised what they'd done, but she took care to massage the data anyway. The official might be unimaginative enough to run their biometrics through his scanner again. Shaking her head, she reviewed the earlier sets of movement orders Haverford had issued. Most of the farmers seemed to be directed to camps near the capital.

She carefully—very carefully—inserted a set of commands into the system, hoping and praying that the enemy didn't have a proper WebHead watching the network. The average official knew little and cared less about how the datanet actually worked, but a WebHead was a whole 'nother story. He might spot her modifications before she could use them and then cover her tracks.

And all we can do now is wait, she thought, as she opened her eyes. Her head swam, just for a second. There was always a faint sense of disorientation between the virtual world and reality, a sense that one of them—the wrong one—wasn't quite real. *And hope that everything goes according to plan.*

"I don't want to sleep," she said, using hand signals to pass the *real* message. "Shall we go sightseeing?"

Phelps nodded, gravely. If something *did* go wrong, they didn't want to be caught in the barracks. "Of course," he said. "We should see the sights before we go onwards."

They walked through the door—the official didn't look up from his terminal; he was playing a card game—and out onto the streets. The temperature was steadily rising, but—unsurprisingly—the defenders were still working hard. Rachel admired their work ethic, even as she silently recorded everything for transmission to the assault force. She heard a pair of gunshots in the distance—everyone tensed, before slowly returning to work—but she knew the attackers were nowhere near the city. Not yet. She wondered who was shooting at whom, then dismissed the thought. It didn't matter.

"Lots of people are going to be caught in the crossfire when we hit the city," Phelps muttered, as they noted defence strongpoints and emplaced weapons. They'd use a burst-transmitter to update the attackers, before they begun the offensive. Hopefully, most of the heavy weapons would be taken out by long-range fire. "They'll be slaughtered."

"Yeah." Rachel grimaced. There was no way to weaken the city first, not if it was imperative to take the city quickly. A gradualist approach, wearing down the defenders while encircling them, was standard procedure…

here, though, it wasn't going to happen. The briefing had made that quite clear. "And there's nothing we can do about it."

She glanced at a refugee camp in a park. A middle-aged woman was handing out supplies, her face a mask of...cold sanctimony. Beside her, a younger girl in her late teens was helping, something trapped and helpless in her eyes. Rachel guessed the girl's life had been turned upside down in the last few days. She looked as if she'd gone from the top of the heap to the very bottom—or as near as made no difference—and still hadn't gotten over it. She might never get over it. Rachel had seen others on her homeworld, struggling to adjust. They'd had help and support. Here...

Lots of people are going to need help, after the war, she thought. A pair of refugees scowled at her as she walked past. She wondered if they knew who she was, then decided it wasn't likely. They were just mad at the universe and everyone in it. She didn't blame them. *And there's not much we can do for them either.*

It was nearly three hours before they returned to the barracks to find that their orders had been trapped in the filter, as she'd expected. She skimmed them quickly, then rewrote them to ensure the four of them were dispatched directly to Haverford itself. The person who'd issued the orders probably wouldn't notice, she told herself, and no one else would have any reason to suspect anything. She read them one final time, just to be sure there were no discrepancies, then allowed them to go to their intended destination. It was unlikely the official on the desk would notice the delay. People who knew nothing about the datanet tended to ignore warning signs that would have had hackers tearing their hair out.

"You're going to Haverford," the official said, shortly afterwards. "And you'll be on the first aircraft out of the city tomorrow morning."

"Thank you, sir," Phelps said. "What do we do now?"

"Sit and eat, or sleep, or do whatever you like," the official said. He sounded as if he didn't give a damn. "Just make damn sure you get on that helicopter. You do *not* want to be late."

"Yes, sir," Phelps said. Rachel was tempted to tell him to take his tongue off the official's boot. "We'll be there."

And then we have a whole different problem ahead of us, Rachel thought. *When we get there, we're going to have to abandon the farmer personas.*

She smiled as she returned to her bunk. She couldn't make many more changes, not from here, but she could get an idea of how the system functioned. And then, when they got there...it would be easy to cut them a whole batch of new IDs. And then...

We can find the enemy bunker, she told herself. The briefing had been long on generalities, but short on specifics. She didn't mind that. There was very little worse than a senior officer who though he knew enough to micromanage his troops from a distance. *And then we can put an end to the war.*

CHAPTER THIRTY-ONE

This did not, of course, help keep the peace. A number of conflicts that had been kept under control by outside forces reignited themselves as the various combatants realised there would be no further outside intervention. Chaos spread, with horrific atrocities following in its wake. Vast numbers of people became refugees, searching for a safety and security that no longer existed.

—PROFESSOR LEO CAESIUS

Earthfall and its Aftermath

"LOTS MORE POOR BASTARDS heading west," Lieutenant Kareem Haiti said, as the Raptor flew over a crowd of refugees. "You think they don't know what's on their heels?"

"I think they do know," Lieutenant Ginny Patel answered. "And that's what's making them run."

She felt naked, uncomfortably exposed, even though she was flying as low as she dared. There was a PDC not too far away and she wasn't entirely *sure* she was below its horizon. A plasma burst that would chew up a starship would vaporise the Raptor so completely, nothing would ever be found. She kept a wary eye on her threat receiver as they left the refugees far behind, watching for active sensors that might signal an HVM team lurking in the forest. The enemy didn't *need* a PDC to ruin their day.

"The groundpounders are punching it up the motorway," Haiti commented. "You think the enemy will be setting more ambushes?"

"Yes," Ginny said. They'd already killed two tanks that had tried to conceal themselves in the undergrowth, unaware that their engines hadn't been shielded properly. A smarter team would be more careful, she was sure. She'd already heard angry complaints about antitank teams that had gone undetected until they'd opened fire. "I'd bet half my salary on it."

Haiti laughed. "Is our salary worth anything these days?"

Ginny shrugged. She'd always told herself, ever since she'd washed out of Boot Camp, that she'd put in a few years as an auxiliary and build up a nice little nest egg before quitting and doing something else with her time, but...Earthfall had derailed her plans. She had no idea where she could go, even if she wanted to leave. And she wasn't sure she did. Sure, her salary might be even less than toilet paper now the economy had crashed, but at least she had a bed, a job and something to *do*. She wasn't one of the poor bastards who'd been caught on Earth, Terra Nova or Kiev when the nukes had started flying. Or starving to death on a crapsack world that couldn't survive without off-world support.

"Fucked if I know," she said. A radio transmission flashed across her sensor. She turned the Raptor, watching carefully for the first sign of enemy attack. "But it could be worse."

"Sure," Haiti said. "We could be down there, trudging through the mud."

"Bite your tongue," Ginny ordered. "We don't want to be cursed."

She had to smile. The planet had seemed nice, but...she'd heard the stories. The whole settlement was carefully planned, an entire infrastructure devoted to keeping the population in line...she shuddered. She would sooner spend her life on a stage-two colony world, perhaps even a stage-one. She would be poor, and expected to have at least four children, but she'd be free.

A team of enemy soldiers appeared beneath them. She flinched, nearly hitting the firing controls before realising they were a band of deserters heading south. Scuttlebutt claimed the local government had told its troops that the marines would torture them to within an inch of their lives, and then shoot them, if they surrendered. It might explain, she supposed, why so few enemy soldiers had surrendered when they could run. The bastards had set their men up to be killed. She watched the enemy soldiers scatter, hoping they had the sense to keep moving until they were far away. They could come in from the cold after the war was over.

Another radio transmission, closer this time. Her eyes narrowed. It looked like an enemy transmitter, perhaps a forward command post. They'd need *someone* to direct the stay-behind teams, wouldn't they? She felt her lips curve into a savage smile as she altered course, again. They'd hit the CP before they realised she was right on top of them, then vanish before any resistance could be mounted. The groundpounders would find it easier to reach the city if no one was coordinating the resistance.

"Ten seconds," she said, as they picked up speed. "Here we go."

"Ready," Haiti said.

• • •

Corporal Sidney Rawhide and his team lurked just under the treeline and waited, readying themselves for the enemy aircraft. The bastards would come soon, if the plan worked, and then…the HVM launcher felt heavy in his hands, pregnant with lethal possibilities. He braced himself, eying the farmer's barn on the other side of the field. They'd set up a radio transmitter inside, programming it to send out random transmissions on command frequencies. The higher-ups had been *sure* the transmitter would attract enemy fire. Sidney rather suspected that a number of *real* command posts had been flattened when they'd made the mistake of signalling where the enemy could hear it.

They might as well have called the enemy directly and ordered one bombing to go, he thought, nastily. He had no love for his superiors and he'd really been looking forward to receiving his discharge papers at the end of the month. It hadn't taken him too long to realise there was no future in the army, whatever rumour might say about planned off-world deployments.

He would just get his ass shot off for nothing. *And if this goes wrong, we might as well have done the same thing ourselves.*

He'd thought, hard, about joining the deserters. He knew enough to remove the implant from his palm, making it impossible to track him unless he was very unlucky. He would have done it too, if he hadn't heard his family farm had been destroyed. His parents and younger siblings had been killed, if they were lucky. He had nothing left, nothing but a desire for revenge. And now, if everything worked as planned, he would get that chance.

Sidney tensed as he heard the faint whine in the air, the whine he'd become all too familiar with over the last few days. The enemy aircraft were quiet, compared to the helicopters he'd ridden during basic, but they weren't completely silent. Once you knew what to listen for, they were easy to hear. He hefted the HVM launcher, scanning the sky for the first glimpse of the enemy aircraft. He didn't want to turn on the seeker head. He'd been warned the enemy were *good* at detecting active sensors and returning fire. The counterbattery fire might start before he even *launched* his missile.

The whine grew louder as the aircraft came into view, swooping down on the barn. The craft looked *odd*, as if a shuttlecraft, helicopter and jet aircraft had mated and produced a thoroughly weird child. He'd seen them fly terrifyingly fast, hover in the air and land on a dime. Heavy weapons hung underneath the craft's stubby wings, half of its racks clearly empty. He ground his teeth in frustration. The bastards had probably shot up refugee convoys as they fled their advance. Damn them. He was *sure* that was what they'd done.

He pointed the launcher at the enemy aircraft as it opened fire, launching a single missile towards the barn. The barn exploded into a fireball, a wave of heat striking his face. He flicked the sensor on, then pulled the trigger. The enemy pilot *was* fast—he threw the aircraft upwards, launching dozens of flares—even as the HVM lanced towards him. He even managed to evade a direct hit! But it wasn't good enough. The warhead detonated so close to the airframe that it took serious damage…

"Got you, you bastard!" Sidney allowed himself a cheer. The enemy aircraft was staggering, clearly unsure if it could fly or not. Smoke was pouring from its rear. "Come on, crash!"

• • •

Ginny cursed savagely as she wrestled with the controls. The HVM hadn't *hit* them—they would be playing harps by now if it *had*—but it had severely damaged her craft. The Raptor was designed to soak up damage, yet...there were limits. She felt her stomach churn as she fought for attitude, knowing it was just a matter of time before the aircraft gave up the unequal struggle and crashed. They were fucked...

"Hit the emergency beacon," she snapped. The controls vibrated in her hands. "Now!"

"Already done," Haiti said. The Raptor lurched to the side. "They're on their way."

"Yeah."

Ginny kept her thoughts to herself. They were well past the front lines, with at least one HVM team prowling around. The rescue team would come in carefully, very carefully. They might not have *time* to reach the crash site before they were captured...assuming, of course, that they survived the landing. If they went down hard enough, they wouldn't live long enough to be captured.

The Raptor lurched again, then started to fall. Ginny threw their remaining engine into a desperate bid to slow their descent, the craft spinning madly as she lost control, but it seemed futile. The ground came up and hit them, the airframe crashing through the trees, smashing them down before finally coming to a halt. Ginny checked her body for injury, as best as she could, then unstrapped herself. Haiti groaned, then started choking. Ginny glanced at him and swore. A piece of metal had driven itself into his chest. She stumbled towards him, but it was already too late. There was nothing she could do.

Fuck, she thought. His body was still warm, but...she knew he was dead. There was no way she could get him to a stasis pod or revival chamber in time. *Fuck. I...*

She heard someone crashing through the undergrowth and froze in horror. She'd done the dreaded Conduct After Capture course—everyone had, if they went on the front lines—but...her instructors hadn't attempted to soften the blow. Captured soldiers—aircrew and snipers, in particular—couldn't expect mercy. They would be tortured, they would be raped—men as well as women—they wouldn't be treated decently, whatever the situation. Insurgents could rarely afford to house prisoners and, worse, they knew the marines would do whatever it took to recover lost personal. The best she could expect was a bullet in the back of her head.

Her hand dropped to her pistol. It had been a long time since she'd fired it—normally, she only fired it on the firing range—and yet, it was her only means of defence. She wondered, as she ducked low and started to crawl towards a gash in the fuselage, if she should keep the final bullet for herself. She kicked herself as she realised she only had two spare clips of ammunition. If she'd been a groundpounder, she would probably have found herself up on a charge for not stuffing every last pocket with bullets. She had the nasty feeling that being court-martialled would be preferable to what was coming her way...

"You in there," a voice shouted. "Come out with your hands up or..."

Ginny ignored the voice as she reached the gash and crawled through, onto the muddy ground. Water was pooling under the aircraft, suggesting that she'd crashed far too close to a lake for comfort. She forced herself to keep moving, hoping she could evade the enemy until help arrived. Her CO would know where she'd crashed, she told herself over and over again. Help would be on the way. She just had to keep away from the enemy and...

Someone jumped her, sending her to the ground. Her pistol went flying. She drew on her training, grabbing hold of his arm and twisting as hard as she could. She was no match for a groundpounder when it came to physical strength, but she was hardly a weakling. Flying a Raptor required strong upper arms too. He howled in pain, giving her a chance to throw him off and hit him in the nose as hard as she could. She had the satisfaction of feeling it break under the impact before someone else shoved a gun in her face. She froze. If they'd intended to take her prisoner, she'd probably convinced them otherwise.

"Don't move," a voice growled. She found herself looking at a young man, probably a year or two younger than herself. "Don't you fucking move."

Ginny forced herself to stay still. She couldn't get the gun out of her face, not before he had a chance to pull the trigger. And even if she did, she was surrounded. There were four other men in the area, all looking furious. One of them held his nose and glared at her. She cursed, inwardly. The most dangerous moments of being taken captive were always the *first*...and she'd already made a bunch of enemies. And if they believed the horror stories they'd been told about the marines not taking prisoners...

Her captor stared at her. "You're a woman?"

"Yes," Ginny said. There was no point in trying to deny it. She was surprised *they* were surprised. She'd been on worlds where the local women were expected to spend their lives as little more than slaves to their husbands, but Hameau had always struck her as a bit more civilised. "Lieutenant Ginny..."

"Shut up," her captor growled. "If you do as we say, you won't be harmed."

• • •

"She broke my fucking nose," Rowan growled. It was hard to understand him. Every word seemed to be slurred. "I'm going to fucking *kill* her."

"No you're fucking not," Sidney snapped. He had no qualms about blowing an aircraft out of the sky, but...he wasn't going to shoot an unarmed woman in the face. Besides, his commander had made it clear that the government wanted prisoners. "Sit down and do nothing."

He glared at the woman. She looked back, as if she was waiting for him to say something. She was at his mercy...he allowed himself a second to savour the feeling, then put it firmly to one side. She'd broken Rowan's nose. She was stronger than she looked, definitely. There was no time for games, not when the enemy might have dispatched a SAR team. He kept the gun pointed firmly at her face as he commanded his team to tie her hands, then search her from top to bottom. She wasn't carrying much, beyond an ID card and a handful of imperial credits. She evidently didn't know they were useless on Hameau.

"On your feet," he growled. He helped her to her feet when it became clear she couldn't stand with her hands bound, then forced her to march into the forest. "Move."

He studied her ID as they walked, listening carefully for the sound of approaching aircraft. Lieutenant Ginny Patel, Terran Marine Corps (Auxiliary). It didn't *look* like a fake, although...he wasn't sure *what* to believe. The higher-ups had snidely dismissed any rumour the planet was being invaded by the marines, let alone the Empire. The Empire was gone. And yet...he eyed the woman's back suspiciously. Female soldiers and aviators were rare on Hameau. He'd only ever met one during his career.

"So," he said, eying the woman's battered face. There was a nasty bruise that was threatening to turn into a black eye. "Marine Corps? Really?"

"Lieutenant Ginny Patel, Terran Marine Corps," the woman said, followed by a string of numbers he assumed to be her serial number. "Yes."

Sidney studied her for a long moment. She hadn't fallen to pieces, not yet. He had a feeling she wouldn't, even if she was thrown to the lions. And that suggested...what? He didn't know much about the Terran Marine Corps. They were supposed to be super-soldiers, but he'd watched enough flicks to take such claims with a grain of salt. His instructors had told him that the flicks weren't remotely realistic—he'd seen enough during his career to know the bastards had been right—but...he shook his head. He wouldn't be deciding her fate. His superiors would make that call.

"Welcome to Hameau," he said, finally. "I hope you enjoy your stay."

• • •

Ginny had forced herself to think, as her captors had marched her further and further away from the crash site, of a plan to get away before they handed her over to their superiors. But nothing came to mind. Her hands were bound, her pistol was lost, her tools, wristcom and datapad had been left behind in the wreckage of her Raptor. A Pathfinder could probably have taken all five of her captors without breaking a sweat, but everyone knew Pathfinders ate iron bars for breakfast and could leap tall buildings in a single bound. She found herself wishing she had a locator implant, although they'd been banned long ago. The SAR team might have liberated her well before it was too late.

She eyed her captors, trying to look for weaknesses. They were rough around the edges, but professional...certainly, more professional than the insurgents who *would* have raped and killed her by now. It was unfortunate that their very professionalism worked against her. If they'd been sloppy, they might have given her a chance to break free. Instead...

They gave her a hat and a battered coat before leading her onto the road. From above, she'd look like just another refugee. She was sure the SAR team was out there, but...

She gritted her teeth. It looked as if she was going into captivity. And escape was impossible.

There will be a chance to escape, she told herself, firmly. *You just have to wait and see.*

CHAPTER THIRTY-TWO

It is impossible to calculate how many people fled their homes, let alone their homeworlds, in the first few weeks after Earthfall. As interstellar shipping steadily collapsed, it became harder for people to board ships and escape. The death toll might well have been in the trillions. We simply don't know.

—PROFESSOR LEO CAESIUS

Earthfall and its Aftermath

"THERE'S NO SIGN OF OUR MISSING PILOT," General Anderson said. "The SAR team found nothing."

Kerri nodded, shortly. "They won't kill her out of hand, sir."

She looked around her ready room, feeling an odd little pang. It felt strange, in some ways, to be worrying about a single life. She was used to watching starships die, each explosion taking dozens of men into the next world. A single life seemed meaningless on such a scale, but she understood the General's concern. The marines had to look out for their fellows. No one else would.

"One would hope not," General Anderson said. "Of course, they *might* have taken her to Bouchon."

"Yes, sir." Kerri couldn't disagree. "And she'll be caught in the midst of the assault."

She shook her head, slowly. "I've got pickets and drones covering all the approaches, sir. If an enemy fleet arrives, we'll know about it before they get into firing range. We've also sent a request for additional firepower, so...we might be able to stand them off when they arrive."

"But we have no way to know when they will arrive," Anderson mused. "They could be coming from *anywhere*."

"Yes, sir." Kerri had put her analysts to work as soon as she heard the news. "It's possible the corporation has controlling interests in a number of other worlds, all within a few dozen light years. They might have intended to snap them up like windfalls after Earthfall, but...we don't know what happened. The plan might have gone completely haywire."

"We don't dare count on it," Anderson said. "And *that* means the offensive has to go ahead as planned."

"Yes, sir," Kerri said. "Good luck."

Anderson grunted. "Have a good one yourself, Commodore. We'll see you on the other side."

• • •

Rachel was already awake when the alarm rang, jerking the rest of the evacuees out of a fitful sleep. The arrival of others—farmers, technicians, corprats—had worried her, if only because some of them might know the people they were impersonating, but nothing had happened overnight. Most of the evacuees looked stunned, as if they knew they'd already lost everything and couldn't hope to get it back. She told herself that most of them would have good jobs, when the war finally came to an end. If they survived...

She rolled out of bed and stood, trying to stumble around like a middle-aged woman who hadn't had enough sleep. She thought she was overdoing it a little, but none of the civilians looked much better. Instead, they were marched into the next room, told to take a ration bar for breakfast and then hurried to the helicopter pad. Rachel chewed her ration bar, trying to conceal her disgust at the taste. She'd always thought the Imperial

Army's ration bars were the worst—soldiers used to joke they were made from cardboard and old gym mats—but these were worse. Somehow. She guessed the procurer had managed to find someone who bid even *lower* to produce the bars. Honestly, she would have thought that was impossible.

A pair of evacuees looked nervous, when they were pushed into the helicopter. Rachel kept her face impassive, snapping her buckle into place without help from the flight crew. The helicopter looked a damn sight safer than some of the aircraft she'd used, during basic training and afterwards. She'd always *suspected* the Drill Instructors deliberately chose aircraft that *looked* as if they were on the verge of falling apart, but she'd never dared ask. It would be odd otherwise. The training budget would easily have covered better aircraft if they'd wanted them.

Phelps sat next to her, his face as impassive as her own. She resisted the urge to start a conversation in sign language, not when someone might notice and start asking why. Instead, she took a deep breath as the helicopter roared to life. A handful of evacuees started moaning behind her as the roar grew louder, the entire aircraft rattling uncomfortably as it staggered into the air. Someone muttered something about the pilot being drunk... she rolled her eyes in annoyance. She really had been in worse places. It certainly beat crawling through a bog, trying to get back to the RV point without being caught. She still had nightmares about the Mohinga. God knew there were trainees who'd gone in and never come out again.

The helicopter stayed low as it roared over the city, heading west. She craned her neck, peering out of the porthole. Bouchon didn't look any better, she thought; the city seemed even more crowded, thousands of soldiers and refugees crowding the streets. A line of lorries made their way out of the city, loaded to the gunwales with refugees...mostly women and children. She hoped the local government had made *some* kind of provision for their food, shelter and security. She'd seen enough refugee camps to know the locals could easily start exploiting the homeless and dispossessed, if the government didn't keep a firm grip on the situation. A sizable chunk of those women were probably going to be sold into sexual slavery.

I want to go to a ghastly little religious world, where I don't have to feel the slightest twinge of guilt for killing the bastards, she thought, although she knew it was unjust. Most civilians on religious worlds kept their heads down, all too aware they'd lose them the moment they raised their voice. *And then I want to go on shore leave to somewhere nice and relaxing.*

She allowed herself to dream of pleasant beaches, hazardous mountain climbs and studs with hot bodies—male or female, she wasn't fussy—then leaned forward to watch the world go by. The western side of the mountains seemed to be considerably more developed than the eastern side, with dozens of towns and hamlets laid out below her. She couldn't spot any defences, but they were too high for her to see much even with enhanced eyesight. The locals were probably pouring everything they had into Bouchon. The city was effectively a bottleneck. If the marines broke through, there would be no natural barriers between them and Haverford.

The helicopter jerked. Behind her, she heard someone being sick. Civilians. She gritted her teeth as the stench wafted towards her, reminding herself that she'd been airsick too when she'd been a little girl. And she'd smelt worse too. There had been times when she'd been convinced the stench of the dead and dying would never leave her nostrils, as if it had embedded itself within her flesh. Her stomach churned, reminding her that she hadn't eaten much. She was going to have to find something as soon as they landed, if she wanted to keep going. She couldn't afford to run out of energy in the middle of the enemy capital.

Not when we'll have to duck out of sight as quickly as possible, she thought. *It would be unfortunate if they actually forwarded us to a farm.*

Her lips quirked as the helicopter jerked again, then started to descend. Haverford came into view, a mid-sized city resting beside a large river. That wasn't uncommon, she knew. Rivers provided cheap transport—and power, sometimes—on colony worlds that couldn't afford more than a handful of basic vehicles. She could see dozens of boats, from small sailing boats to giant barges, making their way down to the sea. It was quite possible their crews had decided to put some distance between themselves and the city until the war came to an end. She didn't blame them. Anyone who wanted to lay siege to the city wouldn't hesitate to start sinking boats to put an end to water-borne trade. Or turn the boats into pontoon bridges.

"Rats leaving the sinking ship," someone muttered behind her.

Rachel blinked in surprise, resisting the urge to turn her head and see who'd spoken. It was rare, in her experience, to hear open dissent. Not here. No one could ever be sure they weren't being recorded, not on a world that was utterly *riddled* with surveillance systems. But…she rather suspected people were starting to realise that the surveillance systems were breaking down. Who knew how much trouble was going to start when it *really* sank in?

She smiled, tightly, as the helicopter dropped lower. The riverside was lined with giant warehouses and barracks, waiting for new colonists who would never come. Earth was gone. The seemingly-infinite supply of new colonists had tapered off. She wondered how the locals would cope, then shrugged. The colony was firmly established. It was the stage-one colonies that would have real trouble.

The helicopter touched down with a bump. She reached for her buckle as the hatch slammed open, the stench of burning hydrocarbons assaulting her nostrils. The helicopter blades were still spinning, whipping through the air in a manner that suggested they were actually sinking. Rachel kept her head low as she ducked out of the helicopter and headed for the nearest building. The complex seemed to be largely empty, but armed guards were everywhere. Getting out would be easy, she thought; getting out unremarked would be a great deal harder.

Another official—she was starting to wonder if they were mass-produced in a cloning tank somewhere—met them as they were chivvied into the building. "I'm afraid that all transport has been seconded to the needs of the war," he said, as if he was unaware of what he was actually saying. "You'll have to remain in the barracks until we can organise transport upriver."

"We quite understand," Phelps said. "Right now, we're just glad to be away from the fighting."

The clerk gave him an odd look. Rachel tensed. She'd made sure to insert all the right documents and permissions into the right places, but she was uncomfortably aware that something could go badly wrong at any moment. A skilled WebHead would have no trouble discovering what she'd done, if he bothered to look. There was a war on. Chances were that normal services had been suspended for the duration. And then it struck her. The clerk was delighted that he too was away from the fighting.

REMF, she thought.

The clerk glanced at her, then back at Phelps. "How much did you see?"

"Not much," Phelps said, shortly. They'd been careful not to make their cover story *too* interesting. The last thing they wanted was to be interrogated by enemy intelligence officers. "We heard the alert and ran for our lives. And when they reached Bouchon they sent us here."

"Where you will stay for the next few days," the clerk said. He sounded disappointed. "You have a set of bunks in the barracks. Stay inside, unless given permission to leave. The city is currently under martial law."

"Drat," Phelps said. "I was hoping to see the sights."

"You'll see the inside of a jail cell if you leave the complex," the clerk said, flatly. "Don't leave the barracks."

"Yes, sir," Phelps said.

He grinned at the rest of the team, then led them down to the barracks. Rachel was almost disappointed. The prefabricated barracks could have been on any world, as if the locals hadn't bothered to reconfigure or replace them over the years. Perhaps it was deliberate, she considered. They'd want to encourage newcomers to get settled elsewhere as quickly as possible. She dropped her knapsack on the bunk—there was nothing in it worth stealing, save for a change of clothes—and glanced into the common room. A handful of evacuees were watching the idiot box. Her lips quirked in disgust as she realised it was a particularly soppy romantic comedy. The lead actress apparently had it written into her contracts that she had to take off her top at least four times per flick.

I'm sure the scriptwriters find it difficult to write around, she thought, sarcastically. *And we'll find it just as hard to tear ourselves away from the box ourselves.*

They exchanged hand signals, then set out to tour the barracks complex. It was just as she'd expected. A handful of buildings, a concrete play area designed for children—she had the feeling that whoever had designed it really *hated* children—and a single dining hall, all surrounded by chain-link fencing and armed guards. She silently counted them as she assessed the situation, trying to decide how best to leave the compound. Getting over the fence and taking the guards wouldn't be a problem. Doing it without their absence being noticed would be a great deal harder.

We might have no choice, she thought, as they went back to the barracks and checked for pickups. The locals weren't even *trying* to hide them. She wasn't surprised to find a dozen in the bathroom block, all carefully positioned so they peered down into the showers. *And the sooner we get out of here, the better.*

"We leave at nightfall," Phelps signalled. "And hide ourselves in the big city."

"Go west," Perkins signalled back. He jabbed a hand towards the distant river, on the other side of the fence. "Let them think we drowned."

"Good thinking," Phelps signalled. "Once we're out of here, we should be able to hide."

Rachel nodded, then hurried up to the roof and looked over the city. The barracks wasn't *that* big, but she still managed to get a good view. The other barracks were being crammed with refugees and, beyond them, thousands *more* refugees crowded the streets. She couldn't see many guards, beyond the handful surrounding the complex. She doubted the locals had enough manpower to secure the streets. There was a faint sense of unease in the air, a sense the shit could hit the fan at any time. She smiled, knowing what it meant. The government's grip on its city was weakening.

They ate a dinner that was almost, but not quite, inedible, then returned to their bunks and waited for night to fall. The locals seemed oddly slack, as if they thought they had too many problems elsewhere to worry about a handful of refugees. Rachel was surprised they hadn't crammed more people into their barracks. She watched the others go to sleep, then joined the rest of the team as they crept into the darkness. The door wasn't locked. She supposed the locals assumed the chain-link fence would be enough to keep the refugees from getting lost in the city. Instead, it barely posed a problem. Rachel scrambled over it with ease. The two guards within eyesight never knew what hit them.

"Got their guns." Bonkowski snickered. "They use palm-readers, sir."

Rachel snorted. The government probably thought that keying their guns to a single authorised user—or a handful of authorised users—would keep them from falling into unfriendly hands. It would work too, if the unfriendly hands didn't know how to bypass the security system. She doubted it would take more than a few minutes with a toolkit to make sure *anyone* could fire the guns. Hell, the system might have been jury-rigged already. The palm-readers were notoriously unreliable. Even the Imperial Army had never adopted them in combat.

"They'll be after us when they realise the guards are missing," Phelps said. He turned and led them away from the barracks. "Let's go."

Rachel nodded to herself as they hurried into the darkness, heading straight for the centre of town. In her experience, the middle and upper class sections tended to be the easiest places to hide. There were fewer friendly people there, fewer people who might look away and keep their mouths shut, but the police were often reluctant to *really* ransack the place. They could break into a house, steal enough clothes and supplies to change their appearance completely and then…do whatever they had to do. If the briefing officers had been right, if General Taggard had been telling the truth…

Don't get ahead of yourself, she thought, sharply. *First things first, in that order.*

They stayed in the shadows as they headed west, deeper into the city. The towering warehouses and barracks were rapidly replaced by apartment blocks, then middle-class accommodation. Haverford had been designed for working professionals, she guessed. There was a curfew, but hardly anyone seemed to be honouring it. She didn't see many policemen—or soldiers—on the streets. Crime didn't look to be on the rise…not yet, anyway. It was just a matter of time. People would start stealing because they were desperate and things would go downhill from there.

And then they will really start losing control of the streets, she mused. The locals seemed to be establishing some defence lines, but…it looked as if they were betting on Bouchon. *And what will they do when Bouchon falls?*

"That house," Phelps said. He pointed to a small two-story house that looked deserted. "If there's anyone inside, take them down as quickly as possible."

"Without hurting them, if possible," Rachel added, quickly. The people living there were unlikely to be dangerous, not really. She didn't want to kill innocent civilians just for a set of clothes. Ideally, the house would be empty. They'd have to check before someone realised they were there and called the police. "We don't want to leave a trail of bodies."

"How true," Phelps agreed. "Let's go."

CHAPTER THIRTY-THREE

The second set of problems, however, came from the worlds that had prepared for trouble. In hindsight, it is clear that a number of Grand Senatorial families—i.e. corporate power structures—had expected a significant collapse for quite some time and taken steps to meet it. Their economies were not unaffected by the chaos, but they didn't collapse.

—**Professor Leo Caesius**

Earthfall and its Aftermath

"DO YOU THINK WE HAVE A CHANCE?"

Derek frowned. The last two days had been spent establishing strongpoint after strongpoint, running around the city and trying—desperately—to plan a defence. No two officers seemed to agree on what best to do to defend their city, with some gambling everything on holding the forward defence line and others assuming the forward line would fall and making preparations for it. Derek rather suspected the latter group were correct, but he knew better than to say that out loud where a senior officer might overhear him. If a Major had been relieved of command and marched off by the security troops for defeatism, he dreaded to think what would happen to a mere lieutenant. He'd probably be shot on the spot, his body left as an example to everyone else who dared disagree...

"I think we need to keep planning for the worst," he said. "And the brass doesn't need to know about it."

He sighed. Whoever had designed the strongpoints was either an idiot or a traitor or both. It wasn't that they were bad designs. They actually looked quite good, on paper. But they were designed, perhaps deliberately, to make it difficult for the defenders to evacuate, if they had to leave in a hurry. The makeshift strongpoints, the converted houses and tower blocks, weren't much better. He'd had to spend hours planning how best to abandon them, when they could no longer be held, and get back to the next strongpoint without either being shot in the back by the enemy or gunned down by his own people. It wasn't going to be fun.

"Good thinking," Loomis said. He looked around the strongpoint. "Do we have enough ammunition and everything?"

Derek shrugged. One thing he hadn't realised—that no one had realised until they'd found themselves fighting a shooting war—was just how quickly soldiers burned through their stockpiles of ammunition. A supply that had been predicted to last for a week had barely lasted two days. The logistics corps had brought in literally thousands of rounds of ammunition, as well as everything from antitank rockets to mortar shells and landmines, but he had no idea how long it would last when the shooting actually started. It was quite possible they'd run out of ammunition midway through the battle. *That* would be embarrassing.

He looked up as a helicopter flew overhead, heading west. A handful of refugees had been flown out of the city, or loaded into lorries and driven out of the city, but...so far, Jenny and her family had remained in the refugee camp. Derek wasn't sure how he felt about that, if he had to be honest. Spending his nights with Jenny was all he'd dreamed of and more, but—at the same time—he knew what might happen to her when the shooting started. His imagination provided too many possibilities, from her being crippled by a bomb blast to being captured by enemy soldiers. But he couldn't send her away. He had no idea who was putting together the lists of evacuees, let alone what criteria they were using. Clearly, Jenny's father wasn't as important as he'd thought.

Loomis nudged him. "You're thinking about her, aren't you?"

"Yeah." Derek smiled, dreamily. "I never knew..."

"Don't get too attached," Loomis advised. "You'd be better trading a ration bar to get your knob sucked than giving your heart to her..."

Derek stared at him. "You've been trading ration bars for sex?"

Loomis smirked. "What am I meant to do with them? Eat them?"

"Well..." Derek found himself at a loss for words. "People actually *take* them? As currency?"

"You'll be astonished just what people will do when they're starving," Loomis said. "Jenny probably feels the same way too."

Derek blinked. "I don't give her ration bars."

"Probably a good idea," Loomis said. "You want her to keep sleeping with you, don't you?"

"Yes," Derek said. He had the feeling one of them wasn't making any sense. He hoped it wasn't him. "What do you mean?"

Loomis winked at him. "You're an up-and-coming army officer who got his troops out of two successive hellholes and is now part of the defence force. Jenny probably thinks you're a good investment."

"Fuck off," Derek said, without heat. "What do you think will happen after the war?"

"You'll get a medal," Loomis said. "And you'll probably be invited to stay in the army."

"Fuck off, again," Derek said. He shook his head. "Maybe she just wants someone to warm her bed."

Loomis laughed, unconvincingly. "You're funny, you."

"Thanks." Derek gave him a sharp look. "At least she wants something more than food from me."

"Keep telling yourself that," Loomis said. "And don't blame me if she fucks you in another way."

Derek ignored the comment and turned to peer into the distance. The flow of refugees had started to taper off as the enemy pressed closer, until they were practically blockading the eastern side of the city. It was pointless—there was nothing stopping the defenders from bringing supplies in from the west—but he had to admit that it was taking a toll on the defenders. The next people they'd see coming up the road would kill them, unless the defenders killed them first. He made sure to keep his head low. The enemy snipers were very good. So far, they'd picked off a handful of senior officers who'd been *sure* they were out of range. His lips quirked, humourlessly. The enemy didn't realise it, but they'd probably helped the defenders.

"Let the troops get some rest, but tell them to be ready to man the defences when the shit hits the fan," he ordered. "And don't let them get into the alcohol."

"Yes, Your Supreme Eminence," Loomis said. "Do you think they'll listen to me?"

"They had better," Derek said. "The greenies whipped two men for drunkenness."

He sighed, inwardly. Colonel Macintyre had sent him reinforcements, a number of men from a dozen different units that had been chopped up and spat out by the invaders. Hardly any of them knew anyone outside their original unit, hardly any of them had been eager to return to the battlefield...Derek himself wasn't keen on the idea, even though he knew his duty. It hadn't been easy to get them to work together and he was uncomfortably aware the entire company might disintegrate when the enemy started shooting. The tactical handbooks claimed they should have had at least six months in the rear, working out their problems before they returned to combat. There hadn't even been time for a few hours of Intercourse and Intoxication.

Although we found time anyway, he thought. He had a sudden impression of Jenny pressing against him, her warm body writhing under his touch. It was so strong that he found himself determined to go to her that very moment, even though they both had work to do. *And tomorrow we could die.*

He calmed himself with an effort. There would be time later, he hoped. Now...

"The scouts say the enemy troops are taking up position," he said. "We could be attacked at dawn."

"Or the middle of the night," Loomis said. Derek *looked* at him. "Think about it. Everyone expects to be attacked at dawn. They"—he jabbed a finger towards the darkening plain—"might just decide to kick things off in the middle of the night, when we're not expecting it."

"I hate you," Derek said.

"Nah, you love me," Loomis said. "Who *else* would stick with you?"

"Oh, fuck off," Derek said. "Go do your job."

Loomis struck a perfect salute. "Sir! Yes, sir!"

• • •

All things considered, Ginny thought, her captivity could have been a great deal worse.

They'd stripped her, of course; they'd searched her thoroughly, leaving no body cavity untouched, before giving her a set of underwear that had clearly been intended for someone shorter, fatter and bustier than her. They'd been apologetic enough about the outfit that she was inclined to believe it was all they had on hand, rather than an attempt to make her feel at risk of sexual harassment. And they'd fired off a handful of questions at her, but not made any attempt to force her to talk. She was starting to think the locals really *hadn't* known they were being invaded by the marines.

As if we didn't tell them, she thought. The chair was comfortable, but the cuffs and shackles around her wrists and ankles made it hard to move. *They probably didn't really believe us.*

She looked around the barren room, wondering if she was being softened up. Her training had made it clear that even *civilised* captors would do their best to make their captives talk, to weaken their resolve to resist and escape when they had the chance. They hadn't tortured or raped her or done *anything*, but...the knowledge that they *could* was lingering at the back of her mind. She knew it was just a matter of time before her captors started considering desperate measures, if they thought there was something locked up in her head that would benefit them. Whatever rules they had about the decent treatment of POWs would be thrown out the airlock in a moment if they thought they had a greater need for answers. And if they did start to torture her, they'd make damn sure she never made it home.

The door clicked, then opened. A short man stepped into the room, wearing an unmarked uniform. Probably a senior officer, she guessed. Someone who expected everyone to know him, in or out of uniform. Or... maybe he was just trying to deny her knowledge. She might be traded back at any moment, if she was lucky. They wouldn't want her blabbing something useful to *her* senior officers. General Anderson didn't need to threaten torture to get her to talk.

"Lieutenant Patel," the man said. "The recorders in this room are off."

Ginny lifted an eyebrow. She'd been pretty sure she was under constant observation before one of her first interrogators had confirmed it. If the locals spied on their own people, with so little regard for their privacy they even watched them in the bathroom, they'd have no qualms about watching a POW. Ginny would have been more concerned about it if she'd been doing something more interesting than sitting in a chair and waiting for something—anything—to happen. And yet...

Her mind raced. The recorders were off? A lie? Or the truth? If it was a lie...she had to assume it was a lie, unless...she winced, inwardly. If someone intended to torture her without authorisation, they'd hardly leave recorded evidence lying around for their superior officers to find. General Anderson would be *pissed* if one of his subordinates broke the Marine Corps Articles of War. She doubted the local higher-ups would be any less annoyed. They might be left holding the bag.

"We studied your ID," the man said. "We put it through all the tests we could muster. And it was genuine."

Ginny knew she should keep her mouth shut. But she couldn't resist. "I told you that."

The man's lips twitched. "Forgive us for not taking your word for it," he said, so dryly that Ginny felt her skin start to itch. "You are, after all, a prisoner of war."

"Yeah." Ginny shrugged. "And now you do know."

"Yeah," the man echoed. "Why are you here?"

Ginny gritted her teeth. "Lieutenant Ginny Patel, Terran Marine Corps, Serial Number..."

"Be quiet." The man cut her off with a wave of his hand. "Why did you invade our world?"

He paused, as if he was expecting an answer. Ginny kept her mouth firmly closed. He wouldn't believe the truth and...he wouldn't like it if he *did* believe it. Besides, she knew she'd already said too much.

The man lowered his voice. "What do you do to POWs? I mean...to the men and women you captured?"

Ginny frowned. She had the odd feeling that a *lot* was hanging on the question. But she wasn't sure she wanted to answer.

"We've been told that you've been shooting surrendering men and raping women and children," the man said. "Is that true?"

"No," Ginny said, before she could stop herself. "It isn't even remotely true."

"No?" The man raised an eyebrow. "Explain?"

"Everyone who surrendered would have been put in a POW camp," Ginny said, tartly. "Once the war is over, they will be released unless they're being held for war crimes against us or local civilians. Prisoners are not generally shot unless they cause real trouble or pretend to surrender in order to get us to let down our guard before they draw weapons and open fire."

"I see," the man said. "And you are sure of that?"

"Yes." Ginny understood, suddenly. "If you surrender, you will be unharmed."

Unless you've committed war crimes, she thought. It was never easy to deal with people who *had* committed war crimes. The urge to hang them for their crimes clashed with the grim awareness that people who thought they'd be hung when they surrendered were likely to keep fighting until the bitter end. It was better, sometimes, to let utter scumbags keep their lives if they surrendered. It saved more lives in the long run. *What have you done, I wonder?*

She kept her amusement to herself. The recorders probably *were* off, then. Her visitor couldn't take the risk of having the conversation watched by his superiors. If they objected to unauthorised torture, what would they say to unauthorised treachery? The poor bastard would be lucky if he was merely shot and shoved into an unmarked grave.

"Right," the man said. "Thank you..."

Ginny looked up at him. "If you get me out of here, if you get me back to my people, there will be a reward..."

The man snorted. "What the hell would they give me? For *you*?"

"Money, if you want money." Ginny held his gaze. "A new life. A new identity. A chance to start your life again, if you wish. Or safety..."

"We'll see," the man said. He hadn't said yes, but he hadn't said no. Few men jumped headlong into treason, even if they thought their side would lose the war. "I'll be back."

He turned and walked out of the cell. Ginny smirked, then hastily schooled her face into blandness. God alone knew what he'd told his superiors, when he'd turned off the recorders. If he *had* turned them off... Ginny had been told that *some* systems were designed to keep recording, even when their owners thought they'd pulled the plug. The poor bastard might wind up in *very* serious trouble.

We'll see, she told herself. The shackles rattled as she tried to get comfortable. Her body ached, painfully. They hadn't put her in a stress position, but...she had the feeling that they'd managed it anyway. And yet...she forced herself to relax. She'd have to wait and see. *Who knows what he'll do?*

• • •

The bed wasn't very comfortable, and the apartment was so dirty that Derek knew his mother would have had a fit if she'd seen it, but he didn't really care. Jenny had found the apartment, and the bed, and a handful of ration bars...he didn't care, as long as he could hold her in his arms. And do other things too, of course. Sex was amazing when you didn't know if you were going to see another morning or not. The days when he'd been a virgin, dreaming of girls who wouldn't give him the time of day, were long gone.

Jenny shifted against him. Her face looked different while she slept, more relaxed...somehow. She rarely relaxed completely when she was awake, even when they were making love. He wondered, suddenly, if Loomis had a point. Jenny might have chosen him for more reasons than the simple desire not to go to bed alone. And yet...he smiled as he saw her breasts, pale and white in the half-light. It didn't matter. He was happy to be with her as long as she allowed. The future could take care of itself.

His terminal bleeped an alert. He sat upright, cursing under his breath. He wanted to stay with her, to make love again...he knew that wasn't possible. He had to get back to the strongpoint before dawn, before the senior officers started their inspections. Loomis could cover for some things, but not for that. It would end with them both in deep shit.

Jenny stirred, her eyes opening. "Do you have to go now?"

"Yeah." Derek told himself she wanted to be with him. God knew she hadn't *had* to take him to her bed, the first time they'd slept together. "I don't want to be late."

"I know." Jenny sat upright. Derek tried not to stare at her bare breasts. They were utterly perfect. "I understand..."

She kissed him, hard. "Come back, all right?"

"I'll do my best," Derek promised. It was hard to think straight. He needed a shower...if they got into the shower together, he'd be late for sure. And yet, the more she kissed him, the harder it was to care. Her breasts pressed against his chest. His hands rose, almost of their own accord, to touch them. "I..."

He broke off. In the distance, he could hear the sound of guns.

CHAPTER THIRTY-FOUR

Those worlds rapidly secured naval bases, garrisons and industrial bases within their sphere of influence, moving so rapidly that they were firmly established before the news had crossed from one end of settled space to the other.
—PROFESSOR LEO CAESIUS
Earthfall and its Aftermath

HAYDN STUDIED BOUCHON through his enhanced binoculars, feeling uneasy.

The city was going to be an utter nightmare to take, if it had to be taken quickly. The orbital and drone imagery had shown that, but it hadn't sunk in until he'd seen the defences with his own eyes. They'd be advancing across a narrow front into the city, marching across terrain that was almost completely barren, bare of anything that might provide even a hint of cover. And then, beyond it…the roads themselves were clear, but the rest of the city was going to be even *more* of a nightmare. Bouchon was so unlike the rest of the planet's settlements that he found himself wondering if the corprats had lost control a few decades ago.

It's an odd place to put a city if you're planning for efficiency, he mused, as he swept his gaze over the defences. *But it's a very good place if you intend to put a cork in the bottle.*

He returned his binoculars to his belt as the sun started to glimmer over the horizon. He'd argued for launching the main offensive at night, but General Anderson had overruled him and ordered the fighting to start at dawn. Not, Haydn supposed, that it had ever really stopped. The snipers had been taking pot-shots at enemy officers and advance missile and mortar teams had been hammering the PDC, trying to force its commander to concentrate on self-preservation. Haydn was mildly surprised the marines hadn't been ordered to take the PDC already. Just sitting there, perched amidst the mountains, it put a dampener on airborne operations.

Mayberry stopped next to him. "Sir? The guns will start in two minutes."

Haydn nodded. "Are we ready to launch the assault?"

"Yes, sir." Mayberry looked as if he wanted to say something, perhaps a suggestion that the company commander should direct operations from the rear, but didn't. Instead, he held up his terminal. "The firing patterns are already set, with the gunners preparing to fire in support."

"Good." Haydn frowned. *Someone* had been sending intelligence from within the city, suggesting targets for the gunners when the offensive began. It was a good idea, on paper, but in practice it would be hard to tell what the gunners had actually *hit*. "And our command net?"

"It's ready, sir," Mayberry said. "Lieutenant Yeller lost the toss. He'll be staying behind."

"He knows what he's doing," Haydn said. "He was earmarked for a company of his own when the shit hit the fan..."

He broke off as the guns started to fire, reaching for his helmet and snapping it into place as the enemy point defence weapons started firing. The skies seemed to light up with fire as hundreds of shells exploded in mid-air, pieces of shrapnel flying in all directions. The defenders were good, he acknowledged. They shot hundreds of shells out of the air. It didn't really matter. Hundreds more would reach their targets, smashing the enemy supply dumps and forcing the defenders to keep their heads down. The sound of explosions grew louder as fireballs washed across the enemy defence line. Many of the strongpoints survived intact, if charred; others, seemingly weaker, were blown open by the direct hits.

"Here we go," he said, as the guns continued to pound. "Lead units…*go*."

He boosted his suit as he ran forward, charging the enemy defences. The enemy guns were opening fire, trying to break up the assault formations while hammering their rear areas, but there just weren't enough of them to make a difference. General Anderson had moved his laser platforms forward, relying on them to provide cover. They'd probably shoot down a lot of friendly shells too—they wouldn't have much time to tell the difference—but it didn't matter. A marine who was hit by a friendly shell would be just as dead as one who was killed by the enemy.

An alert flashed up on his HUD as the enemy brought a plasma cannon online. He hastily pointed his rifle at the enemy weapon and pulled the trigger, launching an RPG towards the cannon. It exploded in a flash of white light—he saw a body flying into the sky, burning brightly—damaging the enemy positions around it. Haydn snorted as bullets started to ping off his armour, the impacts barely slowing him down. Plasma cannons were notoriously unreliable. He didn't blame the locals for keeping them powered down, but it had cost them a handful of precious seconds. Another cannon opened fire, streaks of plasma burning towards the marines. They hit the deck as the rear gunners fired an antitank missile at the plasma cannon. It followed its predecessor into death.

He threw himself forward as he plunged into the first set of bunkers. An alert flashed up—a marine had been hit, wounded badly enough to have to hunker down and wait for a medic—but he kept going, followed by the rest of the platoon. The enemy defenders didn't have armour. Their grenades and antitank charges were more dangerous to them than the marines. He tore through them, pushing normal human feeling aside. There would be time to think about the men he'd killed, crushing their skulls and shattering their bones with blows that would have damaged a *tank*, later. Right now, he had to secure a lodgement before the enemy managed to react…

The ground heaved. He cursed as he stumbled to the floor, catching himself a moment before he slammed into the ground. The enemy had detonated charges…he felt the ground shake again, forcing himself to remain still until the earthquake was over. They were calling down fire on their own positions…their former positions. Whoever was in charge had reacted quickly, ruthlessly and well. They were trying to bury the marines before they had a chance to turn their lodgement into something greater.

Too late, he thought, as the follow-up units started to arrive. They hurled RPGs into nearby buildings, taking no chances at all. A handful of buildings started to totter under the constant bombardment, collapsing into rubble. *Too late, you bastards.*

He kept his armoured head down as the rest of the complex was rapidly secured. The enemy *had* been thinking, damn them. They'd narrowed the passageways, making it impossible for the armoured marines to sneak through. And they'd mined some of the sections…he lost a marine to an IED that, normally, wouldn't have posed any threat. He gritted his teeth, promising himself he'd mourn later as he hurled more grenades into the confined spaces. It was expensive, but better than losing more marines he couldn't replace.

His intercom buzzed. "Objective One, secured," Lieutenant Yeller said. "The enemy is doing his best to impede."

"Then get the third-line units on the way," Haydn snapped. The sound of gunfire was growing unbearable, despite the armour. "Hurry!"

"Yes, sir."

• • •

"I hope the earth moved for you, sir," Loomis shouted. "This…"

Derek barely heard him over the sound of the bombardment. He'd barely made it out of the apartment when the shells had *really* started falling. A chain of thunderous explosions had taken out a supply depot, suggesting the defenders were going to run short of supplies sooner rather than later. He'd kept his head down and ran for his life, trying to ignore the dead and the wounded as he'd hurried to the strongpoint. It had nearly killed him.

A runner appeared at the door, blood streaming from a cut to his forehead. "They're breaking through the first lines," he shouted. "You have to be ready."

"Got it," Derek sounded. His loudest shout sounded like a whisper, compared to the sound of the guns. The constant shaking was getting on her nerves. "Everyone up, now!"

He stood and peered through the gunsights, into the smoke and fire. The enemy had to be in there somewhere, but...they were lost within the haze. He heard mortar rounds falling from the rear, saw explosions blasting up from the bunker...he hoped, as the sound somehow managed to get even louder, they were tearing the enemy to pieces. His men had never been tested. He glanced back and winced as he saw one man lying on the floor, curled into a ball. There was nothing that could be done about him now.

A bullet pinged off the concrete, above him. Derek shivered, unsure if he'd been targeted personally or if it had just been a lucky shot. An *unlucky* shot, he supposed. The enemy shooter had missed. He ducked as low as he dared without losing sight of the forward positions. It had probably been a lucky shot. The enemy snipers were good. He'd been told they could put a bullet though a tiny hole and kill the man behind it.

"Contact," someone shouted. "They're coming!"

Another rocket hit the strongpoint. Derek glanced up, dust falling from the ceiling, then returned his attention to the front. A tank appeared out of the haze, grinding forward with single-minded purpose. Someone fired a rocket at it, missing by a fraction of a metre. The tank's turret responded with terrifying speed, whining loudly as they were brought to bear on the unfortunate gunner. He had no time to run before the tank opened fire.

"Kill it," Derek snapped.

Loomis fired another antitank rocket. This time, it hit the tank and punched through the armour. A lone crewman managed to bail before the vehicle exploded, the remnants of its turret blasting into the air and crashing down some distance from the strongpoint. The lone evacuee had no time to hide before Derek's men shot him. He opened his mouth to rebuke them, but no words came. The tanker would have killed them all, without a second thought, if he'd had the chance. And besides...

A hail of bullets cracked against the strongpoint. Derek returned fire, shooting into the haze without a clear target. There were figures within the haze...he felt his stomach clench as he saw the armoured troopers, advancing forward by leaps and bounds. Loomis fired an antitank rocket at the nearest, but he shot it out of the air with a plasma bolt before it could get within a metre of him. The armoured troops picked up speed...Derek saw bullets pinging off their armour, sparks flickering in all directions as his troops spent their ammunition uselessly. The only thing he had that could scratch them were the plasma cannons and they'd draw fire the moment he powered them up.

He blew his whistle. "Fall back! Now!"

Loomis waited for him by the door as the rest of the men hurried out, heading down the planned escape route. They'd have a chance to resume the fight from a later strongpoint...Derek lifted his radio, babbling firing coordinates to any prowling mortar teams that happened to be listening, then placed a grenade under the plasma cannon. If he was lucky...he turned and fled, following Loomis down the path. Behind him, the ground shook once again. The force of the blast knocked him to the ground. He rolled over, half-convinced he'd been tackled by a gorilla. Instead, the strongpoint was nothing more than a pile of debris and an expanding cloud of smoke.

"We got them," Loomis said. Somehow, he'd managed to remain standing. "They were caught in the blast!"

"Let's hope so." Derek let Loomis help him to his feet. His ankle hurt, as if he'd twisted it without noticing. It wasn't easy to walk, but he had no choice. The enemy would be on them in seconds if they didn't put some distance between them and the former strongpoint. "We have to move."

Behind him, the flames burnt higher.

• • •

General Anderson nodded as the first reports flooded into the command post. He'd expected to lose a number of marines in the opening moments of the engagement...somewhat to his surprise, there had been fewer losses than the projections had suggested. *He* wasn't complaining, but...he scowled as it became clear the enemy had learnt from the first engagements too. They were putting up stiff resistance, then falling back when their strongpoints could no longer be held. Worse, they were actually mounting counterattacks when they thought they could push the marines back. In places, they'd actually succeeded.

Our reputation for invincibility is going to take a beating after this campaign, he thought, sourly. The Marine Corps rarely fought without orbital fire support. They might lose brief engagements, but rarely big battles and *never* the war. Now...it was possible that this was merely the *first* campaign to be fought without orbiting guardian angels. The next one might be under even tougher conditions. *We have a lot to learn from this engagement.*

He watched as another enemy strongpoint was marked off the map. The enemy had fought hard, then withdrawn...this time, for better or worse, they hadn't managed to make it very far before they'd been gunned down. It would have bothered him, once upon a time. Now, the fewer who made it back to their rear areas the better. The city nullified most of his advantages. He didn't need to let the enemy make use of one of theirs.

"Sir, Kennedy's Knowles are requesting additional fire support, danger close," Lieutenant Wiz said. He sounded concerned. He'd served under Captain Kennedy before being reassigned to the CP. "They're hitting tough resistance."

"Do it," General Anderson ordered. Danger close...the shells would be practically coming down on top of his men. No one would call for danger close, unless they were desperate. Their position might be on the verge of being overrun. "And hurry."

• • •

I'm probably being punished for something, Corporal Sidney Rawhide thought sourly, as he and his platoon picked their way through the sewer. They were underground, but not far *enough* underground for his piece of mind. The complex kept shaking, pieces of dust and stone dropping from the roof and falling into the river of shit. *And this place will probably collapse well before we reach our destination.*

He shuddered, trying to breathe through his mouth as they kept moving. The idiot who'd dreamed up the plan had probably never been *in* the sewers, let alone had any real conception of how hard they were to navigate. The platoon had to walk in single file, all too aware that the next earthquake might send them into the sewage. He'd heard stories about alien monsters lurking in the bowels of human civilisation, growing fat on the waste humans threw away. The stories didn't seem so laughable now.

Sergeant Tarn nudged his shoulder. Sidney almost screamed.

"There," Tam said. There was little respect in his tone. "That's the ladder."

"Got it," Sidney said. Tam had joked he'd spent most of his life in the shit. He *worked* in the sewage plant. Sidney honestly wasn't sure why *Tam* hadn't been placed in command. He knew more about the city than Sidney had ever cared to know. "Up there?"

"Aye," Tam said. "I can go first?"

"I should," Sidney said. He didn't want to do it, but he had to set a good example. The lads wouldn't follow someone who wasn't prepared to do the hard work himself, particularly someone they didn't know. "Watch my back."

He scrambled up the metal ladder, trying not to think about the liquid dripping down from somewhere high above. Water or something worse...he *really* didn't want to think about it. The shaft started to narrow as he climbed higher, faint glimmers of light blinking down from overhead…the maps said the shaft opened in a house that had been abandoned hours ago. He reached the top and started to open the hatch, half-expecting to find a rifle shoved in his face. But the basement was as empty as his superior's skull.

"Come on," he hissed. The sound of gunfire was suddenly much louder. The front lines had washed over the house, but they might wash back again at any moment. "We have to move."

He climbed up the stairs to the ground floor and opened the door. The corridor was silent, but he could hear people outside…in the living room. He waited for the rest of the team to join him, then inched forward. Three invaders crouched in the room, peering out of the broken windows. He moved…they spun around with terrifying speed, hands grabbing for their weapons. Sidney opened fire, shooting one of them in the chest. He grunted, as if Sidney had punched him. His body armour had taken the blow…

A giant fist struck *him*. Sidney toppled back, his vision starting to dim. He'd been hurt…no, he'd been shot. They'd shot him. They'd shot him. They'd…he couldn't think straight. His body felt soft as he hit the floor. He'd been shot and…

… Someone loomed over him. He tried to speak, to try to tell him… to tell him what? He didn't know. The prisoner? The woman he wished he'd never found? The words refused to come. He couldn't form a single word, much less a sentence. Someone spoke, but…he couldn't make out the words. It was all so meaningless.

And then the world just faded away.

CHAPTER THIRTY-FIVE

Like the warlords, the new masters of space were ambitious as hell. Unlike the warlords, they had the tech bases to maintain their forces, outproduce their enemies and eventually rebuild civilisation. The real question, of course, was what they would actually do. It should have been clear that the Empire had failed. But what would take its place?

—PROFESSOR LEO CAESIUS

Earthfall and its Aftermath

DEREK RUBBED HIS EYES as he sat up, pushing the blanket aside. He could almost have believed that Jenny was next to him...she wasn't. He was in a bunker, surrounded by his men. A low rumbling echoed in his ears, a distant sound that seemed to be growing ever closer. It had been three days since the battle began, three days since...he felt his head pound as he heard gunshots, far too close for comfort. They couldn't be that close, could they?

Fuck, he thought. His head hurt. He wanted to get up and run, but there was nowhere to go. Security troops guarded the rear, ready and willing to shoot deserters as they tried to run. They'd shot a man yesterday for wounding himself, in the hopes it would get him out of the combat zone. *What the fuck are we fighting for?*

The ground shook. The enemy shelling seemed to be growing stronger, although it was hard to be sure. The higher-ups insisted the enemy would run out of shells at any moment—and Derek believed them, because he knew how quickly his scratch platoons had run short on ammunition—but so far, the enemy appeared to have an infinite supply. It felt like he was playing a multiplayer game, one where the other side was using cheat codes. They seemed to have every edge, and he seemed to have nothing.

He forced himself to stand despite his fatigue as the alarm sounded, waking the rest of the platoon. They'd been promised a solid five hours of sleep, but a glance at the timer told him that he'd barely slept three hours. Derek wasn't sure he'd managed even *that.* The constant pounding, the endless engagements that had boiled down to hand-to-hand fighting, were sapping his strength. He'd seen a couple of officers stand up and walk right into enemy fire, not even bothering to duck before they were cut down. He understood them. He just wanted it to end, too.

Don't show any weakness, he told himself. He was still a lieutenant, but he seemed to be in command of a company...a company put together from survivors of a dozen different outfits that had met the enemy and splintered. He didn't know more than a handful of names and didn't dare try to learn more, not when the poor bastards might be dead in an hour. *Just keep going. Somehow.*

"Wake up, you lazy bums," Loomis said. He was doing a sergeant's job now, but there had been no hint of a promotion. "Breakfast is served!"

The men looked bruised and battered as they stumbled along to the underground mess hall. Derek had no idea how they managed to look enthusiastic. He wasn't expecting anything, beyond ration bars and water. The power had been cut twice, either through enemy shelling or incompetence in the rear. A giant military-grade freezer loaded with meat had powered down, the meat going off before anyone had noticed. Thankfully, no one had tried to eat the spoiled food. Derek knew it was just a matter of time before someone snapped and did just that.

"I'm sorry I had to get you out of bed in the middle of the day, but I'll see you all get extra ration bars instead," Loomis carolled. "Who wants a carrot bar?"

Derek was too tired to find Loomis either funny or annoying. He could barely muster the energy to do anything. It was all he could do to unwrap the bar, then chew it piece by piece. Whatever it was, he was sure it wasn't *carrot*. It tasted more like raw cardboard. Back home, they'd had strict orders to recycle cardboard—and dozens of other things. He had the feeling he knew where the recycled cardboard had gone. The thought made him smile, as he washed it down with funny-tasting water. Someone had probably made a killing selling the army bars it had never intended to actually *eat*.

Although we can't do much else with them, he thought, dryly. *Pigs and goats won't eat them, will they? Only humans...*

He dismissed the thought as he checked his rifle, waited for his handful of subordinates to check the platoons and then led them outside. He'd tried to track down the colonel, to ask for his subordinates to be given the rank that went with their new responsibilities, but there was no sign of the colonel. Half the senior officers seemed to have bugged out, leaving the defence of the city—what was left of it—in the hands of their junior officers. The nasty part of Derek's mind thought that was probably a good idea. The rest of him wondered if he and his men were being left to die.

The sound of shooting grew louder as they emerged from the bunker and made their way down the streets to the defence line. The enemy had secured the eastern end of the motorway and were pushing up it, clearing the defences on either side as they moved. They didn't seem inclined to care about strongpoints to the north and south, but they probably weren't a problem as long as the defenders sat still and did nothing. The enemy wanted to secure the motorway and drive on Haverford, not waste time hunting insurgents in Bouchon. Derek was sure it was just a matter of time until those strongpoints were evacuated, their defenders ordered to go elsewhere. There was no point in leaving them there, waiting to starve, when they could be deployed somewhere a little more useful.

There didn't seem to be much of the city *left*, from his point of view. A dozen skyscrapers were nothing more than piles of rubble, hundreds of defenders buried under the debris. Others were scorched and pitted, their windows smashed and walls cracked by the fury if the enemy offensive. A handful of snipers were up there, he'd been told; they were trading fire with their enemy counterparts as they tried to take out enemy officers. Derek scowled, inwardly, as they reached the defence line itself. Perhaps the officers hadn't fled. Perhaps their uniforms had made them easy targets. He'd already had to rebuke a soldier for saluting him in the middle of a combat zone. God knew the idiot had marked him out as a senior officer. If a sniper had been watching…

"They're bombing and shelling us, but not trying to push though," an officer said. He'd torn off his rank badges, probably in an attempt to hide from enemy snipers. "That isn't going to last."

"I know," Derek said. The line was being pushed back steadily, despite their best efforts. The defences that had taken days to build were being smashed, one by one. "Get your men out of here. We'll hold the line."

He tried to breathe through his mouth as he entered the bunker and peered through the slot. The air stank of piss and shit and fear, the stench of men who knew every second could be their last. Someone had written a series of rude notes on the walls, someone…Derek shook his head. Discipline was breaking down, step by step. It wouldn't be too long before all hell broke loose.

A bullet cracked through the air. He lowered himself, quickly, as he kept looking east. The haze was growing stronger, again. He smelled smoke—and burning human flesh—on the air. The ration bar sat heavily in his stomach, too solid for him to throw up. He heard one of his men retching, but didn't turn to see who. One of the maggots, the newcomers, probably. The others had all seen fighting, even if they hadn't been under his command. You couldn't develop an immunity to combat—an experienced man could die as easily as an inexperienced maggot—but you could get used to the smell…

Loomis nudged him. "Rumour has it that they're trying to outflank the line."

"Fuck." Derek had no idea where Loomis got his information, but he had to admit it was usually good. "What do we do then?"

"Run. Or surrender." Loomis shrugged. "Or die."

Derek winced, inwardly. The stories of just what happened to unlucky men who fell into enemy hands had grown even more lurid as the fighting raged on. It had gotten so bad that some soldiers had openly said they intended to keep the last bullet for themselves. And yet...Derek knew some people could be real monsters, but he found it hard to believe of the enemy troopers. They fought with a bloody-minded determination that chilled, yet...they weren't monsters. They'd been times when they could have shot troopers who were running away and...hadn't.

The shellfire grew more intense, somehow. The ground shifted uncomfortably under his feet. He put his doubts aside, knowing it portended an offensive. The enemy were out there, hidden within the haze. And they'd be coming right at him...

"Get ready," he ordered. Shapes moved within the haze. "Here they come."

• • •

"You know, I tried to volunteer for the Mountain Infantry," Corporal Waters said, as the platoon crept through the enemy sewer. "And they send me here!"

Haydn concealed his amusement behind an impassive mask. The Mountain Infantry were amongst the few army regiments the marines actually respected, if only because they were tough bastards who couldn't be beaten in their bailiwick. He wondered, as they reached the ladder and looked up, just what had happened to their remaining units. Probably disbanded a few short months ago for being too good at their jobs. He'd met too many army officers who'd resented the marines to doubt it.

We could have used them here, he thought, sourly. *I wonder if someone is trying to recruit them.*

He dismissed the thought as he led the way up the shaft, trying not to think about the number of ways the operation could go wrong. The enemy had used the sewers to attack the marines—or move supplies to their strongpoints—but the marines had been reluctant to return the favour. The sewers were enemy territory, terrain they knew too well for anyone's peace of mind. Haydn wouldn't have taken the risk if he hadn't known the enemy were expecting to evacuate a strongpoint through the sewers. They might just pass unnoticed until they were close enough to take out the enemy...

The hatch opened smoothly, revealing an enemy barracks. Haydn grinned, unhooked a stun grenade from his belt and hurled it up, ducking as blue light flashed overhead. He jumped up the second the light faded, holding a shockrod in one hand and his pistol in the other. Most of the enemy troopers lay on the floor, stunned or wishing they were, but a handful were still awake and aware. Their body armour was a cut above the norm for corprat troops. The green tabs on their shoulders marked them as security troops.

No wonder they weren't paying attention, he thought, as he lashed into the survivors with his shockrod. *They're not used to people who can fight back.*

The rest of the platoon joined him as he led the way through the complex. A pair of rooms were barracks, occupied by sleeping soldiers. They slept a great deal sounder after he hurled stun grenades into their rooms and slammed the doors. They'd be rounded up afterwards and shipped to a POW camp. Another room held prisoners, manacled to the wall. He guessed they were would-be deserters who'd run the wrong way. They'd be checked afterwards too.

He reached the outer wall and peered outside. The enemy barracks was just behind the line, nestled behind a strongpoint. He smirked as he keyed his throatmike, sending a hasty transmission to the rest of the assault force. They were right behind the enemy positions and the enemy didn't even *know* it. There were limits to how many men he could move through the sewers, but...he glanced at Mayberry as the rest of the platoon assembled, ready to take the enemy in the rear. The sergeant looked back at him and nodded.

"Quietly, if possible," Haydn muttered. If they could open the way for the assault force, and then get an entire company or two through the gap, they could tear a gaping hole in the enemy defences. The remainder of the defenders would have to run for their lives, or stand and die. He didn't care which. "Now..."

They reached the rear of the strongpoint and hurled stun grenades into the structure. Haydn felt his skin tingle unpleasantly as blue lights flared, the firing slacking off sharply as stunned men hit the floor. He led the way inside, hastily taking out the remainder of the defenders. They hadn't had a chance to sound the alert. He nodded as he sent another update to the assault force, ignoring pleas for information from the enemy communications set. In a flick, he would have picked up the mike and told the enemy CO that everything was quiet on the eastern front. In the real world, such tactics almost never worked.

An enemy mortar team appeared on the far side of the bunker. Haydn grinned as they fell into his arms. They surrendered the moment they saw the guns pointed at them, despite their obvious terror. Haydn felt his smile grow wider. The first platoons were already crossing No Man's Land. They'd be with him in seconds and then...the enemy could run or die. Either way, they were in deep shit...

• • •

"Sir!"

Derek looked up sharply as the runner hurried into the bunker. "What?"

"I just...we just...got word from HQ." The runner was a rat-faced man, but there was no doubting his bravery. No one risked being caught in the crossfire without a considerable amount of physical courage. "They've broken through at Pasteur Square. They're in the rear!"

"Shit." Derek had learnt to read a map in basic and he hadn't forgotten, even after being promoted to lieutenant. If Pasteur Square had fallen, the enemy had broken through the defence lines and was about to make a smashing frontal assault on his rear. "What are our orders?"

"Orders? There weren't any orders." The runner sounded shocked. "They just told me to alert you."

Derek knew he should wait for orders, but there was no point. The enemy might cut their line of retreat at any moment. They'd held the strong-point, repelling two attacks that had come alarmingly close to breaking through the line, but it no longer mattered. The best they could hope for was being cut off and left to starve. Now...he shook his head. There was no *time* to wait.

He blew his whistle. "Everyone, prepare to fall back to Hermit Road," he shouted. The shooting slacked off as his subordinates stood and hurried for the door. "We've been outflanked!"

"Bad move, sir," Loomis muttered.

Derek nodded, mentally kicking himself as he sensed panic running through the company. That *had* been a mistake...he told himself to worry about it later, if there was a later. He opened his mouth to issue orders for a platoon to remain behind long enough to keep the enemy busy, then changed his mind. Issuing orders that wouldn't be obeyed was a bad idea. Instead, he set a pair of machine guns to automatic before following his men out the door. The enemy wouldn't be fooled for long, but it might buy them a few seconds.

The shooting grew louder as he plunged into the open air, following the half-dug trenches towards Hermit Road. A pair of bodies lay on the ground, in the midst of a tiny crater. He stared at them, wondering who they were. Mortar crew, he guessed. Either their mortar had exploded or an enemy sniper had shot them while they were setting up their weapon. He glanced back, feeling a shiver running down his spine as he realised what was *missing*. The enemy weren't shelling their positions. They had to be worried about accidentally shelling their own men.

"Fuck," Loomis said, as they stumbled along. He could hear smaller weapons firing, the sound mixed in with rifle fire. "We're fucked."

"Not yet," Derek said. Behind him, the machine guns fell silent. It wouldn't be long before the enemy took the bunker and gave chase. "Hurry."

Loomis glanced at him, pitching his voice too low for the men to hear. "You want to stay here and surrender?"

"No," Derek lied. He wasn't going to surrender, not now. "I don't know what..."

He froze as he heard the sound of mortars, of shells dropping towards them. They were in the open, caught like rats in a trap...he saw his men starting to run, but his legs refused to move. They were exposed, they were dead...he just couldn't move.

... Loomis barrelled into Derek, knocking him to the ground. He hit the muddy ground hard enough to hurt, tasting muddy water as the ground heaved under him. Loomis shuddered, warm liquid splashing down. Derek shouted at him to get off as the rumbling thunder died away, but Loomis didn't move. His body felt heavy, utterly unmovable. Derek had to struggle to crawl out from underneath him...

... And realised, as blood dripped from his stained uniform, that his friend was dead.

CHAPTER THIRTY-SIX

There was no clear answer to that question. Some factions wanted to reunite the Empire, with themselves as the new masters. Others wanted merely to keep what they already had, assuming they could either come to terms with the other successor states or simply pick up the pieces after the chaos finally died down.

—PROFESSOR LEO CAESIUS

Earthfall and its Aftermath

LOOMIS WAS DEAD.

Derek stared at the corpse, unable to believe his eyes. His friend was dead. His friend...he knelt down, hoping and praying that Loomis was simply wounded. He'd been taught that some injuries looked worse, a lot worse, than they really were. But he didn't have to be a doctor to know that Loomis was beyond help. A piece of shrapnel had struck the back of his head, brains leaking onto the ground...Derek retched, helplessly. He'd seen worse, but this...this was his *friend*. The wounds running down Loomis's back were almost an insult. He couldn't possibly have survived.

A bullet crackled through the air, shaking him out of his trance. The enemy had overrun the bunker, easy enough to do now that no one was fighting them. The jaws were closing rapidly. He turned and ran, forcing himself to zigzag even though he found it hard to care. His friend was dead. The one person who'd been with him from the very moment the shit hit the fan…he wouldn't have mourned, not really, if a bullet had struck him in the back. But the enemy, for whatever inscrutable reasons of their own, let him go.

He gritted his teeth as he reached Hermit Road. An officer he didn't recognise barked orders, directing troops to hurry further to the rear. Derek glanced at a map someone had pinned to the wall and cursed as he realised the enemy had pushed further west than he'd thought. Pasteur Square had merely been the start. They were already outflanking Hermit Road, pushing through defences that had never been intended to meet a serious attack. The entire city might be on the verge of falling…

And Loomis was dead.

Derek ignored the green-tabbed security troopers as he and his men stumbled to the rear. Their old barracks had already been abandoned… he allowed himself a moment of relief that he hadn't left anything *personal* behind, when he'd woken…it felt like *days* had passed since he'd left the bunker. Loomis was dead and Jenny…God alone knew where Jenny was, these days. He hadn't seen her since the enemy had begun the offensive. He hoped she was safe, but…he had his doubts.

"They're coming," someone shouted. "They're coming…"

A gunshot silenced him, forever. Derek barely noticed the body hitting the ground, barely sensed the waves of anger, resentment and panic washing through the retreating soldiers. The enemy shelling grew stronger, suggesting they were trying to impede the retreat. They might draw the line at shooting fleeing men in the back, but…they could hardly allow moral qualms to stop them from killing the retreating soldiers before they could be reorganised, rearmed and fed back into the fray. Derek half-expected to die at any moment. It wasn't as if they were a difficult target…

"Lieutenant," a stern voice said. "Are you listening to me?"

Derek looked up and blinked in surprise. He was in a bunker, a command bunker, with no clear memory of how he'd gotten there. He'd been on the streets, a moment ago…hadn't he? He wondered, briefly, if he'd dreamed everything, then looked down at his uniform. It was stained with bloom, Loomis's blood. His best friend was dead and…

"Lieutenant," the voice repeated. Derek realised, dully, that it was Colonel Macintyre. "Are you listening to me?"

"Yes, sir," he managed. The urge to draw his pistol and start gunning down the officers was almost overwhelming. It was hard, so hard, to resist, particularly when he couldn't come up with a good reason why he *should* resist. "I'm listening."

"Good." Colonel Macintyre sounded officious, as always. "Select ten men from your company. They and you are to be reassigned to my personal guard."

Derek blinked. "Your…*what*, sir?"

"My personal guard," Colonel Macintyre said. "I have orders to leave the city. You will accompany me."

"Yes, sir," Derek said, automatically. A personal guard? Bodyguards? It was difficult to wrap his head around the concept. The idea of leaving the city was tempting, but…he looked at his stained uniform. "I can select ten men and…"

"Meet me at the Secure Block in thirty minutes," Colonel Macintyre ordered. "And get changed into something a little more presentable."

That's my best friend's blood, Derek thought, as Colonel Macintyre walked away. *You utter…*

He controlled his anger with an effort as he located the rest of his company. The officers were already trying to break up the unit, redistributing the rest of his men to formations that had survived the breakthrough relatively intact. He claimed ten men, as per instructions, and ordered them to freshen up as he sought out the officers' washroom. It was surprisingly neat and tidy for a complex in the middle of a war zone. No wonder the officers in the HQ always looked neat and tidy. They lived in luxury while the foot soldiers ate ration bars and died in their hundreds…

Fuck, he thought. An orderly brought him a clean uniform, so crisp Derek was *sure* it had been washed and pressed only moments ago. *What the hell do I do now?*

He tried to tamp down his feelings of resentment as he met up with his squad and led the way to the Secure Block. The security troops on the door seemed inclined to pick a fight until he dropped Colonel Macintyre's name, at which point they practically started fighting over who should have the privilege of kissing his ass. It would have been amusing, once upon a time, but Derek was too far gone to appreciate it. Or make any *use* of it. All the power and pull in the universe couldn't bring his friend back to life.

A large van rumbled towards them and stopped beside the Secure Block. Colonel Macintyre jumped out, nodded to Derek and hurried into the building. Derek looked after him, puzzled. What the hell was going on? He waited, counting seconds and trying to resist the urge to keep looking at his watch. It felt like hours before Colonel Macintyre and two other officers appeared, escorting a young woman in an ill-fitting greatcoat. Her arms were cuffed behind her and her legs were shackled so tightly she could barely walk. She would have fallen, if Colonel Macintyre hadn't kept one hand on her arm.

Derek found his voice. "Sir…?"

"Don't worry about it," Colonel Macintyre said, sharply. "It's well above your pay grade."

I still get paid? Derek frowned, inwardly, as the woman was hefted into the van, plonked on a seat and cuffed firmly to the metal framework. *Who is this woman?*

Colonel Macintyre ordered the squad to climb into the van, then motioned for the driver to start the engine. Derek stared at the woman, studying her through narrowed eyes. Who *was* she? A prisoner, obviously, but…an *enemy* prisoner? He couldn't think of anyone else who would be transported to Haverford…were they going to Haverford? Where *else* would they be going? His eyes crawled over what little he could see of her bare flesh. She was clearly fit and healthy, in the prime of life. Her arms, what little he could see of them, were muscular. It was clear that *she* hadn't been eating ration bars for the last few weeks...

He felt a stab of guilt as the van rattled down the road, clearly heading out of the city. He was leaving his former subordinates behind, he was leaving his friend's *body* behind...he cursed as he realised he was leaving *Jenny* behind. He could have asked for her to be brought with them, or... or what? Colonel Macintyre wasn't likely to do *him* any favours. Why had he even hand-picked Derek and his men to serve as his bodyguard? Didn't he trust the security troops?

Of course not, his own thoughts answered him. *What sort of idiot* would *trust the security troops*?

• • •

The complex looked formidable, if one didn't have body armour, heavy weapons and a certain awareness that there was a difference between *looking* formidable and actually *being* formidable. It would have been impregnable to the average citizen—Haydn had no doubt of it—but the heavy doors were barely a moment's trouble to the marines. The lead platoon blasted the door down, then hurled stun grenades into the shadows as a hail of fire greeted them. It slacked off as blue light flared, turning darkness into day. A handful of security troopers lasted long enough to be shot, but even *they* couldn't slow the marines. Haydn was almost disappointed. He'd heard enough horror stories about the green-tabbed men to feel no qualms about killing any of them who got in his way.

They searched the building rapidly, starting with the basement. There were a handful of cells, clearly designed for multiple occupants; they were almost completely empty, save for a handful of men who'd tried to desert and earmarked for a penal battalion that would now never be formed. Haydn felt his heart sink as he kicked down the next set of doors, grimly aware they might have failed. Intelligence had made it clear that Lieutenant Ginny Patel had been held in the Secure Block, but might have been moved before the city fell to the marines. It looked as if they were right. The remaining cells, designed for prisoners who might kill themselves if left unattended, were empty. One had definitely been in use.

"Check for DNA," he ordered, as he finished sweeping the cell block and hurried back upstairs to the former command post. "Let me know when you have an answer."

The command post looked like something the Imperial Army would have established, once upon a time, although the locals had forgotten the essential precaution of making sure there was no way in hell their enemies could actually overrun their HQ. Parts of the complex looked serious—a map hanging on the wall, terminals formerly manned by staff officers—but other parts were a joke. Luxury furnishings, each one costing more than a low-ranking officer made in a year; a drinks cabinet, the contents either taken or drunk in a hurry when time ran out for the occupants. An empty bottle lay on the floor, the label suggesting it had come all the way from Earth. Irreplaceable, now. He wondered, absently, just who had brought it to the command post and why.

His lips quirked into a snarl as the intelligence staffers started to take the room apart. The enemy had fled in a hurry when they'd realised their lines were coming apart. There was a good chance they'd left something important behind, something that could be used to plan the next stage of the campaign. They might not even have thought to purge their records. The map on the floor was outdated—and growing more and more so by the minute—but everything else *might* be useful. He forced himself to take a step back and wait. It could take hours to uncover something useful.

"Captain." The WarCAT officer sounded tired. "We ran a DNA sweep. I can confirm that Lieutenant Patel was housed here."

"That's something, at least." Haydn had known there was a good chance that Ginny would have been shot out of hand. The enemy officers might not even have had a chance to *order* her shot. Their subordinates might have killed her in a rage and dumped the body somewhere it would never be found. "How was she treated?"

"As yet, I don't know," the officer said. "There's no obvious signs of violence. I didn't find any traces of blood. But the surveillance records have been wiped, the datacores dusted...it's possible they tortured her and then destroyed the evidence. We just don't know."

"We'll find out," Haydn said. "Keep me informed."

He tongued his throatmike, passing the intelligence to General Anderson, then turned his attention back to the map. It *looked* as if the enemy had been moving troops out of their strongpoints, although it wasn't clear what they'd actually been *doing*. They might have been moved west, to help set up defensive lines between Bouchon and Haverford, or they might have been ordered to slip into the mountains and lay the groundwork for a long-term insurgency. The mountains looked like an impassable barrier, but Haydn knew they wouldn't be *that* much of a problem to experienced soldiers, not if they had the right equipment. They'd just have to leave their heavy weapons behind.

And we're going to be heading west, as soon as our logistics catch up, he thought, grimly. He wasn't looking forward to the march, even though it would be easier terrain than the concrete jungle of Bouchon. *And if we don't get there in time...*

• • •

Once, years ago, General Anderson had watched an Imperial Army officer swagger into a city his forces had just liberated from a bunch of insurgents and brutally pacified by putting the entire civilian population into lockdown. The officer had seemed heedless of the damage his forces had inflicted, utterly unconcerned about the civilians who'd been killed or wounded by the crossfire...the man, who had never been near a *real* combat zone, had been an asshole who'd been hated by his troops and despised by just about everyone else. And yet...

General Anderson remembered the man as he walked into Bouchon, finally understanding—on a level he didn't care to recognise—why the man had been so pleased. The city had stood in his way, defying him...he didn't care, not really, that between the occupiers and the invaders a good third of the population had been killed. He'd just been glad it was over, before someone back on Earth started asking hard questions. General Anderson felt the same way, if for different reasons. Bouchon had been a bottleneck. Now it had been opened and his forces could push onwards.

And yet...he couldn't believe just how much damage the city had suffered in four days of hard fighting. Dozens of towering buildings had been smashed, hundreds more were so badly damaged they would have to be knocked down to keep them from collapsing at the worst possible moment...hundreds of bodies lay on the ground, starting to decay under the hot sun. He shuddered as he watched a team of shackled POWs collect the bodies and transport them to the east, where their DNA would be logged before they were dumped in mass graves. There was no time to try and find their surviving relatives, no time to do anything...they'd have to be buried before the marines had a major health crisis on their hands as well as everything else.

And we have too many other problems right now, he thought. The motorway had been secured, but parts of the city were still under enemy occupation. If they didn't surrender quickly, they'd have to be blasted down. *We have to keep the motorway open as we push west.*

He shook his head slowly as the car parked beside a refugee camp. A company of marines had searched the camp when it had been overrun, then provided security for the inhabitants as the defences collapsed and the city fell into chaos. Hundreds of enemy soldiers had gone rogue, drinking themselves senseless or falling on the civilians like wolves on sheep. A handful had been caught in the act and shot, or thrown into the stockade for trial when the war was finally over, but the remainder might well have gotten away with it. The marines simply didn't have the resources to hunt down *all* the looters, rapists and murderers.

"The only thing worse than a battle won is a battle lost," he mused, quietly."

His driver looked up. "Sir?"

"Never mind," General Anderson said. "Just…wool-gathering."

He opened the door and climbed outside. The stench struck him at once, an awful familiar odour he'd hoped never to smell again. He looked around, noticing how many women and young children were looking back at him warily. There didn't seem to be any men over fourteen within eyesight. Most of them had either been conscripted into the defences or were in hiding, trying to evade detection. General Anderson wasn't sure the latter had a hope in hell. Their entire society was terrifyingly transparent.

But not any longer, he told himself. *Not now that we've torn their world apart.*

"Sir." Captain Garth greeted him with a nod. They couldn't risk salutes. "This is Jenny Fothergill. She's pretty much in charge of the camp."

General Anderson frowned as Garth indicated a young woman…she looked as if she were barely out of her teens. Jenny would have been pretty, once upon a time, but her face bore the unmistakable signs of someone who'd seen too much too quickly. And, perhaps, the fear of someone who knew her life was no longer in her hands. Odd, part of his mind noted. That had been true of everyone on the planet long before the invasion had begun.

"General." Jenny's voice was hard, bitter. "What can we do for you?"

"Let us help you," General Anderson said. It wasn't a good answer, but it was the only one he had. "We can provide food…"

"We need to go home," Jenny told him. She sounded broken. "We don't care about anything else. We just want to go home."

CHAPTER THIRTY-SEVEN

It did not help that there was no one alive, at the time, with any experience of full-scale war. The Imperial Navy hadn't fought a real campaign in centuries. Indeed, part of the reason the Empire hadn't been able to quash bushfire wars before they got out of hand was that the military lacked the resources to do so.

—PROFESSOR LEO CAESIUS

Earthfall and its Aftermath

SIMON WONDERED, MORBIDLY, just how he was going to die.

Head Office was not going to be pleased, of course. Failure was bad enough. But a failure that cost enough money to make even a giant interstellar corporation say *ouch* was far—far—worse. Even *he* wasn't sure how much money had been invested in Hameau. He tried to calculate it—he knew from experience that even a stage-one colony was a trillion-credit investment—but drew a blank. The figure wasn't just unimaginably huge. It was completely irreplaceable. The Empire was gone. It was unlikely that anyone, up to and including Onge Corporation, would be investing in another Hameau for a long time.

And they'd have to employ me for millions of years just so I could earn the money to pay it back, he thought, with a flicker of black humour. He knew everything that had happened hadn't been *his* fault, but the corporation would be looking for scapegoats. Maybe everything could be saved, if the relief fleet arrived in time...he shook his head, tiredly. No. Whatever happened, he would be the scapegoat. Too much had been lost. The corporation would want someone to blame. *And that poor bastard happens to be me.*

Sandra tapped on the door, then peeked into the room. "Your Excellency?"

Simon glared at her, taking a twinge of sadistic pleasure in making her flinch. Everyone *else* knew he was a man on the way out, a man who would be lucky if he was *merely* put against the wall and shot. And now... it might not be a figure of speech. Senator Onge had broken men who had failed him, dropped them right into the underclass without a single centicredit to their name...somehow, Simon had no doubt the old bastard's heirs would be just as ruthless. *They* ran an interstellar government now, in fact as well as name. They could do more to him than simply dump his ass on a stage-one colony world no one in civilised society knew existed.

He didn't let the moment linger. "Yes? What?"

"The conference call is ready, sir," Sandra said. "And the *package* has arrived."

"Oh, *goody*," Simon said, with heavy sarcasm. "The *package*. And where *is* the package?"

Sandra coloured. "It...ah, *she*...is being put in the brig. Sir."

"Make sure she is treated well," Simon ordered. "And put the callers through."

He took his seat as the holographic images snapped into existence. They didn't look *quite* as respectful as they should have, not now. Heather MacDonald would be trying to distance herself from him, of course, although she was in for a nasty surprise if she managed to do it so well that Head Office promoted her into his shoes. General Atherton would probably be working hard to pass the buck to his subordinate, no doubt planning to blame Simon for micromanaging from Haverford...Simon was sure that a past master of bureaucratic infighting would come up with a truly brilliant excuse for failure. And yet, if he'd shown a flicker of that brilliance on the battlefield...

Simon let out a heavy sigh. They'd never planned for a full-scale invasion. Their imagination had clearly been somewhat lacking. In the end, no one was to blame. Not really, not in the sense that anyone could be held accountable for the defeat. But Head Office wouldn't see it that way. Someone had to take the blame, so Head Office could put the affair behind it as quickly as possible.

"Well?" His voice sounded weak, even to him. "What's the news?"

"We have lost Bouchon." General Atherton sounded tired. "There are remnants of our forces in the city, with orders to make life miserable for the marines, but...practically speaking, the way to Haverford lies open. They can just drive down the motorway and hit us any time they choose."

"Fuck," Simon said. "I thought you said you could hold the city..."

"I was wrong," General Atherton said, flatly. "We're facing the marines."

Simon frowned. "Are we sure? Now?"

General Atherton nodded. "We have a copy—a thoroughly *illicit* copy—of the military's order of battle, one obtained by Head Office two years ago. We checked our prisoner's ID against the files. She is indeed a marine auxiliary, with four years' service. I think we cannot deny it any longer. We're at war with the marine corps."

"Why?" Heather waved her hand in the air. "What the hell are they doing?"

"They want this world, we think." General Atherton nodded. "I've been reluctant to authorise more...*extreme*...ways to make the prisoner talk. She's unlikely to know too much, Your Excellency, and they will be *pissed* when they find out. And they will."

Simon gritted his teeth. "You can't defend Haverford?"

"I might be able to hold the walls, if the city itself wasn't on edge," General Atherton said, bluntly. "Right now, we're in danger of losing control of the streets..."

"We already *have* lost control of the streets," Heather said. "Some of them, anyway. Too many refugees crammed into our city, too many people with nothing to lose…I think we have to admit we're in trouble. Rumours are spreading faster than we can counter them and…we have to face it. We were never a very popular government. Now that we look weak, the knives are coming out."

"Literally," Simon mused. He'd planted metaphorical daggers in more than one back, when he'd been climbing up the corporate ladder. Now… he wondered what his long-gone rivals would think, if he wound up being stabbed in the back by his people. Laugh, probably. They had good reason to hate him. "We can't come to terms with them."

"Maybe we should," General Atherton said. "Your Excellency, right now…the only thing I can guarantee is that a lot of people, our people, are going to die."

Simon looked at him. "And what will we say when the relief fleet arrives?"

Heather grimaced. "You have the authority to negotiate…"

"I won't." Simon knew he was doomed, whatever happened, but if he stayed true to Head Office…his family would survive. Whatever happened to him, his family would survive. "We have to hope for the best."

"Then, if you don't mind, I need to put the defences in order," General Atherton said. "It won't be long before they reach our walls."

"What walls?" Heather frowned. "We don't *have* any city walls."

General Atherton nodded, curtly. "That's my point."

• • •

So this is how everyone else lives, Derek thought, as he peered around the barracks. It was quite probably the largest barracks he'd ever seen, relative to the number of soldiers who actually *lived* there. There were only twenty bunks, connected to a common room and no less than *four* washrooms. Compared to Eddisford Garrison, it was the height of luxury. *And why are we here?*

He scowled as he paced the tiny room. The drive to Haverford had been nerve-wracking, although they hadn't spotted a single enemy aircraft or drone. He'd still spent most of the journey expecting to be blown up without warning. And yet...as soon as they'd reached the city, they'd been marched to the bunker and pointed at the barracks. They'd even been warned not to risk leaving the underground complex. The datanet claimed that all was quiet in the city, but Derek suspected that wasn't entirely true. The colonel wouldn't have wanted to keep his bodyguards with him if he felt safe.

Cold hatred roared within his breast. Loomis was dead. Jenny...was probably either dead or in enemy hands. He'd tried asking about her, but apparently she wasn't one of the refugees who'd made it out of Bouchon before resistance effectively came to an end. And that meant...he shuddered as it dawned on him that the remainder of his company, the men he'd left behind, were either dead or prisoners too. He thought about the woman they'd escorted to Haverford and felt sick. The thought of Jenny being treated like that...

There will be a chance to do something, he thought. He wasn't sure what the colonel was doing, but he seemed to think that Derek and his men were just...robots. Fine. Derek would let him keep believing that, for the moment. He would do his best to stay close to the colonel until...until he saw a chance to extract revenge. For his parents, for his lover, for his dead friends and comrades...for the lives they'd been forced to live. *Just wait. There will be a chance.*

He lay back on the bunk and closed his eyes. Here, if nowhere else, the surveillance network would be working. Here, he dared not make any open plans. He certainly dared not risk talking to his men. But, by God, he could plan in the privacy of his own mind. They couldn't read his thoughts.

Not yet, he thought, dryly. *And they never will.*

• • •

It had been relatively easy, somewhat to Rachel's amusement, to find a change of clothes and start moving freely around the city. There were so many refugees flowing into the city that a few more strangers would barely be noticed, as long as they were careful. The datanet claimed the enemy—it was odd they never referred to the marines by name—were still on the far side of the mountains, but the inrush of refugees suggested otherwise. They never mentioned *which* mountains, either. Someone who looked at a map would know the marines were within a few hours march of the city.

Assuming no one gets in their way, she mused, as she walked down a street. *A handful of well-trained teams could cause considerable delay, just by sniping at the advance elements and leaving IEDs scattered everywhere.*

She allowed herself a grim smile. The city was on the brink. They'd planned to spread rumours, but there were so many flying around the city that there was no need to bother. Instead, they'd moved to step two. They had to convince the locals that they *could* take up arms against their overlords. Rachel felt her expression darken as she watched for her prey, knowing it was only a matter of time before there was an explosion. Normally, it could take weeks, if not months, to galvanise an insurgency. Here, they would have to do it in a couple of days.

A man glanced at her and whistled, cheerfully. Rachel resisted the urge to draw the gun from her dress and put a bullet between his eyes. The leer on his face suggested he was considering dragging her off the streets...she braced herself, just in case he really *did* try. It would be irritating to have to liberate herself from a would-be rapist, while looking for a particular *kind* of rapist...

She sensed fear running through the crowd. The wolf-whistler turned smartly into a sideway and vanished. Rachel turned, just in time to see a quintet of bully-boys in police uniforms mincing towards her. They looked like people playing at being policemen, not *real* policemen. She guessed they were security officers who'd been pressed into patrolling the streets. Her smile turned cold, then faltered as they saw her. It was important to look weak, to look vulnerable. Human wolves never went after people who could stand up for themselves, or had people who could and would protect them. They went after the weak, the defenceless, the ones who were too scared to fight.

It was easy to pretend to be scared as the makeshift policemen closed in on her. The crowds thinned, some people hurrying away while others stared, unable to intervene and yet unable to look away. Rachel was torn between sympathy and an odd kind of contempt. On *her* homeworld, everyone carried guns. A would-be rapist wouldn't live long enough to stand trial and get a date with the hangman. But here...she knew she should feel sorry for the bystanders. They were helpless against the state and its bully-boys.

A policeman grabbed her arm. He wasn't very strong—she could have broken free even without using her enhanced muscles—but she needed to look helpless for a moment or two longer. Another grabbed her breast, his eyes going wide with shock. Rachel cursed, inwardly. Unless he had no feeling at all in his hand, he had to know she'd padded the bra she'd liberated from the safe house. And that meant...she screamed, pleading for help that—normally—would never come. The policemen gathered around her, one of them already fumbling with his fly. They were going to rape her right in the open...

"Get them," Phelps shouted. He threw himself forward, bellowing an angry challenge. "Get them!"

Perkins followed. The crowd lurched, then charged forward. Rachel grinned, then snapped a policeman's wrist as Phelps and the others attacked. They never stood a chance. The crowd tore them apart, ripping off their uniforms and practically trampling them to death. Rachel felt nothing, even as some of the women castrated the fallen brutes. The policemen had done a great deal worse, she knew. They were only reaping what they'd sowed.

"Kill the police," Phelps shouted. "Kill them all!"

The crowd roared again. They'd scented blood now, they *knew*—deep inside—they were no longer powerless. The mood would spread with the story, as more and more people came onto the streets or out of the refugee camps to join the growing riot. Leaders would emerge, men and women who wanted revenge against the police, the government and everyone who had ever stood in their way. She pulled herself out of the crowd and hurried to the RV point, trying to pull her dress back into place as she ran. Next time, someone else was going to play the damsel in distress.

"You look a mess," Bonkowski said, passing her a pair of trousers and a shirt. "Did you lure them in?"

"Next time, you're wearing the dress." Rachel changed quickly, heedless of their location. "Those bastards were such bastards that they won't even bother to check before jumping on you."

"They'd have to be blind or drunk or both." Bonkowski indicated his muscles. "Could I pass for an attractive woman?"

"I think those people wouldn't care what you liked like, as long as you had a convenient place to stick it," Rachel countered. The thought of Bonkowski in a dress…she snorted. He was right. He wouldn't fool anyone with working eyes. "Just pour on the perfume."

"I don't think there's enough perfume in the world to cover up his stench," Perkins said, as he joined them. "And if he did put it on…"

"I have a very masculine odour," Bonkowski protested.

"That's the point," Perkins said. "You need perfume to cover it up."

Phelps glared them both into silence. "The riots have started," he said. "We have to make things worse for the locals."

Rachel nodded and followed him as he scrambled up the ladder and onto the roof. The buildings were cheap prefabricated structures, so flimsy she was surprised they'd survived more than a couple of years. The locals had probably reinforced them, somewhere along the way. It was a surprise they hadn't simply replaced them, but the government *was* trying to get as many people as possible out of the city. She smiled, rather thinly, as she saw the growing refugee camps in the distance. They were going to be bitterly disappointed.

Phelps jumped from building to building, heading west towards the edge of the slums. The riot was growing louder, spreading from block to block. The policemen on the streets wouldn't be safe, now the crowd had found its nerve. Rachel wondered if they'd have the sense to run. She put the thought aside as they reached their destination, a vantage point at the edge of the slums. Blue lights flashed in the distance as police and fire vehicles made their way towards the riot. They couldn't be allowed to nip it in the bud.

"Grab your bottles," Phelps ordered. "And get ready."

"Yes, sir." Rachel picked up a bottle and primed it. They'd taken two days to gather the materials to make small bombs, each one far more effective than simple Molotov Cocktails, but it been worth it. "I'm ready."

The police convoy came into view. They hadn't realised how serious things had become, not yet. The lead vehicles weren't armoured riot control vehicles, but simple cars. They'd have been better off waiting for reinforcements, if their superiors agreed. Rachel had listened to enough unguarded conversations to be fairly sure their superiors would order the police to throw gas, rather than water, on the growing fires.

"Now," Phelps ordered.

Rachel hurled her bottle. It struck the lead police car and exploded. The entire vehicle caught fire, exploding into a giant fireball. She thought she saw a man dive out, his entire body wrapped in flames, before the rest of the convoy exploded. A pair of policemen from the rear started shooting madly, but she wasn't sure who they thought they were shooting at. The rooftop was an obvious place, yet...none of their bullets went anywhere near the marines.

"Time to go," Phelps said. "Let's see them put out the riot now."

Rachel nodded. Together, they slipped back into the darkness.

CHAPTER THIRTY-EIGHT

They were, in short, in uncharted territory. They simply didn't know what to do. Who should take power, now the Empire was gone? How could they keep their power, now that legitimacy was up for grabs? And what sort of state should they build?
—PROFESSOR LEO CAESIUS
Earthfall and its Aftermath

"THE LOCALS APPEAR TO HAVE VANISHED," Mayberry said.

Haydn nodded as the marines made their way through a mid-sized town that looked surprisingly decent, almost *human*, compared to Eddisford. The buildings were neat and tidy, yet individual; he smiled as he saw a small cottage with a pair of axes hanging over the door. He'd been in places where the owner would have been hauled in for questioning by the police, simply because he appeared to be signalling that he wasn't a mindless little sheep like the rest of the townspeople. But there was no sign of *any* townspeople. The town's population had fled into the countryside.

They'll come back, once the fighting is over, he told himself, firmly. *The real problems will come from army stragglers.*

He scowled to himself as they left the town, picking up speed as they hurried down the road towards Haverford. Hundreds of enemy soldiers were falling back on the city, but hundreds—perhaps thousands—more were scattering into the countryside, taking their weapons and supplies with them. The local government didn't seem to have made any preparations for an insurgency—it certainly hadn't been keen on giving weapons to anyone who didn't work for the government—but it might wind up developing one by accident. It would be a major headache if those men managed to attack the supply columns, let alone start preying on the civilians as the coming winter started to bite. They'd have to be brought in or wiped out before they could make a real dent in operations.

It felt like hours of loping down the road, steadily overrunning and capturing small numbers of enemy stragglers, before Haverford finally came into view. It was the largest city on the planet, sprawling out alongside a river that split into two slightly above the city. Haydn was surprised they hadn't built the city closer to the coast, although he had a feeling the local terrain was prone to flooding. He thought he recognised the signs. Indeed, the drones reported that the terrain to the west of Haverford was almost completely uninhabited. It didn't look to be good farming land. It wouldn't start filling up until the remainder of the planet was populated.

He frowned as he surveyed the city. It was more spread out than Bouchon, presenting multiple possible angles of attack…but it was teeming with people. Smoke rose from a dozen fires, defying the best attempts to fight them…if anyone *was* trying to fight them. The roads were blocked by barricades and armoured vehicles, his sensors picked out a dozen active sensor nodes sweeping the surrounding airspace for potential threats. No drone had survived more than a few seconds when they'd tried to overfly the city. No doubt the sensors had some pretty heavy firepower backing them up.

Mayberry came up beside him as the armoured company slowed to a halt and began to spread out. "Orders, sir?"

"Surround the city, cut off all routes in and out," Haydn said, shortly. The follow-up companies would be joining them shortly, ready to ford the river and cut the city off from the west. A river wasn't much of a barrier to men in armoured suits. "And then ready ourselves for the final offensive."

He shuddered. On one hand, the city's defences looked pretty feeble. They wouldn't stand up to a good solid kick, still less an offensive spear-headed by armoured troopers and heavy tanks. But, on the other hand, hundreds of thousands of civilians were going to be caught in the crossfire and killed. The files claimed that over fifty thousand people lived within the city. Haydn suspected the *real* number was much higher. The refugees alone would make life difficult for the local government. He was surprised they hadn't tried to send the refugees away.

An alert flashed up in his HUD. Snipers within the city were trying to engage the follow-up units as they crossed the river. The marines were returning fire, although they were reluctant to use their heavier weapons for fear of causing civilian casualties. Haydn shuddered, again. That wouldn't last. No commanding officer wanted to tell grieving relatives their children were dead because he'd gone lightly on the enemy. Now, there were no interfering politicians to impose rules of engagement that put troops at risk and made casualties so much higher. Now…

His communicator bleeped. "Situation, Captain?"

"We're encircling the city now," Haydn said. General Anderson knew it as well as he did. He would be following the marines from his command vehicle. "We'll have them cut off by the end of the day."

"Yeah." General Anderson sounded tired. "And then…can we proceed?"

Haydn nodded, slowly. He was the one on the scene. General Anderson expected him to grasp, truly grasp, the reality the maps and holographic displays didn't show. It was astonishing how something that looked tiny on the map could delay an entire offensive in the real world…he put the thought aside as he leaned forward, studying what little he could see of the enemy position. One good solid blow might shatter their defences beyond repair.

"I think so, sir," he said. "We know the way to the enemy bunker."

"Then start making your preparations now," General Anderson ordered. "We move at dawn."

"Yes, sir," Haydn said.

• • •

"We have lost control of the streets," Heather said, flatly.

Simon looked up. He hadn't slept well, not since the first riots had turned into orgies of mass destruction. He'd ordered police and troops to be deputized from the various security and maintenance units, but they weren't trained for crowd control...he cursed under his breath, wondering just how long it would be until one of his subordinates put a knife in his back. The only thing protecting him was the simple truth, he supposed, that whoever took his place would have to deal with the mess in front of him...

He rubbed his forehead. "Just how bad is it?"

"Southside and Westside are more or less completely out of our control," Heather said, grimly. "We have control of the bridges, but little else. Everywhere else...we're barely holding on. We have troops on the streets of Eastside, with orders to kill anyone who steps out of line...so far, that seems to be working. But it won't last."

"And the enemy is surrounding the city." General Atherton looked worse than Heather. He looked like a man who hadn't slept for days. "Right now, Your Excellency, we can't open a single road to the west. It won't be long before we can't get out of the city at all."

Simon felt a hot flash of anger. "I thought you said you could keep the roads open!"

"The units I intended to do it did not survive contact with the enemy." General Atherton sighed, heavily. "Those that didn't get clobbered split up and went underground. They may pose a threat to the enemy, if the relief fleet doesn't get here in time, but...right now, they're no use to us. I have officers attempting to regroup...frankly, Your Excellency, our army was never designed for a long-term campaign in our heartland. It's breaking under the strain."

"Fuck." Simon looked down at his hands. "Can we hold Eastside?"

"We can limit their advantages," General Atherton said. "If they attack, we can hurt them. But we might not be able to keep them out of the city."

"It doesn't matter." Heather shook her head. "They're surrounded the city. They can just starve us into submission."

"They'll be starving the rioters as well," Simon pointed out. "Hell, they'll be starving within days anyway."

"Yes," Heather said. "And that's when they'll force the bridges and pour into Eastside."

"Where there isn't much food to be found anyway," Simon said. The planners had decided there was no point in keeping the algae farms operational, once the *real* farms had been solidly established. They'd been right, until the city had been cut off from the farms. Now…he wished they'd kept the damn things online. "What do we do?"

"We can surrender," General Atherton pointed out. "Or we can hold out and hope for the best."

"And start planning to leave the city ourselves," Heather put in. "Right now, we have to keep the government intact."

And I bet you'd want to leave first, Simon thought. He didn't really blame her, particularly if she succeeded him after the enemy put a bullet through his head. She'd be able to blame everything on him. Head Office would probably give her a promotion. *And I can't allow that to happen.*

"I'll start working on a plan," he said. "For the moment"—he took a breath—"for the moment, concentrate on holding Eastside. Blow up the bridges if you have to. Set traps for the enemy, if they try to breach the walls."

Heather snorted. "What walls?"

Simon ignored her. "And hope the relief fleet gets here in time. Good luck."

He watched their images vanished, then sat back in his chair with a sigh. The hell of it was that he knew he should surrender. Now he knew who they were facing…he shook his head. If he thought the marines would win the overall conflict, he would have surrendered himself—and the entire planet—without a second thought. But the marines had jumped headlong into a fusion core. They had no conception of just how badly they'd screwed up. Simon knew. He was one of the few people who *did* know just how much planning Head Office had made for Earthfall. And the marines were grossly outmatched.

They might have been planning too, he thought, *but there's no way they could have matched the corporation.*

He tapped his intercom. When Sandra appeared, he sent her to find Colonel Macintyre. It was time to start planning for the worst. Hundreds of thousands of people were about to die...he felt a twinge of conscience, mingled with the grim awareness that his family stood hostage for his behaviour. He would sooner sacrifice thousands of people he didn't know than let his family be executed or simply dumped on a penal world for his failure. The idealism of his youth had long since been rejected in favour of cold practicality.

And if that makes me a monster, he thought coldly, *then that's exactly what I am.*

• • •

Derek had spent the morning trying to find out everything he could about the bunker—and about what was happening *outside*. The former was easy—everyone seemed to assume that everyone inside the bunker had a perfect right to be there—but the latter was surprisingly difficult. What little information there was appeared to be heavily restricted, with only senior officers having unimpeded access to the datanet. There were rumours, of course, but most were so wild that Derek found them impossible to believe. The entire planet could *not* have been scorched if senior officers were coming and going all the time.

Although it might as well have been, he mused. *What does the colonel want us to do?*

He sighed, inwardly. Colonel Macintyre had spent a surprising amount of time simply *talking* to him, trying to win his...his what? It was clear that Colonel Macintyre was either *very* well connected or a braggart, and the simple fact they'd been allowed into the bunker suggested the former. But his behaviour was odd. The colonel had gone out of his way to promise Derek all sorts of rewards, from higher rank to a farm and an estate of his own, without actually bothering to tell Derek what he wanted in exchange. It was almost as if he was being courted...

Derek curtailed that thought, rapidly, as Colonel Macintyre peered into the barracks. "Derek," he said. "Come with me."

"Yes, sir." Derek grabbed his rifle, slung it over his shoulder and followed Colonel Macintyre into the corridor. "Where are we going?"

The colonel gave him a sharp look, but said nothing. A woman stood outside, wearing a perfectly-tailored suit that covered everything below her neckline and yet managed to reveal all of her curves. She was so beautiful that she was oddly inhuman, as if she wasn't quite real. Derek felt weirdly ashamed of himself for staring at her rear as she led them down the corridor. She was just so perfect, like a higher being brought down to the mundane world. Jenny wasn't so stunning, but she was real. The lack of imperfection was itself an imperfection.

He schooled his face into a blank mask as they stepped into an underground office. It was surprisingly home-like, for a bunker. Derek felt a stab of bitterness as he surveyed the chamber. The man behind the desk, the man rising to greet them...Derek felt his head spin as he recognised the governor. He'd visited Eddisford...God! It felt like years had passed since he'd been a carefree soldier, looking forward to demobilisation. Loomis had been alive, they'd been equals...laughing and joking together. He had to bit his lip to keep his temper under control. They were being watched. If the security troopers had the slightest doubt of his loyalty, they'd order him removed at once.

"Governor," Colonel Macintyre said. There was something in his voice that suggested a greater degree of familiarity than Derek would have expected. "You sent for me?"

"The city will fall shortly." The governor seemed to sag back into his chair. It was an odd display of weakness, one that suggested he trusted the colonel completely. "Either the starving rioters will tear us apart or the enemy will kick down the door and take us. We have to plan to leave before all hell breaks loose."

Rats leaving the sinking ship. Derek gritted his teeth. It would be so easy to draw his rifle and shoot the bastard, but…he knew it would be a mistake. Now, at least. *You're planning to leave everyone else in the shit.*

"Of course, Your Excellency," Colonel Macintyre said, easily. "When do you intend to leave?"

They talked for quite some time. Derek listened, carefully memorising everything they said while studying the map behind the governor. Haverford was in deep trouble. The enemy had cut them off from the rest of the planet, while half the city was effectively outside their control. Eastside alone could be held, and that wouldn't last. The troops needed to keep the city under control *and* keep out the enemy simply didn't exist.

And the defences don't look that strong either, he mused. *If the enemy took Bouchon, they can take Haverford.*

"It will be done, Your Excellency," Colonel Macintyre said. "We can leave when the city is on the brink of collapse."

"Very good," the governor said. "Be ready."

"We will." Colonel Macintyre looked at Derek. "Won't we?"

"Yes, sir," Derek said.

• • •

The two policemen were on edge, their hands on their weapons at all times. It didn't help them. Rachel moved up behind one of them, so silently that he didn't know she was there until she stabbed her knife through his neck. The other barely had a moment to open his mouth before Perkins got him. He tumbled to the ground, taking the knife with him. Rachel smiled grimly as she dragged her victim into the shadows and started to strip him. The uniform wouldn't fit her very well, but it was unlikely anyone would notice.

Half the men on the streets looked to have been outfitted by tailors who were blind, mad or both.

Her lips quirked. *Which makes them more efficient than the quartermasters on Han…*

She put the thought to one side as she donned the trousers and jacket, silently thanking her parents—and marine medics—that her breasts weren't too big. A little fiddling ensured that the jacket merely looked ill-fitting, as if it had been sewn for someone a little larger and fatter. She could pass for a man for quite some time, provided she kept her voice low and didn't undress. She'd done it before.

"You look very intimidating," Perkins said, as he dressed himself. "That look of sneering disdain really sells it."

"Hah. Hah." Rachel snorted and checked him, making sure he looked presentable. Knowing their luck, they'd run into a police sergeant who'd give them a bollocking for poor presentation. Or something. "We'd better move."

She forced herself to walk in the open, even though all her training argued it was better to stay in the shadows, as they made their way through Eastside. The eastern part of the city was under lockdown, troops and police on the streets chasing anyone they saw breaking curfew without a valid permit. But they wouldn't pay any attention to two more policemen, even if they didn't recognise them. The government had recalled so many former officers—and drafted anyone who was willing to fight—that she doubted *anyone* had a complete list of who was meant to be in uniform. No one would notice two additions to the list…

At least until they find the bodies, she thought. *And then…if they realise what we've done, they'll grow even more paranoid.*

She glanced into the darkening sky. It was obvious the main offensive would begin sooner, rather than later. General Anderson couldn't wait for the city to starve. He had to take it, and the enemy bunker, quickly. And when the assault began…

We'll be waiting, Rachel thought. They'd already scouted City Hall, making a note of the local defences. *And we'll strike.*

CHAPTER THIRTY-NINE

These questions would not be answered in a hurry.
—**Professor Leo Caesius**
Earthfall and its Aftermath

DAWN BROKE LIKE A THUNDERCLAP.

Haydn braced himself as the suit came online, flickering icons appearing in the display and then fading as the suit readied itself for combat. He yawned, despite himself. The night had been quiet—the enemy hadn't tried to mount any spoiling attacks—but he hadn't managed to catch much sleep. The prospect of combat had kept him awake.

Sergeant Mayberry called the company to order as Haydn checked the link to the assault force. The flankers would be mounting a handful of light attacks along the enemy defences, more to keep the enemy on their toes than in hopes of actually making a real breakthrough, but the *real* attack would go straight down the motorway and into the city. He had no doubt the enemy would recognise what they were doing almost as soon as the attack began. There was no point in trying to hide it. They'd be charging at City Hall, ignoring hundreds of other possible targets. The enemy would do everything in their power to stop them.

"All present and correct, sir," Mayberry said, as if there'd been any doubt. A couple of marines had been lightly wounded, but they'd remained in the battle line. The thought of leaving their mates to sink or swim on their own was horrific. They'd sooner die than abandon their comrades. "We're ready."

Haydn nodded, feeling a flicker of excitement mingled with the grim certainty that a great many people were going to die. It had been a *long* time since the marine corps had mounted such an offensive, outside exercises and drills that never quite captured the reality of mobile war. He'd already started cataloguing all the lessons they'd learnt—re-learnt, really—from the campaign. The fighting would be studied for years as the corps—and everyone else—sought to understand the reality behind the story. He had no doubt quite a few officers were going to be embarrassed, but it didn't matter. They had to learn from their mistakes.

He was tempted to give a stirring speech, but he'd never been a wordsmith. Besides, his men were experienced marines. They knew what was at stake. They wouldn't be impressed by meaningless babble, even if he plagiarised from Shakespeare and Patrick Stewart and dozens of other famous writers who'd been largely forgotten in the modern era. They'd want him to get on with it, not waste their time…

"Go," he said.

The guns opened fire, hurling hundreds of shells into the city. Lasers reached up to kill them, but a handful made it through and fell. Explosions billowed over Eastside, each one marking a direct hit. Haydn winced, knowing they might have sentenced hundreds of civilians to death, but…he told himself, grimly, it was a small price to pay to end the war. The fighting *had* to end—and quickly. The supply lines were already stretched too thin.

He broke into a run, the suit powering down the road towards the enemy defences. Alerts flashed up in front of him as the enemy started bringing their plasma cannons online, sparks of blinding light darting towards the marines. The marines returned fire, slamming antitank missiles into the enemy positions. It was massive overkill, but they had no choice. They couldn't let the enemy tear them to shreds. Flashes of light turned into fireballs as the plasma containment chambers exploded, sheets of superhot fire blasting in all directions. He saw a burning man stumbling out of the remains of a makeshift strongpoint, his body being consumed by white flames. He put a shot through his head as a mercy, knowing it might already be too late. The poor bastard had died in screaming agony.

The defence line loomed in front. He hit it with terrible force, smashing though the barricade with all the power his suit could muster. It disintegrated, shattering into a maelstrom of wood, metal and concrete fragments. He glimpsed a number of enemy soldiers—some shooting at him, some running for their lives—as he thrust forward, lashing out in all directions. It wasn't a well-coordinated attack, but it didn't have to be. The enemy didn't have anything that could harm him.

Bullets pinged off his armour as he kept moving, the remainder of the company ploughing through the gaps in the defences. A handful of enemy soldiers threw down their weapons and raised their arms, trying to surrender. Haydn ignored them. The marines didn't have *time* to take prisoners. The poor bastards could shed their uniforms and vanish into the crowd, if they liked, or simply wait for the follow-up units to take them prisoner. They might pose a problem later, but...he shook his head. Right now, it didn't matter.

A tank appeared in front of him, its heavy weapons tracking the marines. He threw an antitank missile at it as it opened fire, taking out a pair of marines with plasma fire. The vehicle exploded a second later, blowing up into a massive fireball. Behind it, two thin-skinned APCs started to reverse as their drivers thought better of throwing themselves into the skirmish. They didn't have time to escape before the marines blew them apart.

He hunkered down and surveyed the situation as the friendly tanks began to arrive, crushing what remained of the outer defences under their treads. The enemy hadn't had enough time to turn every building into a strongpoint, but it looked as if they had shooters everywhere. Bullets kept snapping through the air, ranging from single shots to bursts of fire that looked to have sprayed and prayed in their general direction. Unarmoured men would be in trouble, he thought, as a pair of cars appeared around the corner and drove at the marines. They were quickly blasted down, exploding into giant fireballs that were too big to be natural. VBIEDs? Haydn was surprised. Fanatics used suicide bombers, not corprats. Maybe...he frowned as he realised the truth. The vehicles had been flown by autopilot.

Someone must have edited their code pretty thoroughly, he thought. The vehicles had been civilian, not military. Autopilots rarely did anything risky. They often impeded drivers who had perfectly good reasons for bending or breaking the law. *It couldn't have been easy to convince them to fly into a headlong collision.*

He felt sweat trickle down his back as they resumed the offensive. The tanks took the lead, heavy guns responding to each attack with massive overkill. Buildings crumbled under the barrage, collapsing as their occupants drew fire from the tanks. Haydn saw a building explode, flames spreading rapidly as an improvised bomb exploded ahead of time. He winced, knowing they didn't have time to fight fires either. It would be hours before they could deal with them and, by then, half the city could have burned to the ground. He gritted his teeth as the tanks picked up speed. The sooner they reached City Hall, the sooner they'd be ready to put an end to the war.

And then we can fight the fires, he thought, grimly.

• • •

"Stay down, you damn fools," the sergeant shouted. "Let them get within range before you start shooting."

George Rumford shivered, trying his level best to conceal his fear as the sound of fighting grew closer. He should never have volunteered to join the defences, he should never have put himself at risk...he never *would* have volunteered, if his father's superiors hadn't pointed out that anyone who *didn't* stand in defence of his homeworld would be remembered when the fighting finally stopped. That had been decisive for George's father, who'd ordered his son to join the defence force. The fact that George barely knew how to use the rifle that had been shoved into his hand hadn't been enough to deter him. His career was at stake.

The ground shook. George bit down a whimper, feeling warm liquid trickle down his pants. He hoped no one noticed, particularly not the sergeant. A few hours of listening to the bastard, a man who looked like a gym teacher from Hell itself, had convinced him that the man was nothing more than a bully. George had worked hard to evade conscription when he'd reached the age when he could be taken into the military. To have all that thrown away, when he'd been on the verge of taking the exams that would win him a place at an off-world university, seemed a cruel joke.

He peered into the distance, wincing as the enemy tanks came into view. They were massive, so huge they dwarfed the cars and vans they crushed under their treads. His stomach churned as he saw a school bus smashed in two, the frontal half crushed so flat that it looked like a giant pancake. It would have been funny, if the tanks weren't grinding remorselessly towards him. Behind them, he saw dark-clad figures moving from cover to cover. He felt his stomach churn, as if he was on the verge of throwing up. The advance seemed utterly unstoppable.

"Take aim," the sergeant ordered. He moved from man to man, checking their posture as they took aim. "Prepare to fire!"

George lifted his rifle. It felt heavy, so heavy he could barely keep it aloft. His hands were streaked with sweat. He smelled shit and hoped, desperately, that it didn't come from him. The sergeant barked orders George barely heard. The noise of combat was so loud, even the sergeant couldn't be heard over it. George's legs wobbled. He nearly fell down.

"Fire," the sergeant barked.

George pulled the trigger. The rifle spat bullets. He couldn't tell if he'd hit anything, or if he'd had any effect if he had. The tanks brought their machine guns to bear, spitting a stream of bullets through the air...George threw himself down, a heartbeat before the wall disintegrated. Blood and gore and debris landed around him...he saw the sergeant explode, his upper half wiped away as casually as a man might step on an ant. The floor started to crumple. He grabbed for a handhold, too late. The floor shattered, pieces of debris falling. He fell with it, plunging towards the ground far below...

• • •

Haydn barely noticed the falling building as he pushed down the street, following the tanks as they smashed their way onwards. A dozen bodies fell to the ground, all wearing ill-fitting uniforms and carrying oddly-mismatched weapons. Some were military-grade assault rifles, some were rifles so outdated he'd thought they'd been taken out of service long ago, and some were simple hunting rifles, weapons that hadn't been designed for modern war. It looked like a scratch group of defenders, hastily thrown together in hopes of slowing the offensive for a handful of seconds. He felt a stab of pity for the bastards. It didn't look as if any of them had been experienced. They'd all stained their pants.

Stupid bastards, he thought, grimly. There was a time when bravery became nothing more than foolishness. *You should have run.*

He frowned as he saw a young man, barely old enough to shave. The poor bastard's face was still intact, frozen in a gruesome rictus. Haydn wasn't sure what had killed him, beyond shock. His body was surprisingly intact too. Perhaps he'd had a weak heart, or some medical condition that would have disqualified him for the military if they hadn't been so desperate for warm bodies...

New alerts flashed in front of him. The enemy mortar teams were opening fire again, trying to slow the tanks with HE. Someone else had detonated a bomb in the sewers, sending one of the tanks plunging into the sludge. The crew was fine, but they were going to be the butt of everyone's jokes after they were rescued. Haydn smirked, then started to snap orders as he walked away from the bodies. There would be time to collect and bury them later, once the fighting was over. Everything still hung in the balance.

And if we give them time to recover and devise countermeasures, he thought grimly, *they might drive us back out.*

• • •

Rachel kept her expression under tight control as Phelps led the way towards City Hall. The building was spectacular, the kind of palatial structure she would have expected on a more developed world, but it didn't look particularly easy to defend. Enemy troops had dug trenches in the flower beds and sited weapons behind the walls, yet...they'd be nothing more than a speed bump to armoured marines. The only thing keeping the building intact was the simple fact the attackers *needed* the building. It could have been taken out with missiles or shellfire otherwise, with no need to risk a single marine.

The streets surrounding the complex were, at best, consumed with organised chaos. Green-tabbed men were everywhere, screaming orders at a motley collection of soldiers, policemen and drafted civilians. The confusion was so great—her lips twitched in disdain—that half the officers were issuing orders the other half were countermanding. She'd expected to be challenged well before they reached the walls, but no one got in their way. She suspected it would be a long time before the government managed to restore itself, even if the marines lost the war. It's control over the planet had been broken beyond repair.

A pair of APCs stood at the gates, their guns tracking everyone who walked by. Rachel tensed, despite herself. Enhancements or no enhancements, there was no way she'd survive a machine gun blast at point-blank range. But the crew ignored the Pathfinders as they made their way through the gates. Rachel was minded to write a strong letter of complaint, afterwards. Police uniforms or not, the defenders should have made damn sure to verify *anyone* who tried to enter City Hall.

No one tried to stop them until they reached the doors, where another squad of green-tabbed troopers stood on guard. She couldn't help noticing that their weapons were pointed at the outer layer of defenders, as if they expected them to break and run at any moment. They might well be right. It had been generations since anyone had seen a full-fledged thunder run, outside exercises that bore little resemblance to anything soldiers and marines might have to encounter, but they were unmistakable. It was only a matter of time until the attackers drove their tanks into City Hall. The defenders didn't look remotely ready to meet them.

The leader glared at them. "Papers?"

"Here." Phelps held out a datachip, linked to his implants. "We have orders to report to the command post."

The man's eyes narrowed. Rachel realised, in a split-second, that their cover was blown. She wasn't surprised. The enemy wouldn't be so foolish as to believe their cover, not for very long. God knew they didn't have the time to forge proper papers, or the information to do it with. She triggered her enhancements, charging forward with the rest of her team. The security troopers didn't manage to fire a shot before they were overwhelmed.

"Inside, now," Phelps snapped. They knew where the bunker was, thanks to General Taggard, but would it be sealed? "Hurry!"

Rachel snatched up the officer's communicator as she ran and switched it to an all-units setting. "Scatter," she ordered, deepening her voice as much as possible. "All units, scatter."

She threw the communicator against the nearest wall, grinning as they picked up speed. The enemy would be confused as hell. Some units might even follow her orders and scatter before their officers reasserted control. There was no way to be sure, but it didn't matter. If it worked, it worked; if it didn't...well, it had been worth a try. She unhooked a stolen grenade from her belt and braced herself, ready to throw it to cover their run. The enemy had to be chasing them.

"Good thinking," Phelps called.

"Thanks, sir," she called back.

The interior of the building was surprisingly deserted. It looked as if the staff had been evacuated, after stripping the hall of everything valuable. Faded marks on the walls suggested that, only a few short days ago, they'd been covered with paintings. Rachel wondered, idly, how much they'd cost…and if they were worth anything now, after Earthfall. She put the thought aside as they barrelled down the stairs, straight into a checkpoint. She hurled the grenade ahead of her, running into the explosion. The guards, stunned or killed, provided no opposition…

"Shit," Perkins said.

Rachel looked up. The door to the bunker was closing, fast. She boosted, throwing herself forward as hard as she could, only to slam into the metal with terrifying force. For a moment, her head screamed with pain. Her head swam before her enhancements took control. She was grimly aware that she was going to pay for that later. She'd come very close to knocking herself out. She half-expected to see a dent in the metal, but it was unmarked. It was hullmetal. It could stand up to a nuke.

"Fuck," Phelps said. "Are you okay?"

"Barely." Rachel picked herself up. Enhancements or no enhancements, her head was ringing like a bell. "Did you get the number of the starship that hit me?"

Phelps didn't laugh. "I think we failed," he said. He indicated the hull-metal door. "There's no way we can open it without killing everyone inside. We're screwed."

CHAPTER FORTY

Indeed, as the first post-Earthfall year came to an end, it was not clear if they would ever be answered at all.
—**PROFESSOR LEO CAESIUS**
Earthfall and its Aftermath

SIMON HAD HOPED, as the enemy offensive began, that his defences would be able to keep them out of the city...or, at the very least, bog them down in house-to-house fighting until the relief fleet arrived. But, almost as soon as the enemy began their offensive, the defenders started to crumble. A line he'd hoped would hold for a few hours had barely lasted ten minutes. The reports from General Atherton had made it clear. City Hall would fall by the end of the day.

He stood and picked up his bag. There wasn't *much* he had to take with him, save for a handful of datachips and prized possessions he couldn't force himself to leave behind. The emergency bunker already had a supply of clothes, food and everything else he might reasonably need to keep him—and his staff—alive until the relief fleet arrived. Who knew? Maybe Head Office would realise he'd been plunged into a completely unexpected situation, a conflict he couldn't hope to win. He snorted. Too much had been lost for Head Office to take a sanguine view of the whole affair.

They'd blame him…but they wouldn't blame his family. It wasn't much, but it was all he had.

Sandra entered, looking scared. "Your Excellency?"

"I'm going to the Command Post," Simon said. "Fetch Colonel Macintyre and his team and bring them to me there."

"Yes, sir," Sandra said. "I…"

Simon was tempted to draw the moment out, to make her think that she was on the list of people who would have to stay behind until the very last moment. But Colonel Macintyre was fond of her, in his way, and Simon saw no harm in encouraging it. Colonel Macintyre was practically his nephew, in all the ways that mattered. If he wanted Sandra, why not? She didn't have much between the ears, but…Simon snorted. Who knew? Maybe discovering that her family was a broken reed would be good for her.

"You'll be coming too," he said. "Go."

He watched her go, then took one last look around his office before following her through the door. He'd miss it, if he was allowed to live. He'd enjoyed being a governor, enjoyed having the freedom to make decisions without referring to higher authority. There was no way he'd ever enjoy it again, whatever happened. Head Office wanted him dead. The Marine Corps probably wanted him dead too. And there was no way he could book a one-way ticket to the Rim, not now. One way or the other, he was never coming back.

The Command Post was nearly empty, save for a handful of officers. General Atherton stood in the centre of the room, issuing orders to his staff. Parts of the holographic display were greyed out, showing where the fog of war had overwhelmed the defenders, but the remainder were covered in bright red icons. Simon was no expert, yet even *he* had no trouble in realising the enemy were steadily advancing towards City Hall. A handful of red icons were right on top of the building.

"I've ordered the hatch sealed," General Atherton said. "The enemy attacked City Hall itself."

Simon felt a frisson of fear run down his spine. "What happened?"

"A small group, probably commandos." General Atherton shrugged. "The hatch is sealed. They can't get in, not without destroying a sizable chunk of the city..."

"Right." Simon felt sick. "Can we still leave?"

"The emergency tunnel is open," General Atherton said. "And General Taggard never knew about it."

Simon nodded, shortly. The enemy had known precisely where to go. It could not be denied that someone senior, *very* senior, had fallen into their hands. General Taggard was the obvious suspect...he shook his head. Right now, it didn't matter. General Taggard's treachery was a problem for his successor, whoever that happened to be. He wondered, absently, if Heather had already gone to ground. She was smart. She might manage to get out of the city before the noose tightened.

"Then we go now," he said, finally. "They can take this bunker when it's empty."

"Yes, sir," General Atherton said.

• • •

"It's time to leave," Colonel Macintyre said. "Grab the POW and then go."

Derek nodded, silently putting his own plan into operation. "Billy, take your squad to the brig and collect the POW. Meet us at the tunnel. The rest of us will escort the governor and his staff."

"Good thinking," Colonel Macintyre said. "Coming?"

He sounded distracted, as if he were worrying about something more important than their escape from certain death. Derek allowed himself a moment of relief, then followed Colonel Macintyre out of the barracks and into the corridor. Sandra was waiting there again, her face still beautiful even though it was marred by terror. Derek remembered, suddenly, that he'd seen her before, back before the shit hit the fan. He felt a flicker of resentment as they hurried down the corridor. Back then, the world had made sense.

Back then, everyone knew their place and stuck to it, he recalled, sourly. *And we have learnt hard lessons since.*

He braced himself as they reached the Command Post. There had been no time to put together a conspiracy, not when the slightest whisper might be overheard. Loomis would have understood, Loomis would have followed his lead…Derek sighed, inwardly. Jock Loomis was dead, his body decaying in the ruins of Bouchon. And no one in the Command Post gave a damn. They were more interested in saving their skins than coming to terms with the enemy, the *marines*. Derek had read the reports Colonel Macintyre had forwarded to his ultimate boss. The marines weren't monsters. They'd be willing to dicker with the planet's former rulers…

"Leave your men outside," Colonel Macintyre ordered, as they reached the hatch. "Come with me."

"Yes, sir," Derek said.

He followed Colonel Macintyre into the chamber. The Command Post was shutting down, terminals going dark as their datacores were purged and dusted. The map on the wall suggested that time was rapidly running out. Derek scanned the room as Colonel Macintyre hurried forward to consult with the governor, silently calculating who'd be likeliest to pose a threat. General Atherton had a service pistol at his belt, but he was fat and clearly unfit. His holster was buttoned. It was hard to believe he could get the pistol out quickly enough to make a difference. Colonel Macintyre was far more dangerous. The remainder of the staff officers weren't even armed.

"It's time to go," the governor said. He turned to indicate the map. "Shall we…"

Derek drew his pistol in one smooth motion and shot Colonel Macintyre through the head. The colonel staggered, then fell. General Atherton grabbed for his weapon, then froze as Derek pointed his gun right between the man's eyes. Everyone else stared at him, as if they couldn't believe their eyes. Derek felt a surge of pure hatred and contempt. REMFs. They were in the army, not…he didn't want to think about what they thought they were doing. God! He wanted to kill them all.

"Put the gun down slowly, then back away," he ordered. "Everyone else, keep your hands where I can see them."

General Atherton obeyed, his hands trembling like leaves. Derek felt another surge of contempt. The general had sent countless men like him to die, while remaining behind in a nearly-impregnable bunker. He'd heard the staffers gloating over just how safe they were, under the ground. It would take a nuke to disturb their slumber. Derek wanted to laugh, to rub their noses in their failure. If they'd treated their subordinates better, if they'd expressed even the mildest hint of regret over the men who'd died for them, they might have avoided this.

The governor found his voice. "Young man..."

"Shut up!" Derek pointed the gun at him. "Call the troops. Tell them to surrender, then open the hatch."

"Listen to me," the governor said. "You don't understand..."

"You don't understand." Derek had to keep himself from simply pulling the trigger and blowing the governor's brains, such as they were, all over the room. "Order them to surrender or die, right now."

"I..."

"Choose!" Derek shoved the gun into the man's face. "Surrender, or die?"

The governor wilted. "I'll issue the orders," he said. "And then...you don't know what you've done."

"Fuck you," Derek said. "I know *exactly* what I've done."

He watched the governor like a hawk as he keyed his console, bringing the communications system back online. The governor might not have realised it, but Derek didn't know *that* much about military communications systems. He might issue other orders, if he thought he could get away with it. Derek kept the gun pointed at the man's head as the governor spoke briefly into the terminal, ordering a surrender. A moment later, the hatch was open.

"They'll be here in seconds," the governor said. "I hope you can live with what you've done."

"You won't be living with it at all if you don't shut up," Derek said. He was too bitter and broken to heed vague warnings, particularly when the governor no longer had any power to do anything. The war was over and that was all that mattered. "It's over."

"No." The governor lowered his eyes. "It's not over."

• • •

"They've surrendered," Phelps said, in astonishment. "It's over."

Rachel blinked in surprise as the hatch opened, allowing them to walk into the bunker. The handful of men they saw on the far side surrendered without a fight, handing over their weapons and sitting down. They'd be collected soon enough, Rachel was sure, as they hurried down to the Command Post. She had no idea what she'd find there, but she knew the compound had to be secured as quickly as possible. *Someone* might take control and try to renounce the surrender.

The guards at the door were equally confused, but handed over their weapons when they saw the marines. Rachel kept an eye on them as the inner hatch swung open, revealing a surprisingly basic command centre. A body lay on the ground, the back of his head missing; a man stood in the centre of the chamber, keeping the rest of the men under guard. Rachel had no trouble recognising both Governor Morgan and General Atherton. The rest of the men, including the one who'd surrendered, were unknown to her.

"Congratulations," the governor grated. "The planet is yours."

"Thanks." Phelps sounded more amused than anything else. "Order the PDCs to surrender too, if you please."

The governor's face darkened. "As you wish."

"I missed that," the mutineer said. "Fuck!"

"It's alright," Phelps said. "We have to talk..."

"You have to collect the prisoner," the mutineer said. "She's at the tunnel entrance, or she should be. You can take her home."

Rachel smiled. "Don't worry," she said. "We will."

• • •

The firing died with surprising speed.

Haydn frowned as the remainder of the enemy forces either threw down their weapons and surrendered, or melted away into the underground. They didn't seem inclined to continue the fight, now that their superiors had ordered a general surrender, but not all of them seemed to want to become POWs either. He hoped, as they continued their march towards City Hall, that they'd have the sense to go back to their homes and put their uniforms away. They'd just make people miserable if they kept fighting.

He didn't relax until they reached City Hall, already abandoned by most of the defenders. They'd left their heavy weapons behind, much to his relief. The marines collected them as they secured the building, capturing the remaining defenders. They'd be held prisoner until their ultimate fate could be decided when the clean-up was well underway. He could still hear gunshots in the distance, from the other side of the river. It would be a long time before the city became truly peaceful, once again.

His communicator bleeped. "Status report?"

"They've stopped resisting us," Haydn said. "City Hall and Motorway One are both secure, for the moment. I'm readying my troops to fan out and secure the remainder of Eastside."

"I'm deploying troops to take the remaining PDCs," General Anderson said. "And that will be the end."

"For the moment," Haydn said. He kicked himself for forgetting the PDCs. They were more important than the city. "Sir..."

"I know," General Anderson said. He sounded tired, rather than triumphant. The war had ended on a sour note. "For the moment, it's over."

And not a moment too soon, Haydn thought.

EPILOGUE

"WE JUST RECEIVED AN UPDATE from the planet," Susan said. "The last of the PDCs has been secured."

"Good." Kerri allowed herself a moment of relief. "Deploy troops to seize the orbital industrial nodes and defences."

She leaned back in her chair, feeling tired...and yet, in a way, contented. They'd won. The campaign might have been a mistake—she was grimly aware that the recriminations had already started back home—but they'd won. There would be hard times ahead, unless they were incredibly lucky, yet...they'd won. They'd secured the planet and captured most of the facilities largely intact. Given time, the locals would be won over. If nothing else, the provisional government *wouldn't* be watching them in the changing rooms.

And that would win me over, she thought. She'd had little privacy in her career, but she'd volunteered. She'd known she would have little privacy right from the start. And she'd been a grown adult when she'd signed up. *And if they don't join us, we can send them elsewhere...*

She smiled, tiredly, as the reports came in. There was no resistance. There hadn't even been any attempt to prepare the platforms for demolition. And...given time, they'd be adapted to serve the marines. The campaign might last longer than they'd expected—and probably be fought out on an interstellar scale—but they'd won the first round. It had been worth the price they'd paid…

Thirty-seven marines dead, along with thousands of enemy soldiers; tons of equipment damaged or destroyed…a costly victory, by pre-Earthfall standards, she thought. *Now, it may be only the beginning.*

An alarm bleeped. She sat upright, sharply. "Report!"

Tomas cursed. "Captain, long-range sensors are detecting a sizable fleet," he said. "I count at least nine capital ships, including the battlecruiser. They're heading this way!"

Kerri sucked in her breath. "Signal the fleet," she ordered. "Battle stations!"

• • •

To be continued in

Knife Edge

Coming soon.

AFTERWORD

Those who would give up essential liberty, to purchase a little temporary safety, deserve neither liberty nor safety.
—BENJAMIN FRANKLIN

WHAT WOULD YOU DO if you knew you were being watched all the time?

It's a question that sits ill with me, for a number of reasons. One of them is that I have known a number of extremely religious people (Christians and Muslims) who were constantly on edge, because they believed that God was watching them and judging them every hour of every day. They could not allow themselves to slack, not even for a moment. It wasn't that they wanted to fall into sin—'sin,' as they defined it—but that they were terrified of being found unworthy. They could not let things slide. They *had* to invite people to their faith, they *had* to observe every rule, they *had* to enforce them on their dependents (children), they had...because they feared the consequences if they did not.

And this does tend to be mirrored in the workplace. People who think, rightly or wrongly, that they're being watched all the time tend to resent it. They feel naked, they feel that they have no freedom, no room to make mistakes. The increasing number of open offices, with everyone in one big chamber, has actually led to a fall in actual productivity. There are many reasons for this, but one of them is the lack of privacy. You can't hold a meeting between lower-ranking staff in an open office without everyone overhearing and injecting their comments into the conversation. Nor can you listen to music or scratch your rear without *someone* making a fuss about it. No, you have to *look* busy even when its counterproductive.

Indeed, there was—only a couple of weeks or so ago, at the time of writing—an amusing incident on the set of *Star Trek Discovery* that illustrates my point. Walter Mosley, who is black, penned an op-ed explaining that he quit writing for the show after being harassed by human resources for using the N-word in the writing room. He didn't deny using it, but—as he explained—he wasn't using it to insult anyone (which HR could have reasonably objected to) or even purely for dramatic effect. He was using it to explain something that had happened to him, which caused someone to make an anonymous complaint. As he asks:

"*How can I exercise [both the freedom of speech and the pursuit of happiness] when my place of employment tells me that my job is on the line if I say a word that makes somebody, an unknown person, uncomfortable?*"

The concept of being permanently watched is one that *does* make people uncomfortable, for obvious reasons. We are schooled to believe in privacy, even when we should know better. We are outraged when we learn that perverts have hidden cameras in changing rooms; we are worried when we discover that AIRBNB has a hidden camera problem, when hosts set up cameras and film guests. Indeed, the secrecy is part of the problem. One cannot reasonably object to a declared camera filming people who go in and out of the door. But one can object to one placed in the bathroom, or the bedroom, and if there is one undeclared camera how can the guest be sure there aren't more?

Grappling with the consequences of social change (that which was acceptable five years ago is now *verboten*) and new technology (which isn't always covered by previous laws) is difficult enough. It's difficult to accept, on some level, that your customers might also loathe you and will happily abandon you, if they discover an alternative. (The music industry was practically crippled by pirated music because it was blatantly obvious that they were exploiting their former customers, who accordingly had no qualms about depriving the big companies of their revenues.) However, it is something that we should all bear in mind. The seemingly endless series of data protection scandals are a clear warning that our data is already out there, that it may fall into the hands of people with shadowy motives. And the effects of this can be quite serious.

One simple example, perhaps, would be telling Facebook that you're going on holiday. This seems harmless, right? Not so much if you're being followed by people who want to burgle your house. You've just told them the building will be empty for the next week or so. And then there are the more complex examples, the problems that arise from large-scale data mining. If you have a habit of buying groceries online, a monitoring program can note what you buy and use it to tailor what you're shown. You might be given offers they think will interest you, because you've shown an interest in it, or you might *not* be shown certain offers because they think you'll buy the items at full price anyway. Some of the online supermarkets are really quite cunning. At least two of the supermarkets I've used have a policy that urges you to sign in *first*, on the grounds you'll be shown stuff you can buy. If you don't sign in, you might discover that you can't actually buy some of the stuff in your shopping basket when you check out. But if you *do* sign in, they know who you are and can tailor what you see. The prospects for manipulation are staggering.

Sometimes, to be fair, the results are mixed. I've used Amazon for over fifteen years. I keep getting emails and search results listing books Amazon thinks I will like. However, only a third of them are *good* results, in the sense they're books I might actually buy. The remainder include a number of suggestions that simply don't make much sense, ranging from books that *might* be connected to my purchases if one uses a great deal of imagination to books that have no connection whatsoever. (And that's not getting into the issue of Amazon trying to sell me books by some bloke called Christopher Nuttall.) At other times, however, the results of data-mining are frighteningly accurate. You can build up a terrifyingly accurate picture of someone by tracking their electronic footprint.

It's not easy to see how the big social media companies can *really* rein this in, even if they *wanted* to. Facebook is free to the average user because the *real* money is in advertising. They want—they need—to collect accurate data and sell it, regardless of what *you* think about it. (This is why it's a good idea to limit what you tell them.) To cut down on data-mining would be to cut down their revenues, particularly since it would be difficult to monetise the basic service. A chunk of their users wouldn't be able to pay for it, I think, and another chunk would only pay in exchange for ironclad guarantees the company wouldn't play games with their accounts.

The prospects for abuse are staggering—and already here. Forget tailored adverts and offers; think politics. It's quite easy, if you have a position of power, to slant things in the direction you want them to go, by doing everything from promoting posts you like to actively impeding people who disagree with you. Merely shadow-banning posters can cause all sorts of problems, particularly when it's difficult to be *sure* it's happening. Worse, threatening producers with being kicked off if they refuse to toe the line can force them into resentful compliance. Facebook is riding for a fall, in my opinion, because—like the music industry—it has built up a deep well of hatred from vast numbers of ordinary people. When a replacement takes off, Facebook may collapse as quickly as MySpace.

Indeed, if you want to stay up at night, just think about how many of your gadgets betray your every move. How do you *know* someone isn't looking at you through your computer's camera? How do you *know* you turned the Wi-Fi off? (Funny, isn't it, how modern laptops don't come with a physical on-off internet switch.) How do you *know* Siri or Alexa aren't listening to—and recording—everything you say? (There has already been a scandal with workers listening to people having sex through their voice-activated devices.) How do you know your mobile phone isn't spying on you? Anyone could be watching you, right now.

And this is in the West. It is much worse in China, behind the Great Firewall; it is far—far—worse in places like Iran, Saudi Arabia, Turkey and other repressive regimes where the internet can be turned on and off at will. China has already started building up a social credit system that can be used to keep its citizens under control, a level of intrusion that is right out of *1984*. We should be concerned, very concerned, about this spreading to the West. What could someone do with that level of access and bad intentions? They could tear your life apart, easily. George Orwell was a prophet of the dark side of modern technology.

Every so often, I come across people urging that constitutional and/or legal safeguards should be put aside for the Greater Good. They are opposed to a Really Bad Thing—extremists online, for example—and insist, loudly, that anyone who opposes dismantling such safeguards, in this one incident, is a supporter of Really Bad Thing. It's a maddening argument because it puts anyone who disagrees on the defensive right from the start. And, from a subjective point of view, they might be right. Really Bad Thing is a Really Bad Thing.

But here's the problem. It's *never* just one thing. It's never just the need to stop terrorists or extremists or People Who Dare To Disagree With Me. Once the precedent is set, once those safeguards have been put aside, they don't work any longer. Someone will say "you banned this, now you can ban that." You're heading down the slippery slope, picking up speed as you fall into tyranny. And anyone who dismisses the concept of the slippery slope has more faith in humanity than I do. Once you start making exceptions, you can't stop.

And once you're at the bottom of that slope, do you *know* you'll be at the top of whatever remains?

The problem with a lot of people who advocate such measures is that it never occurs to them that the measures might, in turn, be used against *them*. Whatever your motives, you have to remember that your enemy will feel free to turn your own weapon against you. Once you cross the line, your enemy will consider it permission to cross it too. Or your former supporters will decide you're not *pure* enough and turn on you. You really need to be careful what precedents you set when you're in power. They can be turned against you.

Personally? I say "*Make 1984 fiction again!*"

Christopher G. Nuttall
Edinburgh, 2019

PS.
And now you've read the book, I have a favour to ask. It's getting harder to earn a living through indie writing these days, for a number of reasons (my health is one of them, unfortunately). If you liked this book, please post a review wherever you bought it; the more reviews a book gets, the more promotion.

CGN.

CPSIA information can be obtained
at www.ICGtesting.com
Printed in the USA
LVHW031123141019
634125LV00001B/71/P

9 781695 664890